ONE OF THE FIRST

An ambulance met the flight from Tokyo on the tarmac of Seattle-Tacoma International and whisked Tatsumi Iyama off to the hospital immediately after the simplified immigration procedures had been completed. Iyama was unconscious by the time the representative from the airline arrived to deliver his luggage in person and to confirm that his malady had not been brought on by the in-flight cuisine or by any other cause attributable to the company.

Tatsumi Iyama was a very sick man. An initial examination convinced Dr. Patricia Marston that she was dealing with something completely out of her scope, and she ordered total isolation in the Intensive Care Unit and a series of tests to collect blood and tissue samples, all of which were sent to the lab while she struggled to find the intuition to help her sort this problem out. Her immediate prognosis was meningitis, but until the results came back from the lab, she could not be sure. Meanwhile, Iyama was gradually sinking into a comotose state. . . .

ISOLATION
CHRISTOPHER BELTON

LEISURE BOOKS NEW YORK CITY

A LEISURE BOOK ®

December 2003

Published by

Dorchester Publishing Co., Inc.
200 Madison Avenue
New York, NY 10016

ISBN 0-8439-5295-4

Printed in the United States of America.

Visit us on the web at www.dorchesterpub.com.

*For Michiyo, my wife of twenty-eight years,
whose love, zest for life, and sense of humor
make me want to do it all over again.*

*In loving memory of Lillian E. Belton
October 14, 1916 – March 17, 1999*

ISOLATION

ACKNOWLEDGMENTS

In the interest of fiction, I have taken certain liberties in writing this book; not least of all, abbreviating the time spans and processes that could be expected under normal circumstances. However, the one liberty that I feel most obligated to apologize for is the implication that amending Japan's constitution is the work of a pleasant afternoon. This procedure would, in fact, be more likely to require a period of about twenty years, and even that would be pushing it.

I would also like to thank the following people for their assistance and advice during the writing of this book: Thane and Maiko Papke, microbiologists, Montana State University, for picking me up and putting me on the right track; Lance R. Lindley, Journalist First Class, for allowing me to pick his brains on military matters; G. Miki Hayden, author and prolific correspondent, for enough support and advice to last through fifty writing careers, and for her stern views on vomit; Tony Gregson, translator, teacher, and close pal, for being present when the seed for this book was sown; and to his lovely wife, Mami, for buying more copies of my books than any other person alive; Shane Belton, son and good friend, for reading the initial drafts, acting as a sounding board and providing the best twist of the story. Thanks also to Akiko and Liam, his wife and son, for making him the happiest man on earth; Jamie Belton, son and drinking buddy, for never reading any of my work, thus reminding me that, strange as it may seem, there are still people out there who *do not* like my style of writing.

Chapter One

Movement was sluggish as the killers, sated on rich nutrients, succumbed to the coldness of their confines. The lyophilization process ensured that all water present in the trypticase soy broth was "boiled" off at minus fifty degrees Celsius and at one-thousandth of an atmosphere without damaging its colony of deadly squatters. Soon all motion ceased. The killers were trained to reproduce and kill at room temperature, but the frigid atmosphere robbed them of the incentive to follow their instincts and induced them to lie dormant, patiently awaiting a warmer and more desirable climate.

That would not be long in coming.

Peter Bryant leaned back in his chair and wondered who it was who had said something about life without industry being guilt, and industry without art being brutality. Well, whoever it was, the art he—or she—had in mind couldn't possibly have been prior art. Bryant surveyed his desk with despair. He poked languidly at the reams of paper piled before him with the end of his ballpoint pen, and silently wished away the remaining two hours of his working day. Checking and editing the English translations of Japanese patent applications for the American market was not the most stimulating of occupations, and Bryant often felt his concentration wane around midafternoon. It was not that he disliked his job, just certain parts of it, and recently those parts seemed to be consuming more and more of his time. The problem wasn't so much the two hundred or so pages that made up the application, but the prior art—every single paper and article related to the product that had ever been published—all of which also had to be translated. The prior art was used by the examiner to judge whether the method of producing or developing the product had previously been explained to the public in any shape or form, thus voiding the application on the basis that the information already existed in the public domain. People trained in the field of patents were contracted to translate the actual application, but cheaper, nonspecialist translators were entrusted with the prior art, and mistakes and ambiguities were not unusual.

Bryant sighed deeply and returned to the chore. He was working on the application for Neuraval, an antidepressant in tablet form developed and manufactured by Hamada Seiyaku Pharmaceuticals, Inc., his employer. Neuraval was similar to most of the other antidepressant drugs available on the market, but it eradicated many of the adverse side effects and could be administered to pregnant women and nursing mothers, as well as the elderly and patients suffering from heart problems, liver and kidney disorders, epilepsy, and a wide range of other ailments that usually prohibited their use. When all of the paperwork had been translated and accurately correlated by Bryant, it would be sent across to Hamada Seiyaku's patent attorney in Washington, D.C., who would then check it again before submitting it to the U.S. Patent and Trademark Office. Once the patent had been issued, the exhaustive and expensive clinical trials required to obtain Federal Drug Administration approval could begin.

"Coffee?"

Bryant looked up at his section head, Leonard Drake, and nodded gratefully. Company regulations forbade employees from leaving material related to products for which patents were still pending unattended on their desks, and Bryant was required to lock everything away in his personal safe, even when he visited the bathroom. The people in the office consequently covered for each other as much as possible to save having to bother with this time-consuming procedure, and everybody agreed that the procurement of coffee on behalf of fellow workers was the ultimate display of friendship and camaraderie.

Drake returned with two plastic cups of steaming coffee, handed one to Bryant, and propped his backside on the edge of the adjacent desk. His wire-framed glasses, portly aspect, and smoothed-down hair make him look like a rich uncle in an English stage farce.

"Thanks, Len. Another ten minutes and I would have been asleep." Bryant took a sip from the cup and sat back in his chair.

"Prior art, eh?" asked Drake with a grin, his precise British accent sounding somehow out of place.

"Enough to choke a whale. I'm working on the Neuraval application, and it seems as if every journal and newspaper in the whole of Japan has given it writeups. And some of the translations are deadly. Where the hell do they get these guys?"

"Your guess is as good as mine. I can get Trent to give you a hand, if you like. He's slack at the moment."

"And have him hate me forever? No, thanks. Let him enjoy his brief respite."

"Suit yourself. But you know that Matsuoka is crying out for the Neuraval application. If it's delayed for much longer, he'll be on my tail again." Kazunori Matsuoka was the director of Hamada Seiyaku's patents department.

"Oh, come on, Len. He can't possibly blame me for the quality of all this translation work," Bryant snapped petulantly. "Jesus, man, I've been working my butt off over this."

Drake shrugged his shoulders. "Well, the Japanese patent is now five months old, and you know how touchy he gets when he sees the company losing out on potential overseas revenue. It cost the equivalent of one hundred and twenty million U.S. dollars to develop this drug, and for every month it stays off the American market, the company is losing ten million dollars in unearned income. To say he's eager to start the FDA trials is an understatement. How much longer do you expect it to take? Not too long, I hope."

"That depends on the quality of the rest of this translation." Bryant slapped the palm of his hand wearily on a pile of A4 paper that was still awaiting his attention. "If it's anything like the stuff I've seen so far, it could be as long as three weeks. I've already finished the actual application and documentation on the clinical phase trials. It's just this prior art that's causing the trouble now."

"I'll tell him two weeks. Think about my offer of Trent," Drake said, shifting his weight off the desk and walking back to his own position.

Bryant continued to sip his coffee after Drake had returned to his desk and mused on the unfairness of constantly being accused of costing the company small fortunes because of his inability to cut corners. The department head, Matsuoka, found it necessary to point out on an almost daily basis that a U.S. Patent Office examiner had less than two days to study an entire application, and it was therefore not only good business to take shortcuts, it was also what the company expected of him. Bryant despised this attitude. He took pride in his work and was deeply aware of the importance of the patenting system and everything it stood for, particularly in the field of pharmaceuticals. Though Hamada Seiyaku seemed to feel that his job description should read something along the lines of being a loyal worker who was willing to pull the wool over the eyes of the American authorities, Bryant himself saw it as a position where he was socially and morally obliged to provide the authorities with every item of information that was available in order to help them reach a fair decision. The company also conveniently overlooked the fact that his signature would appear on the application, and if it was ever discovered that he had deliberately tried to deceive the authorities, not only would he never find work in the same field again, he would also be exposing himself to the dangers of public prosecution.

Bryant's office was located on the sixth floor of the Hamada Seiyaku building in Tokyo's Otemachi district. The entire patents department consisted of twenty-six employees, but only five worked on overseas applications: himself, Leonard Drake, Trent Peterson—an Australian—and two Japanese office girls. Bryant himself was a Japanese-American, but apart from his black hair and dark eyes, he had inherited very few Asian features from his Japanese mother's side of the family. He was taller than the average Japanese male, and his face was longer and more finely boned.

Being fluent in both English and Japanese and having majored in patent law at Harvard University, he had discovered three years previously that he could nearly double the salary he was making working for a patent agency in America by combining both of his talents and working for a Japanese company in Japan. Getting the job with Hamada Seiyaku had been easy, for Japan had a marked shortage of bilingual specialists, but he was surprised to discover that the hardest part of the upheaval was waving good-bye to the lifestyle with which he had become comfortable. He was no stranger to Japan, having lived in Yokohama during his junior high and high school days, and the mental image he had retained of small, cold houses and crowded streets was slightly off-putting. Money, however, was money, and the offer of a job with an annual salary of nearly $130,000 had tipped the scales.

But recently he had been wondering if he had made the right decision. He was beginning to tire of the almost dictatorial way in which some large Japanese corporations operated, and strongly rebelled against the idea that he was a company man first and an individual second.

Bryant sighed again and placed his empty cup on the edge of the desk. Whether he liked it or not, he was going to have to get this particular application finished as quickly as possible. He glanced at his watch and wondered what Michiyo would say when she learned that he was going to be at least an hour late for their dinner date with Mike and Carol that evening.

The silence was broken only by a series of humming noises pitched imperceptibly through differing octaves and the rustle of protective clothing. Genta Horie liked the quiet atmosphere within the lab and found a strange comfort in the constant low-pitched hum. He liked to think that it reminded him of the rush his mother's blood had made as it coursed its way through her veins during his period in her womb. At least, that was what one of his coworkers had suggested when he had mentioned the hum a few months previously, and he had no reason to doubt this supposition. In fact, he thought it was a rather cool way of explaining it.

Horie was working at the Class III biological containment hood, his arms thrust deeply into the attached rubber gloves. The cabinet was gas-tight and the supply air HEPA-filtered, but a pinprick hole at the tip of the first finger on the left hand of the rubber gloves had, unbeknownst to Horie, robbed the containment hood of its integrity. The hole was the result of a careless lab technician working with a hypodermic needle the previous afternoon. The negative air pressure inside the hood ensured that none of the internal atmosphere escaped through this hole, but Horie was not the most delicate of workers, and it was only a matter of time before he inadvertently splashed a minuscule amount of the culture he was working with onto his finger.

The first finger of his left hand.

Unaware of the risk to which he had unwittingly exposed himself, Horie continued to transfer the culture, which had been grown to its midlog phase, across to the centrifuge tube so that the bacteria it contained could be spun down to the required pellet before being resuspended in a small amount of Mueller Hinton medium and subjected to lyophilization—a routine and mundane task.

And a deadly one, as it turned out. On his way across the lab to wash up, Horie raised a latex-covered hand to his nose and scratched an itch that could not be ignored.

With the first finger of his left hand.

Peter Bryant reached for Michiyo's hand under the table and directed a grin at his friend, Mike Woodson. Woodson was an attaché at the American embassy in Tokyo, and the two had met up three years previously owing to the procedure for obtaining U.S. patents sometimes requiring an oath or declaration to be made before a diplomatic or consular officer of the United States. Woodson was usually that officer, and the two had become firm friends.

". . . so this innocent-looking teenage girl," Woodson continued, "has on this T-shirt with 'I like lipstick on my dipstick' spread in big, red letters right across her chest. Can you believe that?"

"I can believe anything about this country," Carol Woodson, Mike's wife, said. "I've seen old ladies carrying shopping bags with some of the most outrageous things you've ever seen written on them. Don't they *know* what they say?"

"Absolutely not," said Michiyo Kato, with a laugh. "They would be devastated if they knew. English phrases are just fashionable at the moment. You should see the trouble Peter has trying to buy casual shirts and sports jackets. Everything has English smeared across it nowadays."

"Tell me about it," Mike Woodson said, his eyes briefly glancing up at the shadow-filled ceiling to indicate that he suffered alike.

Peter Bryant swallowed a mouthful of cannelloni and waved his fork at Woodson. "Yeah, it's all right for you embassy types, trotting back to the States every couple of months and stocking up on everything you need. What about those of us whose budgets don't reach that far? You've never in your life had to wear a shirt with 'Let's have jolly day' or 'I'm a plump Mary' written across the pocket."

Woodson grinned at his friend good-naturedly. "Oh, come on, Peter. Don't tell me you don't love those things. And what about that inflated salary you receive in yen? Some of us get paid in dollars and can't *afford* to buy T-shirts in Japan."

The restaurant began to thin out a little as the evening wore on. Woodson ordered another bottle of red wine, and the four friends settled down to the kind of relaxing postdinner chat that is only possible when all participants are totally comfortable with each other. Bryant felt the stress of his working day slowly being purged from his body. His shoulders relaxed and the knot of tension gradually left the back of his neck. He knew that this stress buildup was part and parcel of assuming the role of Japanese salaryman and that he shared this burden with forty million other people on a daily basis, but he found it difficult to avoid the occasional trips down into the depths of self-pity. It took an evening among good company to rid him of these mild depressions. He looked across at Michiyo and felt his heart flutter as she giggled coquettishly at something Woodson had said. Having Michiyo accepted by his friends was the most important thing in the world to him, and there was no doubt that Mike and Carol had taken to her as though she had been a long-lost cousin.

Bryant had met Michiyo two years before at a reception

hosted by the U.S. embassy to welcome a party of tourist industry people from the United States who were in Japan to promote their localities as viable destinations for Japanese travelers. Michiyo had been invited because she was in charge of hotel bookings for a Japanese travel agency. Bryant had been invited because he was always on the lookout for a free drink. Mike Woodson made sure that Bryant got invited to most embassy receptions on the strength that he could provide interesting conversation from an inside angle, and Bryant played his role as "man-on-the-spot" with genial aplomb. After all, a free drink was a free drink, and the embassy, when dishing out the champagne and cocktails, did so with a lavish hand.

Bryant was on his third bourbon when Michiyo had arrived with a pompous-looking Japanese man who was obviously her boss. He felt his eyebrows launch into a little dance routine that he took to be an involuntary display of approval. Her slim figure and long black hair perfectly complemented the sleeveless one-piece dress she was wearing, and her almond-shaped eyes with their glint of mischief managed to make her seem both sultry and fun-loving at the same time. In other words, she was the girl of Bryant's dreams.

It took two more bourbons for him to sidle his way across the hotel ballroom, fending off questions from red-faced men with their bellies hanging over their belts. A hotel owner from Nebraska arrested his progress and asked him if he thought it was a good idea to remove the carpeting from all bathrooms and install drains in the floor in order to attract more Japanese visitors. Nebraska! Bryant said that that was probably the best idea he had ever heard in his life, and then managed to move a few more feet toward his target before being stopped by the director of a luxury limousine service company from Kansas City, who asked if he thought Japanese rice wine should be added to the drink service available in his vehicles. Bryant considered this question and then sagely agreed that something along those lines was almost certain to do the trick. Having excused himself, he kept his head down and managed to edge his way closer to the girl for whom his eyebrows had issued such a positive critique.

"Get you a drink?" he asked in English, having arrived at his destination.

"Um?"

"Would you like another drink?" he repeated in Japanese.

"I do speak English, you know." She turned dark and smoky eyes to him, and he felt his spleen writhe like a salt-sprinkled slug. "I was just trying to be coy. I can't have everybody thinking I'm an easy pickup, can I? Yes, I would love another drink."

They had started dating a week later. Fourteen months after that, Bryant had moved into a larger apartment in Yoyogi, and Michiyo had moved in with him to live as man and wife without verbal vows and official certificates of validation. But Bryant hoped to marry Michiyo soon. Not *too* soon, but soon. Living together was not financially viable when the taxman was into both their pockets for substantial sums. Everybody needed a dependent somewhere along the line to wave in front of the taxman and keep his avarice at bay.

"Snap out of it, Peter. You're staring into the middle distance with an idiotic grin on your face. The waitress wasn't *that* pretty."

Bryant focused his eyes on Woodson with a surprised "who, me?" look on his face.

Everybody laughed, and Bryant's grin expanded. Woodson was right. The waitress *wasn't* that pretty.

"Michiyo has just been saying that you are getting stressed out at work. Burnout at twenty-nine? I thought that only happened in the securities business."

Bryant scratched his head and leaned his elbows on the table. "I wouldn't actually say I was stressed out. It's more like frustration, really. I don't think I have the mental capacity to focus so hard on corporate objectives, although God knows I try. It's not that I don't want the company to be competitive or prosperous; it's just that I have difficulty accepting the fact that one hundred percent of my loyalty must be given only to the company regardless of my own moral conscience. Does that make sense?"

"Been reamed out by the boss, huh?" asked Woodson.

Carol slapped her husband on the arm. "Oh, do be nice, Mike. Can't you see that poor old Peter is having trouble with this?" She turned her attention to Bryant. "Just ignore him, Peter. A lot of Americans—indeed, a lot of foreigners—have trouble adjusting to the almost militaristic style of Japanese management. I have several friends whose husbands complain about the same thing, and it really worries them."

"Whoa, whoa!" Bryant held up his hands, palms out. "You're making me sound like a basket case, Carol. It's not a big problem, just something that's niggling at my conscience. I can handle it. Let's forget it and talk about something else."

"Good idea," agreed Michiyo thankfully. She could see that Peter was uncomfortable in the limelight, and felt a touch of guilt at having exposed him to this scrutiny by bringing the subject up. "If you'll excuse me, I have to powder my nose."

Carol rose with her. "I'm right behind you, Michiyo."

Bryant cupped his hands around his mouth and called loudly after the two girls as they traversed the restaurant: "While you two are powdering your noses, you might also consider taking a pee. It's a long way home."

Michiyo's cheeks flushed as she poked her tongue out at Bryant and continued to thread her way amid the tables to the rest rooms at the back.

Genta Horie felt the vomit rise in his throat, but managed to force it back down into his stomach. His girlfriend, Naomi Ikeda, looked across at him with concern. His face was bright red, but she wasn't sure if that was due to the fever he was running or the three small jugs of sake he had consumed.

"Are you sure you're all right?" she asked.

11

"I'm fine. It's just a touch of flu."

Naomi stretched her hand out and rested the palm on his forehead. "Gen-*chan*, you're burning up. Come on; let's go."

"It's nothing, I tell you. A couple more drinks and a good night's rest is all I need. If I still feel bad tomorrow, I'll go and see the doctor. I promise."

Horie gagged again and covered his mouth with a hand. At the same time a searing pain tore through his abdomen, doubling him over and allowing the vomit to dribble through his fingers.

"That's it!" Naomi said decisively. "I'm getting you home."

She called for the bill and wrapped the uneaten chicken pieces on their wooden skewers hastily in a few paper napkins that were provided on the table. She then helped Genta on with his coat. She could feel his skin quivering beneath his shirt, and wondered if she should get him to the hospital instead of taking him back to his home.

They left the yakitori bar and started to walk toward Horie's apartment. Naomi suggested a taxi, but it was only ten minutes' walk and it would probably take at least fifteen minutes for the cab to arrive. Every ten paces Horie doubled over as another spasm of pain wrenched his stomach. The sweat glistened wetly on his forehead and ran freely down his neck despite the chill of the February evening. Naomi kept an arm around his shoulders to support him, and from a distance it looked like two drunks returning home from a night on the tiles.

"I think I should get you to a hospital," Naomi said, as Horie, overcome by another fit of gagging, was finally able to release the burning liquid from his body and spray it forcefully across the stone-paved sidewalk like a jet of industrial waste. Naomi dropped the pieces of chicken onto the sidewalk in her haste to put a comforting arm around her boyfriend.

Horie coughed twice to force the bitter vestiges of bile from his throat and spat the result into the pool of vomit that lay at his feet. Upchucking was not bothering him as much as the pain in his stomach. In fact, his guts hurt so much that he didn't even notice the tender lesions beginning to form on his arms and legs.

"I'm fine, I tell you. Fine," he said.

By two o'clock in the morning, the edges of the pool of vomit had begun to thicken in consistency. A large number of people returning home from work and from play had stepped gingerly over it and cursed its creator, but now the streets were peaceful and deserted; its very existence was forgotten completely by the passersby who were, by now, tucked up comfortably in their beds. A stray cat crouched on top of a wall that separated the street from a two-acre copse of bamboo trees and thick undergrowth and released a small mewing noise from its throat. A rustling sound in the undergrowth behind it announced the arrival of two kittens that were close to full growth. The mother, having satisfied herself that the area was deserted, silently jumped down from the wall and slowly approached the thickening pool in the hope that she had found supper. She sniffed tentatively at the outer edges and then shook her head briefly, as if trying to remove the vile stench from her nostrils, disappointed at the fact that sustenance would have to be found elsewhere after all. The two kittens followed with less trepidation. One of them discovered the chicken still wrapped in the white paper napkins and began to gnaw through to the meat. His brother, attracted by the low purring sound, joined in and managed to yank a piece of the meat from the wooden skewer. A moment later the mother cat joined them, unwittingly using up the last of her nine lives.

They ate heartily for a few moments, growling softly in their chests as others encroached on their territory, before being disturbed by a dog that had slipped its chain and escaped from its owner's backyard. The three cats wasted no time in darting across the wall and disappearing back into the undergrowth, leaving the dog to triumphantly finish up the tasty meal.

And still some remained—tiny morsels clinging to the wooden skewers—for three small rats and a weasel that appeared from the bushes long after the dog had returned home. All ate their fill before disappearing back into the darkness of the night.

Chapter Two

Shigeru Hamada, president of Hamada Seiyaku Pharmaceuticals, Inc., extinguished his cigarette in the ornate ashtray placed before him and waited for everyone to take their seats and settle down. Beside him sat Masao Ishikawa, director of the Chigasaki Research and Development Center, Hamada Seiyaku's laboratory complex located near the coast of Kanagawa prefecture between the Miura and Izu peninsulas. Hamada noticed the looks of surprise on everybody's faces as they entered the conference room and saw him already seated at the head of the table. His normal style was to effect a dramatic entrance from the door that led off to his office after decorum had been attained, and none of the sixteen directors beginning to fill up the room could remember a time when Hamada had been there before them.

A hush fell over the room as each of the executives opened their notebooks before them and looked up expectantly. Hamada rose to his feet.

"Good morning, ladies and gentlemen. Thank you for assembling at such short notice." Hamada paused with a grim look on his face. His audience shuffled uncomfortably. They recognized that bad news was in the offing, and all began to feel slight twinges of fear over the continuation of their careers. Larger companies than Hamada Seiyaku had been forced to establish crippling restructuring policies in the mid-nineties following the aftermath of the burst of the so-called "bubble" economy, and all instinctively knew that there wasn't a businessman or -woman in the entire country who had one hundred percent confidence in the security of his or her job. "Today we face a grave situation that may have far-reaching effects on the future of Hamada Seiyaku. Known only to myself, the chairman of the board of directors, and Mr. Ishikawa on my left here, Hamada Seiyaku was contracted by the Japanese government some two years ago for the purpose of discovering a biological agent that could be used as a deterrent in the event of an attack of aggression by a foreign nation."

A stunned silence was immediately replaced by a rumble of voices as the executives began to absorb the implications of Hamada's statement. Hamada watched the transformation on the faces of his executives: from polite interest to frowns of mild confusion to full understanding to horror-stricken outrage. It was evident that all had a working knowledge of the international agreements that banned such research. He held up a hand to silence them.

"Before you all start jumping to conclusions, I have something to say," Hamada continued. He waited until the uproar had died down and he was sure he had everybody's attention. "Hamada Seiyaku did not actively seek out this contract. We were contacted by the Defense Agency directly and at first refused to have any part of this unconstitutional project. However, as I'm sure many of you will readily understand, it is not a wise move for a company the size of Hamada Seiyaku to make an open enemy of the government."

The uproar broke out again, and Hamada held up both hands to regain silence.

"We were assured at the time that the project would be nothing more than research, and that no plans for manufacture or deployment existed."

Koichi Nagashima, Hamada's director of administration, stood up and waited until he received a nod from Hamada before speaking.

"I am sure that my colleagues and I will require time to adjust to this—how should I put it?—unprecedented situation. However, I wonder why we have been called together today and provided with this information. If this contract has been in place for two years, why choose now to inform us? May I assume it has something to do with Mr. Ishikawa's presence?"

Several of the executives around the table nodded and looked across at Hamada for an answer.

Hamada looked down at the fingernails on his left hand before raising his eyes to the people sitting around the table. "We have had considerable success with the research, given the limited amount of time that we have been working on it," he said. "But unfortunately, in the past twenty-four hours we have been provided with unwanted proof that our efforts have exceeded even our own expectations."

"Could you be more specific?" urged Nagashima.

"The bacterium has gotten loose, and its first fatality can be expected within the next few hours."

Hamada allowed this piece of information to sink in. He watched Nagashima drop back onto his seat in shock, and then passed his eyes over at the looks of confusion in his audience. He could imagine exactly what they were thinking. *So you screwed up; what's that got to do with us?* They were moving into self-preservation mode. The fact that their company was guilty of breaking international law and flying in the face of Japan's constitution was no longer a problem. The fact that people could, and most certainly would, die as a consequence of their

17

company's actions was no longer a consideration. Their only concern was for their own futures. *How the hell can I distance myself from this?* was written on every face. He despised them all at that moment.

Hamada knocked on the table with his knuckles to bring everyone's attention back to the head of the gathering. "Mr. Okada, chairman of the board of directors, is at this moment briefing the Defense Agency, the Ministry of Health and Welfare, and the prime minister's office on this development, and it may be impossible to keep it under wraps. It is for this reason that I have called today's meeting. We are sure to come in for a considerable amount of media scrutiny over the next few weeks, and I want us to spend as long as it takes to consolidate our official corporate stance. Under no circumstances will I allow outside forces to destroy everything we have worked hard to build up because of something that we were forced into." Hamada ignored the few groans that emerged here and there. His executives had suddenly realized that it was going to be more difficult than they thought to distance themselves from any blame. "Before we start, however," he continued, "Mr. Ishikawa will fill us all in on the background of this unfortunate problem. Mr. Ishikawa?"

Hamada sat down and the attention of all those present moved across to Masao Ishikawa. Ishikawa stood up and walked to an electronic white board situated behind his seat. He cleared his throat and took a telescopic pointer from his top pocket, which he then extended to full length.

"Good morning, ladies and gentlemen." He waited while all of the sixteen executives returned his greeting. "For the past two years, I and a few selected technicians at the Chigasaki Research and Development Center have been involved in isolating a bacterial agent that will induce sickness, and eventual death, at an unprecedented rate. The conditions under which we worked included not only discovering an agent that served our purposes, but also an agent that could easily be controlled

18

through the administration of a vaccine or antidote to prevent it from getting out of hand. This ruled out the existing viruses that cause Ebola and similar forms of disease with high mortality rates. Research has been going on for many years already to control these forms of sickness, and we did not wish to waste time and money by simply joining the back of the queue.

"I do not wish to bore you with the problems we experienced during the first six months of this project, so I will skip to our first hint of success. It became apparent early on in our research that the only way we were likely to achieve success was by genetically altering a bacterium for which we had a good chance of manufacturing an antidote. A team at Harvard University, continuing research initiated by the University of Western Australia, discovered that certain viruses contain a protein known as the UL18 flag. This protein has the ability to trick the body's natural killer cells into believing the virus belongs in the body. They also discovered that this flag could be genetically engineered into viruses and bacteria that do not contain it naturally. Using this concept as a basis for our next step, we then began to look around for a bacterium that could not only be fitted with the UL18 flag, but that would also have a minimal incubation period *and* a high mortality rate."

Ishikawa paused to watch the reaction on the faces of his audience. He moved across to the electronic white board and lightly laid his finger on the button to rotate the surface and bring the concealed area into view.

"And this is what we came up with."

He pressed his finger down on the button, and the words *Neisseria meningococcus* slid from the back of the white board until they came to a halt in the center of the board. Ishikawa tapped the phrase several times with his pointer.

"*Neisseria* meningococcus is a gram-negative encapsulated coccus that causes the disease known as pediatric meningococcemia, or, more commonly, pediatric meningitis. Although between sixty and ninety percent of pediatric meningococcemia is found in children—particularly in children under the age of five—when fitted with the UL18 flag, it will also fool the immune systems of adults into believing that it belongs in the body and trigger the disease."

Kazunori Matsuoka, director of the patents department, raised his hand and got to his feet as Ishikawa nodded to him.

"I understand that meningitis is not a fatal disease and is relatively simple to treat. Surely the bacterium is easily killed by first-line antibiotics."

"Yes, it is, but only if treated before a phase known as the inflammatory cascade—which I shall explain about in a moment—is activated. First of all, however, I would like to give you a rough outline of the symptoms. There are five serogroups associated with meningococcal disease: A, B, C, and the less common W135 and Y serogroups. The serogroup we have selected is the B serogroup, for which no vaccine currently exists. With meningitis, the bacterium causes inflammation of the membranes that surround the brain and spinal cord, and this responds rapidly to treatment. With meningococcemia, however, the bacterium invades the bloodstream and can be fatal within hours. All gram-negative bacteria incorporate poisonous molecules known as endotoxins in their cell walls, and these are released when the bacterium dies. In addition to increasing the virulence factor of our bug by adding a special protein that allows it to colonize the host faster than usual, we have also genetically engineered it to ensure that the bacterium dies after reaching the bloodstream so that the endotoxins are released. This will trigger a runaway reaction by the victim's immune system that is commonly known as the inflammatory cascade, to which I gave mention earlier. Once this inflammatory cascade has kicked in, there is virtually no chance of recovery. The fact that the body's natural killer cells make not even a cursory attempt to fight the bacteria ensures that the inflammatory cascade is activated more severely than in normal cases, so, depending on the incubation period—which could be anything from a few hours to four days—death is almost guaranteed."

Matsuoka slumped back in his seat while Ishikawa looked around for further questions. Yasuko Fukuyama, the director of planning, and Hamada Seiyaku's only female director, caught Ishikawa's eye and rose to her feet.

"I think we all understand just exactly how deadly this disease you have created is," she said with a slight tone of contempt in her voice. "Maybe you could now explain to us the extent of the leak and the company's plan for distributing the vaccine."

Ishikawa paused and closed his telescopic pointer down to pen size. Slipping it into his pocket, he directed his attention at Fukuyama.

"The leak was caused by a faulty containment hood and an inattentive laboratory technician. The first victim of whom Mr. Hamada spoke is, in fact, this technician."

"How could that happen?" Fukuyama asked. "Surely your staff have stringent rules to avoid such careless mistakes."

"For obvious reasons, the technician in question was not aware of the toxicity of the agent he was handling. Although all of our staff are strictly trained in the handling of biohazardous substances, this appears to be a case of several coincidences aligning into a situation that has generated tragic results."

"And the distribution of the vaccine?"

"There is no vaccine," Ishikawa said softly.

"No vaccine?" The shock was evident in Fukuyama's voice. "What do you mean, no vaccine? Surely that was one of the conditions under which you were operating."

Ishikawa removed a white handkerchief from his pocket and wiped it across his brow. "We are still working on it. Certain . . . complications have arisen, and we are no farther on now than we were when we started."

21

"So how is the situation being controlled? Is this disease contagious? Is there the danger of widespread infection?"

Shigeru Hamada got to his feet and waved Ishikawa into his seat.

"You have many questions, Miss Fukuyama," he said sarcastically, gently asserting his authority and simultaneously making it plain that he did not expect any hostile interrogations from his own staff members. "The situation is being handled by containment. So far only the technician has been diagnosed with the disease, and he is safely incarcerated in a special medical facility that is maintained within the Chigasaki Center for situations exactly like this. The only other person who could conceivably have been exposed to infection is the technician's female companion, who is also being closely monitored in another room at the center."

"Voluntarily?"

"I beg your pardon, Miss Fukuyama?"

"Did you receive her consent first, or is Hamada Seiyaku also guilty of violating *habeas corpus*?" Fukuyama's eyes flashed, and the anger in her voice was unmistakable.

"Thank you, Miss Fukuyama. That will be quite enough." Hamada's lips had straightened into thin, pale lines and his eyes were hard and unforgiving. "If you have no desire to help us sort out this problem, then I suggest you leave now. Childish bickering will serve no purpose other than to lengthen the amount of time required to formulate a solution. Although you are obviously giving great consideration to the rights of the victims, your time wasting will invariably result in further infections. Now, do you wish to remain a part of this company, or will you leave now?"

Fukuyama dropped her eyes to the table. Despite her anger, she knew that what Hamada was saying made sense. Whether the company was guilty of gross misconduct or not could wait for a later tribunal, when all of the facts were clear and defensible. What was needed now was swift and decisive action to prevent the problem from elevating into a disaster of unimaginable proportions.

"I'm sorry," she mumbled. "I will stay."

"Thank you. Now what was your question?"

"I wanted to know if the disease was contagious and if there was any risk of widespread infection."

"The disease is highly contagious, particularly at this time of the year when dry-air warnings are constantly being issued. The bacterium thrives in low-humidity environments and is spread through aerosolization or contact with upper-respiratory secretions. We believe that we have so far contained all traces of it through the confinement of the technician and his girlfriend, but we cannot be completely sure. The next few days will be critical in determining our course of action. If no cases are reported within the next seventy-two hours, we can all breathe a sigh of relief and return to our daily work."

Hamada paused for effect, slowly making eye contact with everybody seated around the table in turn.

"On the other hand," he continued, "if one single case of meningococcemia is discovered during that seventy-two-hour period, then the chances are that we will be responsible for hundreds, maybe even thousands, of deaths."

Tatsumi Iyama raised his hand as the cabin attendant walked past his business-class seat. She stopped and leaned over him.

"Yes, sir? Is there anything I can get you?"

"Yes," said Iyama, "do you happen to have any aspirin? I think I have a cold coming on."

"Certainly, sir. I'll bring some right away."

Iyama lay back in his seat, loosened his necktie, and cursed his luck. He hadn't had a serious bout of influenza in several years, and yet here he was, four hours into a flight between Tokyo and Seattle for probably the most important business trip of his entire career, and he could feel the symptoms of a nasty one creeping up on him with extraordinary speed. *Damn!*

23

The cabin attendant returned with two Bufferin and a glass of water. While Iyama chugged the pills, the attendant reached up into the overhead luggage rack and pulled out a spare blanket, which she draped over Iyama's lower body. She could feel the heat of a fever radiating off his skin as she took the empty glass back from him and inwardly sympathized. It certainly was a bummer to get sick just as you were leaving on an overseas trip. "You try to get some sleep," she said kindly. "I'll stick the 'Do not disturb' sign on your headrest and wake you up just before we land in Seattle."

Iyama smiled at her wanly and then closed his eyes, trying to will his body into ignoring the impulse to gag.

Peter Bryant made sure that all important documents had been locked into his personal safe and then walked over to Leonard Drake's desk by the window.

"Coffee?" he asked.

Drake looked up and rubbed a hand across his face. "No, thanks, mate. Had one just a while ago."

Bryant nodded and pulled up a chair.

"Look, I know I said that I'd get the Neuraval application finished within two weeks, but it's not possible. I definitely need three."

Drake clicked his tongue and picked up a pencil, which he rapped in steady rhythm on his desk. "Oh, come on, Peter. You know that's not good enough. Matsuoka will have my balls!"

"I'm sorry, Len, but this thing is killing me. Practically all of the translations are having to be rewritten, and several of them I've had to translate again myself from scratch. It's not as if I'm slouching on the job. I've worked past ten o'clock every night this week. I just *can't* do it any faster."

"Damn, that's just great. Oh, well, if you can't, you can't, I suppose. But I'm not looking forward to telling that to Matsuoka. He holds me responsible for all delays, and I sometimes

24

get a little fed up with making excuses for other people's inefficiency."

"Now, come on, Len, don't you start! If Matsuoka didn't expect everybody to work twenty-four hours a day, he wouldn't have any damn delays in the first place. Jeez, but it pisses me off to get a hard time for slaving my butt off!"

Drake held up his hands in supplication. "All right, all right. Don't take it to heart. I know you're doing a great job, but I have my frustrations, too, you know. How'd you care to come with me when I break this piece of news to Matsuoka? Sound like fun to you?"

"Yeah, let's go, then." Bryant's anger dissipated as swiftly as it had risen. He had no real beef with Drake and knew that he had a lousy job. Drake was expected to act as the bridge between the Japanese management and the foreign workforce, but this was not always an easy thing to do, as it did not entail forcing the management to compromise with the foreigners; it entailed his forcing the foreigners to conform to the management's policy one hundred percent. Although Bryant did not consider himself to be a particularly unruly or radical member of the staff, he was able to recognize the problems that he had caused for Drake in the past by sticking stubbornly to his foreign guns.

Drake looked slightly surprised at Bryant's grin and ready agreement to accompany him, but, sensing that he could score a few points here by letting Bryant see the crap that he had to endure on his and everybody else's behalf, he quickly busied himself by locking all documents away in his personal safe.

The two men were led into Matsuoka's office by a secretary, who waited for her boss's signal before opening the door. Matsuoka sat behind a large wooden desk equipped with a small desktop computer, a blotter, and neat piles of files and paper. He waved them into the seats situated in front of his desk and tapped a few more keys on his computer before turning to them. Balding and with the tired eyes of a Japanese salaryman who had only a few more years before being put out to grass, Matsuoka did not bother to smile a greeting at his visitors.

"Well?" he said.

"It's about the Neuraval application, Mr. Matsuoka," Bryant said, jumping in before Drake could clear his throat. "I'm afraid it's taking longer than I anticipated, and I'll need at least one extra week before it's ready for sending across to the attorney in Washington."

Matsuoka looked across at Drake. "Have you approved this delay?"

"Well, not really, but, well . . . There is a lot of work involved, and Peter has been doing his best—"

"That was not my question."

"Well, not officially, but I can see that there is merit in Peter's argument."

"Let me rephrase the question." Matsuoka removed his glasses from his nose and used one of the stems to scratch the back of his ear. "Do you *intend* to approve this delay?"

"Well, I suppose I—"

"Yes or no?" It was obvious that Matsuoka's patience was wearing thin.

"Yes, Mr. Matsuoka. I believe it to be a valid request."

"Thank God we have that settled. Now, if there is nothing else, gentlemen . . ." Matsuoka turned back to his terminal.

Outside, Bryant slapped Drake good-naturedly on the shoulder and sneered at him in fun. "Yah, you wimp, you! What's all this about Matsuoka tearing you a new asshole whenever you're the messenger of bad tidings? He's a pussy cat!"

Drake, a look of mild shock playing around the grin on his face, laughed and slapped Bryant back. "That is *weird!*" he said. "He's never done that before. That can't be Matsuoka himself. It has to be his doppelgänger or clone or whatever. Or maybe he's gay and just liked the look of your scrawny arse!"

"You wish. I think you just enjoy making everyone believe your job's harder than it really is. It's a sympathy kick."

"Well, whatever it is, you've got your extra week. Just make sure you put it to good use."

The sun was just lifting its face above the horizon out to sea as Yoshikazu Tsunoda walked along the quay toward the *Fujimi Maru*, the vessel that would provide a home for himself and six other fishermen for the following three weeks as they dragged their nets around the Sea of Japan in quest of yellowtail, mackerel, herring, and cod, and maybe even bonito or the occasional tuna that would bring high prices at any of the markets they stopped off at on the way back to port.

Tsunoda had never considered any occupation other than fishing in his thirty-six years. His father had been a fisherman, as had his father before him. His only dream was to save up enough money for a down payment on his own boat, although there was also much to be said for being a hired hand on a vessel owned by somebody else. A flat wage, a commission at the end of each voyage, no worries about the size of the catch, no torn nets to replace, no payroll, no mooring fees, no diesel fees, no maintenance fees, no loan, no insurance, and no threat of barnacles eating into the profits. When he thought of all the anxieties that went hand in hand with captaining one's own vessel, Tsunoda wondered if maybe he shouldn't remain as a hired hand for the rest of his life, as his father and grandfather had advocated.

The cloudless winter sky and the calm sea, sparkling like a million diamonds in the yellow sunlight, generated a warm sense of well-being deep within Tsunoda. He loved the first day of a voyage; especially in such clement conditions. They would leave Hiratsuka on the Pacific coast later in the morning and sail north to cut through the Tsugaru Straits between Honshu and Hokkaido into the Sea of Japan, where they would cast their nets for the first time. The feeling of camaraderie that came with seven men being confined in such small quarters for three weeks was one of the aspects that Tsunoda liked best about being a fisherman. Of course, if he were really honest with himself, he would readily agree that the part of the trip that inspired the highest levels of anticipation and enjoyment was the overnight stopover for refueling in Pusan, South Korea, and the companionship that he and his shipmates would receive at the willing and gentle hands of the hostesses in the various bars that dotted the area.

Tsunoda was brought out of his reverie by a soft mewling sound. He stopped and looked around, trying to locate the source of the noise. Five crab pots were piled in a heap on the edge of the quay beside a crabbing boat, and he slowly walked over to them, craning his neck to see if he could spot the mewler hidden in their shadow. There it was again! He definitely heard a noise coming from behind one of the pots. He hefted his bag off his shoulder, crouched down on his haunches, and gently moved one of the pots aside. Concealed behind it was a bedraggled and very sick cat. The harbor area was usually alive with stray cats, so his discovery did not surprise him in the least. In fact, he was more surprised at the lack of cats, now that he came to think about it. He looked around, but failed to see another feline anywhere. Most unusual.

Shrugging, he grabbed hold of the cat by the scruff of the neck and brought it out into the early-morning sunlight. The cat mewled and put up token resistance, but immediately began to gag and cough up vile-smelling green bile tinged with a hint of blood. It must have swallowed a fishhook and gotten it caught in its throat, he reasoned. He stroked the cat gently on the back of the neck and wondered if he should call the local vet. Not that he would be able to do much, considering the state that the poor thing was already in.

He put his head closer to the cat and tried to comfort it. "Sorry, boy, but you're on your own. I have a ship to catch. You'll just have to try and cough it up on your own."

The cat looked up at him with misery in its eyes, although Tsunoda was sure that he could detect a flash of intelligent gratitude at his comforting words. It mewed softly, and then stiffened as another spasm of pain ripped through its intestines. It began to choke again, and Tsunoda patted it for a last time.

"That's it. Cough that nasty old hook up and you'll be well on the road to recovery. Good luck, cat. You take care of yourself. Hope to see you in a few weeks' time."

Tsunoda stood up, threw his bag across his shoulder, and began to walk toward the *Fujimi Maru* moored thirty meters farther down the quay. He could see activity on deck, probably the captain giving the nets a final check for damage before they set sail. He smiled to himself and his thoughts left the plight of the cat and turned once again to the bars of Pusan and the delights that lay within.

It was getting on to ten o'clock at night when Dr. Masahiro Yasuda realized that he was in above his head. He had initially diagnosed the patient with influenza, but now he was not so sure. He searched through his notes once again to see if he had overlooked anything that might provide a clue as to what the poor man, the middle-aged owner of a yakitori bar down by the coast of Chigasaki, had been inflicted with. It was obviously viral, or so he thought, but apart from that, Dr. Yasuda was completely in the dark.

He picked up the telephone and pressed the button to connect him to the nurses' station.

"Any developments with Mr. Kaneko?"

He listened in silence as the nurse described further deterioration and then hung up. Two hours previously, ecchymotic lesions and petechial lesions had begun to develop on the patient's limbs and trunk, and they were not responding to treatment. There were also indications that the victim was beginning to develop Waterhouse-Friderichsen syndrome, which was characterized by fulminant septicemia and congestive heart failure.

Dr. Yasuda sighed and reached for the phone again. If the

disease was viral, there was a strong chance that it could be contagious and the patient should be isolated. But even so, he had never heard of a virus this rampant. Damn, the patient had actually *walked* into the hospital under his own steam not twelve hours before, complaining of a fever and stomach pains, and now he was all but comatose. Well, it was better to be safe than sorry.

He punched in the number for the nurses' station once again and ordered them to place Mr. Kaneko in total isolation.

"So what do you think is going on then?" Peter Bryant asked in Japanese, washing a mouthful of *tonkatsu* down with a slurp of green tea that he had poured from a dispenser attached to the counter.

Leonard Drake shook a liberal amount of brown sauce over his pork cutlet on its bed of shredded cabbage and pondered the question. "Impossible to say," he replied at length. "Maybe they've made some sort of breakthrough with a new drug. Found a cure for AIDS or something. Who knows?"

"I would say that a problem has arisen," Joji Higashino said. Higashino worked on the Japanese patents for Hamada Sei-yaku, and the three men, who shared the same director, regularly had lunch together. "Matsuoka has been strange recently. Quiet, as if burdened with a substantial load. He spends most of every day in the conference room with all of the other directors, and then sits at his desk until late every night."

"Yes, I've noticed that," confirmed Bryant. "And it's not only Matsuoka. Wherever I seem to go recently, I find a couple of executives huddled up together in conversation: in the foyer, in the elevator hall, by the coffee machines, even in the men's room. Whenever I get close enough to overhear, they clam up and just stare at me as if I were public enemy number one."

"You think we're in for a restructuring or something?" Drake asked. "Maybe they're all going to get the bullet and they're

30

trying to work out a strategy for saving their collective arses."

Higashino refilled his cup from the green-tea dispenser and surveyed his plate and chopsticks somberly. "Well, whatever it is, it's coming to a head. One of the secretaries told me that those daily meetings in the conference room are getting more and more heated. Lots of shouting and angry voices."

"That confirms it, then," Drake said, "a reshuffle." He gulped down a mouthful of tea and belched in satisfaction. "Just as long as the bloody thing doesn't affect me, I don't give a shit!"

The killers wasted no time in colonizing the nasopharynx of their victim. The next step in their deadly invasion was mucosal penetration, which would finally lead into the bloodstream and the body's organs: the meninges, lungs, heart, adrenals, joints, ears, and eyes. They felt no animosity toward their host, as they felt no pity. They were simply going ahead with the task for which they had been designed with a mindless efficiency commonly attributed to machines and robots. They had a job to do, and they were doing it—extraordinarily well.

A colony of the assassins was established in the upper respiratory tract of their host, where they fed heartily off the rich nutrients and multiplied at a frightening rate. Although they did not register the fact, and it in no way diminished their overall power, a certain proportion of this colony was forcibly ejected from the host in an explosive ejaculation of air that propelled them out into the external atmosphere in a phenomenon known as the common sneeze.

Into the mouths and noses of the dozens of people who shared the crowded commuter train from Ofuna to central Tokyo with Yukari Nakagawa, their host.

Norio Kondo felt his wife's hand on his shoulder and leaned back in his chair. He had been so engrossed in watching the conversation evolve on the computer monitor that he hadn't even noticed her enter the study. "Ah . . ." he said as she handed him a glass of warm sake. "Just what I needed."

"Anything interesting tonight?" Shigeko, Kondo's wife, asked.

"Kakadenka was asking for you earlier. I don't know if she's still on-line."

"Let me see."

Kondo moved out of his chair to allow his wife to sit down. She deftly operated the computer mouse to bring up a blank message box, into which she tapped a message. Once she had finished, she hit the post button and the screen was updated to show her message at the top of the screen.

Norio Kondo and his wife had first discovered the Internet in their late forties and were immediately enchanted by its simplicity and far-reaching capabilities. Three years later, they were the Webmasters of an on-line bulletin board that collected members by invitation only. The site, known as the Zen Nippon Otaku Tomonokai, was not registered on any of the search engines—except for those that used on-line spiders to update their databases—and a password was required for entry to keep nonmembers who stumbled across it at bay. Current membership encompassed nearly sixty people, all of whom had been recruited by Kondo himself during his late-night Net surfing through various homepages and public bulletin boards.

"Ah, here she is," said Shigeko as another message appeared at the top of the screen. The message was addressed to Shiwakucha-Baba and was signed Kakadenka. All of the Tomonokai members had self-chosen handles—nicknames that they used to disguise their real identities. Kondo was Gakusha, meaning *scholar*, and his wife was Shiwakucha-Baba, meaning *wrinkled crone*. Only Kondo and his wife knew the true names and occupations of all members, as it was decided at the beginning that anonymity would stimulate conversation.

Norio Kondo sipped his sake and fondly watched his wife read through the message and then type out a reply. Twenty-five years of childless marriage had brought the couple so close together that they were almost inseparable. If somebody had asked him if he still loved her, he probably would have hesitated and registered confusion. His feelings for her had surpassed mere love and had entered the realm of admiration and deep respect. He loved her no more than he loved his own legs, but he could not even begin to contemplate the thought of being separated from those. She was an integral part of him, and life without her was inconceivable. She had put on a good deal of weight over the course of the years and had gained quite a few gray hairs, but then again, so had he. He mostly admired her ready wit and willingness to learn anything new, as well as her easygoing character that had made her a firm favorite on the Tomonokai Web site.

Kondo, a professor of economics at Kanagawa University, had felt relief when his wife had taken so quickly to computers and the Internet. Remaining childless throughout their marriage had affected her more than him, and he had feared for her mental health once menopause had struck just a few years previously. He had hated going off to work and leaving her alone in the house to brood over her own loneliness. His first action had been to purchase a dog, a brown-and-white corgi with a lopsided grin that they had named Gonta and who was presently laid out fast asleep on a square of red carpeting by the wall of the study. Although Shigeko loved Gonta with all her heart and pampered him shamelessly, Norio realized that there was still something missing from her life. He had been introduced to the Internet himself by a colleague at the university and had purchased a computer for home use. One month later, Shigeko had made several e-mail friends throughout the country, and the sparkle of life had returned to the house. Two months later she had mastered the HTML computer language and had set up her own homepage, sharing recipes and other information with anyone and everyone who cared to visit. The idea to open a real-time bulletin board for people who shared the same interests originally came from Shigeko during the summer of the previous year, and the two had spent several satisfying months working out the details and designing the layout until the Zen Nippon Otaku Tomonokai had been launched in October. It had now been up and running for nearly five months.

Norio Kondo was content. Everything in his life was running smoothly. He had a warm house to come home to, an understanding wife, a job he loved, more money than he needed now that the house had been paid up, and sufficient outside interests to keep his life well balanced.

"Kakadenka wants to know how Gonta is getting on," said Shigeko.

At the mention of his name, the corgi lifted his head from his front paws and looked inquisitively at her, his head cocked to one side.

"Tell her he is fat and lazy," said Norio, looking across at the dog with a grin. "Isn't that right, Gonta, old boy? You're fat and lazy, aren't you?" Gonta's ears picked up at the direct communication and he trotted over to Kondo to be petted.

Shigeko laughed and turned back to the computer. She opened a message box and typed in, *Gonta is fat and lazy*. She signed the message, but paused before pressing the post button. As an afterthought she added, *Just like my husband . . .* ☺

Unknown Flu Bug Hits Chigasaki

Yokohama (Kyodo) Local health officials warned Tuesday of a particularly virulent strain of influenza that has stricken twenty-eight people in eastern Kanagawa. Hospitals in the Chigasaki and Hiratsuka regions of Kanagawa prefecture have reported a localized outbreak of what seems to be an unknown strain of flu. Symptoms include temperatures in excess of 39 degrees Celsius, nausea, abdominal pain, and the onset of a fast-spreading rash. So far, twenty-eight cases have been reported, and local authorities are preparing for more.

Chigasaki health officials stress that this outbreak is nowhere near epidemic proportions, but urge anybody experiencing signs of fever, neck ache, or uncontrollable vomiting to contact their doctor as soon as possible.

Although an unknown strain of influenza is considered to be the culprit, authorities have yet to rule out food poisoning and other causes.

Peter Bryant replaced his coffee cup in the saucer and brought the *Japan Times* up closer to his face. He reread the short article and then dropped the newspaper onto the table.

"Mi-*chan*!" he called to Michiyo, who was busy applying makeup in the bathroom. "Come and look at this!"

Michiyo Kato poked her head around the door to their dining room, a tube of lipstick held in her right hand. "You called?"

"Yes. Come and have a look at this. Anything about it strike you as odd?"

Michiyo walked across the room and leaned over Bryant's shoulder to read the article that he was indicating with his forefinger. The fragrance of freshly washed hair and soap wafted over Bryant.

"Looks like a flu warning to me." She shrugged.

"Look at the location. Don't you think that is a bit of a coincidence?"

"Yokohama? Should I?"

"No, not there. Here. Chigasaki and Hiratsuka."

"So what?"

"Chigasaki is where Hamada's R and D center is located. There's a strange atmosphere at work recently and we've all been trying to come up with a reason. Maybe they've had an accident." Bryant refilled his coffee cup and blew on the top to cool it.

"Wow, that's some imagination you have there," Michiyo said with an impish grin. She kissed Bryant on the top of the head and began heading back to the bathroom. "And would you mind putting your dirty shirts into the washing machine for a change? I found three on the chair in the bedroom."

Bryant wasn't listening. He picked up the newspaper and coffee and took them through to the sofa in the adjoining living room. Reaching for the telephone, he quickly dialed the number for Leonard Drake from memory.

"Morning, Len," he said when the connection had been made. "Seen this morning's newspaper?"

"Yes, why?" Drake said.

"Did you see the small article about the flu breakout in Chigasaki? It's in the National News Briefs section on page two."

"No, I didn't. But are you sure? Chigasaki?"

"You find it a coincidence, too, huh? At least it's not only me."

"Hang on a sec; I'll just go and get it."

The telephone clunked and then went silent as Drake laid down the receiver.

Michiyo came into the room, fully dressed and swinging a Gucci handbag from her shoulder. "See you tonight, darling." She kissed Bryant briefly on the cheek. "Don't be late for work, now."

Peter held his hand over the receiver and blew a kiss at her as she disappeared out into the hallway. "I might be a little late tonight," he shouted after her. "Don't wait up."

The sound of the front door closing coincided with a rustle from the phone as Drake picked up the receiver.

"Okay. I've got it," he said. "Seems a bit suspect to me. You don't think that they've been trying out phase trials on a new drug before the animal trials, do you?"

Obtaining patents for new drugs was a lengthy and extremely expensive process. All drugs had to be put through exhaustive toxicity tests on rodents and other mammals before they could be tested on human subjects in clinical trials. Having gotten past the animal tests, the process moved on to phase one, in which the drug was administered to a few healthy volunteers. It then went on to phase two, with a few hundred volunteers, and then phase three, which involved several thousand. Once those three phases had been passed to the satisfaction of the required prescribes, an application for phase four testing could be submitted to the authorities. Phase four trials required hundreds of selected doctors to administer and monitor the progress of thousands of patients over the course of a full year. It was only at the successful completion of phase four that the product could be marketed and the original investment reclaimed. Although it was extremely unlikely that a reputable pharmaceutical company would try to cut corners and speed up the process by shortening the animal trials, both Drake and Bryant realized that they did not know enough about Hamada Seiyaku to completely overlook this possibility.

"That's what I'd put my money on," Bryant said. "There can't be that many strains of unknown flu about, and the location stinks to high heaven."

"So what do you suggest?"

Bryant considered the question carefully. If management discovered that they suspected the company of illegally attempting to force a product onto the market without due process, they would probably be fired on the spot—whether the company was guilty or not—on the basis of disloyalty and troublemaking.

"Well, we obviously can't let them get away with it, but I don't think we should go at this like a bull in a china shop. What about requesting a trip down to Chigasaki to confirm a few of the points on the Neuraval application? It might not do any good, but a look around isn't going to hurt any, either."

"That's no problem. I can make that decision myself. I'll phone up the director as soon as I get to work and make an appointment. Anything else?"

"I also suggest that we make a concerted effort to find out what all of these executive meetings are about. Even if we get caught on that, we can always put it down to natural curiosity. I bet everybody in the whole darned company would give up a month's salary to know what's going on there."

An ambulance met the flight from Tokyo on the tarmac of Seattle-Tacoma International and whisked Tatsumi Iyama off to the hospital immediately after the simplified immigration procedures had been completed. Iyama was unconscious by the time the representative from the airline arrived to deliver his luggage in person and to confirm that his malady had not been brought on by in-flight cuisine or by any other cause attributable to the company.

Tatsumi Iyama was a very sick man. An initial examination convinced Dr. Patricia Marston that she was dealing with something completely out of her scope, and she ordered total isolation in the intensive-care unit and a series of tests to collect blood and tissue samples, all of which were sent to the lab while she struggled to find the intuition to help her sort this problem out. Her immediate prognosis was meningitis, but until the results came back from the lab, she could not be sure. Meanwhile, Iyama was gradually sinking into a comatose state, and all she could do was link him up to the life-support equipment, stuff him full of antibiotics, and hope for the best.

She wondered about the other people on the flight. If the disease were contagious, as meningitis certainly was, then she should contact the airline for a list of passengers and prescribe some preventive medication before it had a chance to spread. She would have to get authorization for that, however, and she decided that her time would be better spent in caring for her patient. She began to make a list of the further tests that she wanted to be run.

Tests that would last longer than the ability of her patient to maintain a grasp on life.

Chapter Three

"Hang on; let me get this straight." Peter Bryant looked incredulously at Leonard Drake and shook his head in disbelief. "You are telling me that you were warned off visiting Chigasaki?"

"That's about the size of it. I couldn't get hold of the director, so I spoke to the administration manager. He told me that they were extremely busy and that they could not accept any visits at the moment. That seemed like a fair comment to me, and if they'd left it at that I probably would have thought no more about it. Thirty minutes later, however, I was called into Matsuoka's office and read the riot act. He was furious, but wouldn't say why. He kept accusing me of meddling in matters that are not my concern."

"Did you mention my name?"

"No, why?"

"Well, let's give it a bit of time to die down, and then I'll go and see Matsuoka myself when you're out of the office and insist that I need to visit Chigasaki to confirm some points. Just to see what he says."

"Okay, if you want. But I think we ought to be careful. I wouldn't be surprised if our initial assumption is correct and they're testing something out there on human subjects. A disclosure of that sort would hammer the company into oblivion, so I don't think they would think twice about firing us to keep it under wraps. I may complain about this job, but I can't afford to lose it."

Drake refilled his glass from the frosted liter bottle of beer and took a deep draft. Joji Higashino waved to the waiter and indicated that he should bring three more bottles to the table—the fourth round they had ordered. They were sitting in a small bar on the Yaesu side of Tokyo Station, a dark and dingy establishment that provided inexpensive solace for the office workers who abounded in the area. When the beer order arrived, Higashino busily filled up each man's glass and wiped his fingers on the *oshibori*.

"So what do you think, Joji?" Bryant asked, turning his attention to the diminutive man.

"Does it matter?" Higashino replied to the question with another question. "I wouldn't be surprised to discover that the company was up to no good, but I don't think that it's our concern. Why can't you just ignore it? It's not our problem."

"Typical!" Drake muttered under his breath, turning his eyes down to the table. "Bloody typical Japanese head-in-the-sand logic!"

Joji looked at Drake, but ignored the barb. "If you think that this is worth losing your jobs over, then I'll say no more. But please count me out. If every company in Japan were placed under the microscope, I'd bet you'd find something illegal in every one. So what? It's of no consequence. That's how business is conducted over here. It harms nobody in the long run, and it stimulates business and the economy. Laws are made by politicians to placate uninformed constituents and the media

40

and few are conducive to effective business. What do they care, as long as they get their inflated salaries and perks? Corporate administration is too important a subject to leave in the hands of mere politicians, so a set of sublaws has been established, and they are observed within certain areas of business. That's the way it works."

"You speak as if you don't care about it, Joji," Bryant said. "Surely you don't think that corporations should be above the law. That would provide the basis for anarchy."

"Maybe, when seen through your American eyes, Peter. But business has been conducted along these lines for hundreds of years in Japan. It is only lately that your tedious set of Christian morals has been adopted by society in general over here, and it's destroying everything that we managed to build up over the past fifty years since the end of the war."

"You seem to forget that I'm Japanese, as well, Joji." Bryant had felt the sting of the reference to his "American eyes." He was proud of his Japanese heritage, and had found that the insult hurt more than he would have imagined.

"No offense, Peter, but having Japanese blood running through your veins does not mean that you are Japanese," Higashino said. He realized that he had just insulted his friend, but there were certain things that just had to be said. "Being Japanese is a state of mind, not a state of body. It's an understanding of things that cannot be explained. It's realizing that for every good, there are debts that must be paid. It's working for the good of generalism, not individualism."

"Oh, come on, Joji. You're talking out the back of your neck!" Drake refilled his glass again and stared belligerently at Higashino. The effects of the drinks were catching up with him. "Look at all of these politicians and executives being arrested lately. They were cheating and getting rich in the process. You think that's good for business? And what about Hamada Seiyaku? Are you seriously telling me that you think it is quite natural for companies to risk the lives of normal people just as long as business is not hindered? That's crap, and you know it!"

"If that's what you think I am saying, then you have misunderstood me. First of all, you have no evidence that Hamada Seiyaku is involved with anything that is risking the lives of normal people. It is your own active imagination that's provided you with this conclusion. Second, do you really think that it's only recently that politicians have accepted bribes from banks and securities companies to ensure favorable handling? Do you think it's only recently that the *Sokaiya* have demanded money from large corporations in return for not disrupting general shareholder meetings? Do you think it's only recently that companies have treated their clients to golf trips and meals in expensive restaurants in order to seal lucrative contracts? No! This is the traditional style of Japanese business, and when left to run its own course, Japan was a thriving concern that earned—deservedly—the respect and admiration of the entire world. As soon as your so-called moralistic Western styles of business were forced upon us, Japan went into free fall, the yen depreciated and the financial systems began to crumble. There are certain things that *must* remain essentially Japanese in order for this society to continue to function. Can't you understand that?"

Drake was becoming more and more incensed. He recognized that this was mostly to do with the amount of beer he had consumed, but he had had about as much as he could take of having all of Japan's troubles blamed on himself, as if he were the sole representative of the entire non-Japanese human race. He had to endure this sort of crap all the time from Matsuoka, who treated him like he had just crawled out from under a damp stone, but he was damned if he had to accept it from a five-foot nobody like Higashino. He slammed his glass down on the table, causing a break in the conversation at the surrounding tables, and waved a finger threateningly in front of Higashino's face.

"Now listen here, you. If you think—"

Before he could continue, Bryant grabbed hold of his finger and squeezed. Drake looked across at him in surprise, as if snapped at by a pet dog. "Calm down, Len. Joji is entitled to his opinion, even if you don't agree with it. There's a grain of truth in what he says. Give the man a chance, for God's sake."

Drake shook his finger free, picked up his glass, and glared at Higashino. "Go on, then. Spit it out!"

"Look, I'm not trying to pick a fight with you, Len. I'm merely trying to explain something."

Drake looked up and nodded, the anger draining from his features. "You're right. I'm sorry. My temper sometimes gets the better of me." He picked up one of the beer bottles and held it out toward Higashino—a liquid olive branch. Higashino swigged some of the beer out of his glass and then extended it toward the proffered bottle so that Drake could top it up. The ritual complete, Bryant and Drake looked expectantly at Higashino, encouraging him to continue.

"You see, there is a sort of subculture that operates within Japanese business. It's undefined, but that's the way it should be. Money changes hands at an incredibly high tempo, which in your culture would be seen as illegal, but it has a curious habit of circulating so that nobody loses out in the long run. A gives to B, B gives to C, C gives to A. You, of course, would label this money as 'graft,' but in my dictionary it is a lubricant to oil the wheels of commerce. It's not a case of one person or one concern getting rich quickly; it's prevalent throughout the entire system and it acts as a stabilizing factor. Everybody is a winner, and it keeps society on an even keel. Take, for example, the recent outrage at companies paying off the *Sokaiya*. Nobody really begrudges them this money. The crime syndicates that run it—the *boryokudan*—would never charge a sum that a company could not afford. The companies pay up and receive certain favors in return, and everybody is happy. Now, consider the fact that your morals have been introduced and these actions have now been outlawed in accordance with the Western style of business. The *boryokudan* have lost a substantial part of their income, so they turn to other interests. What is the result? An increase in drug usage, child prostitution, and violent crime."

Higashino paused to take a sip of beer.

Bryant leaned forward and reached for his glass. "We're not talking graft, Joji," he said. "We're talking about Hamada Seiyaku risking the lives of unsuspecting people. Where does that figure into your scenario?"

"I think you are mistaken."

"What about the flu outbreak?" Drake asked.

"A flu outbreak is a flu outbreak. What do you want me to say?"

Bryant sighed. "Well, let's put it another way. Say, for argument's sake, that we discover Hamada Seiyaku is up to something that would endanger the lives of people. Okay?" Higashino nodded. "Would you feel that it is your duty to help expose the company? Would you be willing to join up with us to make sure that the situation is corrected?"

"No."

"For God's sake!" Drake slapped his forehead with an open palm. "How can we get through to you? Why would you possibly be against correcting a wrong? What is your *problem*?"

Higashino rotated his glass and stared at the top of it. "I have two children and a housing loan," he said.

"So?"

"I cannot afford to anger the company. My children's future depends on me remaining a loyal employee. There is more to Japan's employment system than either you or Peter seem to grasp."

Drake noted the downcast way in which Higashino said this, and invited him to continue. Bryant looked on.

"I, like all other Japanese salarymen, receive my pay on both a monthly scale and a six-month scale."

"The bonus system. Yes, I know. Peter and I also get paid a bonus every summer and winter."

"Well, the cost of land in the Kanto region makes it almost impossible for a normal company worker to obtain a housing loan on the monthly salary, so a system has been established where the monthly payments are kept at an affordable level on the condition that the entire bonus is passed across to the loan company."

"So?"

"A certain proportion of the bonus is discretionary and the company is therefore in a position to prevent me from paying off my mortgage if I don't toe the line."

"But that's blackmail," Drake said.

Higashino shrugged. "It's the way it works. The problem lies with society, not the company. There is also the question of promotion."

"Meaning?"

"It is very expensive to bring children up in Japan. In order to ensure that our children have every chance in the future, it's necessary for them to go to expensive private schools and cram schools so that they can enter prestigious universities. The better the university they go to, the better the job they get when they graduate. My children are small, but already they go to an expensive kindergarten, and my wife has a detailed plan for their entire childhood right through to the age of twenty-two. Her plan has them attending a series of high-class schools until they finally enter Keio University, Tokyo University, Waseda University, or Nihon University. This plan works on the assumption that I will be promoted in line with my age throughout the coming two decades. The costs will increase as they get older, but so will my salary. There is one problem, however. If I'm overlooked for just one promotion throughout this period, it means that I probably will not be able to keep up with the payments, and my children will not be able to enter university. If they don't go to university, they will not be able to get high-paying jobs, so their children will also not be able to go to university. Nor their children, nor their children's children."

Higashino broke off and drank some beer. He looked between Bryant and Drake with a smile on his face as he saw them carefully contemplating his words.

Bryant cleared his throat. "So you're not saying you won't help us. You're saying you *can't* help us."

"Bravo!" Higashino said with a laugh.

"You are being blackmailed by society at large."

"Me and eighty percent of the population."

Drake finished his beer and called for the bill. "Jesus, Joji, that is just about the most depressing thing I've ever heard in all my puff. Have you ever thought of living abroad? How can you stand that sort of pressure?"

"Pressure? What pressure? It's my way of life. I told you, being Japanese has nothing to do with owning a Japanese passport. It is a state of mind."

Drake pulled out his wallet as the bill was delivered to the table and paid the entire sum with a single ten-thousand-yen note, waving away Higashino's protestations. "Well, you've now shamed me into picking up the whole bill. I hope you're satisfied." Drake's frown turned into a grin. "But I'll tell you this. You are a crazy man, Joji Higashino, and I wouldn't trade places with you for a fortnight of passion with a *Takarazuka* troupe."

Higashino grinned back. "Nor me with you," he said.

The sightseeing bus, carrying twenty-two tourists from Osaka, pulled into the restaurant's car park and came to a halt, brakes squealing like irate banshees. The tour guide picked up the microphone and stood to attention beside the driver's seat. She clicked on the mike and informed the passengers that the lunch reservation was not for another forty minutes and that they were free to wander around the Tsurugaoka Hachimangu shrine on their own until that time. "A guided tour of the shrine will be given after lunch, so it may be a good idea to avoid the main complex and just stroll through the surrounding woods. Please make sure that you are back by exactly one o'clock, and please take care when crossing the road. Thank you."

The bus began to empty itself of its passengers. The driver jumped down from his side of the bus, stretched luxuriously, and lit a cigarette before walking across for a chat with three other drivers who were sitting on a bench beside a drink vending machine. The tour guide walked into the restaurant to confirm the reservation and make sure that the group could sit down to lunch on schedule. Several of the male passengers decided that a leisurely cigarette was more important than a stroll through the woods and milled around the bus, chattering among themselves as their wives separated into cliques and crossed the road to the grounds of the shrine.

The Hachimangu shrine was the largest and most famous of Kamakura's numerous shrines and temples and was always crowded with visitors at the main entrance. One of the groups of women turned right at the entrance to the car park and began to walk toward the front of the shrine. Another, consisting of five housewives, crossed the road and entered the precincts of the shrine through a small waist-high gate made of bamboo tied together with twine. The trees immediately baffled the noise of the traffic, and the fragrance of warm compost wafted up from the ground. The group wandered slowly along the path, chattering and bantering loudly in their distinctive Osaka accents and marveling at the cathedral-like atmosphere in which they found themselves. The two hours and fifty minutes they had spent on the bullet train from Shin Osaka station and the subsequent two and a half hours they had spent on the bus had been tiring, and it felt good to be able to stretch their legs.

Movement off to the left caught the eye of one of the women. "Look, what's that?" she said.

The others halted their progress and peered along the line that she drew with an outstretched arm. "Over there! I do believe it's a squirrel. I think it's not well. Quick, help me get over this fence."

She leaned on the shoulder of one of her companions and cocked a leg over the low bamboo fence. Two of the other women followed her, leaving the other two shouting encouragement from the path. She walked slowly over to the squirrel at first to avoid startling it, but increased her pace when she saw that it made no attempt to escape.

"It *is* a squirrel!" she shouted. "But I think it's nearly dead. What should we do?"

Her two friends clustered around and squatted down beside the small creature. "Ah, poor little thing," said one. "It's having trouble breathing. Must have been attacked by a cat or something. Should we take it to the groundskeeper?"

"Good idea."

The first woman picked up the tiny animal and cradled it in her left arm. The squirrel tried to struggle, but was immediately stricken by a spasm that set its body rigid. The two other women looked on in pity, gently stroking the creature's head as its eyes rolled up into its sockets. Its breathing suddenly became more erratic as it strained to force air into its tiny lungs. Mucus clogged its nose and bubbled at the corners of its mouth, until finally its breathing stopped with a final wheeze that sounded like gas escaping from a pipe.

"It's gone," the first woman said softly. "We were too late. The poor little thing is dead." She bent forward and placed a gentle kiss on its head before laying it down on the ground and looking around for something with which to dig a hole.

She found a small branch and snapped off the protruding twigs. Holding the branch in both hands, she scraped a small hole in the hard, red Kanto loam while the other two women searched around for stones to place on the makeshift grave. Their chore finished, they climbed over the fence to join their two colleagues before wandering back to the car park, subdued and strangely disheartened, their walk in the woods totally forgotten.

The small Post-it note on his desk intrigued Peter Bryant. If Joji Higashino wanted to meet him, why didn't he just tell him instead of leaving ambiguous notes stuck to his telephone? He read the memo once more. *I need to speak to you with regard to our conversation the other night. I'll be in the Doutor coffee shop by Yurakucho Station at seven o'clock. Please come. Joji.* Shrugging, Bryant stuck the note onto the diary that lay open on his desk and turned back to his work.

He had an appointment with Matsuoka at three o'clock and wanted to create a viable list of questions regarding the Neuraval patent that could only be asked in person. He had already laid the background to his plans by e-mailing the Chigasaki Research and Development Center with several questions to which he knew they would not bother replying. Chigasaki was notorious for its delay in answering inquiries, and this provided him with a good reason for visiting the plant himself. He hoped that his request for the visit would simply make it appear as if he were striving to keep his part of the bargain by completing the patent application within the time limit allotted to him. Leonard Drake had also played a part in laying the foundations of the plan by taking an afternoon off for a bogus trip to the dentist. With Drake absent, Bryant was obliged to deal directly with Matsuoka himself. He finished off his list and glanced up at the clock. Two-fifty-five. Time to get going.

The dark blue bags hanging beneath Kazunori Matsuoka's eyes were testimony to the strain he was under. Bryant had seen Matsuoka transformed within less than a week from an aging but comparatively congenial salaryman into a husk of a man on whose shoulders rested the woes of the world. Even his suit seemed to hang listlessly from his frame. What was going on? Bryant would have given his right arm to find out.

"You wished to see me?" Matsuoka's question seemed to echo through the room. Even his voice sounded different.

"Yes, Mr. Matsuoka. May I . . . ?" Bryant indicated the seat in front of Matsuoka's desk, and Matsuoka nodded. Bryant sat down and removed his list of questions from a clear folder that contained several sheets of paper. He passed the list across to Matsuoka and sat back while his boss read through it.

"What is this?"

"A list of questions that I need to get answered before I can complete the Neuraval patent. I've e-mailed Chigasaki to try to get the answers, but so far there's been no reply. I'll have to pop down there and sort it out on the spot."

Matsuoka's eyes had narrowed at the mention of Chigasaki. He looked at Bryant suspiciously and worked hard to suppress a bubble of anger that was forming in his gut. "Have you spoken to Drake about this?"

"No, he's off this afternoon. But if I don't get it sorted out soon, I'll never have the application ready in time. Tomorrow is convenient for me, if that's—"

"No!"

The word was almost shouted, like an expletive. Bryant watched in fascination as Matsuoka's neck gradually turned from light ochre to bright vermilion.

"I beg your pardon?"

"What is all this sudden interest in Chigasaki? What are you two up to? I have heard several reports about you two pestering everybody with questions!" Matsuoka's jowls shook with outrage. He found it intolerable that these two *gaijin* should place him in a position where he felt as if he had to defend himself. Could they possibly suspect something? He had to assume that they did. "I have already refused Drake's request for a visit, and now you come waltzing in here with similar flimsy excuses. You have been provided with a desk from which to do your job. If

I wanted you running around the country chasing phantoms, you would have been provided with a car instead. Use your desk, Mr. Bryant, and do the job for which you are paid. Good morning!"

"But—"

"But nothing! Good morning!"

Bryant collected his papers together and stood up. "But I—"

"Good morning, Mr. Bryant!"

Bryant left the office in confusion and walked slowly back to his desk. What had Matsuoka to hide? The request to visit Chigasaki was not unusual under the circumstances, but Matsuoka had nearly had an apoplectic fit at the mere mention of the name. He had expected a refusal—in fact, he had hoped for one, if only to reinforce his own theory that something strange was afoot—but he had not expected it to take such an aggressive form. An uneasy feeling began to swell within Bryant—a feeling that warned him he was in danger of losing his job. Maybe Higashino was right. Maybe he should give up this crazy witch-hunt, after all. It really was none of his business, and he had probably just added another black mark to his work record. What if Hamada Seiyaku were not involved in anything shady? What if Matsuoka's attitude were merely a reflection of Japanese business practices? He was well aware that most companies in Japan operated on a sort of need-to-know basis, with the management keeping their cards close to their chests. Although he didn't think his "American eyes," as Higashino had called them, were simply seeing Reds under the bed, he couldn't really afford to overlook the possibility. Was the job getting so boring that his subconscious was maliciously seeking out phantoms where no phantoms existed, as Matsuoka had claimed? Was the devil finding work for idle hands? Had his resentment toward the Japanese style of business made him look upon himself as a knight in shining armor, arriving in the nick of time to save the populace from the evil machinations of corporate Japan?

But what about the increase in the so-called flu cases down in Kanagawa? The morning newspapers had reported that more than eighty people had now been hospitalized with the mysterious bug, and close to forty were either dead or in critical condition.

He sat down at his desk and sighed heavily. Maybe he should simply give up the idea of linking the company with the outbreak down in Chigasaki and get on with his work. The yellow Post-it note stuck to his diary reminded him of the meeting he had with Higashino that evening. He wondered if it had anything to do with his phantom, and, if so, whether Joji had any concrete information or not. But that was ridiculous! Higashino had made his stance on the subject quite clear in the bar a few nights ago. He had probably just found a good restaurant and wanted to get Bryant's opinion of it. But then why would he refer to "our conversation the other night"? It must be related. *Right!* He would listen to what Joji had to say, and if it was conjecture he would throw in the towel and return one hundred percent of his concentration to his work. He owed the company that, at the very least.

Kazunori Matsuoka removed his handkerchief from his trouser pocket and mopped his face. He was getting too old for this sort of thing. Not that he presumed there was an optimum age for skullduggery, but the pressures of the past week were beginning to catch up with him. He was tired. Very tired.

He ran the conversation he had just had with Bryant over in his mind again. He was convinced that Drake and Bryant suspected something, but he was not quite sure how to go about handling it. Firing them was an option, but what would that solve? It would simply reinforce their conviction that something was going on. Much better to keep them within the company, where a discreet eye could be kept on them at all times. But he was worried. He had already informed the other directors that he suspected Drake and Bryant of delving into the outbreak in Chigasaki, and some of the suggestions for coping with the situation had shaken Matsuoka to the core. One of the directors had actually advocated "removing them permanently." Another had suggested granting them their trip to Chigasaki, ensuring that they were exposed to the bacterium, and then allowing nature to take its course. Although he recognized that this was a form of toadying aimed at gaining favor with Shigeru Hamada, he was also not happy with the way the president was coping with these outrageous suggestions. The man had suddenly become obsessed with keeping the company's name out of the newspapers and was lending an interested ear to every bizarre idea that arose during the meetings. Fortunately, all of them had been overruled up until now, but Matsuoka was grimly aware that the meetings were becoming more and more dramatic and the directors increasingly paranoid. He was obliged to bring up today's conversation at this evening's meeting, of course, but the fact that his reports were pulling the noose closer about Drake's and Bryant's necks was not bringing him any solace. As much as he loathed the direction that the company had taken over this despicable matter, joining the conspiracy instead of standing up for his beliefs during that fateful first meeting had made him as fully responsible as the president himself, and if the natural progression of events eventually led to the cold-blooded murder of these two men, then his hands would be as bloodstained as the rest of them. *Damn!* Why couldn't they have waited until *after* his retirement before getting involved in that idiotic contract?

Matsuoka looked at his watch. Still fifty minutes to go before the next meeting commenced. He reluctantly penciled the words *Drake* and *Bryant* in the margin of his notepad, and then turned to his computer screen to search the Internet for more mentions of the outbreak to add to the twenty-eight he had already located. Today's briefing had all of the ingredients for a long and tedious discussion, and it was shaping up to evolve into one of marathon proportions.

* * *

The unscheduled and unpublicized meeting was held in the prime minister's official residence. Only four men were present: Ichiro Minami, the minister of health and welfare, Naoki Hoshino, the director general of the Defense Agency, Shoji Kubota, the general secretary of the Liberal Democratic Party, and Kiyoshi Aizawa, the prime minister of Japan. They were seated in armchairs that surrounded a low coffee table. All of the chairs were equipped with white antimacassars, but none of the men were leaning back on them. All were hunched forward on the edge of their seats as they read through the two-page briefing prepared for them by the director general of the Defense Agency.

Prime Minister Aizawa removed his glasses and tapped the paper rhythmically with one of the stems. "Why was I not informed of this?" he asked, directing the question at Hoshino.

Naoki Hoshino cleared his throat. "Well, Mr. Prime Minister, the contract was concluded just over two years ago, during the tenure of your predecessor."

"The socialist?"

"Yes, sir."

"Damn!"

The Liberal Democratic Party was formed in November 1955 and was elected into government consecutively up until July 1993, when it was forced to operate as an opposition party for the first time in its history. The Social Democratic Party of Japan took the reins of power from August of 1993, but the LDP managed to get reelected through the formation of a coalition government consisting of the LDP, the SDPJ, and the Sakigake Party in July of 1994. Once the die was cast, the concept of coalition governments followed a period in which tie-ups were considered the norm, and socialist prime ministers no longer triggered the gasps of disbelief that were initially issued by the members of the Liberal Democratic Party in response to the shock received when the leader of the SDPJ was chosen above the leader of the LDP to head the new government for the first time. However, old wounds still rankled.

"But this goes against the constitution. How did it ever manage to get past the General Council and the Policy Research Council?"

"It didn't, sir. The directive to go ahead with implementation was issued by the former prime minister himself."

"And now we hold full accountability."

"Precisely, sir."

Aizawa replaced his glasses on his nose and looked at the two pieces of paper in front of him. "All right. Explain this to me in layman's terms," he said.

Ichiro Minami, the minister of health and welfare, nodded to the other men to indicate that he would take up the briefing. The prime minister pushed himself back into the armchair and laid his head on the antimacassar, his eyes closed and his hands folded in front of him as he prepared his concentration for the forthcoming explanation.

"A contract was concluded between the government of Japan and Hamada Seiyaku Pharmaceuticals, Inc., for the latter to initiate research into a bacterial agent that could be used to slow down an invading army in the event of an act of aggression against Japan. The decision was made soon after it was discovered that North Korea's Taepodong missiles were capable of reaching as far as Tokyo. The idea was to genetically engineer an agent that would be both debilitating and highly contagious within a short period of time in order to infect a large body of men within a minimal time span. Research on a delivery system was scheduled to commence after a suitable bacterium and an effective cure had been isolated.

"The bacterium that was finally chosen is called *Neisseria meningococcus*. The particular strain of the bacterium that was selected induces a disease known as pediatric meningococcemia in small children as a general rule, but it has been genetically engineered to infect adults as well. The disease itself is not usually life-threatening, but it has been made to swiftly lead to a condition known as the inflammatory cascade that is fatal in most cases. Carriage rates during an epidemic are as high as ninety percent, and a large percentage of this number will succumb to the inflammatory-cascade condition." Minami paused and looked up guiltily, as if explaining the situation out loud somehow made him responsible for the contents.

The prime minister opened his eyes. "Go on," he said.

"That's about it, Prime Minister. As it mentions in the report you have, the bacterium was accidentally released from the laboratory, and we are currently faced with the risk of a massive epidemic that could infect thousands of people."

"Is there any antidote or vaccine available?"

"We have preventive medicine in the form of antibiotics, sir, but no cure for the inflammatory cascade. Although inhibitors are available, they do not seem to have any effect on the patient's survival. Hamada Seiyaku is working around the clock to come up with something, but so far without success."

Prime Minister Aizawa sighed deeply and sat upright in the chair. "How far has the epidemic spread? Is there any chance of containing it?"

"Apart from a few isolated cases, the main area of infection has so far been limited to a length of coastline between Odawara and Kamakura in Kanagawa prefecture," said Minami, examining his notes. "We are preparing to issue all hospitals in the area a sufficient supply of antibiotics, but these will be of use only if we can coerce people to visit the hospital to receive them. That means issuing a general health warning, which I feel we should go ahead with. I also think that we should block off the area to prevent people entering or leaving and employ the talents of the Self-Defense Forces to set up distribution centers for the antibiotics in schools and other public buildings."

"Impossible!" Shoji Kubota, the general secretary of the Liberal Democratic Party, said, staring daggers at Minami. "Issuing a general health warning and mobilizing the military would be tantamount to admitting the government's culpability in the affair. Not only would that spell disaster at home, but we would be roasted throughout the world for going against international agreements on biological weapons. The economy could not stand it. The official stance of the government must remain low-profile at all costs."

"What are you suggesting?" asked the prime minister wearily, directing his question at Kubota. "That we simply let the epidemic run its course and watch thousands of people die?"

"No, sir, of course not. I simply feel that we need more time to examine the situation. We have weathered epidemics in the past and we should not overact now and commit political suicide. We should distribute the antibiotics to hospitals and set up a committee to monitor effects. An announcement must be issued to make it clear that the government is working hard to isolate an unknown strain of bacteria, and this announcement can be used to recommend that people in the affected area visit their nearest hospital or doctor for preventive medicine. In the meantime, the committee can draw up detailed plans for how we should cope with the problem."

Prime Minister Aizawa removed his glasses and stared at his knees as he thought the problem through. Despite an outward appearance of clinical calm, he could feel the panic beginning to rise within his chest as the implications of the pending disaster became fully apparent to him. One small mistake in handling the situation, and not only would his political career be over, but he would go down in history as the man who had stood idle when he had the chance to save the lives of countless people and the economic future of Japan. He tried to remove his own personal agenda from the equation—whether he remained in power or not should not be a factor in his final decision—and view the problem coolly from a standpoint of doing what was best for the country. So far he had been presented with two options: he could go along with Ichiro Minami's suggestion and cordon off the affected area, thereby revealing that the government was in possession of more information than it was admitting, or he could go with Shoji Kubota's plan to mislead the public and stall for more time while further options were sought.

The prime minister looked up at Minami and asked, "What are the latest figures?"

Minami ran a finger down a page in his file and said, "One hundred and thirty-two people hospitalized in total, fifty-four of whom have died and another thirty who are listed in critical condition. From what we have gathered so far, the longest period between infection and death is five days and the shortest eighteen hours."

A look of resignation spread itself over the prime minister's face. One hundred and thirty-two people, although terrible, was not a large enough figure to induce him to stand before the world and admit that Japan was guilty of dabbling in biological weaponry. He replaced his spectacles on his nose, collected his papers together, and sat forward on the edge of his seat. "Right," he said decisively. "I want a public announcement drawn up stating that the government is well aware of the seriousness of the mystery disease affecting Kanagawa prefecture and is pulling out all the stops to combat it. I want it to be public knowledge that all hospitals in the entire area have been well stocked with preventive antibiotics, and I want you to make sure that they all are. I want a committee consisting of you four people and as many top-notch experts as are required to be operative within the next few hours. Make sure that someone from Hamada Seiyaku is included on this committee to act as a liaison. I want you, Hoshino," continued the prime minister, nodding at the director general of the Defense Agency, "to formulate a plan for the deployment of Self-Defense Forces into the area within the shortest time frame possible after a go-ahead is given. I want hourly reports on progress and ideas. These reports are to include all latest infection and mortality rates. Is that clear?"

Without waiting for a reply, Aizawa got to his feet and walked rapidly toward the door. Taken by surprise, the three remaining men hurriedly gained their feet and chorused, "Yes, sir," but their voices were drowned out by the slamming of the door.

Peter Bryant glanced at his watch as he passed through the door of the self-service coffee bar and noticed that he was a couple of minutes early for his seven-o'clock appointment with Joji Higashino. He ordered a cup of coffee at the counter and surveyed the dozen or so tables while it was being poured out. Higashino, who had also arrived early, sat with his back to the counter at a table over on the left, his face hidden from Bryant's view. The coffee paid for, Bryant threaded his way through the tables and sat down opposite him.

"Peter, thanks for coming." Higashino seemed genuinely pleased to see him, although there was something in his eyes that Bryant had never noticed before.

"What's with all the cloak-and-dagger stuff, then? Have you been reading too many suspense novels?"

"No, nothing like that. You were out when I came to see you and I was out of the office all afternoon, so I just left a message. Although what I have to say is better said outside of the company."

"Mm, sounds intriguing. Let's have it, then."

The smile left Higashino's face and he looked down at his half-empty coffee cup. "I don't know where to start, really. You know what I said the other night, about me not wanting to get involved if the company was up to anything sinister." Bryant nodded. "Well, I know somebody who is close to the board of directors, and he has sort of got me involved against my will."

"Go on."

"He has asked me to act as a messenger." Higashino looked up at Bryant and tried to gauge how his friend would absorb the next piece of information he had to deliver. "I am to tell you that your name and Len Drake's name have been raised several times during those marathon meetings, and there is a possibility that you could be in danger if you don't take more care."

"What?" Bryant stared wide-eyed at Higashino. "In danger? What the hell does that mean?"

"Oh, damn! I'm not handling this very well. Maybe I should start at the beginning."

"Please do."

Higashino paused to gather his thoughts. "The person I am speaking of is an old family friend. That is why I couldn't refuse his request for help. He has discovered that you and Len are right in your assumption. Hamada Seiyaku *is* responsible for the outbreak down in Chigasaki."

"Damn, I knew it!" Bryant slapped a hand on the table, ignoring the coffee that splashed over into his saucer in his excitement. "What are they doing? Phase trials on human subjects before the animal trials?"

"Worse than that. A mishap in a laboratory has released a highly contagious bacterium. That is the cause of the epidemic. It is a form of meningitis."

A look of horror spread across Bryant's face. "Highly contagious? But that's . . ." Words failed him. He fumbled around in his confused mind, seeking out the questions he should ask, not the statements of indignation that rushed unbidden to his mouth. "Who is your contact? Is he sure about this? How is the company handling it? Why has a warning not been issued? What will . . ."

Higashino shook his head and held up a hand to halt the barrage of questions. "I'm afraid I can't tell you who he is. He himself would be in danger if it were ever discovered that he had passed on this information. He abhors what is happening, but his position prevents him from taking any other action."

"What sort of danger? Are you seriously suggesting that the company would *hurt* us?"

"Apparently, yes. People have died already, and more will certainly die in the near future. The company seems to feel that their involvement in the crisis must be concealed for the time being, and considering the number of deaths that are inevitable, another couple of deaths will not faze them. My contact mentioned that this possibility was broached at last night's meeting. That's why he wanted me to contact you."

"Deaths? You mean murder us? Len and I?" A cold shiver of fear spread rapidly through Bryant's chest. He had never considered death in relation to himself before. He considered it now. He caught his breath as he felt an icy hand of terror grip his heart. If he were killed tomorrow, would Saturday still happen without him? Would Friday's edition of the *Japan Times* still be published without him to read it? Would tomorrow's off-season soccer match between the Kashima Antlers and the Kawasaki Verdy start on schedule? Would Michiyo continue to water his potted *kofuku-no-ki*, allowing it to outlive himself? He cleared his throat and looked up into Higashino's eyes, the fear and confusion within his own openly displayed. "Are you serious?"

Higashino nodded. "I'm afraid so. They are desperate."

Bryant extended the fingers of his right hand and examined them carefully. No shaking. He guessed that would come later. "What should we do? Have you told Len?"

"No, not yet. But my contact asked me to stress the point that you are not in danger at the moment. If you just continue with your work and forget all about Chigasaki, you will be fine." Higashino finished his coffee, placed the empty tube of sugar on the saucer, and got to his feet. Seeing the look of misery on Bryant's face, he sat down again with a sympathetic groan. "Look, Peter," he said, "I don't wish to sound uncaring, but I can't afford to get mixed up in this. If you'll just go back to your job and ignore everything that is going on, you'll have nothing to worry about."

Bryant looked into Higashino's eyes. Did he know more than

he was actually revealing? Higashino's eyes reflected fear, horror, amazement, and persecution—a mixture of ongoing emotions depicting a scenario that he had never imagined could exist. They also reflected deep concern: the concern of one friend for another friend. "I . . . I . . . I don't know if I can do that, Joji," Bryant said haltingly, his thoughts too jumbled to elucidate his feelings effectively. "I can't just stand by and let people die. I have to do something. . . . But what? What the hell can I do?"

Higashino groaned once more. He hated playing the role of messenger and had a passionate desire to distance himself from the situation. He *couldn't* get involved. It was just not possible. He had a wife, two children, and a career to think of. His career notwithstanding, the thought of his wife widowed with two small children to bring up alone did not bear thinking about. Despising himself, he got to his feet, picked up the empty coffee cup, and said, "I'm sorry, Peter, but that has to be your decision. I must leave now, and I would appreciate it if you did not communicate with me anymore in the office or elsewhere."

Bryant looked up sharply. Higashino avoided his eyes and walked across to the counter, where he placed his cup on the service counter provided. At the door of the coffee shop, he turned around once and mouthed a silent *good-bye* before being swallowed up by the darkness outside.

Bryant did not blame Higashino. A threat of physical harm was not the perfect catalyst upon which to base a friendship. He understood that. But he felt lonely. Sad and lonely. A wave of tired misery swept over him, blurring the edges of his vision and making him feel disorientated and dizzy. He gripped the edge of the table hard, as if trying to maintain a hold on a world that was weaving and bucking in an effort to shake him off into a black void. His thoughts were random and disordered, mired in a vat of molten taffy through which the fat and lazy bubbles of coherent understanding floated far too slowly to the surface. A death threat! The threat of death. The possibility of dying. The probability of nonexistence ... A bloated pocket of anger burst through the surface of the molten taffy and Bryant felt the back of his neck and ears burn with righteous indignation. *How dare they, the bastards! What gives them the right to decide whether I or countless other people should live or die?*

The anger served to clear Bryant's mind. He looked about him as if noticing his surroundings for the first time. His emotions were still in turmoil, but his intentions were clear. He could not let them get away with it. He had to do something. Anything!

He got to his feet, returned his cup to the self-service counter, and slowly made his way home.

It was just before three-thirty in the afternoon when Dr. Patricia Marston was paged over the hospital's PA system. She quickly ended her conversation with a young female intern and hurried to her office, where she picked up the telephone and identified herself.

"Dr. Marston? Mark Craven here."

"Oh, hi, Mark. News on the bug?"

"Yes. I ran the tests on the samples from Tatsumi Iyama's autopsy, and they came up with a strain of *Neisseria* meningococcus that causes pediatric meningococcemia."

A frown creased Dr. Marston's brow. "Are you sure?"

"Without a shadow of a doubt."

"So you're telling me that my forty-two year-old patient died of pediatric meningococcemia? A kids' disease?"

"Yes and no," answered Craven enthusiastically. The case intrigued him, and he was, rather perversely, enjoying Marston's surprise. He could hardly wait to drop his barrage of bombshells. "Your patient contracted pediatric meningococcemia, but was killed by a massive drop in blood pressure and organ failure."

"We already know that from the autopsy. But you are now telling me that the organ failure was caused by the meningococcus bacterium? I'll have to check out the carriage rates among adults for that. Sounds improbable to me, though."

"I've already checked them out." Marston detected the hint of glee that Craven was having difficulty keeping out of his voice. She wondered why it was that lab types always seemed to love playing the game of one-upmanship with the doctors. "Between sixty percent and ninety percent of cases are found in children under the age of five, and most of the remaining cases occur in adolescents under twenty. It is extremely rare to find a case in an adult over the age of forty."

"So we either have an extremely rare case or you are mistaken."

Craven ignored the slur. "There's more," he said.

"Yes?"

"I sent out a general e-mail inquiry to hospitals around the country to find out exactly how rare this was, and discovered that four other cases have been diagnosed in adults in the past three days."

"What?"

"And all four of these cases have been Japanese nationals."

"Are you serious?"

"And all have since died."

A sense of puzzlement overrode Marston's irritation at Craven's obvious delight at this piece of news. She hadn't heard of an epidemic in Japan. "Have you been onto the Department of Health? They might need to start quarantining flights from Japan."

"There's more."

"Oh, for God's sake, Mark! Just tell me everything or send down your report. I don't have time to play your silly games."

"The bacterium doesn't match up with any of the known strains or serogroups. There are thirteen serogroups based on surface capsular polysaccharides, but only five associated with

64

meningococcemia. I ran some DNA footprint comparison tests on these five serogroups and the 16S ribosomal RNA gene, and although it identified the B serogroup, it didn't come up with a perfect match. I have ordered an IR spectroscopy and an NMR spectroscopy to identify the polysaccharide, but that will take about two weeks to come back. In the meantime, however, I think I can say without fear of contradiction that we have a brand-new strain on our hands. Maybe they'll name it after me: the MC serogroup. Yes, I like the sound of that."

"Grow up, Mark. What about the vaccines for existing serogroups? Are they effective?"

"Nope. Vaccines are available only for the A, C, W135, and Y serogroups. There is no vaccine for the B serogroup. Probably wouldn't work if there were."

"So we have a new disease on our hands with no way of treating it."

"That's about strength of it. And a savagely dangerous one at that."

Bryant pushed his plate away from him and took a sip of red wine. He had not been very hungry when he arrived home, but had decided that a full stomach might help him think more clearly. It hadn't. Topping up his glass from the bottle of Valpolicella, he took it through to the living room and sat down on the couch. Michiyo was out with friends from work and probably wouldn't be home for at least another couple of hours. Not that it mattered. He wanted to share his problem, but wasn't quite sure if Michiyo was the right person. Sweet and beautiful, yes, but calm and rational? No way!

He picked up the phone and punched in Leonard Drake's number. No answer. Probably exchanging dirty jokes with his crazy pals in the British pub in Takadanobaba. But thinking about it, that was a good thing. The news that Bryant had to impart was not best said over the telephone, after all. *Hi, Len. Watch your ass, mate, 'cause somebody wants you dead. See you tomorrow at the office, man.* Maybe he shouldn't tell him at all. Maybe he should protect him from the agony Bryant himself was going through and just let him take his chances. Was that fair?

Was anything fair . . . ?

Sighing, Bryant picked up the receiver again and punched in Mike Woodson's number. Mike would know what to do.

Carol answered the phone on the third ring, and after exchanging pleasantries, handed the receiver across to her husband.

"Yo, Peter. How's it hanging?"

"To the left. You?"

"Who knows? I try not to look down on the unemployed."

They continued bantering for a few minutes until Bryant detected a break in the conversation and launched into his explanation. Woodson listened without commenting until Bryant ran out of steam.

"Any idea who this person could be? There can't be that many people who'd have access to information like that. One of the secretaries, maybe?"

"I really don't know, Mike. I wish I did. I just don't have a clue what's going on."

Woodson sensed the agony his friend was going through and was filled with sympathy. He didn't actually believe the story, but he couldn't mention that to Bryant without making it sound as if he were mocking him. But it was unthinkable! A reputable Japanese company calmly holding a meeting to discuss ways of murdering their workforce? Preposterous! Still, he had to broach the subject somehow.

"Are you sure this isn't just some sort of joke, Peter?" he asked. "I mean, maybe this guy Joji and that pompous Brit you work with are just twanging on your wires. They might be out somewhere now pissing themselves with laughter over the whole deal. Have you considered that?"

Bryant hadn't. A flicker of light appeared at the end of his tunnel. It had to be something like that. Logic told him that companies could not go around murdering their staff with impunity, but the stress of the recent few days and the sincerity of Higashino's delivered death threat must have culminated in his logic popping out to lunch. But surely Joji wouldn't take part in a practical joke. Quiet, stable, hardworking Joji? Impossible! Higashino was generally known as *majime* within Hamada Seiyaku. Although construed as almost an insult in Western society, *majime*—meaning serious, grave, sober, earnest, faithful, honest—was the highest compliment a salaryman could receive in Japan.

"Mm, I wouldn't put that past Len, but not Joji. I'm sure he wouldn't have any part in something like that. And I saw his eyes, Mike. He believed it, I'm sure."

"Maybe Len has set Joji up, too. Look, you mentioned that he said this deadly disease is meningitis, right?"

"Right."

"Since when has meningitis been a deadly disease? It's curable, Peter. Those people down in Chigasaki are *dying!*"

"Damn, that's a point. I never thought of that." Bryant grabbed at this straw gratefully and felt the huge weight of anxiety being lifted from his shoulders. "Jeez, that bastard Drake is in for some trouble tomorrow. I'll kick his ass from here to Osaka!" Bryant laughed, a short bark of both embarrassment at having been tricked by Drake and relief at having been reprieved from his death sentence. "Meningitis! Why didn't I spot that? That bastard . . . !"

Woodson laughed back. "Well and truly suckered. I always thought you were green behind the ears, Peter, but come on. . . ."

Bryant thanked Woodson and hung up the connection. He shook his head in wonder. *Drake! That rat, Drake! I'll get him for this.*

* * *

The Zen Nippon Otaku Tomonokai Web site was buzzing with news of the epidemic. Most of the members knew that Norio Kondo and his wife lived near the center of the outbreak, and a large proportion of the bulletin board was taken up with inquiries over their health.

Norio Kondo, his left arm hanging limply over the side of his chair as he absentmindedly scratched the top of Gonta the corgi's head, scrolled through the list of messages with a grim smile on his face. He was touched by everybody's concern, but talk of the outbreak was reminding him of his own anxieties. Admittedly, Hongodai, where they lived, was several stops from Chigasaki, but a number of victims had been reported in Ofuna, and that was only twenty-five minutes' walk away.

"*Hoy*, Shigeko," he called loudly. His wife had finished watching her favorite television drama and was in the kitchen clearing up before they went to bed.

"Did you call?" Shigeko Kondo's voice sounded up the stairs.

"Yes. Come and look at this."

It was nearly twelve o'clock at night and one hour into Telehodai time, so the Web site was congested with traffic. Telehodai was the fixed-rate telephone service that allowed unlimited line use between the hours of eleven at night and eight in the morning for a minimal monthly charge and was therefore the darling of Internet junkies.

Shigeko entered the room and walked over to her husband's side. "What is it?" she asked.

"Take a look at these messages."

Norio nudged Gonta out of the way and moved his chair to the left so his wife could pull up her chair. She leaned toward the screen and read the contents in order of arrival.

Attn: Everybody
From: Kyuti
It's just an outbreak of influenza, so the papers say. They'll soon have it under control. Relax . . .

ISOLATION

Attn: Kyuti
From: Totchan
It is not influenza. It is more dangerous. I work in pharmaceuticals, and I know the difference between flu and a killer virus. If you have any friends in that area, I suggest they get out immediately.

Attn: Totchan
From: Kyuryo-Dorobo
I heard that hundreds of people have died already. What is it, then? The news says influenza, but none of the vaccines work. I have some friends who live in Odawara. Will they be safe?

Attn: Gakusha
From: Mairudo-Sebun
Is everything okay with you and Shiwakucha-Baba? The outbreak in your area seems bad. The newspapers are full of it. What's the latest?

Attn: Mairudo Sebun & Gakusha/Shiwakucha-Baba
From: Totchan
Hey, Mairudo-Sebun. We've already covered this. Scroll down and get up to speed. Gakusha, I suggest you move out of your area as quickly as you can. Get out to that weekend cottage in Izu you share with Omotenashi. Things will get much worse before they get better. This disease is a killer.

"Wow, Totchan seems to be taking this thing very seriously. Do you think he is right? Should we get out of this area?"

"I suppose it is worth thinking about, but it seems a bit drastic at the moment. Let's wait for a bit and see what happens."

69

"Mm, perhaps you're right. You'd better let them know we are all right, though. They seem worried about us. Isn't that nice?"

Shigeko left the room to finish up in the kitchen, and Norio quickly punched in a message to calm everybody's fears.

Everybody's but his own, that is.

Kazunori Matsuoka was dragged reluctantly from a deep and dreamless sleep by the muted but persistent digital gurgling of his bedside telephone. He pulled himself up into a semiseated position and fumbled for the receiver. His alarm clock revealed the time to be just after six-thirty, and the gray light seeping around the edges of the curtains confirmed this. His wife stirred beside him, but did not wake.

"*Hai*, Matsuoka *desu*," he said.

"It's Hamada. Sorry for disturbing you, but I need you at the office now."

On hearing the voice of his company president, Matsuoka sat up straighter in bed, his heart pumping faster as he wondered what this day would bring in his ongoing nightmare. The president of Hamada Seiyaku had never phoned him at home before, and he had no reason to believe that this unprecedented call had been made out of courtesy. "Yes, sir, immediately. I can be there within the hour. May I ask what the problem is?"

"An AP report out of Seattle has identified the *Neisseria* meningococcus bacterium in four Japanese nationals in America. The morning papers are full of it and are linking it with the epidemic down in Chigasaki. It's spread all over the front pages, and the government is being accused of covering up. We need to discuss our next step."

Matsuoka shuddered involuntarily. He promised to be at the office as quickly as possible before cutting off the connection, then jumped out of bed, dreading going downstairs and retrieving the newspaper from the mailbox. He looked across at his wife and felt a jolt of envy as he thought of her day, entailing no more anxiety than an increase in the cost of vegetables at the local supermarket.

Mike Woodson sat at his desk in the American embassy in Tokyo amidst a pile of all the English-language newspapers available in Japan, including the *Herald Tribune.* The *Tribune* had relegated the news of the outbreak to a small column on page two, but the Japanese editions had splattered it all over the front pages. Meningitis! So Peter wasn't being hoodwinked after all. The papers made no mention of Hamada Seiyaku Pharmaceuticals, Inc., and did not speculate to any great length on the cause of the outbreak. Most of the outrage was directed at the government, which was accused of dilly-dallying while an epidemic of outlandish proportions—potentially more dangerous than the Spanish flu outbreak of 1918—was developing on their shores. Why, they demanded, had American authorities been able to isolate the bacterium with only four victims, while the Japanese authorities had come up with no better explanation than a flu epidemic with close to two hundred victims at their disposal? The reports also went on to describe outbreaks of the disease in other parts of the country. Sixteen cases of the so-called "flu" had been diagnosed in Tokyo, and a further seven in Osaka. The press were out for blood, but Woodson wondered if such sensationalism was going to help matters at all. Screaming about deadly and incurable diseases was not going to do the economy any good. It could also cause a panic that would spread throughout the entire country as people raced to their doctors and hospitals for every small cough and sniffle.

Woodson realized that he had to speak with Bryant again. He tried to remember all of the details his friend had given him on the telephone the night before, but he didn't have enough information to write a report. He would have to turn his attention to Bryant's plea for help as well. If the bacterium really had been released mistakenly by Hamada Seiyaku, the threat against his well-being could be real. He looked at his watch. Bryant would be on his way to work at the moment, so he would have to contact him later. In the meantime, he decided that he should report the incident verbally at least. He picked up one of the two telephones adorning his desk and asked to be put through to the political section.

Asian Currencies Plunge

Hong Kong (AP) Asian stock markets closed generally lower Thursday as Southeast Asian currencies plunged in a knee-jerk reaction to the plummeting Nikkei index triggered by news of a deadly meningitis outbreak in Japan. The key 225-issue Nikkei index closed at its lowest level in fourteen years, and stocks of all nineteen major banks fell as investors continued to be spooked by the announcement of a deadly epidemic rampant in Japan.

The key Nikkei index fell as low as 7,889.47 before gaining some ground and ending at 8,224.83. The Topix index of all 1,333 first-section issues also slumped to its lowest close in fourteen years. It ended at 763.55, down 60.23 points, or 7.88 percent.

In the rest of Asia, the Thai baht, Indonesia rupiah, Malaysian ringgit, and Philippine peso all hit new lows. Going against the stock markets' falling trend, the main indexes rose in South Korea, Thailand, Australia, and New Zealand. Malaysian shares tumbled 3.83 percent after the local currency slid to a historic low of 4.3200 to the dollar in late trading.

The Kuala Lumpur Stock Exchange's Composite index of 100 blue-chip stocks fell 20.03 points to 526.76. Shares also closed sharply lower in Singapore as tumbling regional currencies dealt a blow to market sentiment, dealers said. The benchmark Straits Times Industrial index fell 56.83 points, or 3.8 percent, closing at 1,439.12.

In Manila, the thirty-share Philippine Stock Exchange index fell 52.24 points, or 2.8 percent, closing at 1,820.60.

In Seoul, the South Korean won rebounded slightly after a weak opening. The U.S. dollar closed at 1,742 won, down from 1,780 won Wednesday.

South Korea shares also closed higher on continued buying by foreign investors. The Koreas Composite Stock Price index rose 9.85 points, or 2.5 percent, to 406.34.

Thai share prices closed higher despite the slump in the baht. The Stock Exchange of Thailand index rose 4.09 points, or 1.1 percent, to 370.27.

The baht was trading at 52.25 to the dollar, up slightly from a morning low of 52.50.

In Australia, a strengthening bond market and the falling Australian dollar prompted a 1.5 percent jump in the key index to its highest close for several weeks. The All Ordinaries index closed at 2,685.3, up 41.0 points.

Chapter Four

Fear can be primed by a single item of information, but it requires more to keep the flame burning brightly. In Peter Bryant's case, imagination was providing the fuel for his own personal conflagration of gut-wrenching fear. He was imagining himself dead. And, having imagined himself dead, he was trying to determine whether his parents would have him cremated in Japan and sent home in a ceramic jar, or whether they would go to the expense of shipping his remains back to the States intact. He decided that his destiny lay in a cream-colored jar, bouncing about on his mother's lap as she sipped her glass of chilled white wine aboard the international flight to Los Angeles, a jumbled mass of ashes and dust, with his ear brushing against his sternum and his big toe intermingling with his fourth vertebra. And then turbulence three hours out of Narita, shaking the contents about and laying his dusty old nose right beside his dusty old asshole. *Sheesh!*

Michiyo Kato laid a cool hand on his brow and kissed the lobe of his ear. The sound of this emitted so close to his inner ear sent a shiver through Bryant and made him jump. He turned his head toward her with a gentle smile.

"I guess I'm not being very good company tonight, am I?"

"You never are," Michiyo replied, matching his smile. "You are a miserable old brooder who prefers the company of his own thoughts to anything else, but that doesn't make me love you any less." She leaned close again and pecked him on the cheek. "Although I suspect that tonight's thoughts are darker than usual. What's the matter, Peter? Are you still worried about work?"

Bryant shifted forward and reached out a hand for the mug of coffee cooling on the incidental table beside the couch. He was still in a quandary about how much he should tell Michiyo. He was worried that the death threat against himself would be extended toward her if she possessed the same information. He wanted to protect her with the mantle of ignorance. The word *meningitis* spread across the previous day's newspapers had shocked him to no little extent. The word had seemed to pass through his mortal tissue and explode within his brain like a starburst shell. If the meningitis part of it was true, then he presumed that the death threat was also true. Should he tell Michiyo about Hamada Seiyaku's involvement in the outbreak? She had read the papers and knew all about the situation, although she seemed to have forgotten about his reference to it a few days before. And what about Len? He still hadn't informed Drake about the threat. He really ought to speak to the man as soon as possible. Maybe he would arrange to meet up with him early on Monday morning before work and tell him everything he knew.

"Peter . . . ?"

He blinked and turned his attention to Michiyo.

"You're daydreaming again. What *is* it?"

"I'm sorry, Mitch. Things have just been a little hectic lately. I'm also worried about this epidemic down in Kanagawa prefecture. The newspapers say there are indications that it's spreading up into Tokyo. Maybe you should go and visit your parents until it's all over. It could be dangerous, you know."

"Rubbish! You worry too much. It's just typical media sensationalism. It'll soon blow over. Anyway, I have a busy week coming up. We have started taking the bookings for Golden Week, and we're having trouble getting sufficient accommodation in several European cities. I couldn't possibly take time off now."

Bryant hadn't expected her to agree anyway. "I think you should consider it if things get any worse. This is much more dangerous than flu, you know."

"Yes, yes, yes," Michiyo said, slapping him lightly on the leg. A beeping noise was heard from the direction of the bathroom, indicating that the tub was full. "Your wish is my command, oh king. But in the meantime, I'm going to take my bath. Maybe you can think up some interesting conversation by the time I get back." She unfolded her legs from beneath her and left the room, leaving Bryant all alone with his demons.

He sighed. He had been sighing a lot lately. Every time his mind returned to his predicament, he heard—and felt—himself release a deep and dramatic sigh. Why was that? he wondered. Just another of those inexplicable human traits that nobody had ever bothered looking into, he supposed, but there was no doubt that a good sigh seemed to clear the air a bit.

He finished the coffee and fumbled for the newspaper to see if anything worth watching was on the television. His expectations were low, as most of the Saturday-night viewing in the Kanto region sucked, in his opinion. The baseball season wouldn't begin for another couple of months, so he was left with a choice of variety programs in which everybody would shout as loud as they possibly could, a couple of quiz shows that used cute animals, or a few lousy television soaps. He decided to wait for the news broadcast at eleven o'clock. Maybe they would have an update on the outbreak.

He was replacing the newspaper on the table when the telephone rang. He picked up the receiver. "*Moshi, moshi,*" he said.

"Mr. Bryant?"

"Yes."

"I contacted you via Joji Higashi the other day. I believe you received my message accordingly."

Joji's contact! The beat of Bryant's heart increased its pace.

"I . . . well, yes, I did. May I ask your name?"

"I would rather not say, if you don't mind. It would serve no purpose."

Male. Well educated. Tokyo accent. Probably middle-aged, although the voice was slightly muffled and it was difficult to say for sure. Bryant guessed the man was speaking through a handkerchief or some other device in order to disguise his voice. Did that mean he knew him? Well, if he worked for Hamada Seiyaku, the chances were that he did know him. No surprises there.

"I'm afraid that things are getting out of hand," the voice continued. "My conscience won't allow me to sit back and ignore this train of events, so I have come to you for help."

"Help?" A wary note crept into Bryant's voice.

"Yes. I want you to pass on some information."

"Why should I? What about the threat against Len Drake and myself? Surely that would put us in more danger. Why don't you just phone the police?"

"You are safe. Attention has been taken away from you by other events. You are forgotten for the moment. And I cannot go to the police. They would ask too many questions and would not believe my story."

"And just what is your story?" Bryant asked, beginning to think that this guy was nothing more than a wimp on a power trip. He certainly liked to inject a good deal of drama into his conversation. "Why should I help you? I don't even know who you are."

"I want you to pass on an item of information to your embassy friend, Mr. Woodson."

"You know Mike?" Bryant said in shock. *Jesus, what is happening?*

The voice ignored the question. "I want you to inform him that the meningococcal bacterium was genetically engineered. The American authorities seem to have overlooked this, and we *must* have help in producing a vaccine. Tell him that a protein was included to override the NK cells. It is known as the UL18 flag. It makes the body believe that the bacterium belongs there. Are you taking this down?"

"Eh . . . what?" asked Bryant, who wasn't.

"Mr. Bryant. Please get a pen and paper and take down what I say. This is extremely important."

Bryant tucked the receiver under his chin and retrieved his briefcase from its position against the wall behind the couch. He fumbled around inside and brought out a red pen and his diary. "Okay," he said once he was seated on the couch with the pen poised over a blank page. "Go ahead."

"The meningococcal bacterium was genetically altered to contain a protein known as the UL18 flag to trick the body's immune system into believing it is not harmful to the host. Got that?"

As he feverishly scribbled down the message, Bryant was aware of a change in roles. He had started off in a superior position, but here he was now, meekly taking orders from the mystery man. But Bryant was not stupid, and he realized that what he was hearing was probably very important indeed. No macho stuff needed. Just get on with the job.

"Got it," he replied.

"Virulence factors were also engineered into the organism to speed up the incubation time. Okay?"

"Okay."

"And finally, it was modified so that the bacterium dies soon after it hits the bloodstream, releasing inherent endotoxins into the body and triggering the next stage of the disease."

The voice became silent while Bryant rapidly wrote down this last sentence.

"Is that it?" asked Bryant when he had finished. "Will they understand all that?"

"Yes. They should have no problem at all."

"May I ask why you are doing this? You are part of Hamada Seiyaku, I take it."

"I am, but I wish I were not. The company suddenly has the power of life and death over others, and they are wielding it badly. Paranoia has produced a collection of monsters, and I cannot sit back and allow it to happen. If you do not believe me and think that I am trying to provide you with misinformation, then I do not blame you. However, the American authorities will be able to discover if I am telling the truth relatively easily by testing a sample of the bacterium they have in their possession. I am simply pointing out the place to which they should direct their attention. The papers are calling it meningitis, but it is a much more dangerous disease known as meningococcemia."

"Why don't you contact the authorities yourself? And why the American authorities? What's wrong with the Japanese authorities? Surely they would be better suited to your purposes."

Bryant detected hesitation on the other end of the phone. He could hear the man's muffled breathing and guessed that he was working out how he should continue with the explanation.

"I . . . er . . . Mr. Bryant, what I have to say may shock you, but I need you to understand the seriousness of the situation. One of Hamada's directors will be murdered within the next couple of days, charged with a lack of sympathy for the company's dilemma." He paused for a moment, awaiting Bryant's response. Encouraged by his silence—Bryant had been rendered speechless—he continued. "Should it be discovered that I had contacted the authorities, that same fate would certainly await me. I chose you as a conduit because I know that you would feel strongly about correcting this situation, and because I am in a position to monitor all discussions that concern you inside the company. I can therefore protect you from within. I need you, Mr. Bryant, and I plead for your understanding."

Shaking his head to clear his thoughts, Bryant tried to stay focused on the overall picture. "So why not the American authorities?" he asked.

"The Japanese authorities are aware of the situation and do nothing to correct it. I'm afraid that corruption is no stranger to Japanese politics, and I do not know who to contact."

"And the condemned director? Will you let him die?"

"I'm afraid so. I have not been made privy to the details of the execution, so do not know where, when, or how it will take place. I only know that the end result will suggest a suicide."

Random thoughts rattled around inside Bryant's brain as he tried to make up his mind whether to trust this man or not. The explanation was plausible, but he couldn't shake the idea that he was being set up. But for what purpose? Surely relating the story to Mike Woodson wouldn't put him in any hotter water than he was in now. The news that the company had lost interest in him and Len had come as a relief, but the bearer of the initial death threat was the selfsame man, so there was a very real chance that he was being played for a patsy. But could he afford to ignore the plea?

He thought not.

"Okay, I'll pass your story on to Woodson. Is there any way I can contact you in case he has any questions?"

"I'm afraid not. Telephone numbers can be traced back to their owners. But I'll keep in touch with you as the situation develops. Thank you very much, Mr. Bryant. You will not regret it."

The caller hung up.

Bryant replaced the receiver in its cradle thoughtfully without releasing it. Things were heating up, and he was not sure that he cared for his role as middleman. But he had to pass this piece of information on before Michiyo returned from her bath. It would not do for her to be in the same room when he described murder and conspiracy over the phone. He picked up the receiver again and punched in Mike Woodson's number from memory. Before he hit the last digit, he broke the connection and flipped open his diary to the list of addresses at the back. He wanted to check something out before he spoke to Mike. Running his finger down the page until he found the entry he sought, Bryant laid the receiver on the table and phoned a Montana number.

The phone was answered on the fourth ring.

"Hello?" said a sleepy voice.

"Thane, hi, there. It's Peter."

"Peter?"

"Peter Bryant. I'm phoning from Tokyo. How are you, man?"

"Peter! As well as can be expected, considering it's six o'clock on a Saturday morning. What's happening?"

Thane Robertson was a postgraduate microbiologist at Montana State University. Bryant had attended junior high and high school with Thane's wife, Maiko, and the two had met up and become firm friends some ten years previously.

"Sorry about the time, Thane, but I want to pick your brain. Would you rather I phoned back later?"

"Nah, go ahead. I'm awake now, anyway. Maiko's *oka-san* invariably calls at weird hours, too. What's up?"

Bryant flipped back to the page of his diary on which he had written the mystery caller's message. He quickly scanned his scribbled notes and asked, "If I asked you to genetically engineer the meningococcal bacterium so that it was even more contagious and dangerous than usual, what would you suspect my motives to be?"

"Which one?"

"Which one what?"

"Which meningococcal bacterium?"

"You mean there's more than one?" A frown creased Bryant's brow.

"Yup."

"Jeez, I don't know. Any one. The baddest-assed one."

"Mmm, a strange question, but I'd probably suspect you of being crazy."

"Okay, let's put it another way. If you found a serious outbreak of meningitis and discovered that the bacterium had been genetically modified to make the disease not only more virulent, but also fatal, what would you think?"

"What would I think? Jesus, Peter, what's with the riddles? Are you suggesting that such a bacterium exists?"

"Well, yes and no. It's all pretty hypothetical at the moment, but I am trying to figure out why anybody would go to the trouble of creating a disease that would spread rapidly and be deadly at the same time."

"Well, I can think of three reasons off the top of my head with the information you've given me."

"Go on."

"My first guess would be biological warfare, my second would be profit, and my third would be a bad case of the crazies. Depends who's behind it, really."

"I'm listening."

"If it was a government, then biological warfare would be the obvious motive; if it was a company, then profit; and if it was a loony with a grudge against society . . . well, I guess you get my point."

"Tell me about profit. How in hell's name could a company profit out of disease?"

"If, for example, it was a pharmaceutical company, then they could have a cure waiting in the wings. If an epidemic actually broke out, they'd make a fortune."

Bryant became silent as he digested this piece of information. That would certainly fit the scenario. Could Hamada Seiyaku have actually triggered the outbreak deliberately so that they could cash in on a vaccine? But surely he would have heard about that. They couldn't market a vaccine without a patent, and he'd never heard of any recent drug that would combat meningitis. Unless a patent had been applied for only on the Japanese market. He would have heard of it only if an application had been filed for the U.S. patent. He'd have to check that out. Joji Higashino would know. If, of course, he would speak to him . . .

"Thane, that's fantastic. I really appreciate it. How's Maiko, by the way?"

"Fine. She's learning to drive at the moment, so you can expect a sharp decrease in Montana's population over the next few months. You'll probably read about it in the newspapers. But what's all this about genetically engineered bacteria, anyway?"

"Nothing to worry about. Just checking up on something a pal said the other day. Thanks a lot, Thane. Love to Maiko . . ."

Bryant hung up before Robertson could ask any more questions. Things were falling into place. At least he now had a motive to append to the message for Mike Woodson. He heard the hair dryer whir into action in the bathroom and guessed that Michiyo had finished her bath and would be out soon. He estimated that he had about ten minutes. *Right!* He would phone Mike first and then call Len Drake to set up an early-morning cup of coffee before work on Monday.

Mike Woodson sat in Robert Rasnick's office and waited while his report was read. Rasnick's graying hair flopped over his forehead and obscured his eyes from view. Nearing fifty, Rasnick was proud to still be in possession of a full head of hair, and liked to keep it slightly long to emphasize its existence. This slight touch of vanity was completely out of character for Rasnick, the chief of the political section in the American embassy, who was usually brash and rarely bothered about the comments on his invariably rumpled suit and general state of hygiene. He looked even more incongruous than usual this Sunday morning, wearing slacks and a polo shirt that failed to conceal his growing stomach or the wad of gray chest hair that protruded from his collar.

"Damn, this is some report, Mike," said Rasnick, looking up in wonder. "Genetic engineering? Willful release of a biological agent? Death threats? Murder? Are you sure your contact is not living on a different planet? Can you verify any of this?"

Woodson shifted in his seat. "No, but I can vouch for him. It is possible that somebody is setting him up, but I can guarantee that he believes every word of that statement. And, you can't deny the fact that an outbreak of this disease is in progress."

"Any reports of a murdered director yet?"

"None so far."

"What about these motives? Have you had a chance to check out this allegation about Hamada Seiyaku releasing the bug because they have a cure for it?"

"Yes, briefly, but no patent has been filed for a vaccine or any other drug related to meningitis or meningococcemia by Hamada in the last two years."

"Which will rule out the profit angle. What are we left with? Biological weapons and terrorism." Rasnick brushed his hair out of his eyes and stared at Woodson. "What's your call, Mike?"

"Well, biological weaponry would mean that the Japanese government would have to be involved, and that sounds a bit far-fetched. On the other hand, a prosperous company like Hamada Seiyaku would hardly get mixed up in terrorism if they didn't stand to profit from it. I really don't know. Maybe there is another motive."

"Biological weaponry wouldn't necessarily have to involve the Japanese government. Maybe Hamada Seiyaku has been commissioned by a foreign government. That would take care of the profit motive. In fact, something like that has a better ring to it than trying to profit out of a cure."

Woodson shrugged his shoulders.

"Okay," continued Rasnick, "I'll get some of my people to run a check on this company. If any shady relationships with foreign countries exist, they'll find them. I'd also like to send this report back home, but there are too many loose ends. Can you get your contact, Bryant, to come in for a full debriefing? It shouldn't take more than an hour or two."

"Sure," said Woodson. "I'll arrange it for tomorrow night. You want to be present?"

"Yeah, why not? Around eight would suit me fine."

Yasuko Fukuyama sat before her computer and allowed her attention to wander across to the rain-splattered window of her office. Nine o'clock on a Sunday evening and she was still at her desk. But not for much longer. Given the circumstances, she doubted if the president of Hamada Seiyaku would force her into completing her statutory month after she had handed in her resignation, especially after the open confrontation she had had with him late on Friday night. No, it was certainly in the company's interests to get her out of the building as soon as possible. This would be her last trip up to the fourteenth floor and her sumptuously appointed office.

Her mind wandered back to the pride she had felt at becoming Hamada Seiyaku's first ever female director. Twenty-five years of hard and dedicated work had finally paid off when she was elevated to her present position as director of planning some three years previously. She had been surprised at the amount of support that she had been afforded in those three years. Of course, there were a few of the older men who still tried to make things difficult, but overall she had felt an integral part of the company's administration and had been given a free hand to pursue the company's best interests. She had done a fine job and had been extremely proud of her commitment to Hamada's prosperity.

Until recently.

She still found it impossible to believe that the company could change practically overnight from a caring and socially responsible corporation striving to overcome the diseases of the world into a pit of wickedness and evil. People were dying, and the only concern was to protect the company and its damn executives. She hated Shigeru Hamada with a passion born of disgust. How could he have subjected so many innocent people to this despicable disease and then display absolutely no remorse whatsoever? She couldn't stand it any longer. The sooner she had finished typing out her resignation and placed it on Hamada's desk, the better. She returned her attention to the computer screen.

A noise in the outer office disturbed her concentration as she reread her resignation. Apart from the security staff, nobody should be in the building at this time on a Sunday night. Maybe her secretary returning for a forgotten item. She stood up to move around her desk, but before she could complete the movement, the handle of the door turned and it was thrown back against the wall. Two men, whom she did not recognize, stood in the frame, one holding a child's futon under his arm and the other holding a small pistol that was pointing directly at her. She gasped in fear and indignation.

"Who are you? What do you want?"

The two men entered the room without answering and closed the door. She noticed that both were wearing latex gloves. The one with the gun threw a packet approximately twenty-five centimeters by fifteen centimeters onto her desk.

"Open it!" he said gruffly.

She looked down at the packet and noticed that it was a double pack of panty hose. She looked up in confusion, but the man simply waved the gun at it and repeated the order.

Picking up the package and a paper knife from her desk, she slit open the top before looking up again.

"Remove the contents."

Fear was beginning to override her sense of indignation. Her heart thumped and she was at a loss what to do. Her first instinct was to grab the phone and demand that these men be thrown out, but the presence of the gun made her realize that they would hardly stand meekly by while she explained the situation to security. How the hell had they managed to get into the building, anyway? And what did they want? Was this a robbery? But she kept nothing of value in the office. Of course, they wouldn't know that, so it was a possibility. Or could she possibly be the victim of a rape attack in the safety of her own office? The panty hose and futon seemed to suggest something kinky, but for God's sake, she was fifty years old! She looked into the man's eyes, searching for an indication of lust, but it was like staring into the eyes of a shark: cold, no emotion. He nodded toward the package in her hands, and she reluctantly removed two pairs of panty hose, the cardboard shape retainers falling to her feet.

The other man came around the desk and approached her from behind. She closed her eyes tightly in terrified anticipation of searching hands, and was surprised to receive a heavy buffet that pushed her legs up against the desk. The man extended the child's futon around her from the back until the edges overlapped in front of her.

"Hold that!" The command grunted sharply into her ear made her jump. Fear triggered her responses, and she grabbed hold of the futon and held it in place before her. "No, leave your arms inside. Hold it from the inside!" She complied, and the man then began to wind rope around her, tugging it tight until she was cocooned from knees to shoulders in restrictive wadding.

Kidnappers! I'm being kidnapped! It all made sense. A high-level executive with a company like Hamada Seiyaku would be a prime target for kidnappers. She didn't know whether to feel relief or dread. At least the indignity of rape was no longer a consideration. That alone caused hope to blossom within her. Hamada would soon pay the ransom; she was sure of it.

And then she remembered her resignation displayed on the screen of her computer.

"Excuse me." Her voice quavered and cracked, and she had to say it again. "Excuse me, but would you mind if I erased that file from the computer? You might not get your money if it is left there."

The man with the gun looked at her quizzically. He leaned over the desk until he had a view of the monitor. Understanding flooded into his face. "No problem," he said. He shifted the gun to his left hand and grabbed the computer mouse. Leaving the letterhead with Fukuyama's name, he highlighted the main text and then pressed the delete key. Fukuyama breathed a sigh of relief.

The man who had tied her up retrieved the two pairs of panty hose from the desk. He aligned them carefully and then slipped both pairs over Fukuyama's head so that the crotch piece of both lay beneath her chin. She looked swiftly at the man with the gun, trying to discern his intentions from his eyes. Nothing. A jolt of horror flooded through her as the legs to the panty hose were tied together behind her neck and pulled tight, causing her to gag.

They were going to kill her! The futon was to prevent her from struggling!

The scream that erupted from Fukuyama's throat was cut off by a strong hand being clamped violently over her mouth.

"Be careful! Don't mark her!" snapped the man with the gun.

The pressure eased a little, but Fukuyama was unable to fill her lungs with the air required to scream again. She began to struggle, but the tight wrapping of the futon made it impossible. She tried to lash her head backward and forward, but the man

88

held her firmly. A piece of cloth was jammed into her mouth and another piece was used to tie it behind her head. The noises she did make were now muffled and would never be heard outside of the office.

The first man laid the gun down on the desk and came around to help his partner. They grabbed one side of the futon each and dragged her over to the window. One of them closed the blinds with one hand and used his body to press Fukuyama into the wall while the other went to get a chair from the opposite side of the office.

Once the chair was in position beside her, they manhandled her up until she was standing on top of it. The futon made it impossible for her to move, and all she could do was try to lean all of her weight off to one side and hope that the chair would topple over.

It didn't.

The second man used the windowsill to lever himself up until he was almost standing beside her. He grabbed the four loose ends of the panty hose that snaked down her back and threaded two of them through the loop of the metal fitting that held the blinds in place. Pulling hard, he forced Fukuyama to move up onto her tiptoes while he tied the ends firmly together.

He jumped down from the windowsill and kicked the chair out from under her in the same movement.

Yasuko Fukuyama began to die.

Grunting in satisfaction, he moved back over to the desk and seated himself in the chair. Placing his gloved hands on the keyboard, he proceeded to type out a suicide note that was short on specifics but long on emotion. He pressed the save button to ensure that his efforts would be written over the original resignation letter, effectively erasing it from the hard disk, and then turned his attention back to his partner, who was cutting the rope tied around the limp and grotesque figure that swung up against the wall.

With the futon and gag removed, Fukuyama looked small, defenseless, and very, very dead.

Leonard Drake's initial reaction to Bryant's story was to laugh. He threw his head back and laughed heartily until the corners of his eyes were moist with tears. People at the other tables in the coffee bar turned toward him, but averted their eyes again when they realized he was a *gaijin*. *Gaijin* were strange and their bad manners not worth dwelling upon.

Bryant shifted uncomfortably and leaned farther across the table. "Len, give it a rest, for God's sake! I'm telling you, it's true!"

Drake wiped the corner of one eye with the back of his hand and tried to control his laughter. "Are you serious?" he asked at length. "Oh, come on, Peter, that's ridiculous! This is Mickey Mouse country. The land of virtual pets and single-ply toilet paper. A company like Hamada might try to bend the rules so that they can avoid the phase trials, but the deliberate release of contagious diseases, death threats, and murder? No way!"

"Keep your voice down!" hissed Bryant. "I'm telling you, it's the truth! I'm going to try to find out from Joji if a meningitis vaccine has recently been patented, and if it has, then we'll have a motive. But if we're found out, we're as good as dead."

The smile left Drake's face. He could see that Bryant was deadly serious, and despite finding the concept utterly preposterous himself, he knew he had to respect his fears. "You really think that Hamada Seiyaku would have us killed? Two office clerks?"

Bryant looked down at his coffee cup. "I guess I don't really know for sure, Len, but I don't think we can afford to take the chance. All I'm saying is that we should keep as low a profile as possible and just carry on with our jobs as if we suspect nothing. Just as a precaution."

"I think you're wrong. If any of this is true, then I think we should have it out with Matsuoka. In fact, that's what I intend to do the moment we get into the office."

"No . . . !" Bryant looked up sharply. Maybe he shouldn't have told Drake after all. He should have guessed that Drake's low boiling point and flash temper would prevent him from humbly admitting defeat and retiring into the background. Drake harbored a slimy sort of superiority complex that made him jump to conclusions and lash out at anything that conflicted with his own point of view. He was not the perfect confidant. "You mention this to *anybody*, let alone Matsuoka, and I'll personally kick your spine out through the top of your head! I don't need you or anyone else putting my head in a noose."

A look of surprise spread across Drake's face. "Well, well, well," he said, "Do I detect a touch of passion creeping into the conversation? You really are riled up about this, aren't you, Peter? But, if you think that I am going to sit back and allow a bunch of ineffectual corporate cretins to issue threats that concern my safety, then you've got another think coming, pal. If you want my opinion, you are talking out of your arse, but I'm not going to leave it up to conjecture. I'm going to see Matsuoka or even Hamada himself if necessary, and get to the bottom of this. Now, are you coming or not?"

Drake finished his coffee and stood up, staring defiantly down at Bryant, whose shoulders slumped dejectedly. *Damn, what a mistake!* How could he possibly have thought that Drake would have nodded his understanding and gone about his business as if nothing had happened? Bryant sighed his fourth sigh of the morning.

Outside, Drake walked to the edge of the road and looked about for a taxi. Bryant stood beside him and stared at the serenity of Hibiya Park across the road, trying to think of a way to change Drake's mind. By confiding in Drake, he had now put himself in even more danger.

"Let's walk," he said finally.

"What? It's a twenty-minute walk to Otemachi."

"It's probably a twenty-minute wait for a cab, too. Come on, walk off some of that fat, you slob."

Drake grinned and slapped Bryant on the back. "Okay, but if a taxi comes along, I'm hailing it."

Bryant stared at the rain-slick sidewalk as they walked side by side. The heavy rain of the previous evening had let up, but the sky was still bloated with angry-looking clouds threatening another downpour in the not-too-distant future. Drake, typically, clicked his umbrella rhythmically on the pavement as he walked, almost as if he felt it was his duty to play out the role of the British stereotype. Bryant hadn't even bothered bringing one. Umbrellas had been the last thing on his mind when he had left home that morning.

"Listen, Len," said Bryant after they had walked in silence for two hundred meters, "I want you to give me two days before you approach Matsuoka."

"What's the point? What can you possibly expect to achieve in two days?"

"Think of it as a compromise. If, as I was led to believe, one of the directors is found dead between now and Wednesday morning, then you will concede the fact that the information I have is at least correct in part. If, on the other hand, nothing has happened by Wednesday morning and I haven't managed to collect any other evidence, then I'll concede the fact that I'm being led up the garden path and will accompany you when you visit Matsuoka. How's that? Fair?"

Drake stopped walking and turned to Bryant. He placed the tip of his umbrella between his parted feet and rested both hands on the handle, looking for all the world like a slightly plump Gene Kelly in *Singing in the Rain*. "Look, Peter, I don't want to be offensive, but you are on a bloody wild goose chase. There is no point in prolonging this. You're torturing yourself. I can see it in your eyes. Think how much better you'll sleep tonight if we can get this thing out into the open once and for all." He placed a hand behind Bryant's elbow and started walking again, propelling him forward.

"What if it's true?"

"Eh?"

"What if you approach Matsuoka, who is bound to deny it anyway, and then somebody kills you on the way home tonight? That will certainly get everything out into the open, and there is no doubt that you'll sleep better tonight."

Drake continued to walk in silence, but Bryant was pleased to notice that his sarcasm had put a frown on Drake's face. At least he was considering the idea.

"Okay, Wednesday morning," said Drake after a few moments. "But you'd better come up with something good by then."

Bryant smiled at his victory. He had nothing to smile about, really, considering that all he had gained was to revert the situation back to the point where it stood the moment before he had confided in Drake, but he was pleased. The thought of Drake storming into Matsuoka's office and demanding an explanation had sent an icy torrent of fear coursing through his veins, and it was a relief to know that he had managed to avert that scenario.

The two men walked in silence. Bryant watched an empty cab pass; Drake had forgotten all about an alternative form of transport. Fifteen minutes later they turned right onto the street leading down to Tokyo Station, and both noticed the ambulance and the two police cars stationed immediately outside of Hamada Seiyaku's main entrance simultaneously. They looked at each other and shrugged.

The main foyer of the building was bustling with people. Two policemen were standing at attention in front of the bank of elevators. Young office girls huddled in cliques with their handkerchiefs pressed to their mouths, shoulders slumped as if cowering from something unspeakable. Groups of salarymen also stood about, some of them smoking nervously. A low buzz of conversation permeated the hall, but individual interactions were muffled and indecipherable. The people standing around had one thing in common—they were all staring at the floor indicator located over the left-hand elevator. Bryant looked up at the indicator and saw that the fourteenth floor was illuminated. The directors' floor. He spotted his colleague, Trent Peterson, among a small group of people over by the emergency stairs. He tapped Drake on the arm and nodded toward Peterson. The two men walked over.

"Morning, Trent. What's happening?" Drake asked.

Trent Peterson nodded a greeting and returned his eyes to the elevator. "A suicide," he said in his soft Australian accent. "Fukuyama hanged herself in her office."

"Fukuyama?" Bryant repeated, his brow furrowed as he tried to place the name.

"Yasuko Fukuyama, the director of planning."

Bryant choked back the gasp that threatened to burst from his mouth and spun around to Drake in horror. Drake's mouth had dropped open and the shock was evident on his face. Despite his own battered emotions, Bryant wryly realized that he now had an indefinite extension to his Wednesday-morning deadline.

The atmosphere of abject terror around the conference table was tangible, a thick cloak of sickly-sweet, cloying fear that hung in the air like a cloud of flies around a decaying corpse. Shigeru Hamada could actually smell it. The fifteen directors sat around the table in total silence, each concentrating on his inner thoughts and studiously avoiding the eyes of the president. They looked pathetic, he decided with joyful zeal. And all because he had total power over them—a power that he had never dreamed existed before: the ultimate power of life over death. Or, as he preferred to think, death over life.

Having let them stew in their own juices for several more minutes, Hamada finally got to his feet and waited until all eyes were directed at him. He saw a plethora of emotions in those eyes, although disgust, hate, and fear were predominant.

"By now you will all have heard of the death of Ms. Fukuyama," he said. "A sad but necessary demise, as I'm sure you will all agree. I hope you will believe me when I say how sincerely I hope that this will be the last casualty from among our ranks." Hamada swung his eyes slowly around the table, looking at each of the directors individually as he allowed his unspoken threat to sink in. He would have to be careful from now on. In having Fukuyama killed, he had passed an invisible boundary from which there would be no return. He had no doubt that all of the fifteen people sitting around the table at the moment were his enemies and would not hesitate to turn him in to the authorities if they thought they could protect themselves. Fortunately, he didn't think the police would believe them anyway. Not a mark had been left on Fukuyama's body; her fingerprints were on the panty hose packet, there had been no sign of a struggle in her office, and the suicide note had been concise and easily comprehensible. The government would protect him as well. By assisting in covering up the crime and setting up one of their stupid committees to "cope" with the situation, the LDP had signed on as an equal partner and could no longer allow Hamada or Hamada Seiyaku to be denounced. No, as far as the National Police Agency was concerned, Yasuko Fukuyama had committed suicide during a deep depression, and Shigeru Hamada was as pure as the driven snow.

The director of administration, Koichi Nagashima, slowly rose to his feet and cleared his throat nervously. Hamada nodded in his direction. "Yes, Mr. Nagashima? You have something to say?"

Nagashima cleared his throat again. "I would like to say on behalf all of us here today how much we regret the loss of Ms. Fukuyama's life." He looked Hamada in the eye and felt his mouth go dry as a frown appeared on the president's forehead.

"I would also like to say," he continued hastily, "that our conviction to the company is not lessened by this unfortunate incident, and that you can count on us as being loyal to the company's interests."

Hamada's brow smoothed over and a small grin turned up the corners of his mouth. "Well, thank you, Mr. Nagashima. I am flattered that you should take the trouble to state your convictions. Your statement, I take it, goes for everyone in the room. Correct?"

One by one, everybody seated around the table nodded their heads in the direction of the president. Nagashima sat down, hating himself for his bland kowtowing but more concerned about his physical safety than a brief moment of humility. As one of the senior directors, verbally vowing allegiance on behalf of everybody was expected of him. He suddenly realized that he had firsthand experience of what it would be like to be a politician in a dictatorship. He had read of the consequences of crossing swords with leaders in certain countries in the world, and he had no doubt that he had been thrust into a similar situation. He was still shocked at how quickly Shigeru Hamada—who had earned his loyalty and respect up until now—had turned from a competent chief executive officer of a reliable company into a tyrant who wielded his power with a total lack of compassion for human life. He had become a madman whose ideal of protecting the company had turned into a blazing obsession. Didn't he understand that nothing would ever be the same again? Didn't he know that the truth would eventually be brought into the open? Didn't he know that he would not be allowed to escape punishment for his wanton disregard for human life?

"Now, if you don't mind, gentlemen, I'd like to commence the meeting." Hamada picked up a folder from the table in front of him and began to read from it. "The total number of infections so far is six hundred and seventy-eight, with five hundred and forty-two already dead. That is only within Japan.

We also have another fifty or sixty cases diagnosed overseas, and a particularly virulent outbreak in Pusan, South Korea, triggered by a Japanese fisherman who has since died." Hamada paused and looked around the table. Everybody was busy writing down these figures. "The Chigasaki Research and Development Center has unfortunately not made any headway in developing an antidote, but you'll be pleased to know that the government has stocked all hospitals in the Chigasaki region with Rifampin, Sulfadiazine, Ciprofloxacin, Minocylcine, and Cefriaxone, the only forms of preventive medicine that are currently available. As the disease also seems to be spreading to other parts of the country with alarming speed, they are also planning to establish massive stockpiles of these drugs and set up a network for immediate distribution if and when necessary, and—"

A telephone located on the wet bar behind Hamada began to ring, interrupting his brief. He nodded to the man sitting on his immediate left, who walked over to the bar and answered the call. He listened for a moment before placing his hand over the mouthpiece. "It's for you," he said to Hamada.

Hamada clicked his tongue in annoyance at being interrupted and walked over to accept the phone. The rest of the room remained in silence while Hamada listened to the caller without making any comment. Having hung up the receiver, he walked thoughtfully back to the table, where he placed the heels of his hands on the edge and leaned his weight onto his arms, his head bowed.

Breaking out of his reverie, he glanced at his watch before lifting his face to the fifteen directors. "It seems, gentlemen, that we have another problem to take care of. Ten minutes ago, at nineteen fifty-five exactly, Peter Bryant of the overseas patent department was seen entering the American embassy in Tokyo." He looked across at Kazunori Matsuoka. "Anything suspicious in his movements today?"

Matsuoka stood up self-consciously, his face reddening

slightly. "No, sir. Both Bryant and Drake spent the day working as usual, and neither has mentioned Chigasaki since last week."

Hamada nodded thoughtfully, and Matsuoka sat down. These two damned foreigners were becoming an unpleasant and persistent irritant. Although he doubted they had made any headway with their quest for information out of Chigasaki, they were proving to be a distraction that he could no longer afford. Today would make the third time their names had cropped up during the meetings. Well, they would live to regret it. *Three strikes and you're out!*

"Well, I'm afraid that it is about time Mr. Drake and Mr. Bryant met up with a little accident. We cannot afford to take any chances. If you will excuse me for a few minutes, gentlemen, I shall set up the logistics from my office. Please entertain yourselves in my absence."

Chapter Five

"*Tadaima!*" Bryant shouted as he opened the door to his apartment. A pair of gray Cuban-heeled leather shoes in the *genkan* informed him that Michiyo had already arrived home. He was rewarded with a muffled "*Okaeri*" from the kitchen.

Michiyo Kato was pottering around preparing a snack as Bryant pushed open the door and entered the room. She was dressed in the flimsy robe that he had bought her for her birthday the previous June, and he noted her slim lines as she stretched up to get another glass and a plate from the cupboard above the sink. He walked up behind and wrapped his arms around her, grunting appreciatively at her delicious fresh-from-the-shower fragrance. She felt warm and familiar, something exotic to take his mind off events. A pocket of love burst within him, threatening to overcome his senses and cause him to drag her off to the bedroom and reacquaint her with his undying devotion. Instead he laid his chin on her shoulder and squeezed her hard. She looked over her shoulder and pecked him on his proffered cheek. "Hungry?" she asked.

"You bet! I've been at the embassy for over an hour, and apart from several gallons of coffee, I've had nothing since lunchtime. What are you fixing?"

"Well, it doesn't take much intelligence to work that one out," Michiyo said, spreading her arms expansively over the worktop, upon which a stick of French bread, a wheel of Brie cheese, a packet of tortilla chips, and a bottle of red wine were laid out, ready for transportation into the dining room. "Are you sure you have an IQ of one hundred and forty-five?"

"Less of your lip, woman." Bryant tightened his fingers and dug them into the sides of her slim waist, causing her to giggle and squirm out of his reach. Before she had moved too far, Bryant caught hold of her hand and pulled her to his chest, enfolding her in his arms and burying his face in her neck. The action seemed to give him stability. He had endured the last few days of his life with a stoic sense of disbelief—almost as if he had had an out-of-body experience—and the simple pleasure he obtained from being held tightly was like balm to his raw and tattered nerves. He was surprised to realize that he was on the verge of breaking into tears—not tears of self-pity, but tears of love and emotion. He wanted to hold Michiyo forever, to absorb the love she exuded and curl up in her warmth like a puppy protected from the world by an over-possessive master.

Unfortunately for Bryant, Michiyo had other ideas. She bit him sharply on the ear and pushed him away. "Not before dinner, Peter," she said reproachfully, an impish grin on her face as she turned back to the worktop. "You get the wine and glasses, and I'll get the rest."

Bryant smiled ruefully as he complied with her command. He should have known better anyway. Although as passionate and expressive in the confines of the bedroom as any woman he had ever known or read about, Michiyo's Japanese upbringing restrained her from displays of affection elsewhere, her policy being that there was a time and place for everything. This had worried him at the beginning of their relationship, and he had experienced occasional pangs of anxiety over the thought that she did not really love him as much as she claimed. She even refused to hold hands in public and would look away coldly if he tried to kiss her good-bye at the station at any time. He had since discovered that this was not uncommon. Michiyo was neither cold, uncaring, nor asexual. She was simply following the dictates of her culture. But he couldn't help but feel dejected whenever she refused his advances. Especially at a time like this.

Bryant was halfway through his first bite of French bread and Brie when the telephone rang. Hastily rinsing it down with a mouthful of wine, he walked across to the phone in the adjoining living room and answered it.

"Mr. Bryant?"

"Hold on a moment." Bryant covered the mouthpiece with the palm of his hand. "Work. I'll take it in the bedroom," he said to Michiyo by way of explanation as he left the room. He had recognized the voice of his mystery caller.

Sitting on the edge of the bed in the small bedroom, he said into the receiver, "I'm back. What do you want this time?"

"Mr. Bryant, you must leave your apartment now. You were seen going into the American embassy tonight and you are to be the target of an accident. You must get out of there as quickly as possible."

"What?" Bryant blanched as if hit over the head with a baseball bat, the fears that he had managed to forget for twenty minutes flooding back. "Are you serious?"

"I am afraid so. I have prepared some money for you and Mr. Drake. Two million yen each in cash. You can use this to move somewhere else in the country or even return to your own countries. I am sorry it's not more, but that is all I could raise in cash at such short notice."

"But, that's impossible. I *can't*. What about my girlfriend, my *everything*?"

"You can decide on that later. At the very least, I want you to move out of your apartment with your girlfriend and check into a hotel away from the Yoyogi-Shinjuku area tonight."

"Why the money?"

"I feel that it is the least I can do. I want you to know that all Japanese are not as bad as the president of Hamada Seiyaku. Consider it severance pay. Now, do you have a mobile telephone?"

"Yes."

"Let me have the number. I want you to be waiting outside of Minami Shinjuku station on the Odakyu line at"—a pause—"eleven-thirty. Take your telephone with you. I will contact you when you get there and let you know where to pick up the money."

"How do I know that you are not just setting me up for the accident?"

"Why would I bother? If I were arranging for your demise, it would be much easier to carry out in the confines of your home. Remember that I know exactly where you are at the moment. You must trust me."

Bryant conceded and gave the caller the number to his mobile phone.

"Thank you. There is one other thing that I want you to pass on to Mr. Woodson, although you must promise me that you will do this by telephone and not try to approach the American embassy again." Bryant promised. "I didn't bother mentioning it the other day because I didn't think it was important, my only concern then being that America help us manufacture an antidote. However, I have now realized that things are likely to escalate, and it would be helpful if your government were aware of a simple fact."

"Go on."

"The Japanese government is responsible in part for this outbreak. The bacterium was commissioned by the government as a potential weapon for slowing down an invading army during war. That is why I cannot approach the Japanese authorities."

Shoji Kubota's unexpected visit coincided with the prime minister's nightcap of whisky and water. An aide brought another glass and placed it on the tray next to the bottle of Bunnahabhain, the two bottles of Suntory mineral water, and the small bucket of ice. Kiyoshi Aizawa pushed aside the laptop computer, poured the general secretary of the Liberal Democratic Party a drink, and passed it across the desk.

"Smooth," said Kubota, having taken a sip. "Very nice indeed."

"Single malt whisky is one of my few indulgences," said Aizawa dreamily. He loved this time of the day, and despite the fact that he was not overjoyed at the interruption, Kubota's presence did not completely dissipate his feeling of relaxation. "Although most Scotsmen would be extremely distressed to see me polluting it with ice and water. I have heard that in their eyes, watering down a good whisky is like putting milk and sugar into Japanese tea."

Kubota laughed briefly. "A nauseating thought. I myself prefer a good cognac, although I must admit that this is exceptional whisky."

"Would you like a brandy? I can get a bottle brought in, if you wish." The prime minister leaned across to the telephone.

"No, no, no. This is fine, thank you."

The two men sat in silence as they savored the scotch. The lights had been dimmed in the main part of the study, and a single wall light behind Aizawa and a desktop lamp provided the only illumination in the wood-paneled room. No matter what time the prime minister returned home from his official engagements, he always made a beeline for this room and relaxed over a couple of drinks before turning in.

"Do you bring news on the outbreak?"

"Yes and no," said Kubota, shifting uncomfortably on his

seat. "I just thought it fair to warn you that I will not be supporting you if the situation gets out of hand, as seems likely at the moment."

Aizawa looked down at his drink and listened to the ice cubes tinkling against the crystal glass. "I see," he said at length. "And may I ask why?"

"We will need a scapegoat, and you, unfortunately, are the perfect choice. Although I should mention that I have nothing against you personally. I am simply doing my job as I see it."

The prime minister nodded. He was not really surprised. Being the leader of the Liberal Democratic Party—or any other party in Japan, for that matter—was a tenuous position. Election to the post did not always mean that the best person had been chosen, simply that political favors had been returned. The entire ranks of Japanese government were split into small factions headed by people of differing levels of power, and the stronger of these people were known as kingmakers. In order to get sufficient votes for his own election, Aizawa had lobbied all of these factions, notably the factions headed by powerful kingmakers, with the promise of high-ranking positions in his cabinet being made available to certain people of their choice. A faction with a large number of cabinet ministers was in a position to consolidate its power base even further, so the reformists and other politicians who really could do some good were kept in the background through lack of support from the people who preferred personal political power to capable government. Aizawa had gained the support of Shoji Kubota, the leader of the *Kubota-Ha* and a renowned kingmaker himself, during his election campaign, and his present position was, in part, thanks to him. However, these so-called kingmakers were also capable of becoming kingbreakers, and Aizawa recognized that his time was drawing to a close.

"And if the situation does not get out of hand?" he asked.

"Then you have no worries. But I think you will find your confidence is falsely placed. The number of victims is increasing daily, and it is only a matter of time before the media discover the government's involvement. It has been decided that you and the socialist shall be held responsible."

"Today's figures show less than seven hundred casualties, and the preventive medicine is being distributed according to plan. Things have not yet reached anywhere near disaster levels."

"The experts tell me that the epidemic is claiming victims in increasing multiples. Seven hundred today will be one thousand four hundred tomorrow and two thousand eight hundred the next day. Within a week we will have ninety thousand victims, and nothing to treat them with. Within two weeks, one million one hundred and fifty thousand. Within three weeks more than ten percent of the entire population. Do you want me to continue?"

Aizawa slumped further into his seat. He took a sip of whisky, but it failed to provide any solace. He was an accessory after the fact to mass murder. Would the situation have been different had he been more aggressive in his actions when the outbreak first became known? It was possible, but that would have meant admitting that the government was responsible, and the basic rules of politics forbade the telling of damaging truths. He was caught in a vicious circle.

"We will continue supporting you until it is no longer possible. We will then demand a vote of no-confidence in the Diet and pull you down. I am sorry, but that is the way it has to be."

Aizawa nodded again.

"Of course," Kubota added, raising his eyes slyly to Aizawa to gauge his reaction, "it would save a lot of time and trouble if you would consider resigning."

Aizawa leaned forward and placed his elbows on the desk. "Never," he said quietly, his voice no more than a whisper in the large room. "If you think I am going to retreat into the background like a whipped puppy just when the going gets tough, then you have misjudged me, Kubota. I shall do everything within my power to put this country back together again, and damn the consequences. If you wish to play your foolish games in the background, then that is your prerogative, but do not expect any help from me. I have a job to do, and I will make sure it gets done."

"Your stubbornness will do nothing to help this country, Aizawa, no matter how good your intentions are. You will simply be taking the focus off more important matters and wasting everybody's time. You are finished already, and delaying the inevitable is not a prudent course of action to take at this time. I hope you will reconsider."

"Never!"

"So be it." Kubota sighed inwardly. Not that he was expecting servile acquiescence from Aizawa anyway. He had just thought it a gambit worth trying, and the result did not surprise him. "In the meantime, I think it would be prudent if the government were seen to be taking a firmer hand with the situation. Maybe the time is ripe for mobilizing the Self-Defense Forces to set up distribution sites for the medicine at strategic locations. We must also turn our attention to the economy. The Nikkei index is plummeting and the yen depreciating at an unprecedented rate. The financial sector is already screaming blue murder, and—"

"I can do without the lecture, Kubota," Aizawa said louder than was necessary, interrupting Kubota's monologue. The air in the room was suddenly thicker, charged with the particles of anger and contempt. "I am not totally ignorant of what is going on, you know. I have already received Hoshino's plan for military deployment, and it will probably be activated within the next couple of days. I am also considering hauling the bridge-bank concept out of mothballs to cope with any bankruptcies that might arise in the financial sector." He placed the empty glass on the desk and steepled his hands beneath his chin, staring directly at Kubota. "One other thing that you don't know is that I will scream at the top of my lungs for international help if the problem worsens. This is no longer a game played for political benefit, and protecting my own hide is not sufficient reason to keep me silent. I will admit to everything, and to hell with the consequences. People are dying, and it is my job to prevent that."

"I would strongly advise against that, Mr. Prime Minister," said Kubota. His eyes had hardened and he matched Aizawa's stare unwaveringly, fury not far from the surface. "You do not have the right to destroy everything the party has achieved over the past fifty years. I will see that you are labeled unstable and run out of town before I allow that to happen. You will be out of politics forever."

Aizawa smiled. "That is your prerogative, Kubota, but I wonder if you have the time. According to your own scenario, the entire population will be dead within a few weeks. If you think that I can live with that on my conscious, then you are a very bad judge of character. If I believe it to be the only way, then I will stand up and sing."

"Then you leave me with no choice, Mr. Prime Minister. I'm afraid that I am compelled to commence procedures to have you removed from office immediately."

"Fine! Go ahead. But my only hope is that you are elected in my place so you can understand what it feels like to be responsible for the lives of so many people. Now, if you'll excuse me, I would prefer to be left alone."

Kubota placed his glass on the desk and stood up. He stared at the prime minister for a moment longer, clenching and unclenching his fists, before turning on his heels and walking briskly out of the office without another word. The door banged loudly behind him.

Aizawa chuckled and flicked the edge of his glass, the melodious ring produced by the lead crystal somehow soothing. He had certainly rattled that pompous old bastard's cage. Kubota's threat had left not a dent on him. The chances of his being able to rustle up enough support to run a vote of no-confidence through the Diet within a reasonable time frame were remote, to say the least. Not that it mattered if he did; Aizawa would still have enough time to ensure that the correct decisions were made to overcome this sticky period in Japan's history. Aizawa was determined to sort the problem out once and for all. Although he didn't feel that the time had yet arrived for him to admit to the government's culpability, he knew that it would come in the near future, and he also knew that at that time he would do what was best for the country, not his own political beliefs.

He reached across for the bottle of Bunnahabhain and topped off his glass.

It was not unusual for Norio Kondo to arrive home from a day's work at the university after eleven o'clock at night, but it was unusual for him to find his wife sobbing inconsolably on the sofa. Dropping his leather briefcase by the door, he rushed to her side.

"Shigeko, what is it? What's the matter?"

Shigeko turned her face toward her husband, her chin quivering in her attempt to control the sobs that racked her body. "It's Akiko-*chan*."

"Akiko-*chan*? What's wrong with Akiko-*chan*? Has she had an accident?"

"She's . . . she's dead." Shigeko crumpled back onto the sofa, her hands covering her face as her body heaved up and down.

"Dead? How? What happened? What about Seiji-*kun*? Is he all right?" Seiji and Akiko Kuwano lived next door. They were young—still in their early thirties—and were battling hard to keep up the payments on a house that was, all things considered, well out of their price range. They were a pleasant, hardworking couple, and Norio knew that Shigeko had struck up a firm friendship with Akiko.

"I don't know where Seiji is. I haven't seen him since he left for the hospital this afternoon."

"What happened? Tell me quickly!"

"It's the disease. That damned meningitis thing. Akiko-*chan* visited the hospital yesterday to pick up some of that medicine they are giving out. She had to queue up for more than three hours, she said. She must have caught it then. She woke up early this morning vomiting, so Seiji took her to the hospital. She died early this afternoon in terrible pain."

"Oh, my God. That's awful!" Norio ran his fingers through his hair. "When is the funeral? We'll have to help Seiji-*kun* out financially. He'll never be able to afford a proper funeral or a burial plot. Oh, dear, how awful . . ."

"There won't be a funeral. The authorities told Seiji that his wife's body is a biological hazard and cannot be released to him. They will arrange for the cremation and tell him when to come and pick up her ashes. If he comes back, that is . . ."

Norio looked at his wife quizzically. Her face was still buried in her hands, but the shaking was beginning to calm down. "What do you mean, 'if he comes back'? Why shouldn't he come back?"

Shigeko raised her face and touched her husband gently on the cheek. "There are rumors," she said softly. "Everybody knows at least one person who has died from this horrible disease, and all of the victims' family members mysteriously disappear, it seems."

"Oh, come on. That is ridiculous! They have probably just moved out of town for fear of their own safety. What are you trying to suggest?"

"They say that the authorities spirit them away somewhere because they are potential carriers of the disease."

"Stupid old wives' tales!" Norio dismissed the rumor with a wave of his hand. "How can you possibly believe things like that? This is modern-day Japan, for God's sake! Not some small third-world dictatorship."

"I'm scared, Norio. I think we should leave here. Get far away from this horrendous illness."

Norio looked into his wife's eyes and saw the depths of her fear. He nodded gently and stroked a hand along the back of her head. He had been thinking along the same lines for several days now, and had been patiently waiting for the correct timing to broach the subject himself. "You're right, of course. We must leave. I'll e-mail Omotenashi and see if he wants to join us in Izu Kogen. It will take us a few days to stock up on supplies. It might also be a good idea to change the car for something larger and set ourselves up with a portable computer so we can continue to communicate with everybody. We might have to stay there for some time."

Shigeko smiled thinly through her tears. She knew she could count on her man to sort everything out. She herself simply wanted to lie down and not think about anything. She returned to mourning her friend.

Mike Woodson was still in his office, reading through the typed-up transcript of Peter Bryant's debriefing. He was still having trouble believing that a company like Hamada Seiyaku could be responsible for even half of the allegations that Bryant had made, but the conviction with which Peter had stated his case was giving him real cause for concern. There was no doubt that Peter believed every single word of it. The evidence was also beginning to pour in. Not only was the outbreak down in Chigasaki irrefutable proof that something was going on, but tests on the bacterium in America had confirmed the fact that it had been genetically engineered in the exact way that Bryant's mystery caller had claimed. And he must not forget that a Hamada Seiyaku director was now dead, as prewarned.

All that remained now was for an attempt to be made on the lives of Bryant and Drake, and to come up with a feasible motive for genetically engineering a deadly bacterium. True to his word, Robert Rasnick had had Hamada Seiyaku checked out to see if they had any dealings with foreign governments, but it had turned up nothing. In fact, Hamada Seiyaku was as clean as any company in Japan, and cleaner than most. There had been one or two rumors about *Sokaiya* connections, but nothing serious enough to stain the company's reputation. Woodson had also run a more substantial check on the patents the company had applied for over the past five years, and there was nothing that pointed to a vaccine or cure for any meningitis-related disease. It was ridiculous! There had to be something. Reputable companies like Hamada Seiyaku would not spend time and money creating a bug that served no purpose. And if they *had* gone to all this trouble, then why had they not come forward and admitted that they were responsible in public, instead of keeping it quiet and allowing valuable time to be wasted while people died? What did they have to hide?

Woodson shook his head in bewilderment and picked up his pen to sign the bottom of the report. He had finished signing the document and was reaching for his coffee cup when the phone rang.

"Mike, it's me, Peter. Listen, I don't have much time. That guy phoned me again and told me to get out of the apartment. Hamada Seiyaku has put a contract out on me and Drake."

"Whoa, whoa, whoa! Slow down a bit. . . ."

"I don't have the time, Mike. They are going to try to kill me! I have to get out of here as soon as possible. Now listen to what I have to say."

Woodson noted that his friend was close to panic and remained silent.

"I have the motive. The bug was commissioned by the Japanese government for biological weaponry."

"What . . . ?"

"The idea is for it to slow down an attacking force in the event of war. That's all I know at the moment."

"Peter, I want you to come to the embassy. Now! If what you say is true, then I must add it to this report and send it over to the States as quickly as possible. You'll also be safe here from any attempts on your life. I can protect you."

"I can't, Mike. I was seen entering the embassy tonight. That is the reason for the death threat. They're sure to be watching. Mitch and I will find a hotel on the other side of town for tonight. I'll contact you once we have checked in and let you know where we are. We can talk about protection then. In the meantime I want to stay as far away from the embassy as possible."

Woodson ran a hand through his hair. Bryant's near-hysteria was contagious, and Woodson was feeling his fear. "Peter, listen. I'll come and pick you up. Get out of the apartment and I'll pick you up somewhere else. *Anywhere* else! Just name the place."

"I'm sorry, Mike. I have one other thing to do tonight, and I still haven't managed to contact Drake. I have to let him know about this. I'll keep my mobile phone close by in case you need to contact me, but otherwise I'll phone you after we have found a hotel. It'll probably be late. Speak to you later."

The line went dead before Woodson could object. Woodson opened his diary and copied Bryant's mobile phone number down onto a small piece of paper, which he then folded and placed inside his wallet. He wanted to keep it close at all times. He was deeply worried for his friend and felt completely impotent at not being able to do anything constructive to help him. He looked at the wall clock. Nearly eleven o'clock. He presumed it would take at least a couple of hours for Peter to phone him back, and he resigned himself to a long and tedious wait. But before he could settle down to his tedium, he had something to do. He flipped open his address book, picked up the receiver, and punched in Robert Rasnick's home number.

"Rasnick."

"Robert. It's Mike. I think we have our motive. I know it's late, but would you mind stepping into the office for an hour or two?"

* * *

112

Bryant kept his hands jammed deep inside the pockets of his coat to ward off the chill of the night. His breath plumed dramatically before him as he hurried down the street back to his apartment. He had left Michiyo in a flood of tears, cramming clothes and other essentials haphazardly into a large sports bag. He didn't want to leave her alone longer than necessary.

The pickup had gone smoothly, and a small leather clutch bag containing four million yen in cash was tucked under his arm beneath his coat. At least, he presumed that was what it contained; he had not bothered checking. At first he had thought that the mystery man was observing him from inside a building near the station, but the instructions to walk along the road and then back again had shown that he had been right behind him at a distance of no more than a hundred meters. Upon Bryant's return, the clutch bag was leaning up against a vending machine outside of the deserted station. It certainly had not been there before, for Bryant had purchased a cup of hot coffee from the machine while waiting for the call.

Spooky.

He pulled his mobile phone out of his pocket and pressed the redial button to make another attempt at contacting Drake. The time was nearing midnight and the stupid bastard still wasn't home. *Damn!* Was he out drinking every single night of the week? He replaced the phone and huddled further into his coat for warmth. A fresh breeze had sprung up and was finding its way into every available opening. Just another two blocks and he would be home. And then what? Another thirty minutes explaining and consoling Michiyo? Well, she did have a right to know the depth of the situation, he supposed. It wasn't every day that someone was told to leave home or face death. But she would have to wait until they were out of the apartment and on their way to another part of town in a taxi.

Bryant didn't notice the parked car waiting ten meters away from his apartment building when he turned onto his street, but he noticed the three men climb out of it as he walked past. He stopped and his heart seemed to jump out of his chest like that of a cartoon character. He looked about frantically, futilely willing an escape route to suddenly appear from nowhere. There was no doubt that the men's total interest was concentrated exclusively on him. Two of them were standing directly in front of him, blocking his passage, and he sensed that the other had walked around the car and come up behind him. The crash on the back of his neck still came as a surprise. The pain exploded in his head and he stumbled forward into the two men in front. A fist flashed out of the darkness and caught him squarely on the side of the face, lashing his head over to the left, where it came into contact with a fast-moving foot. A few more flashes of pain that seemed to come from nowhere made Bryant realize that he was in big trouble. Since he'd never gained much experience in street fighting or bar brawling, his reflexes were not swift enough to parry the barrage of kicks and punches that his body was being subjected to, and he sensed that it was only a matter of time before he was ground to a pulp. He hurt. He hurt like he'd never hurt before, but knew instinctively that he had to remain on his feet. Once on the ground, he would stand no chance of defending himself. Ignoring the pain, he pushed as hard as he could with his feet and slammed his shoulder into the chest of one of his attackers. The man was taken by surprise, but Bryant's low stance prevented him from using his fists to inflict the damage that he had intended. The man stumbled back a couple of paces, but soon recovered and grabbed a handful of Bryant's hair. A powerful kick to his testicles from behind crumpled Bryant's body, and he wheezed in pain as he felt his head being pulled back by his hair. The next moment, the side of the parked car was rushing toward his face and everything went fuzzy around the edges. He had lost. He was as good as dead, and he didn't give a damn. The pain in his body had robbed him of the zest for life. He no longer cared. . . .

Adding a few extra kicks for good measure, the three men grabbed hold of Bryant's supine figure and dragged him out into the middle of the street, where they dropped him face-down. Bryant was dimly aware of the asphalt being hard and unyielding, but strangely comforting. It felt cool on his face, cool enough to make it a perfect pillow. He felt sleep washing over him. A good sleep was all he needed, really. A couple of hours' shut-eye and he would be in perfect shape again. Ready to enter the ring for the next round, even.

Two conflicting noises invaded his sense of peace. One he recognized as the revving of a car engine. The other he recognized as Michiyo calling his name. The voice seemed to come from somewhere above his head, so he guessed she was calling from out of the window of their apartment. Now wasn't that nice of her? He was certainly lucky to have found somebody who was so concerned over his well-being. He would tell her just how much he appreciated her concern after he had had his nap. A small smile creased the corners of his mouth.

Before Bryant could give in to the pleasures of slumber, a strong hand seized the collar of his coat, and he felt himself being dragged swiftly over the asphalt. A split second later, the wind of a fast-moving car washed over his body, clutching at the edges of his coat and flapping them crazily in the false breeze.

"Quick, you have to help me," a frantic voice pleaded in his ear. "They are trying to run you over. They want to kill you!"

A screech of brakes sounded twenty meters down the road.

Bryant painfully raised his head and looked into the frightened eyes of his neighbor from the first floor of his apartment building. Feeling justly embarrassed at having been observed in such an unsightly situation, Bryant smiled coyly and said, "Hi!"

The man swore and grabbed hold of Bryant's collar again.

Bryant felt himself being dragged until the middle of his back bumped into the curb. He grunted slightly in discomfort as the curb grazed along his spine, and then, suddenly, there were two pairs of hands on his collar and he was lying faceup on the sidewalk. The newcomer was screaming in a high-pitched, hysterical voice.

"Police! Police! Somebody call the police! Help!"

Reason was beginning to return to the throne. Bryant shook his head and shifted himself up onto an elbow just in time to see three men standing uncertainly a few meters away. Lights were being clicked on in the surrounding apartments, and people were opening windows. Michiyo stood between him and the three men, screaming at the top of her lungs. The men looked around at the sudden interest in their activities, and, realizing that things were not working in their favor, directed final looks of pure hatred at Bryant and his screeching protector before turning on their heels and racing back to the car.

A moment later the sound of the engine died away and was replaced by Michiyo's sobs as she draped herself over Bryant's stiff and pain-racked body.

"Oh, Peter, what have they done to you? Is anything broken? Where does it hurt?" She cupped his battered face in her hands and surveyed the damage, her tears dripping freely onto his neck.

"It's my . . ." Bryant looked up past Michiyo and into the faces of his rescuer from the first floor and several other interested parties. What he had to impart was not something he would like to have admitted in public under normal circumstances, but Michiyo seemed worried, and he thought he ought to let her know.

"Yes, my darling? What is it?"

"Well, it's my balls," he said in an exaggerated whisper. "I think they're growing larger."

* * *

116

Raymond DeBerry, the president of the United States of America, sat at his desk and listened to Wayne Jeffers deliver his bombshell without any discernible change in expression. He glanced across at the chairman of the Joint Chiefs of Staff and the secretary of state and noticed that they were having more difficulty in concealing their emotions. Dale Lindley, the chairman of the Joint Chiefs, was spluttering like a valve with a faulty gasket.

"But that's just not possible," Lindley said. "The Japanese government carrying out research into bioweapons? They wouldn't dare!"

"I'm afraid so, Dale," answered Jeffers, the director of the Central Intelligence Agency. "This report came in from Robert Rasnick in Tokyo, and anything he says you can take to the bank."

Patrick Watson, secretary of state, cleared his throat. "Just what international treaties is that in violation of?"

Jeffers shuffled some papers on his lap and began to read. " 'The protocol for the prohibition of the use in war of asphyxiating, poisonous, or other gases, and of bacteriological methods of warfare, commonly known as the Geneva Protocol, and which came into effect on February eighth, 1928.' " His finger moved farther down the page. " 'The Biological and Toxic Weapons Convention that came into force in 1975. The Australia Group of 1985 . . .' "

"Do they ban research into biological weapons, or only deployment?"

Jeffers had expected this question and was prepared. "Well," he said, referring back to his notes, "if the contents were written in stone and placed on Mount Sinai, they would probably read, 'Thou shalt not develop biological weapons; thou shalt not produce biological weapons; thou shalt not stockpile biological weapons; thou shalt not acquire biological weapons; and thou shalt not retain biological weapons.' " Jeffers looked up and grinned. "I guess that sort of covers it, wouldn't you say?"

DeBerry slapped his hands on the desk. "Damn," he said, "just what we needed right now. Okay, pull the Japanese ambassador in and run him through the mill. Give him the normal bullshit about how distressed we are to hear this news and how we are expecting a full report on it at his earliest convenience. If he denies it, wave the United Nations in front of his nose. In the meantime, Wayne, get your boy in Tokyo to send us some proof. I won't bother contacting the prime minister until I have the ambassador's reaction and a more detailed report from Tokyo. Now, let's get onto this damn bug itself. Is it still spreading?"

"Yes, sir," answered the secretary of state. "The latest figures from Tokyo show nearly eight hundred victims, and most are either dead or close to death. Initial projections expect this number to rise dramatically over the next few days. We have also had fifty-two cases registered in America, not to mention several hundred in different locations around the globe."

"How are we intending to deal with that?" asked the president.

"Well, sir, I think we need to set up quarantine zones at all ports of entry to screen arrivals from Japan. This disease is one deadly son of a bitch, and we can't afford to let it get loose over here. There's bound to be a big outcry, but we'll have to just roll with the punches. Isolating the bacterium is not as simple as pissing on a piece of litmus paper, and these people will have to be kept against their will for anything up to twenty-four hours. Maybe more. That will require space, so we'll have to set up makeshift testing bays in areas well away from main terminal buildings. We'll therefore require the assistance of the military."

DeBerry made a note on a legal pad. "Okay, you and Dale can work out the details of that later. Consider it authorized. Bring me anything you need signed as soon as you can. What else?"

"I think we need to work out a detailed plan for the mass

evacuation of Americans from Japan," said Wayne Jeffers. "If this bug really gets a grip, we ought to have a plan that can be deployed at a moment's notice."

"Surely plans for that are already on file. Isn't that correct, Dale?"

"That's right, Mr. President, but they could be a little out-of-date. It wouldn't do any harm to bring them out and dust them off. We'll also have to take the evacuation of our allies into account, seeing as we are the only foreign nation with military air bases and naval bases within Japan. A list of priorities for the use of airstrips will have to be worked out afresh, now that the end of the Cold War has increased our number of allies. I'll get somebody on that right away."

"Fine, you do that. Now let's get back to this report from Tokyo. You say that your man has a mole working in the company that created this monster?"

Wayne Jeffers nodded. "He is being run by one of Rasnick's men, a guy called Mike Woodson."

"Is the mole an American?"

"Yes, sir."

"Okay, give this guy everything he needs: money, equipment, backup, whatever. He is now employed by the United States government, and his job is to find out every single piece of information he can and pass it across to us."

Peter Bryant, the U.S. government's newest employee, winced as Michiyo applied antiseptic to each of his wounds in turn. He was sitting on the bed in a nondescript business hotel located close to Iidabashi station, completely naked except for a small hand towel draped delicately over his swollen testicles. It was three-thirty in the morning, and all he wanted was to sleep. His eyelids were heavy and difficult to control, and if it were not for the series of sharp stings caused by Michiyo's cotton pad coming into contact with his contusions, he probably would be asleep already. Fast asleep.

"There, that should just about do it." Michiyo leaned back on her heels and inspected her handiwork. Bryant had refused her offer of Band-Aids, as the only open wound was a cut on his inner lip. The rest were bruises and a lump on his forehead that was large enough to plug a hole in a ship. "I'm afraid there's not much I can do for your, um, other injury," she said, waving a limp hand at the towel on his lap with a small grin on her face. "You'll just have to wait for the swelling to go down."

"If it ever does," said Bryant morosely.

He stood up and groaned at the pain. There was not a single area of his body that he was not painfully aware of. He wouldn't be able to move for at least a couple of days, he was sure. His muscles were already beginning to seize up and scream in protest, something he hadn't experienced since the day after playing ninety minutes of soccer for the embassy team during a charity cup eight months before. With his legs spread wide apart—much to the delight of Michiyo—he managed to hobble across to the adjoining bathroom and survey himself in the mirror. He groaned again. One eye was almost completely closed up, and the rest of his face and upper body was a mass of yellow-blue bruises. He resembled a sunrise he had once seen coming up out of the ocean on the island of Oahu.

Hobbling back into the bedroom, the hand towel clutched before him in a futile attempt at modesty, he picked up his coat and fumbled in the pocket for his mobile telephone. The leather clutch bag containing the cash given to him by the mystery caller fell to the floor. He didn't have the energy to pick it up. In fact, he was lucky to still have it. His benevolent first-floor neighbor had come across it lying near the curb just before the police had arrived and had returned it to him. If the police had discovered it, he might have had a bit of explaining to do. Not everybody walked around the streets of Tokyo with four million yen in cash tucked under his arm in the dead of night, and he was sure it would have aroused the interest of the constable who had taken his statement. He switched on the telephone and selected Mike Woodson's embassy number from the list of preprogrammed numbers.

"Hello?"

"Mike, it's me. . . ."

"Where the hell have you been? I've been trying to contact you for hours! Why did you switch your damn phone off, for God's sake?"

"I'm sorry, man. We had a bit of trouble. Three guys tried to kill me."

"*What?* Are you all right? Where are you? I'll come over and pick you up right away. Jesus, what happened?"

"Calm down. I'm fine. Just a few scratches and bruises, and maybe a slight concussion, that's all. We are in a business hotel in Iidabashi, just down the road from the Tokyo Dome."

"What's the name? I'll come and get you."

"No, Mike, not tonight. I'm exhausted and must get some sleep. I've got money, and Mitch is with me. We are safe for the moment. I'll need to rest up for a couple of days until my body starts working again. Nobody knows we are here, and it is probably a lot safer than the embassy or your house, which they're bound to be watching. I'll phone you tomorrow after I've rested."

"Okay, Peter. I understand. But you be careful. And there's one other thing. . . ."

"Yes?"

"Well, I don't quite know how to say this. Especially over the phone."

"Yeah, yeah, I know. You love me, right?"

"Peter, I have some bad news."

Bryant lowered his head and clutched the telephone as hard as his aching body would allow. He had a hunch that he knew what was coming. "It's Drake, isn't it?" he whispered slowly, his heart full of dread.

"I'm afraid so. He apparently jumped off the platform at

121

Akihabara station, right into the path of the Sobu line train. He was killed instantly. He was seen scuffling with two men just before that, but nobody knows if he jumped or was pushed."

"He was pushed, Mike," said Bryant with conviction, "And the poor bastard didn't even know it was coming."

Chapter Six

Kiyoshi Aizawa surveyed his cabinet and found it wanting. He doubted if there was a country in the entire world that could boast such a morbid collection of misfits who were in their present positions only because they had attended prestigious universities and discovered powerful mentors early on in their careers. In fact, most of the people present came from political families and had been propelled up the ladder by their own relatives. The job of running the country had been turned into a cottage industry, for God's sake! An elite group of twenty highly paid men and women, and not a true politician among them. At least, none that could qualify for the title of statesman, as Aizawa defined it. They were nothing more than the sons, daughters, nephews, and nieces of past politicians. If talent was produced from common gene pools, then where were the present-day Shakespeares, Beethovens, Renoirs, and Edisons? Surely their descendants would also be capturing the eyes of the world if ties of blood were sufficient to produce a similar genius in their offspring. The emergency cabinet meeting had been called to act as an informal briefing of events so far, but already they were intent on reaffirming their connections with the various factions and were bickering heatedly across the polished table, each trying to gain an extra few points in the childish game of one-upmanship that Aizawa despised.

He decided to wait until the hubbub had died down naturally, instead of calling the meeting to order. Maybe he could score a few points himself by not lowering himself to their level. Or maybe, by expecting to garner a few points, he already was at their level. That was certainly something to think about.

He pointedly removed his wristwatch and laid it on the blotter before him, its strap acting as a rest to tilt the face toward him. He propped up his chin with his right hand in as bored a manner as he could muster and stared at the people sitting around the table, slowly shifting his gaze from person to person. The arguments were batted back and forth across the table for several more minutes, but gradually the noise began to abate as the cabinet ministers noticed that the prime minister had not yet called a start to the meeting and turned their faces toward him out of curiosity.

When the last smattering of voices had finally died out, Aizawa picked up his watch and glanced at the dial. "Six minutes," he said aloud. He raised his eyes to them and continued, his voice rippling with sarcasm, "I'm glad you all think that we have six minutes to spare. The situation obviously can't be as bad as I was given to believe. There must be hope after all." Several of the ministers lowered their eyes to the table in embarrassment, but he also noticed a few—notably the older members with affiliations to the larger factions—puffing out their chests like pigeons and subjecting him to glares of indignant outrage. Well, if they wanted to act like children, let them be treated like children. "Now, if you don't mind, I'd like to start the meeting. Minister Minami, maybe you would honor us by speaking first."

Ichiro Minami, the minister for health and welfare, got to

his feet and nodded a brief thank-you to the head of the table. Aizawa lay back in his chair and steepled his fingers beneath his chin as Minami launched into a speech that lasted thirteen minutes. He mentioned the 7,000 victims of the disease and the 5,800 fatalities, as well as providing a breakdown of these figures by region. It was obvious, he opined, that the problem was no longer restricted to the confines of eastern Kanagawa, but affected the entire country in varying degrees of severity. He explained how the Self-Defense Forces were assisting in distributing the preventive drugs that were available and the problems they were having in coping with the huge queues that were building up outside hospitals and other medical facilities. He went on at length—and left nobody in doubt as to his personal feelings—about the large percentage of what he referred to as "low-level hospital workers" who were no longer turning up for work for fear of being exposed to the bacterium, and he paused to pass detrimental comment on the number of criminals who had broken into government stockpiles and stolen large quantities of the drugs, which were now being sold on the black market for substantial sums. He finished up by making it clear just how astounded he was at the depravity of those who would stoop so low as to steal from their fellow human beings.

But Aizawa had heard it all before. He was getting hourly updates on infection figures, carriage rates, and distribution patterns, and he couldn't give a damn how astounded Minami was. Let him be astounded to hell and back, for all he cared. If Minami thought that a few stolen drugs were the biggest problem they faced, then the country was in bigger trouble than he had imagined. Now that the American press had gotten hold of information that pointed to the government's involvement in the development of the bacterium, Japan was in the biggest hole of its postwar career. Already several countries in Asia had reacted with powerful but predictable outrage at Japan's so-called warmongering and had then followed this up by banning all flights and shipping out of Japan and removing Japanese produce from their stores. The economic implications of that alone were staggering, and it would not be long before a record number of small- to medium-sized companies that relied on exports began to file for bankruptcy. The American and European governments had been a little subtler in their condemnation of Aizawa and his government, but the discrimination had already started with local workers boycotting Japanese-run factories to prevent them from operating. The press in each and every country of the world was having a field day.

And Minami was worried about a few stolen drugs.

Minami regained his seat at the table and Aizawa nodded to Hidenori Tamura, the minister of finance. "Minister Tamura. May we have your report, please?"

Tamura stood up and opened his notes. He peered at all of those present in turn with a weasely jerking movement of his head, like a news anchor trying to drag out the moment of suspense. "The situation is not good, I'm afraid," he said eventually, having satisfied himself that he had everybody's attention. "The value of the yen against the dollar has hit the one-hundred-and-eighty mark despite yesterday's market intervention by the U.S. Treasury Department and the Federal Reserve, and the Nikkei index has dipped into the eleven thousands. This is, unfortunately, having a dire effect on other Asian countries, and I fear we must face the possibility of a devalued Chinese currency. The reason for yesterday's intervention was to avoid this eventuality, but unfortunately it appears not to have had any effect whatsoever."

Aizawa faded out the droning voice of Tamura and returned to his own tortured thoughts. It was not that he found the details uninteresting; it was just that he already knew most of the facts. In any case, the full reports would be condensed and made ready for him later in the day, so he would not miss out on anything of importance. His attendance at the meeting was mostly cosmetic. It had been called mainly for the reason of bringing all ministries up to speed on the present situation, and did not, in truth, really need to be chaired by the prime minister himself. But Aizawa had insisted on attending in order to gauge the attitudes of his cabinet. True to his word, Shoji Kubota, the general secretary of the LDP, had already started his campaign to pull down Aizawa and had begun by lobbying the ministers in order to gain their support. Of the twenty ministers present, Aizawa knew he could rely on only four or five as staunch allies, but he had hoped that he would be able to recognize at least a touch of sympathy in some of the others. All knew perfectly well that he could not be held responsible for the initial research and development of the meningococcocus bacterium, so he thought that a spark of humanity might be ignited within a few to make them realize that Aizawa had not only been landed with a bum rap, but the time and energy that a potential vote of no-confidence and reelection required was not in the best interests of the country at the present moment in time. He realized now, however, that he was expecting common sense where none existed. He could see it in their eyes. Knowing of Kubota's intentions, none, apart from his own allies, were willing to go down with this particular ship. They would wait patiently for the next, doing nothing more than prolonging their own agony and ignoring the needs of their country. So be it. It did not alter his own agenda one iota. He would continue to work for the benefit of the country regardless.

He noticed that Tamura was coming to the end of his report and tuned his mind back into the last few sentences. Tamura was suggesting that they heavily reduce the amount of overseas development assistance that was being paid to third-world countries in order to retain enough in the coffers to bolster up Japan's own financial institutions. A stupid idea, but nothing less than Aizawa expected. The Japanese psyche was not geared to worry about other people—particularly other people in other countries. He had observed it all through his life and even recognized it in himself. He had on numerous occasions seen a newscaster somberly report on an air crash claiming the lives of two hundred people somewhere abroad and then end the report with a reassuring smile and the words, "Thankfully, no Japanese were involved." He had seen documentaries about the possibility of dead-in-the-air satellites falling to earth end with the fervent hope that it fell on any country other than Japan. He had seen footage of Japanese celebrities visiting famine victims—with their expensive gowns, sparkling jewels, and eyes glistening with crocodile tears—conclude with the statement that, having witnessed this sadness, they were glad they had been born in a civilized country like Japan. It was not that Japanese people lacked compassion. In fact, they had compassion to spare, under certain circumstances. It was simply that when push came to shove, they counted their blessings and looked out for number one.

But not in this case. Japan was the world's top provider of financial assistance to a total of 162 countries, and cutting off funds to these countries would merely pull the rest of the world into the quagmire. Aizawa was determined not to let that happen. He made a small note on his memo pad reminding him to stanch this flow of stupidity the moment he got back to his office, and then acknowledged the end of Tamura's report with a slight inclination of his head.

Next in line was Sayaka Morishita, the minister of home affairs and the eldest of the four women in his cabinet. Aizawa glanced at his watch. Already the meeting had been going on for nearly thirty minutes, and they were up to only the third speaker. He wondered when the aide he had recruited before the meeting was going to appear. He had specifically instructed him to deliver the message after the meeting had been running for thirty minutes, but there was still no sign of him.

He listened to Morishita explain about the problems the private sector was experiencing with absenteeism and about the small riots that had broken out here and there in anger over the government's involvement with the epidemic. She then went on to describe an increasing tendency for the public to stockpile certain commodities, and his mind turned back to 1973 and the oil shock, when not a roll of toilet paper could be had anywhere. Even his wife, he remembered, had been guilty of going out on extensive shopping expeditions to buy up as many rolls as she could find. This time, however, it was not toilet paper that was being hoarded; it was barbecue briquettes, lighter fuel, safety matches, camping gas cylinders, kerosene, and gasoline. The newspapers had spread their rumors of a breakdown in utilities as well. The entire country was convinced that the water, electricity, and gas supplies were due to be shut down at any moment, owing to a lack of staff to run them. The media had conveniently overlooked the fact that a government press release had assured them that the military would be mobilized, if necessary, to keep the utility lifeline operational, but that such an eventuality was nowhere near in sight. They had instead run with only half of the story, and headlines stating that the government had admitted that there might be a possibility of reduced services, were plastered all over the front pages. Typical!

The door over to the right-hand side of the room was opened approximately thirty centimeters and a studious-looking young man with a neat gray suit and rimless glasses entered. He walked quietly along the length of the room toward Aizawa and handed him a small piece of paper folded into four before retracing his footsteps and disappearing back through the same door.

Aizawa balanced his spectacles on the end of his nose and examined the piece of paper thoughtfully. He frowned and rose to his feet, nodding apologetically at Sayaka Morishita for interrupting her. "I am terribly sorry, ladies and gentlemen, but I am afraid I have to attend to some other business. Kindly carry on without me. Thank you."

129

Collecting his papers together in a small bundle, Aizawa bowed slightly to all those present and swiftly left the room. The aide in the rimless glasses was standing outside with a slightly puzzled look on his face. He had never been called upon to deliver a message to its author within a stipulated time frame before.

Once the door was closed, Aizawa turned to the aide and said, "Thank you very much. What is your name?"

"Ishibashi, sir. Susumu Ishibashi. Mr. Kubota's secretary, sir."

"Well, Ishibashi, today you have performed well and saved me from a fate worse than death. You will go far." Aizawa slapped the aide on the back, grinned broadly, and stuffed the note into the man's top pocket conspiratorially before striding off down the corridor. Once the prime minister was out of sight, Ishibashi removed the piece of paper from his pocket and looked inquisitively at it. He then turned it over and looked again, the corners of his mouth turning up into a knowing smile as he crumpled the paper up into a ball and bounced it up and down for a few moments on the palm of his hand. Chuckling gently to himself, he slipped the ball into his pocket for later disposal.

The paper had been blank on both sides.

Peter Bryant laid down G. Miki Hayden's *By Reason of Insanity* and went to answer the knock at the door. Five days of resting up in the hotel room had gotten rid of most of his aches and pains, but his genital injury was still causing him to walk with a slight hobble, and he was beginning to have serious doubts that he would ever be "serviceable" again. He wished Hayden's Dr. Astin were present. He would certainly know what drugs to prescribe, even if only to ease the mental anxiety caused by his status as a potential eunuch.

Bryant's caller was Mike Woodson. He strode into the room and sat down on one of the beds, plainly amused to see Bryant's wide-legged gait. It was his third visit since the day after the incident, and his initial shock at seeing the extent of Bryant's injuries had been tempered by the fact that Bryant, apart from his debilitating nether region, seemed to be no worse off for his ordeal.

"Where's Mitch?" he asked, leaning across and helping himself to a handful of small chocolate candies from the bedside table.

"She's out shopping for lunch," said Bryant, easing himself gingerly down onto the bed opposite Woodson. "And if she comes back with another one of those revolting bento boxes they sell outside the dome, she and I are going to fall out. I no longer wish to fraternize with cold rice and dried-up fish."

Woodson nodded sympathetically. He had only ever had two cold-rice lunch boxes in his life before, and neither had particularly impressed him.

"So to what do I owe the pleasure of this visit?" Bryant asked. Woodson had been laden with newspapers, magazines, paperback books, and candy on his previous visits, but this time he appeared to be empty-handed.

"Just a visit," Woodson said, shrugging his shoulders non-committally and continuing to pop the small candies into his mouth. "I just thought I'd drop by and see how you were doing. How are your . . . er . . . things, by the way?" He nodded at Bryant's loins to indicate the subject of his inquiry.

Bryant was not fooled by the banter. He noticed that Woodson seemed uncomfortable with something and suspected that he wasn't going to enjoy this conversation one little bit. "Better every day, thanks. Wanna see 'em?"

"No, no, no . . ." Woodson said hastily.

"Then tell me why you're really here. You've got something on your mind, haven't you, you crafty old devil? Something you are reluctant to tell me. Right? You didn't come all the way over here to ask after my balls."

"Okay. You asked for it." Woodson popped the last of the chocolates into his mouth, rubbed his hands together, and leaned forward with his elbows on his knees. "I do, in fact, have something to tell you, but I'm not quite sure how you're going to react to it. I get the feeling that you are not going to be too happy about it, and I just wanted to confirm that your nuts are still painful enough to prevent you from making a dive for me."

"Tell me more."

"You see, Peter, you are now employed by the United States government."

Woodson left the words hanging in the air and concentrated on Bryant's reaction.

"What?"

Woodson nodded and watched Bryant's raised eyebrows dip down into a frown.

"What do you mean, employed by the government? Are you offering me a job at the embassy?" The frown disappeared from Bryant's face and was replaced with a thoughtful smirk. "Actually, that's not a bad idea, now that I'm out of a job. When do I start?"

"Not at the embassy, Peter. Something a bit more, um, adventurous."

"Adventurous? You mean like a courier or something like that?"

"Try CIA field agent."

Bryant lapsed into silence as he digested this piece of information. He looked at Woodson with a lopsided grin on his face, waiting patiently for him to drop the punch line. Woodson remained silent.

"A CIA field agent? Me? A spook? This is a joke, right, Mike?"

"No joke, Peter. You will be provided with all the equipment that you could possibly need. This has come down from the president himself. They want you to find out as much as you can and report back to Washington."

"But that's ridiculous! What about you guys at the embassy?

132

What about all those other trained personnel they have at their disposal? Why me, for God's sake?"

"There is a very strong possibility that an evacuation of all American citizens from Japan will be carried out in the near future. The embassy will close down and we'll all be sent back to the States. We do have other operatives, as you say, but none with your inside knowledge of Hamada Seiyaku, and certainly none who can speak Japanese as well as you."

"Oh, cut me some slack here, Mike! That's the most ridiculous thing I've ever heard in all my life. You are joking, aren't you?" Bryant waited for assurance, but none was forthcoming. Woodson remained motionless on the bed and simply stared at him. Bryant ran a hand through his hair, the realization that Woodson was on the level finally coming home to roost. "No, Mike, I'm sorry, man. I just can't do it. Anyway, I can hardly turn up to work at Hamada Seiyaku as if nothing had happened. Something tells me that I should keep as far away from those bastards as possible."

"We realize that."

"So what other information could I get? I have no training, Mike. What possible use could a damned office clerk be to the government, for Christ's sake?"

"They want you to keep in contact with your mystery caller and report on everything he says. This guy is obviously in the know, and he is too valuable to lose. The shrinks have analyzed this guy and think that the chances of his switching his loyalty across to somebody else are practically zero. They also say that he obviously feels a deep sense of responsibility toward you, and this would be exacerbated if you stayed on."

"And what makes you think I'll stay behind after the evacuation, anyway? Damn, if the government thinks things are that dangerous, there's no way I'm going to stay on and risk my butt."

"Oh, you'll be staying, Peter." Woodson spoke softly and

133

averted his eyes down at the dingy red carpet to avoid his friend's questioning stare.

"What in hell makes you say that?"

"Michiyo . . ."

The single word stopped Bryant in his tracks. His mouth gaped open as he realized the implications of what Woodson was saying. "You . . . you would prevent her from leaving with me? Just to keep me here?"

"No, of course not, Peter. Nothing like that. It's just that in an evacuation scenario, only American citizens and their spouses are taken care of. Non-American nationals would not be included in the order."

"But that's crazy! I couldn't leave without her."

"Exactly."

"Oh, Jesus, Mike! How can you sit there calmly and say things like that? We're friends, aren't we?"

"I'm sorry, Peter. I hate this every bit as much as you do. But this order has literally come down from the very top. Your name has been spoken by the president in the Oval Office, man! The powers that be have decided that you are the perfect person to provide information on the situation within Japan both before and after the evacuation, and my disliking it is not going to change their minds. Look, I realize this must have come as a bit of a shock, and you are perfectly within your rights to refuse. But before you do, just think about it for a few days. You won't be expected to do any Flash Gordon sort of heroics. You'll be provided with a computer and a satellite linkup so you can send off reports whenever you have anything you think is worth reporting on. Although it would be a great help if you could manage to forge a closer friendship with the mystery caller. We have about ten zillion questions to ask him. We'll also need details on local conditions so the government can work out ways of controlling the situation and getting the economy back on the rails. Sometimes you'll be asked to check something out, but that's about the extent of it. No dangerous stuff, I promise you."

Bryant stared at Woodson in silence. He saw the sense in the request, but that didn't help him come to a decision. The thought of running around with high-tech equipment, play-acting the role of a secret agent, scared the britches off him. Especially when he knew that there were people out there who wanted him dead. He couldn't possibly do it. It was just too ridiculous for words.

"Just give it a few days' thought, Peter," Woodson said kindly. "I'm really sorry to spring this on you, but things are sort of escalating and we need somebody on the spot over here."

"Yeah, sure. Okay, Mike, I'll think about it, but I can't prom-ise anything. Darn it, I'm nothing but a desk jockey. An office clerk. Did I mention that? An office clerk, Mike. I shuffle pa-pers all day and then go home at six o'clock when a bell rings. Are you sure the president knows that?"

"Actually, he doesn't. He seems to think that you are a mole being run by our resident CIA officer. You've no idea how pleased he was to discover that you were American."

Bryant chuckled in spite of himself. "A mole? Shit, man, a mole is a rodent! A blind rodent! They eat worms and things. Yuck! You can tell Mr. DeBerry from me that I take that as a very personal insult and shall be voting Republican in the next election."

Woodson laughed, too. He stood up to slap Bryant on the back just as a key turned in the door and Michiyo walked in.

"Hi, Mike. Nice to see you again." She walked over to allow Woodson to peck her on the cheek and then removed two brightly colored boxes from a plastic bag. Passing one across to Bryant, she offered the other to Woodson. "Are you staying for lunch, Mike? We're having grilled eels today. I can get another one for myself later."

Woodson stared at the bento lunch box and held the palms

of his hands out in refusal. "Sorry, Mitch, but I have a lunch engagement. Peter can have mine." He grinned across at Bryant and said, "See you, buddy. Think about what I've said and take care of that cluster."

As he walked across to the door, Woodson was forced to suppress a giggle as he heard Bryant sigh deeply and mumble to himself, "I guess mole cuisine has its good points after all."

The crowd of nearly six hundred people outside the Hiratsuka General Hospital was becoming more and more unruly by the minute, and the six police officers assigned to this location were not doing a very good job of controlling it. Had they stopped to analyze their methods, they might have realized that the main cause of this unruliness was their own heavy-handed handling of the situation. Makeshift barriers had been set up to guide the people into the hospital in an orderly queue, but the sheer number of people pushing and shoving against each other was simply too large for these slim and inadequate corridors to confine. Whenever one of the barriers toppled over, two or three policemen would rush forward shouting and cursing and lean all of their weight against the surging crowd in an effort to force it back through the narrow hole, a task not dissimilar to forcing toothpaste back into the tube.

So far three people had been admitted to the hospital for unforeseen injuries caused by this stupidity: an old lady with a broken arm, a small child who had inadvertently placed his left eye a touch too close to the end of an umbrella, and a middle-aged asthma sufferer who had incurred the wrath of the crowd by having the misfortune to be seized by an attack of coughing.

And still the policemen considered the crowd to be at fault. They rallied together and tried to force the people into an even smaller area of the hospital's driveway, obviously feeling that the less space they occupied, the less trouble they would be.

They were wrong.

For these people were not criminals. They were simply members of the public who had answered the pleas on television and in the newspapers to visit their doctor for a supply of medicine to—hopefully—prevent them from contracting the killer meningitis disease that was decimating their neighborhood. Their numbers included people from all walks of life, from infants not long out of the womb through schoolchildren, office clerks, housewives, train drivers, bank tellers, business tycoons, would-be rock musicians, shopkeepers, scientists, and construction workers, to one old man of ninety-three years old who seemed on the verge of expiring with or without the threat of the dreaded meningococcemia. Normal people who were being pushed to the limits of their patience.

Had the policemen looked around, they would have seen real crimes in progress. Two men in dark suits not one hundred meters away were accosting every person who left the special door that was reserved for the hospital's satisfied customers and offering them five thousand yen for the packs of Rifampin and the other drugs that they held clutched tightly against their chests. Most refused, but some, realizing that an extra two hours in the queue for an additional prescription would work out to a satisfactory hourly wage, eagerly sold their wares. These were then passed across to another dark-suited man, who offered them to newcomers for the outrageous price of twenty thousand yen per prescription. They sold like hotcakes.

Just around the corner, concealed from the crowd by a small copse of trees, a group of four high school boys was busily mugging everybody who was in obvious possession of the white prescription bags and who was smaller or weaker than they were themselves. Anybody who satisfied these two stipulations could expect to be depossessed of their hard-earned drugs and sent unceremoniously down the road with the threat of bodily harm if they so much as raised their voices or took a step in the direction of the police officers. Once every twenty minutes or so, one of the two men in dark suits would trot around the corner and purchase the drugs from the boys at a going rate of three thousand yen a shot. Business was brisk.

But the policemen had been told to control the crowd, not scour the streets for crime, and until a senior officer told them otherwise, their duty, as they saw it, was to contain six hundred people in an area that logic and a simple knowledge of physics dictated could contain only five hundred.

Strangely enough, the first person to rebel against authority was a thirty-four-year-old housewife who appeared ill-equipped to say no to a door-to-door salesman, and certainly not up to the rigors of beating up policemen. The pressure of the crowd had forced her out through the gap between two barriers, and, despite her efforts, she could not gain reentry. The policeman who tried to help unwisely placed his left hand on her right breast and his right hand on her left shoulder before applying as much pressure as he could. The woman took umbrage at this familiarity and lashed out with her handbag, catching the young officer painfully on the ear with the metal clasp. Incensed, the officer immediately released her and brought his arm back with the hand clenched into a fist. Before he could release this makeshift weapon, however, three men, closely followed by several dozen others, had burst through the barrier and had pounced on the officer, dragging him to the ground and kicking him repeatedly around the head, chest, and legs for having the temerity to raise his hand to a defenseless woman. In times of stress, the underdogs tended to take care of one another.

It took only a few moments for the other officers to realize the problem and come running, but by then it was too late. The crowd surged through the barriers like a living single-celled organism and began to take out their frustrations on the unfortunate policemen. The battle raged for thirteen minutes until reinforcements dressed in riot gear appeared on the scene and waded through the crowd with candy-striped riot sticks flailing. After seeing the punishment their colleagues had taken, they were not in the mood for taking prisoners.

One of the hospital's administrative staff, scenting business, announced over the PA system that all orderlies were to collect every spare stretcher the hospital had and bring them down to the main entrance as soon as possible.

The doctors and nurses on duty rushed to the windows to see what the ruckus was and sighed collectively at the sight that greeted them. Not two o'clock in the afternoon, and already the neighborhood's third riot of the day.

Harold Bowes, the master of the *Miyamoto Spirit*, sat at the desk in his quarters and read through the news update concerning the epidemic in Japan, a look of concern spreading across his smooth-shaven but suntanned face. He looked up at the bank of three clocks affixed to the forward bulkhead, one displaying Greenwich mean time, one Japan time, and the other Saudi Arabia time. Four hours before the estimated time of arrival at the pilot boarding position. The twenty-four-hour and six-hour messages informing the port authorities of the ETA had been sent through to the Yokohama Hoan MSA Station on schedule, and he had another hour left before the last of the mandatory three messages had to be transmitted. An hour in which to make up his mind.

The *Miyamoto Spirit* was a single-hulled VLCC—Very Large Crude Carrier—and had been assigned to Pier A at the Negishi Refinery, owing to the fact that it was the only berth in Yokohama capable of handling the vessel's two hundred and eighty thousand tons. Bowes had checked the BA 3548, 3109, 3108, and Admiralty Pilot NP42A charts and discovered that Negishi was closer to the heart of the outbreak than he was comfortable with. In addition to the responsibility of delivering his cargo on time, the master of a vessel was also responsible for the safety and well-being of his crew.

He read through the news update once more. Although the hub of the epidemic remained in the coastal region between

Odawara and the tip of the Miura peninsula, a comparatively large percentage of victims had been recorded in Yokohama and Tokyo. Negishi was midway between Yokohama and the Miura peninsula. Or, as Bowes perceived it, slap-bang in the middle of the danger area. The fatality rate stood at nearly twenty-one thousand people with an additional seven thousand people hospitalized, and almost 80 percent of those had been recorded in the area in which he had been instructed to berth his tanker and allow his crew ashore.

Was it worth the risk of bringing a deadly disease on board for the empty run back to the Middle East?

He thought not.

He reached across the desk and picked up a notepad and pen. Having scribbled out his instructions and torn the page off the pad, he rang for his first officer.

Jonathan Lemieux, the first officer, knocked on the door and entered, smartly saluting the master and standing at attention.

"At ease, Jonathan," said Bowes briskly. Despite the fact that he had spent his entire life in the merchant navy and had never served his country other than in the role of taxpayer, Bowes liked to maintain a sort of naval style of discipline aboard ship. He held out the message to Lemieux. "Pass these instructions across to the chief, will you? You'll also need to inform the crew and tell the port authorities that we no longer require their services."

Lemieux read through the message and didn't even bother to conceal his surprise and disappointment. Every sailor dreamed of shore time during a long voyage, and to have it snatched away when it was only four hours off the starboard bow was like having Christmas canceled just before the midnight Mass. "With all due respect, sir, are you sure this is wise? The Yokohama agent will scream blue murder, and the company will be none too happy at having a full cargo returned to Saudi."

"I'm afraid they will just have to lump it. The Yokohama

agent can take a running jump, for all I care, but check to see if the company wants us diverted to a different destination so they do not lose out entirely on the voyage."

"And the crew, sir?"

"You'll just have to convince them that I am working in their best interests. Now, if you please, Jonathan."

"Sir!" Lemieux snapped off a smart salute and left the master's quarters.

Twelve minutes later, an almost imperceptible change in the movement of the *Miyamoto Spirit* was felt as she about-turned to put Yokohama off her stern and headed back out to sea, her cargo of undelivered crude oil secure in her massive tanks. The duty officer of a passing freighter transporting a cargo of cereal into Honmoku watched the supertanker glide gracefully past and scratched his head in confusion. He had never seen an oil tanker outbound from Japan riding so low in the water before, and the sight was somehow unsettling.

Shigeru Hamada was in a foul mood. His hands shook with fury as he read through the memorandum that had been delivered to his secretary by a scruffy express cyclist a few minutes earlier. The note was from Hiroshi Okada, Hamada Seiyaku's chairman of the board, who was currently a member of the government ad hoc committee set up to monitor the spread of the meningococcemia disease. Okada was the sole liaison between the government and the company, and it seemed to Hamada as if he was enjoying his role as conduit a little too much. He was forgetting where his true loyalties lay. The sense of importance from sharing a round table with several government ministers on a daily basis had filled Okada with a false air of superiority that grated heavily on Hamada's nerves. Already he had taken to addressing the president as "Hamada-*kun*," instead of "Hamada-*san*"—the "*kun*" being an honorific that was usually reserved for younger people and underlings. Although a four-year age advantage technically gave him the right to do so, he had always balanced his use of honorifics with the president's superior position and called him by the more polite "*san*." Until he began to hobnob with top government officials, that is. Hamada, who had personally handpicked Okada for his present position, saw this as a sign of disrespect and loathed him for it.

Hamada read through the memorandum once again, the muscles in his jaw rippling with emotion. The committee had decided that a criminal investigation should be made into Hamada Seiyaku's involvement in the affair in order to placate an angry populace, and the investigation was to be launched on the following day by the National Police Agency. Okada, in his note, had recommended that Hamada himself cooperate with the investigators to clear the matter up as quickly as possible so that more time could be spent on containing the disease. The very *cheek* of the man! How dared he meekly side with the government and suggest that Hamada Seiyaku take the fall instead? Okada's job was to protect the company, not help the damn government save face, and to placate an angry populace. Damn, he could not remember being so mad!

Before he could control himself, he had lashed out at the contents on top of his desk and sent a nearly overflowing ashtray and a small table lamp crashing to the floor. "*Bastard!*" he screamed out loud, impervious to the fact that his secretary in the outer office would surely be able to hear him. He felt the anger beginning to take control, building up within him like a bright crimson tidal wave, blurring his vision and speeding up his respiration until his breath came in short bursts. His pulse pounded in his ears as he clenched and unclenched his fists, searching the office for something—anything—on which to vent his fury. He kicked out at the wastepaper basket and sent it skidding across the office until it came to a stop by the wall, its contents scattered haphazardly throughout the path of its trajectory. And still he hunted for something to punish. Something to hurt. Something to kill.

Until the feeling passed as swiftly as it had arisen, as it always did. Abruptly and without fanfare. He slumped down into his chair, shaking his head in wonder and fear. It was only in the past few weeks that his anger had begun to get the better of him, but he realized that he should be worried about it. He hoped it was not a tumor or anything else that would affect his physical health. He should probably get a medical checkup, but he just couldn't spare the time. It would just have to wait until he had steered the company through this period of unrest and back onto the road to recovery. But how could he be expected to do that when all around him were incompetent and constantly stabbing him in the back? First of all there was the woman Fukuyama, then those two *gaijin*, and now Okada. Why did everybody want to betray him? Didn't they realize that he was only trying to rescue the company and secure them all gainful employment? It was crazy! The things he detested more than anything else in this world were double standards and a lack of loyalty from the people he knew and trusted. A person could either be for the company or against it. There was no middle ground. And anyone who was against it was a sworn enemy.

Still, Fukuyama and one of the *gaijin* had paid the price. That left only Bryant and Okada to deal with. His men were already scouring Tokyo for Bryant, so that was one problem he could put to the back of his mind for the moment. He was lucid enough to realize that he was being a little on the obsessive side about that, but he couldn't allow Bryant to go free. Not because he posed any significant threat to Hamada Seiyaku anymore, but because it was necessary for his directors to see that he was capable of carrying out his promises as stated. He needed order in the ranks, and Bryant's death would remind them that he would not stand for disloyalty in any shape or form and rally them together to fight for the future of the company.

So that left Okada. What was he going to do about him? It

would take only a single phone call to put a permanent end to the traitor's toadying, but there was no doubt that an acting member of the ad hoc committee was an extremely useful asset to have. Not only did it provide Hamada with inside information as to the government's intentions, it also served the purpose of showing that Hamada Seiyaku was cooperating fully with the authorities. Would they allow a replacement in the event of Okada's suddenly and irrevocably becoming unavailable? Well, why not? The government needed the contact as much as he did. Surely they would not cut off their link to the only organization working around the clock to develop a vaccine for the bacterium. No, of course they wouldn't. What had he been thinking of?

Hamada reached for the telephone.

"You know, I somehow feel richer than I ever have in my life. Do you know what I mean?"

Shigeko Kondo finished arranging the boxes of mineral water in the back of the minivan and stepped down out of the vehicle. "Yes, I believe I do. Not so much rich financially, but rich in other ways. This reminds me of packing up to go on vacation when I was young. It's sort of exciting."

Norio Kondo rested an elbow on the handle of the cart in which he had wheeled the boxes out of the supermarket and smiled at his wife. "Yes, that too, although I was talking about money." He nodded his head at the small sports bag on the passenger seat, just visible from his position. "Lots and lots of lovely money," he said, a look of feigned avarice playing across his features. "It seems to have so much more value outside of the bank than it does in it."

The bag contained just over eighteen million yen in cash—the equivalent of approximately 100,000 U.S. dollars since the rate of exchange had plummeted to one-eighty to the dollar. Norio Kondo and his wife had had a busy day. They had spent the morning visiting the three banks in which they kept their money and withdrawn everything except for a small sum sufficient only to keep the accounts open. After a hasty meal in one of the family restaurants dotted around their neighborhood, they had driven to La-Ox in Totsuka and spent an enjoyable thirty minutes purchasing a laptop computer with a built-in modem, a spare battery, a printer, spare ink cartridges, paper, and floppy disks. The rest of the afternoon had been taken up with driving around various wholesale outlets, supermarkets, and liquor stores to stock up on as many supplies as they could carry. They had even managed to find one store that still had a supply of kerosene and had bought seventy-five liters divided between three plastic tanklike containers. The back of the minivan—purchased two days earlier in a part exchange deal with their Toyota Crown—was chockablock with cardboard boxes and other supplies of varying sizes.

"I'll just return this cart and then that should just about do it for today," Norio said. "We can spend tomorrow repacking everything so I can see through the back mirror, and then it's off the next day."

Driving back toward their home through the mostly deserted streets, Shigeko said, "I must admit, I'll certainly be glad to get out of this place. Everything seems so scary now. It's like something out of a science fiction movie."

"Yes, well, it won't be long now. We'll soon be up in the mountains and away from Yokohama."

"Will Omotenashi be coming out to the house as well?"

"Not straightaway, but he said he would join us soon. I guess it's not as bad up in Tokyo yet, so he is not as anxious to get out as we are."

Omotenashi—the on-line handle for Toshio Otsuka—was one of the first members to join the Zen Nippon Otaku Tomonokai, owing to the fact that he had been at school with Norio Kondo and had been one of the first people invited by Kondo to join. Otsuka owned a small private hotel near Nishi-Nippori in Tokyo together with his wife, Harumi, and two years previously the two couples had joined forces to purchase a four-bedroom *besso*—or weekend house—at the foot of Mount Omuro in Izu-Kogen, 130 kilometers southwest of Tokyo.

"I hope they come soon. It would be nice to have some other company out there. Maybe we could invite Totchan as well. He lives in Tokyo, doesn't he?"

"Totchan probably has his own plans, although I'll ask him, if you want."

"Yes, do. The more the merrier. He is married, isn't he?"

"Yes, I believe so."

"Any children?"

"I can't remember. I'll check."

The dusk was well advanced by the time they reached home. They carried everything from the minivan into the house in the dark. Although the chances of the van's being stolen were slim, they both felt safer storing all of their new purchases away from prying eyes. They had to be repacked anyway, and they didn't want to tempt fate unnecessarily. Gonta was ecstatic to be reunited with his owners after a long day of solitary confinement and hindered the operation by constantly getting under their feet. It was nearly seven o'clock before they sat down and flipped the top off a bottle of beer. Norio filled his wife's glass and then handed her the bottle so she could fill his.

"Here's to the open road and a life of freedom."

Shigeko clinked her glass against his. "*Kanpai*," she said. "Although I'm not too sure about this open-road stuff. We will come back once it's all over, won't we?"

"Yes, of course we will. We'll be back before you know it. Honestly."

Peter Bryant looked across at Michiyo's sleeping form and smiled fondly. Her long hair partly concealed her face, but he could still make out her natural beauty in repose, her lips parted and her eyes relaxed in total serenity. It was not much after ten o'clock at night, but she had already been asleep for more than thirty minutes. She had taken to going to bed early out of pure boredom since their enforced confinement in the business hotel. He also suspected that she preferred the blissful sanctuary with which sleep provided her to the stark reality of wakefulness and consequently slept longer than usual out of simple self-defense. Their own problems notwithstanding, she was seriously upset about the direction in which her country of birth was heading. The government seemed to have made no progress whatsoever in its attempt to find a vaccine for the disease, and the death toll was mounting daily. The front-page headline of the *Asahi Evening News* that lay on the bed beside him pronounced more than forty thousand fatalities and an additional twenty thousand victims hospitalized. The general atmosphere in the streets resembled a country under siege. The government had announced plans for the rationing of dwindling imports, and that had triggered a spate of panic buying by general consumers. Neon lighting for advertising purposes had been made illegal, as had air-conditioning, and companies had been ordered to change their business hours to eight o'clock in the morning until five o'clock in the evening to save on electricity consumption. Overtime had been banned, nearly sparking a riot outside of the Diet Building and necessitating thousands of stick-wielding policemen to be brought in to control the mob of twelve thousand enraged people who relied on overtime pay to meet their bills. There were even a few reports of people being attacked in the streets simply for sneezing in public. Society was falling apart and paranoia was taking over.

Bryant leaned across and splashed another shot of Japanese whisky from the black *daruma* bottle into his plastic cup. He wasn't usually much of a whisky drinker, but the four walls of the room seemed to be closing in on him with every passing hour, and a little something to turn his mind away from the tedium was proving to be a blessing. He had also discovered a certain amount of solace in the bottle after hearing of Drake's death. He sipped the whisky and grimaced. He really should get some mineral water to dilute the spirit down a little. If there was any left in the shops, of course. He doubted it.

"Peter?"

"Yes, honey?" He watched Michiyo loop her hair back over one ear and push herself up onto one elbow.

"When are you going to bed? The light is annoying me."

"Soon, but it's still a bit early for me. If I sleep now, I'll be up at four o'clock in the morning. Turn over onto your other side. It's darker there."

"What are you drinking?"

"Whisky. Would you like some?"

Michiyo swung the covers back and pushed herself up into a sitting position. She sat cross-legged on the bed and rubbed the sleep out of her eyes with her knuckles, like a chipmunk washing its face. "Yes, please. Just a small one."

Bryant collected another plastic cup from the low chest of drawers, slopped a finger of whisky into it, and passed it across to Michiyo with a smile. She sniffed lightly at the contents before raising the cup to Bryant. Bryant picked up his cup and returned the toast. "To Japan," he said softly.

"To Japan," echoed Michiyo.

The ritual complete, Bryant sat down on his bed and slapped the newspaper with the back of his hand. "From Monday all public transport services will end at eight o'clock at night. Central Tokyo will be a ghost town. We'll stick out like sore thumbs. Maybe we should move a bit farther out of town. Maybe to one of the Urayasu hotels in Chiba. What do you say?"

Michiyo took another sip of whisky before answering. "I don't know, Peter. Your injuries are not totally healed. I think we should stay here for at least a few more days."

"We might not get the opportunity. Have you noticed the funny looks the hotel manager has been giving us? The rest of the hotel is empty, and I don't think he appreciates having to stay on duty only for us. If the death toll continues increasing like this, they are likely to close the place down and throw us out. I think we should preempt them. Anyway, I'm feeling fine now. Most of the aches and pains have disappeared, and the swelling down there has almost gone. I feel great!"

"Well, I must admit that I wouldn't mind a change of scenery. Maybe it's not such a bad idea after all. Do you think those men are still looking for you?"

"Nah," he said with more conviction than he felt. "Any threat I did pose to them has been completely removed now that I'm out of Hamada Seiyaku. All of the information I have is also now spread all over the newspapers. I know about as much as the general public. I'm sure they've given up on me."

"Then why are you worried about us sticking out like sore thumbs?"

Damn, she'd gotten him again. "Just being cautious, really. Anyway, we have tons of money, so why not live it up a bit in one of those flashy resort hotels down by Disneyland?"

Michiyo suddenly looked happy for the first time in several days. Her face seemed to light up at the thought of getting out of dirty downtown Tokyo and into a bit of luxury. She had deliberately put off thinking about the future for fear of what it contained, and the routine of living in dismal accommodation with only lunch boxes and convenience-store sandwiches for sustenance had depressed her more than she had realized.

"Yes, why not?" she said. "That sounds wonderful. I think we deserve a change, don't you?"

She placed her empty cup on the floor next to her bed and moved over to sit next to Bryant, who pushed the newspaper out of the way and extended his arm so that she could cuddle up to him. He gently brushed a stray lock of hair off her forehead and craned his neck around to kiss her on the cheek. Anticipating his intentions, Michiyo turned her face to him and met his lips with hers.

Silence reigned.

Moments later they both shifted back onto the bed so that the wall provided a support for their backs. Bryant stared contentedly up at the ceiling, Michiyo nestling cozily into the crook of his right arm with her head snuggling up against his chest.

"Peter?" Michiyo said softly.

"Yes, sugar?"

"Do you think things will ever get back to normal again?"

Bryant considered the question. "Probably not," he answered honestly. "Japan has made a lot of enemies with this, and there're a whole bunch of countries out there with long memories. Particularly in Asia."

"I don't just mean politically. I mean socially. I've never seen Japanese people this"—she paused to select a suitable adjective—"intense. This frantic. This . . . afraid."

"Of course, Mi-*chan*. Everything will work out okay in the end. We Japanese are a resilient people."

Michiyo giggled. She loved it when he included himself as a member of the Japanese race.

"We'll bounce back and be singing our *enka* from the top of Mount Fuji before you know it. Another couple of months and we'll be drinking sake under the cherry blossom trees and complaining about the language used by high school girls. By May we'll be slinging our cameras around our necks and visiting Australia. A little thing like this can't hold us back. We were born to survive."

Michiyo snuggled deeper into his embrace. He had his faults, but she'd never met anyone as gentle, considerate, or reassuring as Peter in her entire life, and she loved him dearly. She placed the tips of her fingers on his knee and began to walk them slowly up the inside of his leg.

"You know you said that the swelling had gone down and you were feeling great?" she said slowly.

"Yes," he replied dreamily.

"How long do you think it will be until you are ready for the ultimate test?"

Her fingers continued walking until they could go no farther. The motion of her fingers changed from a walking action to a gentle caress. Bryant sighed audibly and reached across with his left hand to cup her chin and tilt it up toward him.

"Another minute or so should do it," he whispered throatily, leaning over to kiss her gently on the lips. "Or maybe even less . . ."

Chapter Seven

It had snowed in the night, and the grimy traces of it could still be seen in the gutters and up against the edges of the walls as Peter Bryant and Michiyo Kato left the hotel to look for a restaurant that was still open. The bento vendors in front of the Tokyo Dome had decided that their trade was better plied elsewhere, much to Bryant's delight, and the local convenience store no longer seemed to have a supply of fresh bread for sandwiches. It was either eat out or exist on a diet of potato chips and candy bars.

Despite his elation at having escaped from the room that had been his prison for nearly a week, Bryant shivered in the icy wind and pulled his coat closer around him. He slipped an arm around Michiyo's waist and the two began to walk briskly toward Iidabashi station, where they hoped there was a higher chance of finding an open restaurant.

"Did you see the relief on the manager's face when I said we would be checking out tomorrow?" asked Bryant.

"I certainly did. That's the first time I've ever seen him

smile. Do you really think he'll close the place down?"

"I wouldn't be surprised. It obviously doesn't belong to him, and it can't be much fun keeping all the amenities available just for us."

"Amenities? What amenities? They don't even have room service, and everything has to be bought out of vending machines at vastly inflated prices."

"Just think of all that happiness he exudes. That's an amenity. Without us he can return his face muscles to storage and be as miserable as he likes."

They walked past the Big Egg and Korakuen before turning left onto the street that would take them down to the station. The gloominess of the day was heightened by the lack of cars necessitated through the rationing of gasoline. Usually on a weekday the area would be teeming with trucks and private cars, but today the roads were practically deserted. The audible whistle of the wind as it forced its way around man-made structures seemed to make the streets throb with a dark malevolence. Bryant shivered again. There were still a certain number of people out and about, but nowhere near the number that had occupied the area prior to the epidemic. They bustled down the street as speedily as possible as they made their way to and from offices, their eyes trained on the sidewalk before them, studiously avoiding eye contact with other people. Many of them had the lower halves of their faces covered with mufflers and white surgical masks that were commonly sold in pharmacies to prevent the spread of influenza. None smiled.

It came as a shock for Bryant to realize that the people were this worried about the outbreak. From the confines of the hotel, the disease had not seemed to be an imminent hazard. It was something that was happening on the other side of the prefecture. Hell, on the other side of the *planet*, even. He had not realized just how fast it had crept up to their doorstep to pose a potential threat to their health. He now understood Michiyo's depression and feeling of impending doom. Her daily excursions out into the streets must have sapped her emotions more than he had known, the poor kid.

"What if the hotels out in Urayasu are not taking reservations?" Michiyo asked, interrupting his thoughts.

"What do you mean?"

"Well, Urayasu is only a little way outside of Tokyo, and if the hotels in Tokyo are closing down, why should the ones in Chiba stay open?"

"Oh, come on, you can't equate four-star international hotels with that dump we're staying at. They'll be open. Take my word for it."

"Mmm," she said, not entirely convinced. "I certainly hope so."

They continued to walk in silence until they reached an overhead walkway that took them across the Kanda River and the main road that passed in front of the station. They had just finished climbing the steps when Michiyo gasped and pointed a shaking finger down into the river, her other hand held over her mouth in horror.

"What is it?" asked Bryant, his nerve ends tingling with anticipation. The atmosphere of the streets was beginning to get to him.

"Look, there! Floating in the water. It's a man."

He followed the line of her pointing finger. "Oh, my God!" The words came out in English, despite the fact that they always spoke Japanese together when alone. The shock of seeing a fully grown adult male floating facedown in murky brown water had caused his first language to burst to the foreground. "Come on," he continued, correcting himself and reverting to Japanese, "let's get to a telephone and call the police before he floats too far away. There's bound to be one near the station."

"What about your mobile phone? Can't you call them on that?"

"I left it at the hotel. Come on, quick."

He grabbed her hand and pulled her behind him as he rushed across the walkway and down the steps to Iidabashi station. Two green public telephone boxes were located by the side of the steps. He yanked open the door of the nearest one and pushed Michiyo inside ahead of him. Michiyo picked up the receiver while he struggled to close the door to the confined space and punched in the one-one-zero number for the emergency services.

"Come on, come on . . ." she muttered as she waited for the call to be answered. "Police, please. I wish to report a dead body floating in the Kanda River. At the intersection in front of Iidabashi station." She clicked her tongue in exasperation as she was put on hold. Ninety seconds later a voice came on the line. Michiyo listened for a few moments, and, with a final, "*Hai, wakarimashita. Arigato gozaimasu*," she hung up.

"They didn't even ask my name," she lamented outside of the phone box. "Apparently this is the twenty-third report of a dead body in the Bunkyo ward since nine o'clock this morning. The police services are stretched to their limits, but they promised to send a patrol car to investigate as soon as one is available." She grabbed hold of Bryant's arm and held on tightly. "This is getting scary, Peter. Maybe we should move to Chiba today."

Bryant placed his hand over hers and squeezed. "I'm beginning to doubt that Chiba is far enough. I want you to go back home until this is all over, Mitch. Would you do that for me?"

"Home? You mean Fukushima?"

"Yes, you'll be safe there until things have panned out."

"I'll go if you come with me."

Bryant squeezed her hand again and looked ahead. They had entered a mall beside the station, and he was pleased to see that most of the restaurants were still open, although presumably not for much longer, if deliveries were not getting through. Michiyo's family lived on the outskirts of the city of Aizu Wakamatsu in Fukushima prefecture, and the thought of escaping the gloom and despondency of Tokyo and curling up amid the beautiful mountain scenery of her hometown was an attractive thought. Aizu Wakamatsu was just under three hundred kilometers from Tokyo, but it could have been on the far side of the moon, as far as the outbreak was concerned. They would be safe there. It certainly was tempting. Very tempting. But what about Mike Woodson? He had promised to think about his proposal to stay on and maintain contact with the mystery caller, and he still hadn't come to a decision on that. There was something else niggling at the back of his mind, as well. He still had the four million yen that the mystery caller had given him, but half of that money had been destined for Leonard Drake, who no longer required it. He felt obliged to return it, even though he was sure the mystery caller did not expect it back. His own conscience simply would not allow him to keep it. Ignoring the call of his government and a moral obligation in order to run off and hide in the mountains would solve absolutely nothing at all. He would never be able to live with himself again. "I have a couple of things I need to sort out before I can leave," he said. "I need to contact Mike and a few other people. You go first and I'll follow on. I promise."

"When?"

"As soon as I can. A week, tops."

Michiyo remained silent as they walked into a noodle shop and ordered tempura udon with side dishes of rice. Once the steaming bowls of fat, white noodles topped with deep-fried prawns had been delivered and the waitress had withdrawn, she said, "I'll wait with you. Surely another week won't matter."

"No, Mi-chan. Please. I want you to go home. Today. This afternoon. Things in Tokyo are different now. Strange. I don't feel safe here. I'll be okay in the hotel in Chiba, but I might have to come into Tokyo a couple of times, and I don't want to have to worry about you while I do so. Please."

"You promise you'll come just as soon as you can?"

"I promise."

"And you'll keep out of trouble? Avoid all risks?"

"Cross my heart."

Michiyo ate a mouthful of rice and stared into Bryant's eyes miserably. She could see the love and compassion there and knew that he would keep his word, but that did little to dissipate her feeling of dread at being separated from him. A tear ran down her face and moistened her cheek. "All right, I'll go," she said at last. "But don't you dare switch off your mobile telephone. I'll be checking up on you every day, and you must join me if things get worse. Deal?"

Bryant leaned across the table and gently wiped the dampness off her cheek with his thumb. "Deal," he said softly.

The man sitting on the wall outside of the Tokyo Dome flicked his cigarette away and stared intently at the couple walking toward him. He waited until they had passed by before taking a photograph out of his inside pocket and scrutinizing it intently. Satisfied, he whistled to his partner, who was standing by the curb eating a candy bar, and nodded in the direction of the couple. Without speaking, the two men swiftly fell into position and began to follow them at a distance of sixty meters. Five minutes later, the couple turned into the entrance of a dingy business hotel and the men came to a halt. They crossed the road and faded into the shadows of the doorway of a small printing company that had long since closed down. One of the men removed a leather glove from his right hand and pulled a mobile telephone from his pocket. He punched in a number and waited for the call to be answered.

"Hamada, sir. I think we have located our target. . . ."

The situations room had been set up in the gray corridors of the underground complex in the White House to monitor all information coming out of Japan and to collate it into legible intelligence. In fact, it consisted of a suite of three rooms staffed by fourteen men and women, but nobody deemed it necessary to adhere to the dictates of English grammar by calling it the clumsier—but grammatically correct—situations rooms. The three rooms were therefore referred to in the singular.

The high-tech meeting room contained a long polished table into which twelve computer monitors had been imbedded at an angle to shine up into the faces of the people present: five along the length of each side and one at each end. Only six were in use. A larger monitor was suspended from the wall at the far end of the room, and next to it stood an extremely nervous middle-aged man who was obviously having trouble controlling the shaking of his hands and knees. He licked his lips repeatedly as he waited for the secretary of state to introduce him to the other five occupants of the room. Six, if he counted the pale but attentive technician who sat at an impressive console over by the wall. The technician, he had been informed, was able to project anything he wanted onto the monitors by flicking a few buttons on his console, from prepared documentation to video clips, and even live satellite pictures of almost any place on earth.

Patrick Watson, the secretary of state, looked across at the president and raised his eyebrows. Raymond DeBerry nodded back in answer to the tacit question. Watson pushed back his chair and rose to his feet.

"Good morning, Mr. President, gentlemen. The main part of this meeting will be held after we have had a full briefing on the characteristics of the meningococcal bacterium from Professor Stanley Donnelly of Western Washington University. The professor has been provided with all information we have on the outbreak in Japan and has spent the past few days analyzing it. He will also be in charge of a group of biologists and scientists at the university who have come together in order to start work on finding a cure for the disease. A full verbatim report will be handed out later, together with a glossary explaining all of the technical words that the professor uses, so I would appreciate it if you would keep your inquiries confined to the matter at hand and not question the vocabulary." Watson looked across at Donnelly. "Please go ahead, Professor Donnelly; you have our attention."

"Thank you and good morning, gentlemen," said Donnelly as Watson sat down. "I realize that your time is at a premium, so I will try to keep this explanation as brief as possible. The disease we are dealing with is known as pediatric meningococcemia in America and meningococcal septicemia in Europe. As the name implies, it is a disease mostly found in children, but it has been genetically engineered to affect adults as well. I will start by saying that this disease is extremely dangerous and is capable of killing within hours. It is caused by a certain strain of the meningococcus bacterium, *Neisseria* meningococcus, which is also the most common cause of meningitis. But there the similarity ends. Meningitis attacks the meninges, the membranes that surround the brain and spinal cord, but meningococcemia attacks the blood, releasing a poisonous molecule known as an endotoxin that results in a runaway reaction by the victim's immune system. Once this runaway reaction, called the inflammatory cascade, has been triggered, there is very little hope of recovery. To put that into simpler terms, meningococcemia does not kill the victim. Death occurs as a direct result of the inflammatory cascade. The bacterium is simply the catalyst to ensure that this state comes about." Donnelly paused and reached for the glass of water that stood on the table in front of him. Having taken a sip, he nodded at the technician, and the first of the documents he had prepared was displayed on the computer monitors and the large screen behind him.

"From what I can gather from the information with which I have been provided, the B serogroup of the meningococcus bacterium has been genetically engineered as follows." He picked up a pointer and used it to indicate the first item at the top of the screen. "One, to trick the body's immune system into believing that the organism belongs in the body. The result of this is to get a certain percentage of bacteria into the bloodstream as swiftly as possible before the body can begin fighting back and before the victim realizes that he or she is ill." He moved the pointer down to the next item. "Two, to increase the virulence of the disease. Without further information I am not able to say exactly how this has been done, but I presume the amount of time the bacterium requires to adhere to the mucosal membranes of the nose and throat has been speeded up." The pointer moved to the bottom item. "And three, to kill the bacteria as quickly as possible after it hits the bloodstream in order to firmly establish the inflammatory cascade within the victim before he or she can be treated."

Dale Lindley, the chairman of the Joint Chiefs, cleared his throat and raised a hand. Donnelly nodded at him. "I have two questions, if I may, Professor. First of all, could you please clarify the relationship between killing the bacterium and establishing the inflammatory cascade for us? I don't quite see the connection."

"Certainly." Donnelly took another sip of water. "The endotoxin that triggers the inflammatory cascade is an integral part of the bacterium's cell wall and is not released unless the organism dies. If the bacterium remains alive within the victim's bloodstream, the disease will not advance to the deadly second stage. This will provide time for the bloodstream to be injected with a bactericidal/permeability-increasing protein that is normally produced in white blood cells and that kills gram-negative bacteria in such a way that it effectively neutralizes the endotoxins. In other words, if the endotoxins have not been released by the time the victim is diagnosed, the chances are that he or she can be treated successfully to a full recovery."

"I see. You also mentioned that a 'certain percentage' of the bacteria make their way into the bloodstream. Why not all?"

"It is necessary for some of the bacteria to remain in the upper respiratory tract in order to ensure that the disease is passed onto other hosts so that continued existence is guaranteed. If all of the organisms entered the bloodstream at the same time, there would be none left to infect other people and the disease would, for all intents and purposes, be committing suicide. Although it is difficult for me to hazard a guess as to how this has been achieved, I would not be surprised to discover that the organism will not attempt mucosal penetration until a certain stage of growth has been reached, allowing it to remain in the nasopharynx and reproduce for the required period, thereby ensuring that a next generation is established before its own demise. This would be made possible by controlling the concentration of homoserine lactones secreted by the bacteria. A phenomenon known as quorum sensing allows the bacteria to recognize when a required set of conditions have been met, and this activates certain genes to determine their actions. In this case, I presume the amount of the homoserine lactones secreted into a chemical pool will determine when migration into the bloodstream is to commence. If there are too few bacteria, the chemical will simply diffuse away from the bacterial cell."

"Thank you, Professor," said Lindley.

Donnelly was beginning to get into his swing now, and he noted with pleasure that his knees had stopped shaking. He nodded at the technician once again and a new document was displayed on the monitors.

"Next we come to control. Prophylaxis of the immediate population is vital in preventing the spread of meningococcemia, but it can also be achieved through isolation. From what I have seen of the reports from Japan, prophylaxis with Rifampin and other drugs of choice is not having a whole lot of effect on this particular strain, but that may be due to delayed distribution methods and a lack of supervision over dosages. However, as we have to work with the data we have, isolation is the only other means I can suggest to prevent further spread of the disease. Meningococcemia is population-dependent and therefore cannot exist for long outside of a host or controlled laboratory conditions. In fact, I believe Mr. Lindley will back me up when I say that our military takes the spread of this bacterium into consideration when spacing bunks. Isn't that correct, sir?"

Lindley nodded. "That is correct, Professor."

"Excuse me, Professor." DeBerry held up his hand, and Donnelly felt a jab of self-importance at the thought that the president of the United States was acting like a fourth grader before him. "Although I understand perfectly well your suggestion for isolation, unfortunately we are talking about one hundred and thirty million people crammed into an area the size of California. The epidemic has already spread to most of Japan's major cities and to quite a few rural areas. Isolating the victims is totally out of the question."

"I realize that, sir, but—"

"What I want to know is, what are the chances of us getting a vaccine developed for this thing? In your valued opinion, what would be involved and how much time would we need to come up with something to fight it with?"

"Well . . ." Donnelly paused to gather his thoughts. This was going to be a tough one to answer. "First of all, I ought to mention that a vaccine won't work unless the protein that tricks the body's natural killer cells into preventing the immune system from mounting an attack against the bacterium has been neutralized."

"Throw that one past me again."

"A vaccine is used to prime the body's immune system before a disease is contracted. An attenuated organism is injected into the body to teach the immune system exactly how to mount an attack in the event of a real infection. The second time the immune system 'sees' the organism, it mounts a hyper response that destroys it before it can make the victim sick. In this case, however, the bacterium contains a protein that persuades the body's NK cells not to attack, so the lessons learned from an attenuated organism will simply be ignored and the vaccine will not serve the purpose for which it was designed. What we need is either a vaccine that will teach the immune system not to be fooled by this protein or an antidote that is capable of mounting a postinfection attack on the bacterium with a chemical compound."

"Whatever. So I have the same question about an antidote or anything else that can stop this bastard."

"Unfortunately, despite the fact that we have been tipped off to the utilization of the UL18 protein, we still have absolutely no idea how it was engineered into the bacterium in the first place. It will take us at least another week for the nuclear magnetic resonance results to come through, and without those we know nothing of the special relationships between the atoms involved. And even once we get this data, it won't be conclusive. Basically, we will have to reverse-engineer the entire structure of the organism and analyze all of its components before we can even think of beginning work on finding a way to neutralize it. That could take months. Years, even."

"What if we get all of the documentation made during the development of the bacterium? Would that help?"

"Yes, most definitely. It will certainly save time, but . . ."

"But . . . ?"

"There is still no guarantee that it will help us find an antidote."

"But it will take us one step closer toward it, right, Professor?"

"Yes, sir. That is correct."

DeBerry nodded and looked over at the secretary of state. "I think we've heard enough, Patrick. Unless anyone else has any questions, maybe you would show Professor Donnelly out and then return so we can continue with the meeting." He turned back to Donnelly. "Thank you very much, Professor. You have been most helpful, and I'm sure all of us here today wish you all the luck in the world in coming up with something to crush this damned disease."

Donnelly collected his papers and was led out of the door by Watson. The president waited until the secretary of state had returned and was seated at the table before continuing.

"Right, so we now know exactly what we are up against. A disease that kills you before you know you are ill. Can we have the distribution map up on the monitors, please?"

A map of Japan appeared on the monitors. Approximately 20 percent of it was colored in red, notably around the Kanto and Kansai regions. The rest of it was pale yellow. Beside it was a table listing mortality rates by region. The grand total at the bottom of the table read one hundred and thirty-five thousand.

"How the hell do you go about isolating that much of a country?" said DeBerry in disgust. "You can't just dig a trench a mile wide around the most populated areas and leave everybody in them to die. There's got to be a better way. Any ideas?"

"With all due respect, sir," said Lindley, "I do believe that isolation is the only way we can handle the situation."

"Oh, come on, Dale. Do you have any idea of the logistics that would be needed to isolate twenty percent of an entire nation?"

"I wasn't thinking along the lines of twenty percent, sir."

"Go on."

"I was thinking of one hundred percent."

A silence fell around the table as everyone present digested the meaning of Lindley's words.

"You mean just throw them to the wolves? Forget all about them as if they never existed? Come on, Dale, that is not possible, and you know it."

"Actually, Mr. President, it is no different from what we are doing right now. All I am saying is, let's activate the evacuation order, put a stop to all flights in and out of Japan, and then see what we can do from this side of the pond. Professor Donnelly and his team will begin work immediately on trying to formulate a vaccine or antidote, and at the same time, we can throw all of our resources behind trying to shore up the global markets. We mustn't overlook the fact that Japan is not the only victim here. There are many countries in the world that are being annihilated by the collapse of the financial markets, and this indecision is having a worse effect on financial systems than a clear, out-in-the-open policy would have. In the end, the only difference would be that we had pulled American citizens out of a hazardous region. Surely that is within our rights."

The president examined the backs of his hands while he thought things through. He was sure that Lindley was simply going out on a limb to verbalize what everybody else was thinking, and for that he didn't blame him. Decisive action was the order of the day, but abandoning a country like Japan was an enormous step—more potentially controversial, even, than the order to drop the atomic bombs on Hiroshima and Nagasaki. But what if he didn't order the evacuation and stayed close by Japan in her hour of need? What good would that do? The situation would, as Lindley had pointed out, be exactly the same, with the only difference being that a large number of American nationals would be infected and die as a result.

"You make a strong case, Dale. All right, you win. Activate the evacuation order, but don't announce it until I have had a chance to speak with the prime minister. I also want somebody to liaise with this ad hoc committee they've started up so we can get hold of the documentation used to engineer this bug. You can sort that out, Dale. Make sure everything is ready to ship out by the time the last flight leaves Japan. Sooner, if possible. And you, Wayne." DeBerry looked across at Wayne Jeffers, the director of the CIA. "Get your mole to work right away. We need every single piece of information that is available. Make sure he establishes firm contact with this mystery guy and bleeds him for everything he knows. Maybe he'll be able to provide us with information that the development documentation doesn't contain. I also want him to report on general conditions after the evacuation order goes through. From now on, he is to act as our ears and eyes in Japan. Get him on it immediately!"

"Yes, sir!"

Hiroshi Okada, sixty-four-year-old chairman of Hamada Seiyaku's board of directors and part-time government committee member, was flying through the air to his death, and he didn't have a clue as to why he should find himself in this dreadful predicament. At least he knew how it had come about; what he didn't know was why. Less than ten seconds earlier he had opened the door to two unknown men who had grabbed him by his arms and rushed him backward through his eighth-floor condominium until they reached the French doors leading out onto the balcony, his heels scraping comically against the wooden flooring and occasional rugs. He had been speechless at this effrontery and had tried to fight back as one of the men unlocked the catch on the window, but his puny struggle had failed to have any effect on them in the least. Once the window had been opened, it had taken only a brief moment for the men to manhandle him out onto the balcony and toss him off into space. And now here he was, speeding through the air at a fair rate of knots with an unyielding concrete courtyard racing up to meet him. Twenty-four meters of nothingness culminating in a whole lot of hurt.

Although there was not a great deal of time to reflect on past actions during a twenty-four-meter fall, Hiroshi Okada's mind was working overtime, and each individual thought was conceived, pondered on, and discarded in favor of the next within a fraction of a second. The thought that ten seconds earlier his only worry in the world had been what necktie to wear with his pale blue shirt rankled especially. Why had some-body tried—tried?—to kill him? What had he done to deserve it? Realizing that he would never know the answer to that and that time was at a premium, he turned his mind to more practical matters for the final eighteen meters of his life. Did his wife know where to find the insurance papers and bankbooks? Did he ever tell her that he kept the deeds to the condo in his safety-deposit box? Did he have a recent photograph for use at the funeral? Would the police realize that this was not a suicide but a murder and track down the culprits? Would his son—

And then he no longer cared.

Kazuya Amano pulled back slightly on the throttle of his thirty-two-foot fishing boat and reached for his binoculars. He was right: a large and very fast boat was coming directly toward him out of the west. He presumed that this signaled the fact that they were no longer in international waters but encroaching on South Korean fishing grounds. He stuck his head out of the wheelhouse window and waved across to the skipper of the *Kushiyama Maru* not twenty meters off his port side. The skipper waved back and Amano pointed ahead in the direction of the fast-approaching boat. He waited for an acknowledgment before going across to the starboard window and performing the same ritual for the skipper of the *Arashio Maru*, and then once again for the *Hotei Maru* situated thirty meters off his stern.

The mainland of Japan, one hundred and seventy kilometers behind them, was no longer visible, but Amano was afforded a faint glimpse of the South Korean coast from the peak of every swell. Another hour's sailing. He presumed that the approaching South Korean patrol boat would simply check them out to make sure they were not dragging their nets and then leave them alone, but he had ordered the radio silence before leaving Hagi in Yamaguchi prefecture so that there would be no danger of them being accused of defying an order to turn back. One could not defy an order that one could not hear, after all. At least, that was the logic behind Kazuya Amano's plan of action.

Amano squinted through the hazy sunlight at the gray Pae Ku–class patrol boat. It was now close enough for him to see the sharp bows slicing neatly through the ocean, sending two individual plumes of froth skyward, and the two long whip aerials bending back toward the stern of the vessel. He felt a momentary stab of anxiety. If the patrol boat did manage to turn him around, he would have to refund all of the money collected from the seventy-eight passengers spread between the four vessels, and he certainly didn't want to do that. He had been amazed at the amount of money some people would pay for a simple trip across the Sea of Japan. Most of them came from the big cities, of course, the fools. The people of Yamaguchi took life at a slower pace, and nobody was overly worried about the epidemic that had broken out in other parts of the country. And even if they were, none of them would be stupid enough to pay him several million yen for a two-hundred-kilometer run across to South Korea. Once word had gotten out that he was available for hire, they had come running. His son had helped there by posting a message on his homepage, or whatever he called that newfangled computer thing he was always playing with. He even had a couple of people on board who had come from as far north as Akita prefecture. It certainly beat fishing; of that there was no doubt. He had amassed more money with this single run than he could expect to earn over the course of the next fifteen years, even taking the two million yen he would have to pay each of the other three skippers into consideration. If all went well on this maiden run, he was thinking about arranging another run for the following week. He would be richer than he ever thought possible in his life.

The military patrol boat reduced speed as it neared the fleet of four fishing boats and then slewed around in the water like a reigned-in Thoroughbred until it was following the same course one hundred meters off their starboard flank. Amano could see activity on the deck. One of the seamen was waving both of his arms and then pointing up to the array of satellite dishes and antennae on the mainmast that sprouted out of the middle of superstructure. Amano chuckled to himself. How pathetically impotent man was without his backup of modern technology. By simply keeping the switch to his radio firmly at the off position, a multibillion-yen high-tech military craft was about as useful as an umbrella in a typhoon. Amano watched the man throw his arms up in frustration as it became obvious that the fishing boats had no intention of communicating. Another sailor came onto the deck with a spherical black tube under his arm. He aimed it at the boats and began to operate a lever on one side to open and close a louvered panel covering the front of a powerful flashlight. Despite the sunlight, Amano was able to see the light emitted, but as he didn't understand Morse code, it didn't really matter whether he could or not.

The fleet forged onward without reducing speed. An older man, whose air of authority led Amano to believe he was the captain, appeared on the deck of the patrol boat and stood staring across the distance that separated them, his legs splayed wide to compensate for the movement of the vessel, his hands placed dramatically on his hips. He cóntinued to stare for a moment longer before speaking into a small handheld microphone. His voice boomed across the ocean: "You are ordered to turn back," he said in English. "You are considered to be a biohazard and you will not be allowed to reach the South Korean mainland. Slow down and turn back."

Amano's uninterest in learning Morse code also stretched to the English language. He had no idea what the captain was saying.

The captain repeated his order three more times before giving up and disappearing back into the superstructure. A moment later two seamen emerged. They ran aft to a contraption located near the stern and busied themselves out of Amano's line of sight. Curious, Amano walked over to the wheelhouse window and peered across at the patroller. He could see the sea-to-sea missile launchers clamped to the transom and the harpoon launchers immediately behind the superstructure, but the two seamen were engaged in something between these weapons, and he couldn't quite make out what it was. He stood on tiptoe and craned his neck to catch a glimpse of the seamen, and a moment later his curiosity was satisfied as the cannon's fearsome barrel swiveled around in his direction.

Amano blanched and stumbled back to the helm. He had been expecting some sort of capstan or winch. He felt something move deep within his bowels, but failed to recognize it as terror. They wouldn't dare fire! The fleet was not doing anything illegal, and they had every right to be here. They had not been fishing, and every person who was to be let off in South Korea was in possession of a passport. He had checked them himself. He knew that the Koreans were being a bit touchy over this outbreak thing, but not even they would go as far as firing on unarmed maritime traffic. It was a bluff. It had to be a bluff. Well, if they wanted to speak to him that urgently, they would just have to wait until he was moored in their harbor and stuffing himself full of their grilled meat and *kimchi*.

The captain reappeared on deck and his voice echoed across the water once again: "You are ordered to turn back. This is your last chance. Slow down or we will open fire."

Amano kept his eyes and the bows of his fishing boat trained on the western horizon.

He heard the whistle of the shells before the staccato *thwack-thwack-thwack* of the cannon and instinctively ducked his head. *The bastards!* They were actually shooting! *Bakayaro!* The shots smacked harmlessly into the sea thirty meters ahead and Amano breathed a quick sigh of relief. He looked across at the captain of the patrol boat and made a gesture with his right hand that left the recipient in no doubt as to his opinion of this turn of events. The captain gestured back by using the palms of his hands to press downward onto an imaginary force, indicating that he wanted them to reduce speed.

Amano could hear the moans of terror coming from his nineteen paying passengers down on the deck of the boat. He poked his head out of the wheelhouse door and looked down on them huddled together in their attempt to make the smallest possible target. *"Daijobu da! Shinpai suruna!"* he shouted over the noise of the engine. *"Zettai fune o utenai kara! Daijobu da!"* Somewhat placated by his confidence that the South Koreans would not open fire on the boat, the passengers relaxed a little and smiled fearfully up at him.

Amano regained his position at the helm just as three more shells whistled overhead and landed not ten meters in front of his bows. They were getting closer. He hoped they didn't misjudge the distance and hit his boat by mistake. A perforated hull certainly wouldn't aid his passage back to Japan after they had made the drop-off. He glanced back over to the patrol boat and saw that the captain was still gesturing for him to slow down. He flipped him the bird once more and smiled grimly as the captain gave up and replaced his hands on his hips again. Amano could practically feel his frustration across the distance that separated them. Served the bastard right! He hoped the swine was court-martialed for taking potshots at unarmed ships.

The captain suddenly swung on his heel and shouted something to somebody concealed within the superstructure. Amano's heart nearly surged out through his throat as he saw the barrel of the cannon swivel around until it was pointing directly at his wheelhouse. But despite a nagging sense of anxiety, he still felt confident. They *couldn't* shoot on friendly ships! It just wasn't allowed. A moment later he revised this opinion as he saw the captain bow deeply from the waist, as if in abject apology.

The bastards were going to open fire!

Amano was splayed alive by the first shell as it came crashing through the window of the wheelhouse. Before the remains of his lifeless body had time to drop to the wooden deck, the barrel of the cannon had swung downward and was strafing the side of the boat, causing horrific carnage among its nineteen passengers as it sought out the engine block. Two seconds later, the entire boat was lifted out of the water by a huge explosion that rained shrapnel, debris, and unspeakable organic matter down on the occupants of the other three boats.

And still the compact PGM 586-591 cannon sought a target. Slowly, methodically, it worked its way through the three remaining boats until nothing protruded further than twenty centimeters above the surface of the water and the only sound was the steady thrum of the patrol boat's engines. The South Korean captain remained standing on the deck of his command and surveyed the result of his day's work, tears of remorse streaming unhindered down his face. He had carried out his orders to the letter, but that was little consolation to him. He had just witnessed something that he knew he was destined to see night after night for the rest of his life. He hoped he had the fortitude to withstand it.

Norio Kondo pulled the minivan off the road onto the gravel driveway and allowed it to coast slowly down the slight slope to the garage located beside the house. He switched off the engine and smiled reassuringly across at his wife before opening the door and jumping out. The cold wind immediately snapped at his heels and wrapped icy tentacles around him, but he stretched luxuriously and allowed it to cleanse him of the despair that had built up during the drive from Yokohama to Izu Kogen. They had taken Route 134 through to Odawara and then joined Route 135 to bring them south past the city of Ito and up into the mountains of Izu Kogen, and the journey had been fraught with anxiety. The sight of the closed-up shops and burned-out buildings as they had passed through Chigasaki and Hiratsuka had brought home the extent of the disaster to both of them, and they had driven through in silence, occupied not with each other's company but by their own individual dark and dismal thoughts. They had seen groups of people roaming the streets aimlessly—some armed with batons, baseball bats, and other makeshift weapons. A group of youths on motorcycles had roared past them at high speed as they had crossed the bridge fording the river Sagami, and they had run into them again thirty minutes later as the gang ransacked a service station and gleefully set fire to the cars in the car park. The hard shoulder of the highway was littered with cars abandoned by their owners when they had run out of gasoline and discovered the tanks in the service stations empty. Many of these cars were now hollow, burned-out wrecks, as were the hearts of the people caught in the midst of the calamity.

Gonta, the corgi, leaped from the van and began to run in joyful circles on the lawn, his tongue lolling from his grinning mouth as the fallen leaves swirled up around him. Shigeko joined her husband on the gravel path and watched the antics of the dog. "Well," she said, "at least it didn't take long for one of us to get over his depression."

"And so shall you soon. You'll see." Norio placed an arm around his wife's shoulders and squeezed gently. "We made the right decision. We are well out of the way up here. And just look at that view! Come on, let's get the place aired out."

The Kondos' *besso* was a four-bedroom timber-frame house set into just under five hundred *tsubo* of green and wooded land. It had a large living room with an eight-tatami-mat room leading off it, and the bathroom was supplied with hot springwater that stayed at a constant temperature of forty-two degrees Celsius. They had not visited the house for over two months, and everything was slightly damp and musty. Norio swiftly moved from room to room opening the windows, while Shigeko pulled all of the futons out of their *shiire* cupboards and stripped them of their sheets for washing. As Shigeko crammed the sheets into the washing machine and set the cycle to full wash, Norio collected the empty tanks from all of the kerosene heaters and lined them up for refilling in the garage. They then began to unpack the minivan, bringing the food supplies and computer equipment into the house and storing everything else in the garage. It was nearly five o'clock and close to dusk when they were able to close the windows and allow the house to heat up. Gonta was already laid out exhausted in front of the kerosene heater in the front room as Norio returned from his last chore—opening the spigot to the springwater and allowing the bath to fill up. Shigeko poured out cups of green tea and they sat sipping them as their bodies responded to the comforting heat and slowly began to unwind.

Norio looked across at his wife. She was getting old, her body was becoming shapeless, and the wrinkles were clear to see on her cosmetic-free face, but to him she looked more beautiful than any scrawny model who had ever sashayed her ass down a fashion-show walkway. Her beauty did not lie on the surface for all to see, but penetrated straight through to her core before bouncing back and emanating from her in a golden aura that Norio was especially aware of.

He stretched out an arm and covered her hand with his. "I love you," he said almost inaudibly.

Shigeko looked up in surprise. She couldn't remember the last time he had uttered those words. It was just not his style. Norio, like most Japanese men, did not feel comfortable expressing his emotions verbally, and she had become adept at sensing his feelings through small actions, not spoken confessions. She knew he loved her dearly, but she had never expected to hear him say so again as long as she lived. She was touched, and a tear spilled from her eye. She clasped her free hand over the top of his and squeezed.

"Do you remember when we were first married and used to get in the tub together?" Norio asked, a mischievous grin on his face. "You'd scrub my back and I'd scrub yours?"

Shigeko nodded shyly, getting the drift of his meaning.

"Well, the tub's ready, if you'd care to join me. . . ."

Gonta raised his head and watched them leave the room hand in hand. Although not overburdened with intelligence, Gonta was able to recognize that they were not heading for the kitchen, so logic informed him that food was out of the question. He lost interest and went back to sleep.

Peter Bryant was not sure he cared for the look on the hotel manager's face. There was something shifty about it, as if he were trying to conceal embarrassment or guilt. Bryant had merely asked for the room key and requested that his bill be made ready for his departure in one hour, but the manager's eyes had flickered between the countertop and Bryant's face repeatedly without once looking him steadily in the eye. What was he trying to hide? Maybe he had entered Bryant's room during his absence and helped himself to something he shouldn't have. Or maybe he was intending to pad the bill to make a little pocket money on the side. Or maybe he was just a naturally shifty character. An image of the small leather bag containing four million yen on top of the bedside cabinet floated into Bryant's mind, and he suddenly felt the urge to get up to his room as swiftly as possible. Nodding a puzzled thank-you, he grabbed his key and made for the stairs up to the second floor.

The Daimaru carrier bag, containing a rucksack that he had purchased from the department store located in Tokyo Station to replace the sports bag Michiyo had taken with her to Fukushima, banged against his legs as he ran up the stairs and down the corridor. Michiyo had left Tokyo at three-thirty-two aboard the Yamabiko bullet train for Koriyama, and even with the time required to change trains at Koriyama, she would still be at home in Aizu Wakamatsu before seven o'clock that evening. At least that was one thing off his mind, although he was already missing her and felt a tad lonely.

The door to his room was locked, but that came as no surprise, considering the hotel manager had his own set of *aikagi*. He slipped the key into the lock and turned the handle. A rustling noise from within alerted him to the fact that he had visitors, but before he could react to this information, the door was yanked open and the intruder had grabbed hold of his collar and dragged him inside. Instead of resisting the forward motion, Bryant ran into it, surprising his assailant and causing him to stumble backward into the bed, where he was unable to avoid sitting down unceremoniously. The moment he was in the lower position, Bryant pulled back his fist and let the man have it as hard as he could on the side of his head. The man sagged and released his hold on Bryant's collar, his hands instinctively flying to his head, and Bryant brought his knee up as hard as he could, connecting satisfyingly with the burglar's jaw. He felt, more than heard, the jaw crack, but before he was able to take advantage of his superior position, two arms grabbed him from behind and heaved him backward onto the carpeted floor.

Damn, there are two of them!

Bryant wriggled like a gaffed fish and slammed his head back as hard as he could into the second man's face, glancing briefly off a cheekbone. This failed to do much damage, but it alerted the man to the fact that Bryant was not going to lie still while they beat the shit out of him, and served to prevent him from releasing the bear hug around Bryant's chest for fear of the consequences.

Bryant was pissed—*really* pissed—but the only words that flashed repeatedly through his mind were, *Oh, dear God, not the balls again. Please, please, anything but the balls!*

A foot lashed out from the first man, who was still sitting on the bed, and caught Bryant squarely on the side of the face.

The stars swam in front of his eyes, but they did not prevent him from noticing that the man on the bed had pushed a hand inside his jacket and pulled out a small but eminently serviceable pistol. Bryant began to struggle even harder. He didn't want to die in a dingy old hotel room—in fact, he didn't want to die anywhere—but the way things were going seemed to point exactly toward that possibility. He began to hammer his feet up and down, like a child throwing a tantrum, in an attempt to connect with his assailant's legs, and although he felt his heels land against solid shinbone on several occasions, the man merely grunted and hung on grimly. Rubber Reeboks, it seemed, were not the ideal medium for inflicting pain.

The man on the bed stood up and smiled grotesquely through his misshapen jaw and the blood that ran from his mouth. He straightened the arm that held the pistol and pointed it directly at Bryant's head, closing one eye and squinting along the barrel in aim. Bryant cursed loudly in English and began to rock from side to side, providing the man holding the gun with an alternating view of Bryant's and his own colleague's head. "Hold him still!" the man shouted in exasperation, his voice muffled by his injury. "I can't get a good aim."

The man increased the power of his bear hug, but the rocking motion was providing Bryant with a modicum of leverage on the floor with his elbow. He put all of his strength into raising himself up and throwing all of his weight over to the other side. The man clinging steadfastly to his back was not of great build, and this enabled Bryant to flip him over comparatively easily. Pleased with the results of this, Bryant cocked his elbow for the return journey and then lay still, breathing heavily as if his exertions had exhausted him. Seeing his chance, the man with the gun swiftly took aim at Bryant and pulled the trigger.

But Bryant was swifter. Timing his move perfectly, he lurched off the floor with his elbow and swung the second man across his back. The noise of the gun was loud in the small room, but before Bryant could register the uncomfortable sensation in his inner ear, the tightness around his chest relaxed and something warm and wet ran down the back of his neck and into the collar of his shirt. Guessing—hoping—that the warm and wet stuff was not leaking from his own body, he shrugged the weight off his back and rolled over, the skin all over his body cringing in dreaded anticipation of the second shot.

It never came.

The man with the gun stood staring at his dead companion in puzzled surprise, the gun hanging limply by his side. Realizing that he had been presented with an opportunity, Bryant hauled himself up onto one knee and launched himself at the weapon. His life depended on disarming this crazy bastard, and he was not about to let a chance like this slip from his grasp.

This time the gunman was swifter. Before Bryant could grab hold of the gun, he had whipped it upward and then brought it down on the top of his head. The pain seared through Bryant's brain and the stars sparkled before his eyes for the second time in as many minutes. His momentum kept him moving forward, but he knew the only thing that awaited him at journey's end was a bullet. He fell to the floor and braced himself for the piercing pain.

The noise, when it came, made him jump and then whimper softly. It was loud and sounded nearby, but it did not cause the same pain in his inner ear that the first shot had. He opened his eyes and looked up, scanning the area in front of him where the gunman had stood. The room was empty. The man had fled, slamming the door behind him.

Bryant lay on the floor for a few more moments while he gathered his wits. A trickle of blood flowed from his hairline and ran into his left eye, blinding him temporarily and forcing him to get up in search of something with which to wipe his face. One of his unwashed T-shirts was draped over the back of a chair placed in front of the television, and he picked this up and mopped up not only his own blood, but also the blood from his dead assailant that had run down the back of his neck. Having managed to remove as much of the gore as was possible, he looked around again and noticed the half-empty whisky bottle standing beside the television. Throwing the soiled T-shirt onto the bed, he grabbed hold of the bottle, unscrewed the cap, and poured a generous amount into a plastic cup. He gulped a mouthful down and choked as it burned a path down his throat. Moving across to the bed, he sat down and sipped the rest slowly. His hands were shaking and he could feel a rippling wave of indecipherable emotion rising to the surface. The backs of his eyes prickled, and he tried to hold back the tears. Tears of what? Pain? Relief? Rage? Loneliness? Self-pity? He didn't know. He knew only that he had seen the brink of death and had lived to tell the tale, and as far as he was concerned, that was good enough reason for weeping.

So he wept silently, his shoulders shaking with the effort until his body had been exorcised of the primeval desire to simply cry for undefined reasons.

The T-shirt was employed for a second time; this time to dry his cheeks. He felt slightly ashamed at the uncontrollable outburst and was glad nobody had seen him. He finished off the last gulp of whisky and tossed the empty cup onto the bed. It was time for him to get out of there in case the gunman had called reinforcements. Damn, why hadn't he thought of that before? There could be an army of armed men rushing down the street at this very moment, all intent on putting him into an early grave.

Forcing himself to move, he ripped open the carrier bag containing his new rucksack and began to stuff all of his belongings into it. He quickly checked to ensure that the money was still in the clutch bag before ramming it inside, and then rushed into the bathroom for his toothbrush and shaving gear. Giving the room a final once-over, he picked the room key up from the floor where he had dropped it and walked toward the door.

And then it struck him. What the hell had these two men wanted? The cash was in the exact same place where he had left it, so they probably were not searching for valuables. Knowing the reason for the visit could be important, he propped the rucksack up against the wall and moved back into the center of the room. Dropping down onto one knee beside the corpse, he turned it over and began to rifle through the dead man's pockets. Most of the contents seemed inconsequential—cigarettes, lighter, handkerchief, pen—until Bryant found the man's wallet. He flipped it open and studied the driver's license. Takashi Kamio. Thirty-four years of age. Bryant opened one of the pockets of the wallet and began to sift through the credit cards, old receipts, and business cards contained therein. He pulled the credit cards out and checked the name on each one. Takashi Kamio. As burglars went, he was either extremely unprofessional or very, very confident. The last item of plastic was not a credit card, but a company ID card. An unsmiling photograph of the man looked out at him, and the name written beside it was the same, but Bryant's attention was not on this item of information, but on the company name and logo situated at the top of the card.

Hamada Seiyaku Pharmaceuticals, Inc.

Bryant was not sure whether to be surprised or not. Although he had more or less guessed that his visitors had not been simple burglars, he had tried to suppress the thought, as it would provide proof that Hamada Seiyaku had not yet given up on its quest to kill him. Proof that he would rather not have.

But why hadn't he been killed when they had the chance? What was their motive for entering his room if only to flee the moment the going got rough? The gunman could easily have finished him off before leaving if he had really wanted to. *Weird* . . .

Bryant decided to ponder on that riddle later. At the moment his priority was to get out of the room before reinforcements came, but his curiosity overcame his instinct to run. He began to scrutinize the area around the fallen assailant for anything that would provide a clue. A flash of red plastic by the bed caught his eye. It was mostly concealed beneath the shadow of the quilt, but it was not anything that Bryant recognized. A closer inspection revealed it to be the handle of a small wire cutter. He looked deeper into the shadow and his eye fell on a small screwdriver. Overriding a sense of panic and a loud voice in his head telling him to get out of there immediately, he crawled over to the bed and peered underneath.

It was too dark to make out the fine details, but he instantly recognized the contraption for what it was. A bomb! It was the first time he had ever seen one in the flesh, so to speak, but as an avid fan of action movies, he was left in no doubt that his guess was correct. It was a prayer book–sized lump of explosive wrapped in brown greaseproof paper with two detonation caps protruding drunkenly from the top. Wires connected the detonation caps to a square battery. He presumed there was also a timing device, but he couldn't make it out in the gloom.

He swallowed hard. Had the thing been primed? Did he really want to know? He crawled slowly backward until his feet bumped up against the body lying in the middle of the floor. Primed or not, this was no time to linger. He stood up and retrieved his rucksack. Walking gently across to the door, he exited the room and made his way down to the foyer.

The manager avoided his eye. Bryant was tempted to leap across the counter and beat the hell out of the guy, but logic informed him that it was not a good idea to waste any more time or complicate matters. He smiled as he approached the counter.

"Is my bill ready?" he asked calmly.

"Er, yes, sir. Right away, sir!"

Bryant pushed his credit card across the counter after inspecting the bill. All seemed to be correct. The manager took the card and ran it through the authorization machine, his fingers trembling slightly. He had heard the shot and seen the man who had slipped him 100,000 yen for the passkey run panic-stricken from the hotel and had feared the worst. He had never expected to see this *gaijin* again, at least, not in an upright position, yet here he was, paying his bill as if nothing had happened. The manager noted the blood drying on his hairline and his stained shirt collar and gulped as he pushed the receipt across the counter for a signature.

Bryant reclaimed his credit card, and began to walk toward the door. Just before he disappeared from sight, he stopped and turned back to face the man.

"Oh, yes. I nearly forgot. There was something else."

"Sir?"

"There's a bomb under the bed in my room."

"A bomb?" Bryant found the look of surprised horror on the manager's face extremely pleasing. "What do you mean, a bomb? What do I do if it explodes?"

"Well, that is up to you, but you might try jumping ten meters into the air and then spreading yourself liberally over that wall there. Have a nice day, now. . . ."

Chapter Eight

The sudden ring of the mobile telephone startled Peter Bryant and had his heart pumping in his chest. He fumbled in his pocket with fingers numbed from the cold of the evening. "Hello?"

"Mr. Bryant. You are still here?" *The mystery caller!* "After I heard of the bungled attack on your life, I thought you would have put as much distance between yourself and Tokyo as possible."

"No, I'm still here. There was another attempt this afternoon."

"I know. That is what made me try your number again. I had no idea you were still here; otherwise I would have contacted you earlier. Are you all right?"

"Just, although I shouldn't be by rights. The guy had me cold and could easily have shot me, but he simply ran out the door. I still don't understand why."

"You interrupted a Hamada Seiyaku employee and a small-time crook, Mr. Bryant. Hamada's usual contact refused to have anything to do with explosives, so he improvised. The man who was killed was the Hamada employee. The crook, I understand, hasn't stopped running yet. You were very lucky. Where are you now?"

"Around. Why do you want to know?"

"Mere curiosity. Do you intend to stay? Even after the evacuation?"

"Evacuation?" So they had gone for it after all, as Mike Woodson had forewarned. Why was he not surprised?

"Yes, it was announced this afternoon."

Bryant hesitated before answering. He still hadn't officially made his mind up whether to stay or not, but there was something inside him that knew he would remain behind. He really needed more time to think the problem through, but if the evacuation had already been announced, then he would have to come to a decision in the very near future. An image of Michiyo flashed into his mind. Could he leave her and fly back to the States without even saying good-bye? *No way!* The shot wasn't even on the board. "Yes, I will probably stay behind." *Damn!* He hadn't meant to say that with so much conviction.

"I see. And where will you be staying, may I ask?"

Bryant detected a note of concern in the caller's voice. It both surprised and comforted him. It established a bond between them and made him want to pour his heart out to this man who had been in his corner from the beginning. The loneliness induced by Michiyo's absence, the ordeal he had been through that day, the freezing conditions, and a fat chunk of self-pity were bubbling up inside him, generating a craving for sympathetic human society. He also recalled Mike Woodson telling him that the caller felt loyalty and responsibility toward him and that he was expected to forge a closer relationship. He decided that it was time to dismantle his barriers and level with his newfound friend. "I have no idea, to tell the truth," he said. "In fact, I am homeless at the moment. All of the hotels I contacted are refusing reservations. I am sitting on a park bench that is destined to be my bed for the night."

"Mr. Bryant, you must get off the streets before it gets too late. It is dangerous for you to be out after dark. There are many tales of mugging and looting."

"Yeah, tell me about it." Bryant had witnessed a mugging outside of Shinagawa Station not twenty minutes earlier. The victim, a man in his fifties, had been set upon by six youths, who had not only taken his wallet and other valuables but had also smashed his spectacles out of what seemed to be pure spite.

"I can give you the address of a small private inn in Tabata. The owner is a friend and will let you stay. I will contact him to let him know of your arrival. How far are you from Tabata?"

"About thirty minutes."

"Then you must make your way there immediately."

"Do you have a name?"

"For the inn?"

"No, for you."

The caller hesitated. "A name? What do you mean?"

"Any name. Just something I can call you."

Another brief hesitation. "Maybe you would like to choose one yourself."

"Me? Sure, why not?" Bryant thought for a moment or two before continuing. "How about Kagemusha?"

"Ha, I see you know your Kurosawa, Mr. Bryant."

"Actually, no. I've never seen his movies. I am going from the Chinese *kanji*. The shadow warrior. It seems to suit you."

"I am flattered, but I should mention that I am no warrior. Not by any stretch of the imagination. I am but a frightened child concealing himself behind a facade of anonymity."

"I owe you my life. If you hadn't contacted me I would probably be dead by now. I am grateful for that."

"I did what I deemed to be best. I neither need nor deserve your gratitude, Mr. Bryant."

"It is yours anyway." Bryant could tell that the caller was pleased at having his actions recognized. There was something in his voice that indicated pleasure, not smugness—more a sort of relief at hearing a third party confirm that his decision had been correct. Bryant felt close to him: two strangers brought together for the sole purpose of vicariously experiencing each other's pain and hardship. "I ought to tell you that I intend to stay on in Japan so I can report back to the American government. If you have any information that could be of use, it would make my job easier, Kagemusha."

"May I ask the purpose of the reports?"

"Well, to help, I guess. They are working on a cure for the disease and need as much information as possible. They also need details on local conditions to formulate political strategies for saving the economy. That's all I know, really, but I should be able to find out more later. They will be providing me with certain equipment to stay in touch with them, but apart from that I know very little at the moment. If it is important, I'll contact Mike Woodson and let you know."

"I'm afraid I won't be of any use for much longer. Tomorrow will be my last day at Hamada Seiyaku. Things have gone too far, and I fear for my own safety. Another of our number was killed earlier today—Hiroshi Okada, the chairman of the board. Hamada had him killed for sympathizing with the government. I cannot stand this wanton killing any longer. I have friends who will look after me. Hamada was taken into custody this morning for his involvement in the release of the bacterium, but it will take him only a few days to make bail. I intend to be gone from Tokyo by the time he is released."

"Is there anything I can do?"

"No, Mr. Bryant. Although I thank you for the offer."

"I still have the money you gave me for Leonard Drake. I must return it. Can we meet?"

"Keep it. You deserve it."

"I want you to stay in touch with me. Is that possible?"

A silence met Bryant's request. A few moments later the voice said, "Yes, I will keep in touch for as long as the telephones remain functional. Now, do you want the address of this inn or not?"

"Kagemusha?" Bryant said when he had finished writing down the address and had replaced his diary in the rucksack.

"Yes?"

"Take care. And thanks."

"Thank you, too, Mr. Bryant. I wish you well."

The words being broadcast by the American Forces Far East Network differed slightly from those used by NHK, CNN, the BBC, and all other broadcasting networks available within Japan, but the gist was the same: An executive order from the White House initiating the evacuation of all American citizens from Japan was now in effect, and all people eligible for the order were to calmly make their way to Yokota and Misawa air force bases and to various other domestic airports—a list of which was read out—with their passports or other forms of identification. All foreign spouses of American citizens requiring inclusion in the order would be obliged to provide marriage certificates or proof of marriage before being allowed aboard outgoing flights. Luggage must be kept to a maximum of one suitcase and one item of hand baggage per person. A list of telephone numbers was also provided for those who had inquiries not covered by the announcement.

The exodus had begun.

Bryant slid the glass-paneled door closed behind him and stood on the slate slabs that made up the *genkan* to the small inn. "*Gomen kudasai*," he shouted. "Anyone home?"

He heard a door slam out of sight down the corridor, and a moment later a gray-haired middle-aged man came into view. "Ah, Mr. Bryant. We have been expecting you. Please come on in out of the cold."

The man hastily took a pair of blue slippers from the top of the shoe box and laid them out on the floor. Bryant murmured his thanks, removed his shoes, and stepped up into the inn.

"Please come this way, Mr. Bryant. My wife is laying out your futon, but if you would like something to eat, that can easily be arranged. We don't have much in the way of entertainment, but I can promise you excellent homemade cooking and as much sake as you can drink." He winked conspiratorially and mimed the action of raising a small cup to his lips.

"Thank you very much, Mr. . . . ?"

"Otsuka. Toshio Otsuka, although Totchan probably referred to me as Omotenashi."

Bryant ignored the ambiguity of this statement and followed his host down a dimly lit corridor to his room. The door was open, and a middle-aged woman was inside smoothing down the sheets to a futon laid out in the middle of the eight-tatami room. Leaving their slippers outside, the two men entered.

"My wife, Harumi."

"A pleasure to meet you, Mr. Bryant. Any friend of Totchan's is a friend of ours. Please make yourself at home. We have one of the few *onsen* hot baths in Tokyo, so please feel free to take a dip before dinner. You are our only guest, so you will be quite alone. It is just down the corridor on your left. You can't miss it. You will find the towels on a rack just outside the bathroom door. You will eat with us after your bath, of course. Unless you prefer to eat in your own room, that is? I wouldn't like to force you."

"No, no. That will be fine. Thank you very much indeed. I didn't expect such hospitality. I am truly grateful. Would you like me to sign the check-in book or something?"

Otsuka was horrified. "Of course, not, Mr. Bryant! How could you possibly say such a thing? You are our guest, not a customer."

Before Bryant could voice his amazement, Harumi said, "Your Japanese is beautiful, Mr. Bryant. Where did you learn to speak so well?"

"I . . . er . . . my, er, mother is Japanese. I spent my youth here."

"Ah, yes, that would explain it. I have always heard that Japanese is one of the most difficult languages to learn. It's the *kanji*, you know. Do you read and write *kanji* as well?"

"Well, yes, I do. But not as fluently as I would like, although I read it a lot faster than I write it."

"Now, isn't that just amazing? You must have studied very hard. When I first heard from Totchan that you were an American, I must admit to feeling a little worried. Neither I nor my husband speak English, you see, and I was anxious over how we would communicate. But now that I know you speak such perfect Japanese, I have nothing to worry about at all, do I?"

"I suppose not. Listen, I hope I'm not—"

"Well, I must pop off and get the dinner ready," interrupted Harumi, "I have laid out a *yukata* for you, so please take your time and join us after your bath. I'm sure my husband will enjoying sharing a cup or two of sake with you. It is not often that he gets the chance to relax without guests, and he does like his drink of a night."

"That is very kind of you. Thank you very—"

"*Anata.*" Harumi had already turned her attention to her husband. "Come, let us leave Mr. Bryant in peace. He must be very tired and wanting his bath. We'll see you again soon, Mr. Bryant."

The door slid shut behind the garrulous couple before Bryant could respond. A broad grin cracked his face as he ran the conversation over in his mind. Whoever the mystery caller was, he certainly had good taste in friends. He couldn't think of a couple more aptly suited for the job of running a small inn. Shaking his head in delight and wonder, he rummaged through his rucksack for a change of underwear and grabbed the *yukata* robe from the bed.

Five minutes later, having rinsed himself down with the shower provided and scraped the dried blood from his hairline,

Bryant gingerly stepped into the steaming bath. The sound of the water dripping from his sodden hair echoed eerily around the bathroom as it splashed into the water. Even the sound of his own breath reverberated inside his head as the humidity of the steamy atmosphere set a wheeze in his throat. He moaned blissfully in sheer pleasure as the hot water rose to cover his entire body right up to the neck. The bath was large enough for three or four people, so he was able to stretch out comfortably. He began to run his hands over his legs and torso to see if he had sustained any lasting damage from his run-in with the so-called burglars, but apart from the bump on his head and a thumping headache, he seemed to be in pretty good shape.

All he had to do now was decide his next step. He couldn't stay with Mr. and Mrs. Otsuka for too long, as he was sure they would soon be wanting to get out of Tokyo. It was also dangerous. If Hamada had tracked him down to his last hotel in Iidabashi, the chances were that he would have no trouble discovering this new hideout. It wouldn't be fair to subject these kind people to any danger attributable to his own selfishness. He would have to telephone Mike Woodson and seek advice. Now that the evacuation order had been issued, he presumed that Mike himself would soon be leaving the country. He had to sort something out before then.

Dreamily deciding that he would telephone Mike after dinner, Bryant closed his eyes and submerged his chin in the luxurious warmth of the hot springwater, for the moment safe, warm, and in good company.

Dinner consisted of a deep-fried prawn tempura, an impressive plate of red and white fish sashimi, and several small side dishes of pickles and assorted boiled vegetables. Toshio Otsuka was constantly plying the one-point-eight-liter bottle of Gekkeikan, and Bryant was fast becoming a fan of the tasty beverage.

"So how did you first meet Totchan?" Toshio asked, his face

bright red and jovial from the effects of the sake.

Bryant wasn't sure how to answer the question. He presumed they were referring to his mystery caller, but would it be safe to admit that he didn't know him from Adam? Although he couldn't imagine them suddenly turning frosty and throwing him out on the street for admitting to never having met the man, he didn't want them to feel that he was enjoying their hospitality under false pretenses. "Well, to tell the truth, I've never actually met him, per se. . . ." Bryant closely examined their faces to detect any change in expression. To his surprise, they both clapped their hands together and burst out laughing.

"The same as us. We've never met him either. Are you a member of an anonymous on-line board? That's how we know Totchan."

"Well, yes, something like that." Bryant spotted his chance to unravel a part of the mystery and pounced on it readily. "I don't even know his real name. Do you?"

"No, no, no. All we know about him is that he works in pharmaceuticals and lives in Tokyo."

"And that's about exactly what I know." Bryant, although disappointed at not finding out the true name of Kagemusha, relaxed a little more. Discovering that his mystery caller was an Internet geek offered a new dimension to his character. The image of him sitting alone at night, conversing via computer with people like the Otsukas, placed a sort of homeliness on him and made him seem less threatening. He was beginning to feel very fond of the man.

"Does he use the same handle? Totchan?"

"I'm sorry . . . ?"

"Totchan. What name does he use on your bulletin board?"

"Ah, yes. We know him as Kagemusha."

Toshio and Harumi laughed again. "That's just typical of him," said Toshio, pausing to take a gulp of sake. "He does have a taste for the dramatic. Actually, we might get the chance to meet up with him soon. I wonder what he looks like?"

"I bet he's young and handsome," said Harumi. "Unlike you, you ugly old warthog."

Toshio took the insult in the playful manner in which it was delivered and chuckled sheepishly. "Well, if he is, you can forget all about him. He wouldn't look twice at a wrinkled old witch like you."

Harumi roared with laughter and slapped Toshio on the arm.

Bryant smiled politely, marveling at their companionship, but, not wanting to allow the subject to change, said, "How will you get to meet him? I'd like to meet him myself if possible."

Toshio poured another glassful of sake for them both and raised his glass for the umpteenth time. "Harumi and I own a *besso* up in the mountains of Izu," he explained. "It is a sort of joint-ownership thing with the people who run the bulletin board we are on. Now that this damned disease is everywhere, we will all move up there for safety. Gakusha, the list owner, and his wife have already moved up there, and we will follow them in a couple of days. Gakusha has also invited Totchan to come and stay, as he is the only other member who lives in either Yokohama or Tokyo. I don't know if he has accepted or not, though."

Bryant turned his mind back to his conversation with Kagemusha earlier on in the evening: *I have friends who will look after me. I intend to be gone from Tokyo by the time he is released.* Had he finally tracked Kagemusha down? Did he at last know where he could find him? On the other hand, did he have the *right* to find him? If the man didn't want to be found, what gave Bryant the right to disturb his peace and come running after him? Yet another problem that would require deep pondering. But maybe it wouldn't hurt to just establish some sort of line of contact. He didn't have to use it if he finally decided to leave Kagemusha in peace.

"That is nice," said Bryant casually. "Listen, will you be taking your computer out to Izu with you?"

"That depends on Gakusha. We might not bother if he is taking his. Why?"

"I was wondering if you could let me have your e-mail address. You know, just so I can thank you formally for your kind hospitality and keep in contact. I'd also be very curious now to discover if Totchan is, in fact, young and handsome."

"Of course. I'll go and write it down. I'll also give you Gakusha's address in case we don't take our own computer with us. You can always contact us through him."

Toshio got unsteadily to his feet and walked across to a door at the back of the room. "If you want," he called from the small room that served as an office, "I'll let you have Totchan's address, too. If he does come out to Izu, he is sure to bring a computer with him."

Kiyoshi Aizawa walked onto the stage and took his place at the lectern. He looked down upon the sea of heads spread out before him and squinted into the flashing camera strobes and dazzling television lights. He was about to make a historic speech, and he knew that the eyes of the entire world were trained upon him. The gentle hum of voices died down to a perfect silence, broken only by the rustling of clothing. Steeling himself, he grasped both edges of the lectern and leaned closer into the array of microphones.

"Today is a sad day for Japan," he said, his amplified voice ringing out loudly in the large room. "One hour ago a bill was passed amending our constitution to enable me, the prime minister, to announce a state of emergency that is the precursor of martial law." A rumble of voices spread through the crowd of reporters. Aizawa raised his hand for silence. "Our police services are no longer able to contain the wild outbreak of crime and civil unrest that is afflicting our streets, so their numbers will be augmented by the Self-Defense Forces. In addition to this, the SDF will set up field hospitals in all affected neighborhoods to dispense preventive medication and to cope with the increasing number of meningococcemia victims. The SDF will also be called upon to take over the operation of certain facilities that supply the nation with indispensable services if—and when—their assistance is required. This will ensure that the entire country continues to enjoy electricity, gas, and water supplies, as well as maintaining other vital utilities, such as communication and transportation services."

"Excuse me, sir." A young female reporter in the third row raised her hand.

"Yes?"

"You mention that the Self-Defense Forces will be used to augment the police forces. Does that mean they will be under the jurisdiction of the National Police Agency?"

"No, they will come under the jurisdiction of the Defense Agency and operate independently of the NPA. They will simply be there to enforce law and order on the streets."

"And when will this state of emergency come into effect?"

"From midnight tonight."

"So soon?"

"Yes, so soon." Aizawa held up his hand to halt the barrage of questions that erupted from the floor. "If you will allow me to continue," he said, speaking above the din. "You will all be provided with a press package outlining the details of these unprecedented measures before you leave. I believe that all of your questions will be more than adequately answered by these fact sheets, so I would appreciate it if you would save your inquiries until after you have read them. Another press conference has been scheduled for nine o'clock tomorrow morning, when you will be allowed to ask any questions you wish concerning the contents."

The room became quiet again as everybody turned their attention back to the prime minister.

"A crisis headquarters will be set up inside the Diet Building, from which the present state of emergency will be directed. Myself, my entire cabinet, and all vital staff will move into these headquarters tomorrow so that we can address ourselves to the problem twenty-four hours of every day. We have three main priorities: to discover a cure or a method of controlling the meningococcemia disease, to control the rampant inflation and restore both domestic and global financial markets to their former state, and to eradicate the wave of crime that is sweeping the country. The details of this are also in the press packages that will be distributed later, so I do not want to answer questions at the moment. I will simply end by saying that the government is determined to solve the problems that we are now facing within the most expedient time frame possible, and that these seemingly drastic measures have been initiated solely to ensure that we are not diverted from our objectives. I am sure we will have our critics, but the time for vacillating has passed. It is now time to act. I thank you for your time, ladies and gentlemen."

Aizawa left behind a roar of shouted questions and walked off the stage. A female aide handed him a damp hand towel with which to wipe the thin layer of pancake makeup from his face and neck.

"You are making a mistake." Shoji Kubota's voice sounded softly beside him. "It is madness to turn the country into a fort under siege. You will merely panic the public and run everything into the ground."

Aizawa had not noticed General Secretary Shoji Kubota approach. He looked up and stared him in the eye, noting that his narrow face appeared even more gaunt than usual. "Well, I'm sorry you think that way, Kubota. Presumably you still believe that the government should stick its head in the sand and hope everything will go away? Am I not right? Well, I'm terribly sorry if an unexpected stay in the Diet Building will mean you have to curtail the events and functions you attend to fill the party coffers, but we have more important things to do."

"Flippancy does not become you, Aizawa. You will regret crossing me. There are many people who are not happy about moving into the Diet, and most would be glad to see you replaced."

"There are also many who are quite happy to escape the threats of violence and the thrown vegetables caused by the government's inactivity. It is important for the people to know that we are serious in our efforts to overcome this."

Kubota laughed sarcastically. "Huh! You think that hiding behind closed doors is the way to show our seriousness? You are losing your mind, Aizawa, and I will not allow you to drag us all into the pit with you. Support for me is growing stronger with every day, and your time is drawing to a close. As much as you may dislike hearing it, you are playing directly into my hands. Enjoy your final days, my friend."

"Under martial law, I could have you arrested for speaking to me like that, Kubota. Treason would be the charge." The corners of Aizawa's eyes creased into a smile. "But that would be no fun at all. I would miss your scintillating conversation over breakfast every morning, and we can't have that, can we?" He draped the soiled hand towel over Kubota's shoulder before turning on his heel and heading back to his office, leaving the general secretary cursing under his breath in frustration.

The bright sunlight glinted off the Lockheed C-130E/H Hercules, the C-9A Nightingales, and the C-141B Starlifters as they taxied slowly across the tarmac to their loading positions. The air was filled with the sound of strained voices shouting through loudspeakers as they tried to herd the thousands of civilians into orderly queues. The competing roar of high-powered engines made for an environment of high tension and frayed nerves. The 374th Aeromedical Evacuation Squadron and the 630th Air Mobility Support Squadron were in charge of the actual airlift for the evacuation, but the 374th Airlift Wing was responsible for ground control. Everybody involved in the everyday operation of Yokota Air Base, located twenty-eight miles northwest of Tokyo in the foothills of the Okutama Mountains, had been press-ganged into helping handle the crowds, from the recruits of the Airman Leadership School to the services divisions of the Samurai Café and the Tama Lodge. Many were young, most were inexperienced at crowd control, and all were armed.

Maurice Higgins felt his anger rising to the limits of his ability to control it. The pushing and shoving was driving him crazy, and he knew he was near breaking point. The smartass just in front of him wasn't helping any, either, spouting off his knowledge of military affairs to everyone who would listen. Who gave a damn whether the seats on the Nightingales and Starlifters faced the front or back anyway, for God's sake? *Jerk!*

Higgins, his wife, and his four-year-old daughter were trapped in the middle of a massive queue of Americans and Japanese leading from the gates of the base to a large gray tent that had been set up for administrative and baggage check-in purposes four hundred yards away. At the pace the queue was moving, Higgins knew that they would have to endure at least another five hours of shuffling along with other people's baggage banging up against his legs, listening to ex–air force grunts spouting out garbage the whole time. And even when they finally managed to get aboard and airborne, they still had the prolonged indignity of quarantine to face once they reached American soil.

Sachiko, Higgins's Japanese wife, viewed his pursed lips and scarlet neck with trepidation. She recognized the signs of a major confrontation, but was powerless to do anything. Maurice was a good husband and father under normal circumstances, but once his blood started boiling, there was no safety valve other than to just let him rip. It was nearly six weeks since his last rampage, and that time he had overturned a table in an Italian restaurant in Roppongi and broken two of the waiter's teeth for providing bad service and lousy food. Sachiko decided that it would be better to wait on the peripheral edge of the queue until the storm had blown itself out. Their daughter, Monica, was only knee-high to the milling crowd, and she could be in danger of being trampled if Maurice started any trouble. Firmly grasping Monica's hand, she began to edge her way through the hordes of people until they were standing out in the open.

And not a moment too soon. She heard her husband's voice raised in sarcastic anger above the whining aircraft engines and general hullabaloo.

"Hey, asshole! Why don't you just shut your mouth! I don't give a shit about you or this damn base. All I wanna do is get on one of those planes and get my ass out of here. D'ya hear?"

"Screw you, pal!"

Sachiko winced. That was certainly not the way to appeal to Maurice's better feelings. She heard her husband's roar, closely followed by a squeal of rage emitted from the unwitting antagonist, and an erratic wave began to work its way out from the center of the trouble in ever-increasing circles, like a stone dropped into a bowl of mercury. Sachiko pulled Monica back out of trouble's way as the crowd expanded outward. She was furious with Maurice for causing trouble on this day of all days and stood back tapping her foot on the asphalt in anger. Didn't the stupid slob realize how traumatic this all was for her? She was being forced to leave the country of her birth without even saying good-bye to her parents to go and live abroad for God knew how long, and all he could think about was the inconvenience of having to queue up before being allowed on the airplane. All those company-paid first class tickets on his business trips had spoiled him. They had turned him into the selfish baby boomer that he himself had always proclaimed to despise. *Blast him!*

The sound of footsteps behind revealed a dozen young airmen rushing to the scene to break up the fight. It was the fifth fight of the day, and they were getting used to it.

Sachiko felt a tap on her shoulder and looked up into the face of a staff sergeant. "May I see your identification, ma'am?"

"My identification? Yes, of course." She took her passport out of her bag and handed it across.

"This is a Japanese passport, ma'am. Do you have an American passport?"

"No, I don't. I never bothered having one issued."

"I'm afraid I'll have to ask you to leave, ma'am. Only American nationals are allowed through onto the aircraft."

A twinge of fear hit Sachiko. Maurice had all of their papers, but he was obviously still busy, if the noise coming from the center of the crowd was anything to go by. "My husband is American," she said hastily. "He has our marriage certificate and all other papers."

"And where is your husband at this moment, ma'am?"

"He is in the crowd there. He is involved in the fight."

The staff sergeant looked skeptical. He had been warned to be on the lookout for unqualified Japanese nationals trying to party-crash the evacuation, and this woman's story seemed just a little too pat. "Well, he can come and find us when he's finished. Would you come with me, please, ma'am?"

"But why? What have I done?" Panic had begun to creep into Sachiko's voice. Her husband would kill her if they had to join the back of the queue again. "I'll get separated from my husband if I go with you."

"Looks like you're separated already, lady." The respect had disappeared from the staff sergeant's voice and been replaced with a curtness that openly displayed his suspicions. "Now follow me."

"Please just wait a moment until he comes. He won't be long, I promise."

Monica, picking up on her mother's distress, began to cry and clung to Sachiko's leg.

"I won't ask you again, lady!" The sergeant grabbed Sachiko's upper arm in a firm grip and began marching her briskly over to the gate. "And shut that damned bambino up! She's driving me crazy!"

Maurice Higgins was frog-marched out of the crowd by three airmen, one on each arm and one carrying his suitcase. He was disheveled, had blood dripping from his nose, and was panting heavily. Once they were ten yards away from the queue, the airmen released him and spun him around. The one with the suitcase dropped it and held a stern finger under his nose. "You are one lucky fella. If anybody had been hurt in that circus, I would have had to book you. You hear what I'm saying?" Without waiting for a reply, the airman pushed his face close to Higgins's. "Another squeak out of you, pal, and you're out of here. You understand me?"

Higgins nodded and straightened his coat. He knew when he was beaten, and he didn't want to lose the chance of getting a flight out today. "Sure, I understand. I'm sorry. I just got a little worked up, that's all. It won't happen again."

"You're damned right it won't."

With a final menacing stare, the airmen walked off, leaving Higgins to look around for Sachiko and Monica. He scanned the entire area, but couldn't see them anywhere. He walked back to the crowd and asked a few people if they had seen them. Nobody had.

Collecting his suitcase from the place where the airman had dropped it, Higgins began to walk around in aimless circles, searching everywhere for a glimpse of his wife and child. He could feel his anger rising again. If the bitch was keeping out of his way deliberately to make a statement on how she felt about his involvement in the fracas, he would be very mad indeed.

"Maurice!"

The voice was faint, but he had definitely heard it.

"*Maurice!*"

There it was again! He swung around in the direction of the gates and caught sight of someone in a red coat scuffling with a uniform. Sachiko was wearing a red coat. He began to run, discarding the suitcase, as it hindered his movement. His wife was only about one hundred yards distant, but it seemed to take forever for him to get there. He saw Monica being handed out of the gate into the arms of one of the Japanese policemen, her face screwed up and her tiny fists jammed into her eye sockets. Sachiko was still struggling with the uniform, desperately trying to avoid being pushed through the gates. The guy in the uniform was getting fed up with her. Higgins was still ten yards away when the man grabbed her by the shoulders and slammed her into the gate, her head jerking backward and striking the metal. She sagged to her knees, but the uniform immediately pulled her to her feet, her head lolling to one side like a rag doll's.

Higgins was seething, his peripheral vision clouded over with a red veil of rage. He sprinted the last few yards and launched himself onto the back of the uniform. The staff sergeant staggered forward and tried to turn around to see what had hit him, but before he could, Higgins had passed an arm around his neck and thrown him backward over onto the hard and unsympathetic ground. The moment he was on his back, Higgins jumped on top of him, closed his fingers around his throat, and began to bang his head rhythmically against the hard concrete. Two other airmen came running and tried to pull Higgins off, but his grip on the man's throat was too firm and all they succeeded in doing was to contribute to the sergeant's misery.

"Get him off me! Shoot the bastard!" the sergeant wheezed through pain-distorted lips. "Shoot him quickly!"

Airman First Class Jeff Konowalchuk unshipped his M-16 from his shoulder, checked that it was set to single shot, and slipped off the safety catch. "Move away from that man or I'll shoot!" he ordered. "Now, mister!"

But Higgins was not in the mood for taking orders. In fact, he didn't even hear it, so engrossed was he in destroying the person who had dared to lift a finger against his wife and child. Releasing one of his hands from around his victim's throat, Higgins brought his arm back and smashed a fist into the sergeant's face.

"I'm warning you! This is your last chance! Get off that man or I'll shoot!"

Higgins hit the sergeant once more, and Monica Higgins, five years old on her next birthday, was forced to witness a scene that would haunt her dreams for the rest of her life: the tragic and unnecessary execution of her own father.

"Where will you go?"

"I'm not sure yet. That's one of the things that is really worrying me at the moment. It would be foolish to stay in Tokyo, but that is where the mystery caller is, and it's probably not a good idea to move too far away from him."

Mike Woodson kicked at a small pebble and watched it tumble down the side of the grass bank before looking up and squinting into the sunlight reflected back from the Tama River twenty meters distant. "Any leads as to his whereabouts yet?"

"Two small ones. I have his e-mail address, which I can use if all else fails. I haven't used it yet for fear of alienating him. I don't want to scare him off. There is also a chance he will be moving out to the Izu peninsula sometime in the near future to stay with friends. I guess I could follow him down there, but it will mean passing through the infected area, and as I have no transport, I am a bit worried about that. The trains are still running, but I don't want to catch this disease myself."

"I've brought some drugs to protect you, but we're not sure if they work or not. You'd better not risk exposing yourself to the bug in case they don't, Peter."

Peter Bryant nodded and watched a C-9A Nightingale claw

its way slowly into the sky from Yokota Air Base three miles to the east. "How's the evacuation going?"

"As well as can be expected, I guess. The biggest problem is that most of the Americans who live in Japan are concentrated in the Kanto area, so Yokota and Yokosuka are getting the brunt of it. They have started ferrying some of the people out to other locations in the UH-1N helicopters to ease the congestion, but that is likely to take forever."

"What about you and Carol? When will you leave?"

"The day after tomorrow. There's a priority list for embassy staff evacuation, and I'm not very high up on it. I have to stay around until the end and help close down the embassy."

Bryant squatted down on the grass and nodded toward the two bags that Woodson had brought from the air base. One was made of corrugated steel, about the size of a small suitcase, and the other was a canvas zip-up bag. "They look heavy. I was hoping to travel light."

"You can probably discard the case. It is mostly padding to protect the computer and satellite phone from the air force, who love nothing better than to practice thirty-yard passes with things like this. The canvas bag is packed full of drugs—something called Rifampin. You'd better start taking it right away. You'll need four six-hundred-milligram doses taken orally every twelve hours. The instructions are typed on each pack in case you forget. Any that you don't need, give out to whomever you wish, but don't let them think it will make them immune to infection. Make sure that Michiyo and her family get some, if you can, but tell her to remove her contacts. This stuff stains body fluid orange and will screw up her lenses."

"Thanks, Mike. I appreciate it. You'd better show me how to operate the computer, as well."

Woodson sat down on the bank, hefted the steel case onto his lap, and slipped open the catches. The case contained fitted foam padding into which a laptop computer and an iridium satellite telephone were imbedded. He pulled out the telephone first. It looked like any other cellular telephone, but a thicker-than-normal battery pack on the back ran the entire length of the unit, and the knob on the end of the aerial was bulbous and had a diameter about the size of a coat button. "A satellite phone. We don't know how long the telephone system will survive this upheaval, but whatever happens, this baby will make sure you can contact us." He removed a small yellow wire-bound notepad from his pocket and tossed it across to Bryant, who caught it deftly. "Every number you need is written in there in order of priority, although I have already programmed all of them into the phone for convenience's sake. If you can't get through to the first number, try the second. If the second doesn't work, then go on to the third, et cetera. In case the notepad falls into somebody else's hands, the first three words you must say whenever you ring any of these numbers are 'bright light rubies.' Got that?" Bryant nodded. "If you don't start off with those three words, the line will be disconnected immediately. We sort of figured that no matter how well a Japanese person learns the English language, they are always going to get caught up on those Rs and Ls and tip us off; hence 'bright light rubies.' "

"Sneaky."

Woodson replaced the telephone inside the case and pulled out the computer. "This will be your main means of communication. It's thin, light, and extremely durable. It works in much the same way as any other computer, but has been set up so the communication screen is displayed immediately. The satellite telephone plugs in here." He indicated a socket at the back of the case. "When you want to type out a message, all you have to do is press this icon to display the text-input screen. You can save the file under any name you want and it will appear here on the right-hand side. To send it through to us, highlight the file and press the send button. The computer will automatically compress the file, telephone the correct number, and 'squirt' it up at the satellite before hanging up.

To receive messages independently, simply hit the receive button. Otherwise, messages will be automatically downloaded if they exist when you send. It's as simple as that."

"What about the browser I asked for? I have managed to get hold of the mystery caller's e-mail address. I'll need that to contact him."

"Man, you have been busy. I'm impressed. It's this icon here. The machine will automatically dial you into the Internet whenever you start up the browser. From there you will be able to surf the Net just like you were sitting at home. The connection will be cut off when you end the program."

Bryant stared at the screen for a moment longer before nodding his understanding. "Seems simple enough."

"I've written a brief set of instructions into this file here." Woodson indicated a file on the screen with his forefinger. "If you get stuck on anything, just open the file and it will tell you everything you need to know."

Bryant packed the computer back into the case and snapped the lid shut. He sat down on the grass next to Woodson and stared across the river. "I guess that's about it, then."

"I guess it is."

Neither of the men wanted to end this final meeting. A wave of loneliness swept over Bryant, and he wondered, not for the first time, if he were doing the right thing.

Woodson picked up on Bryant's thoughts and said, "What made you decide to stay? Mitch?"

"Yeah, although there is something more that I can't explain. If it had only been Mitch, I would have gone with her to Fukushima and stayed well out of harm's way. I just feel, well, sort of responsible in a way. I don't even know if I will be of any use, but I feel that I owe it to Japan to try. Does that make sense?"

"Not in the least."

Bryant chuckled. "It doesn't to me, either. It may sound corny, but this country is just so full of nice people, and I hate to see it destroyed in this way. If staying in contact with the mystery caller will help bring an end to these atrocities, I can't just turn a blind eye. I have to do everything I can."

Woodson placed a hand gently on Bryant's back. "I understand, Peter, and I commend you for the decision. I just hope everything works out all right."

"You think it won't?"

"I don't know, Peter. I really don't. My heart keeps telling me that everything will end up well, but when I read the figures, logic tells me that it's going to need a miracle to get this country back on its feet again."

"What are the figures?"

"Five hundred and forty thousand dead, and maybe double that number infected. It's spreading like wildfire."

"Jesus . . ."

"I have to get back to the embassy." Woodson slapped his hands on his knees and stood up. He extended a hand to Bryant and pulled him to his feet. "You take care, buddy. You hear?"

Bryant nodded, suddenly feeling like the last guest left at a party. "Sure. You too."

Woodson grabbed Bryant by the shoulders and pulled him into a hug, his right hand slapping gently on his back. "I'll see you back in Washington," he said softly, "I'll make sure those frosties are lined up right along the bar."

"I'll hold you to that. See you, Mike."

"Good-bye, Peter."

Bryant turned and picked up the two bags. He looked over his shoulder, winked once, and then started walking along the grass bank to the station and his train back into Tokyo.

Chapter Nine

Having returned to Tokyo after his final meeting with Mike Woodson, Peter Bryant spent the rest of the afternoon lying on the tatami in his room, trying to formulate his next plan of action. He knew the Otsukas were intending to join their friends up in Izu Kogen in the near future, so he had to think of something before the end of the day. Not a pleasant prospect. Although they had not said anything specific, he had somehow received the impression that they would have left today had it not been for him, and he was feeling a slight twinge of guilt. He considered asking them if they would allow him to stay on at the inn unchaperoned after their departure, but he decided that such a request would be difficult for them to refuse and certainly not fair under the circumstances. They had been too kind already, and he didn't want to spoil the relationship they had built up over the past twenty hours. On the other hand, maybe they would be able to suggest somewhere else that he could stay. He would be of no use to the U.S. government whatsoever camping out on the streets and providing a perfect target for the muggers and looters that abounded.

A knock on the wooden door frame was followed by the door sliding open. Toshio Otsuka stood in the doorway with an expectant and somewhat out-of-character look of seriousness on his face. "May I?" he asked.

"Of course, Otsuka-*san*. Please come on in."

Bryant hastily got to his feet and retrieved a flat *zabuton* cushion from a small pile by the wall. He laid it on the floor in front of the table and invited Otsuka to sit down. A moment later Harumi Otsuka brought in a pot of green tea and then mysteriously left the room with a brief but seemingly sympathetic smile. Bryant began to feel a premonition of bad tidings. Otsuka poured the tea and pushed one of the cups toward Bryant, who was sitting on a cushion on the opposite side of the table.

"I have been in contact with Gakusha and Totchan," said Otsuka after taking a sip of the hot tea. "Gakusha is the joint owner of our *besso* in Izu. I think I told you about him."

Bryant nodded.

"We had a very interesting conversation, Mr. Bryant. Totchan told us all about you."

"All about me? What do you mean?" Bryant's premonition of bad tidings burgeoned, and he began to feel slightly uncomfortable. Otsuka was displaying no animosity—in fact, he seemed as congenial as ever, if not more so—but if the mystery caller had mentioned the death threats, he was probably working himself up to throw Bryant out of the inn to protect himself, his wife, and his livelihood.

"I hear people have tried to kill you." *Damn!* So he would be on his own earlier than expected. "That is terrible. My wife wept when she heard that. Apparently you were injured, too. Are you still hurt?"

"No, I'm fine, thank you. That was over a week ago. Just a few minor aches and pains remaining, that's all." Bryant looked down at his hands spread on the table before him, like a naughty schoolboy being interviewed by the headmaster. "Look, I'm sorry. I should have told you, I know. I could have brought danger to your home, and that is unforgivable. I'll leave immediately. And please accept my deepest apologies."

"Tomorrow will be soon enough," Otsuka said kindly. "Nobody knows you are here yet. There is no immediate rush."

Bryant looked up into Otsuka's eyes, detecting something in the man's tone of voice. What was it? Concern? Compassion? Sympathy? A mixture of all three? "That is very kind of you, Otsuka-*san*. I appreciate it very much."

"You are welcome, Mr. Bryant. Totchan also mentioned that you were in contact with the American government to help overcome this disease that we are afflicted with. A sort of secret agent or spy."

Bryant lowered his eyes again and nodded. It was the first time he had heard himself referred to as a spy, but once he thought about it, that was exactly the role he was playing.

"He said that you were a normal office clerk who was placing himself in grave danger simply to help us out. A man of indescribable moral conscience from whom we all had something to learn."

Bryant raised his eyes, surprise outlining his features. He had never expected such good press from Kagemusha, and he felt a glowing warmth. "He said that?"

"And more." Otsuka fumbled in his pocket and brought out a sheet of paper folded into four. He laid it on the table and pushed it across toward Bryant. "This is an e-mail message addressed to you from Totchan."

Bryant reached out for the paper and unfolded it. Raising quizzical eyes to Otsuka and receiving an encouraging nod in return, he read through the message briskly, his mouth dropping open in wonder, and then read it again.

Dear Mr. Bryant,
    I have been considering your situation and have de-

cided to do everything within my power to help you. Unfortunately, Japan is incapable of sorting out this problem alone, and I believe we should welcome the assistance of the United States. As I mentioned on the telephone the other day, I will be leaving Tokyo soon to stay with some friends. One of these friends is the person who just gave you this message, somebody I refer to as Omotenashi, but whom you will know under a different name. He speaks very highly of you, and I am now convinced that your motives are pure and that you are interested only in finding a cure for the meningococcemia disease. I know you have many questions to ask me about the bacterium, and I am willing to provide you with any information I have if it will further the efforts of the American government.

I have discussed the matter with my friends, and we have decided to invite you out to Izu Kogen to stay with us. We will be in contact with many people throughout the entire country and will therefore be able to supply you with the details you need on local conditions on a much wider scale than you were originally considering. Omotenashi will be leaving for Izu tomorrow, and I respectfully ask you to accompany him. You will be safe with us and will accomplish much more than you will on your own.

I hope you will accept. I myself intend to arrive in a couple of days, and I look forward to seeing you then.

Your friend,
Kagemusha

Bryant was dumbstruck. He read through the message for a third time, a look of total disbelief spread across his features. Kagemusha had come through for him again. With a simple message, he had solved all of Bryant's problems and instilled him with a confidence that he had not expected to experience anytime in the near future. With the benefit of hindsight, Bryant realized that his most pressing anxiety had been a fear of not being able to provide the U.S. authorities with the information they needed and being denounced for a fraud. Simple reports on dead bodies floating in Kanda River would do absolutely nothing to further their cause, and he had even passed his mind over fabricating certain harmless details into his reports to make it seem as if he were earning his keep. Ridiculous, he knew, but every man had his pride, and Bryant was no exception. He looked up at Otsuka incredulously. "But this is . . . this is just . . . I don't know what to say. . . ."

"But you will accept, won't you, Mr. Bryant?"

"Well, yes, thank you. Of course I'll accept, Otsuka-*san*! You've no idea what a relief this is to me!" He reached over the table, clasped Otsuka's right hand in both of his own, and shook heartily. "I didn't have a clue what to do after leaving here, but now I have a clear itinerary. It's wonderful!"

"*Hoy!*" Otsuka managed to free his hand from Bryant's grasp and shouted for his wife, but before his voice had died out, the door to the room slid open and Harumi Otsuka, a huge and delighted grin spreading across her face, entered with a tray bearing a large bottle of Gekkeikan and three small china cups. Otsuka frowned at her. "Listening at the door, eh?" He turned back to Bryant. "What shall be done with nosy women, Mr. Bryant, eh?"

Harumi was not perturbed. "Well, what did you expect me to do? Sit in the kitchen and wait for your call? Anyway, I knew Bryant-*san* would not refuse, and I wanted to be prepared."

"Well, you certainly *are* prepared," Bryant said with a laugh, "But I don't think I could handle a drink at the moment. It's still the middle of the afternoon. The tea is fine for me."

"Nonsense! We must celebrate. You are now an honorary member of the Zen Nippon Otaku Tomonokai!"

"The *what?*"

"The Zen Nippon Otaku Tomonokai, although we usually

211

call it the Tomonokai for short. That's the name of the Internet bulletin board owned by Gakusha."

"I see. But, *otaku?*" Loosely translated, the Zen Nippon Otaku Tomonokai meant the All Japan Nerds' Friendship Society, although *otaku* could also be translated as *geek, fanatic,* or *maniac,* none of which appealed greatly to Bryant's Western sensibilities. He would have to figure a way of sending this piece of information across to Washington without turning himself into a laughingstock. He could just imagine the look on Mike Woodson's face when Bryant announced that he was an honorary nerd.

"That's what everybody calls people who enjoy playing about with computers and the Internet," Harumi explained, mistakenly assuming that Bryant's question indicated that he did not understand the meaning of the word. "It's mostly used for young people, but we thought it was rather applicable. Come, come, here's your cup."

Bryant accepted the cup and allowed Toshio Otsuka to fill it to the brim with cold sake.

Once the toast had been made and everybody had clinked cups together, Toshio Otsuka said, "Tell me, Mr. Bryant, do you really think the American authorities will be able to discover a cure for this awful disease?"

"Frankly, I have no idea. The only thing I do know is that they will leave no stone unturned in their effort to try."

"That is so nice of them," Harumi said. "Why would they be so concerned over us when the Japanese government does nothing?"

"To tell the truth, I think you'll find that they are more interested in protecting their own economy, and helping Japan just happens to fit into that scenario."

"Oh, no! I'm sure you are mistaken, Bryant-*san.*"

"Don't get me wrong. I'm sure they would help anyway, but the state of the American economy helps increase the priority level."

"Well, we must all be grateful for that and do everything we can to help. How long have you been a spy?"

Bryant nearly choked over his sake. "For about three hours, actually. Although I have yet to start my official duties."

"I must say, you don't look much like a spy. How did you get the job?"

"*Hoy, hoy*, Harumi," interrupted Toshio, glaring at his wife. "Leave the poor man alone. I'm sure you'll get to understand everything about him over the next few weeks, so don't bother him with all of your questions now. Shouldn't you be getting dinner ready or preparing for our departure or something? Leave the man in peace."

Harumi poked her tongue out and pouted, but stayed where she was.

"I don't mind answering your questions," said Bryant diplomatically, not wanting to be the cause of a marital tiff. "Anything you want to know, please just go ahead and ask."

"There, you see? Such a nice man. Are you married, Bryant-*san*?"

"Enough!" Toshio banged his open palm on the table. "We have more important things to speak about. I'm sure Mr. Bryant wants to know everything about the Tomonokai and Izu Kogen. Isn't that right, Mr. Bryant?"

"Well, yes, I suppose I do, but I am quite happy to answer any questions you have about me. And please call me Peter."

Toshio raised his hand to halt the question that was about to spring from Harumi's lips. "You live dangerously, Peter-*san*," he said with a chuckle. "By the time we get to Izu Kogen tomorrow, I can assure you that my wife will know every single detail of your life, including how often you wash your underwear."

"And why not?" said Bryant, raising his cup in a salute to friendship. "We are now all spies together and should know everything about each other."

"Spies?" The look of wonder on Harumi's face displayed her

appreciation of this idea. "You're right. I suppose we are. . . ."

"And before you ask, Harumi-*san*, washed once a week, but changed every day."

Free Fall Continues in the Global Meltdown

Hong Kong (AP) Markets around the world continued to plummet Thursday as Japan's doors to the rest of the world were closed and Moody's Investors Service, Inc., downgraded the Japanese government's rating level from Baa3 to E plus. This marked the second downgrade in just one week after Japan was cut to the Baa3 rating from the highest Aaa rating last Friday in the wake of financial turmoil caused by the meningococcemia outbreak. Other Asian countries struggled to cope with the vacuum left behind by this, but all efforts seem to have had little effect. By the time trading ended in Asia and began once again in Europe, it was clear that the free fall had yet to reach its peak.

In Hong Kong, the Hang Seng index dropped 52.20 points in the first fifteen minutes of trading and remained in negative territory throughout the entire session to close 124.63 points, or 2.3 percent, lower at 6,865.62. Trading volume reached an all-time high of Hong Kong $79 billion (US $10.13 billion,) but 80 percent of this was estimated to be government buying in its weeklong battle to prop up the local stock and stock futures markets, as well as to punish speculators.

In Singapore, the benchmark Straits Times Industrial index crashed through the crucial 900-point level to end the day at 834.36.

Worries over the health of Thailand's financial institutions also saw a drop of 23.18 points in the Stock Exchange of Thailand index to 221.42.

The Kuala Lumpur Stock Exchange's Composite index

fell 32.62 points to 411.58, its lowest close in twelve years.

In other parts of the world, the Dow Jones industrial average in New York tumbled more than five percent Thursday to 8,106.65 as the United States government closed all flights in and out of Japan. On the New York Stock Exchange, declining issues swamped advances 2,988 to 244 on heavy volume of 936 million shares. The technology-heavy Nasdaq Composite reflected these tendencies with an 81.72-point, or 4.6 percent, decline to 1,574.63. The Russell 2000 index, which tracks small companies, was the hardest hit of all indexes as investors fled to the safety of larger, seemingly safe havens, such as IBM, General Electric, and other blue-chip issues. It had fallen 18.61 to 302.17 by the end of the day's trading.

In Frankfurt, the Xetra DAX index plunged 6.4 percent to 4,236.32. In other European bourses, the London FTSE 100 index also dropped 5 percent to end the day at 4,948.6.

The only area that seems to be benefiting from this turmoil is bonds, as money sought out safety and continued to pour into U.S. government securities. The thirty-year Treasury bond, which moves in the opposite direction of prices, soared to its lowest level since regular issuance was started in 1977. The Bellwether bond was up $11.87 on a $1,000 bond to yield 5.34 percent.

Toshio Otsuka drove the white Toyota past the Izu Kogen station and then turned right to take them up into the mountains beyond. The crisp March air provided excellent visibility, and Bryant was able to see Mount Omuro in its entirety through the front windscreen. Its steeply sloping sides and flattened peak made it resemble a gigantic loaf of bread, but it lent the area a touch of dignity as it majestically watched over its domain with solid and reassuring immobility. They drove in silence, all conversational threads having been exhausted long before as they had driven through the affected area and been rendered speechless by the sights that had met them. None had wanted proof of the extent of the outbreak, but they had been unable to avoid it and had been taken unawares. Even Harumi Otsuka, whose nonstop chatter and endless questions had amused Bryant enormously on the drive between Tabata and the coast of Kanagawa, was subdued and silent, content to reflect on the conversation that continued within her own mind.

Ten minutes later, the car turned right onto a small country lane and continued for two hundred meters before coming to a halt outside a timber-frame house with a neatly trimmed lawn. The front door of the house opened and a middle-aged couple walked out onto the wooden deck, followed immediately by a brown-and-white corgi, which dashed across the lawn toward the car as if chased by a pack of wolves.

Bryant waited in the background until the two sets of friends had completed their greetings—pretending to busy himself with removing the luggage from the trunk—before walking across the lawn and up the steps to the deck.

"Mr. Bryant," exclaimed Norio Kondo, his hand outstretched as Bryant neared. "I have heard much about you from our mutual friend, and you are welcome in my house. This is my wife, Shigeko."

"Gakusha-san. I have also heard much about you from Mr. and Mrs. Otsuka. Thank you for the invitation to stay. It is my fervent hope that I can be of use."

Inside the house, Bryant was shown upstairs to his room and invited down for coffee as soon as he had settled in and taken the shower that he had requested. Thirty minutes later, refreshed and with damp hair, he walked into the front room and found Norio Kondo and Toshio Otsuka sitting on the floor around a low table in the adjacent eight-tatami-mat room.

"Ah, Mr. Bryant. Please come and join us. Coffee?"

"Yes, please. Thank you very much."

Bryant took his seat at the table and looked around the room with curiosity while Kondo went to the kitchen to request an additional cup of coffee. Apart from the table, it was completely devoid of furniture, and the focus of the room was on the vase of flowers and hanging calligraphic scroll within the *tokonoma*—a small floor-level alcove stretching up to the ceiling approximately one meter wide and sixty centimeters deep at the back of the room. The windows were concealed behind latticework screens covered in white *washi* paper that diffused the outside sunlight and created a warm and intimate atmosphere within the small room.

"It's beautiful," said Bryant, accepting his coffee from Kondo. "I love the scroll. It does say '*oikaze*,' doesn't it?"

"You read Japanese as well, Mr. Bryant? You are a very talented man. Yes, *oikaze*, or tailwind. It is a pet fantasy of mine to consider myself carried along by the wind and never lagging behind. To take opportunity when it arrives without actively seeking it out. The simplicity of the concept appeals to me greatly. I have no ambitions to lead any field, just to keep up when developments are made and not be left behind. To run with the wind, not try to outpace it."

"That is fascinating."

"Not really. I am basically a very boring man who just likes to justify his existence by speaking grandly. That scroll was, in fact, presented to me by our mutual friend, along with the suggestion that I make more of my life." Kondo grinned mischievously, lifted himself slightly off his cushion, and broke wind loudly. "And that, I'm afraid, is about the only tailwind we will find in Japan until we help you and your government sort out our problems."

Bryant's obvious surprise delighted Kondo. Kondo laughed aloud and slapped his knee. Toshio Otsuka groaned and placed his hand over his eyes.

"Oh, Peter-*san*, you played right into his hands," said Otsuka. "Nobody escapes the *oikaze* joke, but usually Gakusha has

217

to bring the subject up himself. It still amazes me how he manages to control the timing."

"Discipline and training, my friend. Something that you will never understand." Kondo turned his attention to Bryant. "Now, Mr. Bryant, I'm sure you have many questions to ask. What can I tell you?"

On reflection, Bryant realized that he didn't have many questions at all. Toshio Otsuka had already given him a rough outline of the Zen Nippon Otaku Tomonokai, and, not being a stranger to Internet communications himself, he had picked up the concept readily and without problem. He understood that the idea was for all of the Tomonokai members spread throughout the country to send in daily updates on local conditions, and Bryant would correlate these into a cohesive report for sending to Washington. The members would also be encouraged to search the Internet for any relevant information that could be of use and pass it on.

"Well, first of all, I'd appreciate it if you would call me Peter."

"Fine. Peter-*san* it is."

"Otsuka-*san* has already explained the workings of the Tomonokai, so there's not a great deal more I need to know. My government has asked me to pass on details of conditions within Japan, and if the members could help me with that, then I should not cause you too much trouble. Apart from that, my questions at the moment are minimal."

"Our mutual friend mentioned that you will be wanting to question him on certain matters as well. May I ask which matters?"

Bryant paused. He didn't know exactly how much information the others had on the mystery caller and wasn't sure if they knew of his connections to Hamada Seiyaku Pharmaceuticals. He didn't want to let the cat out of the bag if Totchan was trying to keep this a secret.

Before he could speak, Kondo said, "Totchan told me that

you worked together in Hamada Seiyaku. Can I presume that the questions you need to ask are related to the epidemic?"

Bryant smiled gratefully. "Yes, that's right. My people in Washington will be sending me a list of the questions that they'd like him to answer to help them come up with some sort of cure. They already have a team working on the problem, but there appear to be several points on which they are unclear. They are hoping that Totchan will be able to help. Which reminds me . . ." Bryant knew he was pushing his luck, but curiosity was burning a hole in his gut. "Do you know Totchan's real identity yourself?"

"Yes, I do."

Bryant took his chance. "You have referred to Totchan as 'our mutual friend' on several occasions, and also just said that he and I worked together. It may sound strange, but I'm still not perfectly clear on who, exactly, Totchan is. Would it be possible for you to let me know his real name?"

Kondo looked at his watch. "Mm, fifty-five minutes. Totchan said that you'd probably ask that sometime within the first hour, and he just got his nose under the wire. A very impressive man indeed. Unfortunately, Peter-*san*, Totchan has specifically asked me not to tell you. He wants to surprise you himself."

"But why?"

"I have no idea, but I get the impression that he is looking forward to it very much indeed, and he obviously thinks that you will be completely astounded. Why, I don't know. But surely you must have some idea. If you worked together with the man, you must have your suspicions."

But he hadn't. He had racked his brains for many hours to come up with somebody who fit the mold of the mystery caller, but it could have been anybody. However, now that Kondo had suggested he would be astounded to discover the identity of Totchan, that probably meant that it was someone Bryant knew relatively well, not just someone with whom he shared a nodding acquaintance. His first thought was Joji Higashino, but he quickly discarded it. Joji, although perfectly capable of passing information down a telephone line and maintaining contact with a bunch of Internet addicts, was not close enough to the top of the tree to be in possession of the information the mystery caller had so liberally scattered about. It had to be somebody who had access to the minutes of the directors meetings, and that ruled Joji out. In any case, Bryant was sure he would be able to recognize Joji's voice on the telephone, no matter how much he tried to disguise it. No, it had to be somebody else. But who would have access to the minutes of the meetings? The president's three secretaries, all of the sixteen directors' secretaries, plus any of the maintenance staff in the computer section who, he presumed, would be able to check the contents of any file within the system. He could rule out the women. Whatever his traits, there was no doubt that Totchan was male. Even his on-line handle—Totchan—proclaimed his gender. Totchan was an affectionate name for *father*, not dissimilar to the American *pa*. Well, that would narrow it down to four people—three in the computer section and one of the president's secretaries—but apart from a brief conversation with the president's secretary at the previous year's *bonenkai* party, he didn't know any of these people. Certainly not enough to be "astounded" when they stood revealed. He shrugged his shoulders and looked across at Kondo. "No, I don't. I can whittle it down to a few contenders, but none who seem to fit the bill."

"Then you are in for a shock tomorrow. Totchan informs me that he will arrive sometime in the afternoon, so you have only one more day to suffer."

"I shall look forward to it."

Shigeko Kondo poked her head around the edge of the door frame and cleared her throat. The three men looked up at her expectantly.

"If you have finished with the *oikaze* routine, one of you

might come and help me carry in some supplies from the garage."

Prime Minister Kiyoshi Aizawa sat at his desk and stamped his personal *inkan* seal onto the top sheet of a wad of documents. He had claimed the State Ministers' room on the second floor of the west-central section of the Diet Building as his own and had had a cot set up in one corner so the room could act as both an office and as sleeping quarters. His cabinet ministers had been allocated smaller offices/sleeping quarters in the First Members' office buildings, but the other staff members deemed necessary to run the nation had not been afforded the luxury of individual quarters. They were currently sharing cramped sleeping conditions in the five House of Representatives committee rooms and the eight other committee rooms located in the annex building. Both the Members' Office buildings, of which there were three, and the annex building were connected to the diet by underground passageways.

Construction of the National Diet Building was completed in November 1936, and it had been used as the seat of national parliament ever since the seventieth session of the imperial diet had convened in 1937. Standing three stories high, with one basement level and a 65.45-meter domelike tower dominating the central structure, the building exuded an aura of history, pomp, and majesty.

Aizawa liked the historical atmosphere of the building and still fondly recalled the first convocation day after his election to the House of Representatives some thirty years before, when he had walked through the great bronze doors of the central entrance and been presented with his buttonhole pin. He remembered staring up at the statues of Hirobumi Ito, Shigenobu Okuma, and Taisuke Itagaki in the central hall and wondering if his career would ever culminate in a statue of himself being placed among such venerated company. Now he knew the answer.

221

Never in a million years!

For Aizawa was under no illusions as to how history would record his tenure. In a mere twenty-six days, Japan had been transformed from a prosperous and powerful supereconomy into a crime-ridden and near-bankrupt collection of dysfunctional autonomous bodies, and there was no doubt that he would be assigned the blame for this. Eighteen of Japan's forty-seven prefectures were already in a state of near-crisis as people stayed away from work and the basic lifeline infrastructure began to systematically break down. Agricultural produce was rotting in warehouses, shops were not being restocked with basic necessities, and power cuts were affecting the areas that relied on fossil fuels for electricity and had yet to be plugged into the national grid. The Self-Defense ground forces were helping out by manning the telephone exchanges, nuclear power plants, and water supply facilities, but the logistics involved in getting the men to the right places and then making sure they had sufficient rudimentary training to take over the jobs of the absentees erected further obstacles to coping with the situation. Hyperinflation was also a burgeoning problem. As more and more shops closed their doors, the black market was the only place where people could obtain the food and supplies they needed, and prices were shooting through the ceiling. That wouldn't last for much longer, however. Aizawa had put his stamp on an order for all banks and financial institutions to close their doors just that very day in order to halt the cash runs that were bringing the banks to their knees, but this would also provide an unexpected, albeit slightly cruel, bonus. Without access to their money, the populace would not be able to fuel the avarice of the black markets for very long. Aizawa hoped that this gambit would make the black marketeers reduce their prices or disappear completely and not simply result in good people going hungry. He supposed that a rationing system of some sorts would have to be worked out in the near future. He already had a small group of staff working on that problem.

The only good news that Aizawa had received all day was an indication that the carriage rates were dropping drastically. People were staying off the streets and avoiding all contact with other people, and this was having an enormous effect on hindering the spread of the epidemic. The estimated figures for the day had been more than thirty percent less than the projected rates—seven hundred and fifty thousand as opposed to one-point-one million—and this information punched into the desktop simulations had shown that similar rates of decline could be expected in the following weeks. *Thank God for small mercies!* The mounting death toll had placed Kanagawa prefecture in deadlock, and the rest of the Kanto region and the Kansai region would not be far behind if things were allowed to continue as they were. There were insufficient beds for the number of people who had contracted the disease, and the hospitals that did have the space were not equipped with the intensive-care facilities required to isolate the victims from other patients. Handling the corpses was also proving to be a huge job, as they remained biologically hazardous right up until the moment of cremation, and people in the private sector were refusing to have anything to do with them. Yet another job in an ever-lengthening list of chores for the Self-Defense Forces.

Aizawa flipped to the next stack of papers and began to scan through them briskly. They were summaries of the reactions recorded abroad since the announcement of a state of emergency and martial law. Predictably, all Southeast Asian countries—without exception—were unanimous in condemning Japan for its so-called warmongering. Riots had broken out in all major cities, and the Japanese embassies in a total of fourteen countries were currently under siege by picketers and demonstrators. Molotov cocktails appeared to be the weapons of choice, and already a large amount of property had been seriously damaged. The strongest reactions had, naturally, come from South Korea and North Korea. It was almost too surreal for words to imagine those two countries agreeing on a single issue, and yet here they were, issuing official comments that could have been penned by the same speechwriter. How ironic it was to think that that the problem had started through a fear of North Korea launching an invasion against Japan but had turned into a catalyst for bringing the two sworn enemies to agreement for the first time in more than half a century.

The prime minister removed his spectacles, laid them on his desk, and rubbed his eyes with the heels of his hands. He suddenly felt a craving for a drink—not whisky or any other spirit, but something light. A soothing glass of beer, maybe. Or even a glass of red wine. His working day had started well before five o'clock that morning, and it was now ten minutes past midnight. He knew that physical exhaustion would not help him function rationally under present conditions, but there was just so much to do. He couldn't *afford* to sleep. It was as simple as that. Mental exhaustion was also taking its toll. Shoji Kubota was facing him down on every issue in an attempt to impress his followers and to wash more sand out from beneath Aizawa's foundations, and despite the prime minister's avowal not to let this bother him, he was becoming increasingly exasperated over the frustration that it was generating. He had more important things to think about than internal party politics, but Kubota was not yet ready to let him off the hook. It was also beginning to turn personal. Kubota's focus had been taken completely off matters in hand and retuned into a single all-consuming objective that reeked of paranoia: to bring Aizawa down at all costs. Although here Aizawa was able to recognize that he could be accused of goading the man and was therefore not totally guilt-free himself. His attitude toward Kubota had become more and more sarcastic as the days had passed, and he now seemed to look forward to the opportunity of showing him up in public with an almost perverse sense of

enjoyment. But, when viewed realistically, that was simply prolonging the amount of time required for the government to
apply itself to the huge number of outstanding problems, and
he knew he must make a serious attempt to control himself.
Maybe it was time to throw down the olive branch. Would
Kubota accept a truce if it were worded correctly? Although
pigheaded and puffed up with his own importance, he was nev-
ertheless a public servant and could not overlook a plea for
help to save the country from complete and utter ruin. At the
very least, Aizawa felt that he should speak to the man and
see if he could appeal to his better instincts.

Aizawa reached a hand out for the telephone and rang
through to the aide on duty seated at a desk outside the door
to the State Ministers' room.

"Sir?"

"Get me a bottle of red wine and a bottle of brandy. Not
the Beaujolais Nouveau that they are still serving up in the
dining hall. That passed its peak two months ago. Something
warmer, more mellow."

"Yes, sir."

"And ask the secretary general if he would mind coming to
see me for a few minutes, would you? Tell him it's important."

"Yes, sir. Right away, sir."

Aizawa sat back in his chair and shuffled the papers around
into three separate piles: those that he had already attended
to, those that required his perusal, and those that needed his
authorization stamp. He would work on those first thing in the
morning. Folding his hands behind his head, he leaned back
in the chair and stared up at one of the two chandeliers that
decorated the ceiling. He could feel his eyelids growing heavier
with fatigue and hoped that Kubota would not take too long
in coming. It would never do to be caught napping at his desk,
providing Kubota with even more ammunition for his snide
and hurtful remarks.

The knock at the door came six minutes later. Aizawa hurriedly smoothed down his hair and straightened his position in the chair. "Come in," he shouted.

The aide entered with a decanter of wine, a decanter of brandy, and two crystal glasses on a silver tray. He placed the tray on one of the round tables nearest to Aizawa's desk and bowed. "The secretary general sends his compliments, sir, but regrets that he is too busy to come at the moment. However, he suggests that you might like to visit him, if you have nothing better to do."

Seething inside, Aizawa declined the invitation and dismissed the aide. So that was how Kubota wanted to play it, was it? He walked around the desk and poured himself a large glass of wine, which he sipped gently, frantically trying to suppress his anger and concentrate on the slightly acidic taste of the grape.

Aizawa couldn't remember the last time he had been this angry. In his mind's eye, he saw Kubota at that moment, surrounded by his creeping minions and laughing heartily over his ready wit. *If you have nothing better to do.* Oh, that had hurt. That had really hurt.

But at least Aizawa was now clear on one thing: No matter how bad the state of the country became, Shoji Kubota would not be willing to call a truce.

So be it.

Peter Bryant placed his mobile telephone on the small table in his room and lay back on the floor. The room was comparatively small, but more than sufficient for his purposes, and even boasted a beautiful view across to Mount Omuro. The phone call he had just made had not been easy. Michiyo—her voice already picking up the rising inflections of the Fukushima accent, as it always did when she returned home for any length of time—had been mortified to hear that he would not be joining her in Aizu Wakamatsu, as originally planned. She had felt betrayed and had made no secret of this.

"But Peter," she had said, her voice raised in a plaintive whine, "you promised! You said you would be here within the week."

"I know I did, Mi-*chan*, but I have been given the opportunity of helping out here. I might be able make a difference. A big difference."

"What's wrong with making a difference in Fukushima? Please, Peter, you said you would come."

And so the conversation had continued, Michiyo moodily reminding him of his promise with every sentence and Bryant valiantly trying to come up with reasons that sounded plausible enough to explain away his absence. It was a no-win situation. No matter how much he explained that he would be safe, Michiyo wanted him beside her, and his safety was not serving as a convincing catalyst for his not being there. Rerunning the conversation through his mind once again, Bryant realized that he wasn't even convincing himself. He wanted to be beside Michiyo as much as she wanted to be beside him.

But he had a job to do. By agreeing to provide the U.S. government with information, Bryant had committed himself to giving of his best, and in the present situation, his best would mean remaining in Izu Kogen as an active member of the Tomonokai. He couldn't go to Fukushima. His conscience would not allow it. He loved and was loved, but his duty seemed to be on a slightly higher plane. Love lasted forever, but duty demanded immediate attention. It surpassed feelings of affection and personal gratification. He could love and be loved once all of this was over, but he knew he would never be able to forgive himself if he turned his back on his self-proclaimed duty at this point in time.

Bryant rolled over onto his side, propped his head up on his hand, and began to pick morosely at a loose piece of straw protruding from the tightly woven tatami mat. He was feeling miserable. Although he had not expected Michiyo to give in easily and accept an enforced separation without a battle, he had hoped that she would be able to make a little more effort in trying to see things from his point of view. Why couldn't she understand that he was not following this course of action simply because he didn't want to be with her? Surely she knew that he loved her dearly and would give almost anything to be by her side.

Almost anything . . .

The problem lay in the word *almost*. Michiyo was having trouble accepting the fact that she was not his top priority at the moment. She had a rival—a rival named *duty*, which was being guarded from external interference by a sentinel named *conscience*. Bryant tried to imagine what he would do if placed in her situation, but the concept was too ambiguous to grasp with any true accuracy. He *wanted* to think that he would display perfect understanding and commend her for her unselfishness, but he was not convinced that he would be able to do this. He put the thought out of his mind, his sentinel once more coming to the rescue.

But he hadn't wanted the conversation to end in an argument.

"Peter, I *demand* that you get on the next train to Fukushima. Who do you think you are? One of the regulars from *Mission Impossible?*"

"Michiyo, please listen to me. I have committed myself to this. I have made promises that I cannot break. . . ."

"What about your promise to me? You had no trouble breaking that one."

"Mi-*chan*, I am going to hang up now. I'll phone you again tomorrow after you have had a chance to think this through."

"Don't you *dare* hang up on me, Peter. I need you here. Now! I don't want you running about playing Robin to Mike Woodson's Batman!"

"I'm sorry, Mitch. . . ."

"Peter . . . ?"

He pressed the button to break the connection.

And had never felt more like a louse in his entire life.

Tiring of picking at the straw, Bryant rolled over onto his back and folded both hands behind his head. Logic informed him that dwelling on the problem would serve no purpose, but it was difficult to get his mind off it and onto a new subject. He *couldn't* go back on his word to Mike Woodson. Besides, his decision to remain behind in Japan now encompassed a wide range of people who would be going out of their way to help him. It was no longer a single promise to a friend, but a multitude of commitments at varying levels to different people spread throughout two or more continents. He *had* to go through with it. People were relying on him.

Feeling slightly placated by this reasoning, Bryant stood up and retrieved the laptop computer from its steel case lying on the floor by the wall. He would spend the rest of the time up until dinner composing his first-ever report to the U.S. government, appraising them of his success at having established contact with the mystery caller and a group of people with contacts throughout the country.

Slipping into spy mode, Bryant discovered as he typed the report, was easier than he had expected. Michiyo's ire was still boring a hole into his soul, but concentrating on something else seemed to dampen its importance, relegating it to a mild irritant as opposed to a major mental upheaval. He had made the right decision; he was sure of it. He would make it up to Michiyo when it was all over and he could place love once more at the top of his priority list.

For the time being, however, love came second.

Chapter Ten

The black Nissan Cedric drew up to the curb and the engine fell silent. All members of the Zen Nippon Otaku Tomonokai had come out to greet the new arrival, and only Peter Bryant remained on the deck, allowing the others to greet the mystery caller first. He felt slightly nervous, as if standing at the back of a stage waiting for the spotlight to illuminate his existence. Would he recognize the man? Would he be recognized?

He did not have long to find out.

Bryant's mouth dropped open in disbelief as the man climbed out of the car and walked into view, bowing deeply to the Kondos and Otsukas. Bryant watched as if in a trance as the short, balding man opened the rear door of his car and pulled an enormous suitcase from the backseat. Toshio Otsuka leaped forward to take the case from Kagemusha, and the group began to walk toward the house. The mystery caller was wearing an Aquascutum plaid shirt over a pair of dark slacks, and his feet appeared inordinately large in their white sports shoes—clothing that Bryant would never have imagined this man having in his wardrobe in a million years. He had only ever seen him in a business suit and necktie before.

As the group reached the steps to the deck, Kagemusha looked up into Bryant's eyes and grinned. Leaving the others standing on the grass, he slowly climbed the four steps and held out his hand.

"Mr. Bryant," he said, "I have been looking forward to this moment for some time, and the look on your face has exceeded even my own high expectations." Grasping Bryant's hand firmly, he reached over his shoulder and pulled him into a gentle hug. "Please accept my sincerest apologies for all of the trouble to which you have been subjected. My thanks also."

Released from the hug, Bryant hitched up his drooping jaw. "Mr. Matsuoka? But . . . but . . . I was expecting . . ."

"Somebody else? Who, may I ask?"

"Well, nobody in particular. Somebody young and handsome, actually . . ." He looked over Matsuoka's shoulder and winked at Harumi Otsuka, who quickly brought a finger to her mouth to shush him up, a look of embarrassed shock on her face. "But this is incredible. I would never have guessed if my life had depended on it. I thought you were a secretary, or one of the system engineers." It was his boss! Kazunori Matsuoka, the director of the patents department! But that was unthinkable!

"Come, come, Mr. Bryant. I gave you several clues. Do you not remember me mentioning 'another of *our* number' when I informed you of Hiroshi Okada's death? I would not have said that if I were a secretary."

"But you were so angry when Len Drake and I started investigating Chigasaki. You couldn't possibly have faked that."

"Ah, yes. So I was. But only because I was obliged to report on your movements, and you were being about as subtle and secretive as an Osaka *manzai* team. You were forcing me to become instrumental in causing both you and Drake harm. Had I failed to report you and word of your actions had somehow gotten back to the president, my own life would have been in danger. Wouldn't you have been angry under the same circumstances?"

Before Bryant could answer, Norio Kondo walked up the steps, closely followed by the others. "Come, you can finish this conversation inside. It is too cold out here, and I'm sure you would like a hot drink after your long journey."

An hour later, the six members of the Zen Nippon Otaku Tomonokai assembled in the living room for their first official meeting. While Shigeko Kondo disappeared into the kitchen to brew the coffee, Norio Kondo explained how to use the laptop computer, set up on a desk beside the window of the living room, and log on to the system with the highest authority rating. By the time Shigeko returned, all five were sitting around the dining table.

"First of all, I am sure I also speak for Mr. and Mrs. Otsuka when I say welcome to our two unexpected guests. Our home is honored by your presence."

Matsuoka and Bryant bowed their thanks.

"Now, to clarify our objectives, we are here to help gather information on Mr. Bryant's behalf so that it can be sent across to the American authorities in the hope that it assists them in discovering a cure for the meningococcemia disease. Mr. Bryant assures me that work has already begun on this, and any extra pieces of data we can provide may prove to be extremely important. Second, we also need to pass across details on conditions throughout the country in order for the American government to have a clear idea of carriage patterns and local lawlessness in the event that the U.S. military is used to deliver any medication that becomes available. Immediate distribution of an antidote or vaccine will be imperative to halt the spread of the epidemic, and it is here that we can be of most use."

Toshio Otsuka raised a hand and waited for Kondo to acknowledge him. "If I may ask," he said after receiving the acknowledgment, "why does the American government need us to provide this information? Surely the Japanese government could provide more accurate information."

"An excellent point. Maybe Mr. Bryant would like to answer that one."

Bryant leaned his elbows on the table and cleared his throat. "Well, from what I can gather, we are being regarded as a sort of backup for information being provided by the Japanese government. Given the virulence of this outbreak, there is no guarantee how much longer the government will be able to function properly, and maintaining constant contact with a foreign power may lose its priority. Also, it appears as if politics is playing a role in the supply of information, and a much rosier picture than actually exists is being painted."

"But why does the American government *need* this information? If a cure is found, surely it will be distributed by the Japanese authorities anyway?"

"That is true, of course, but America will offer to help with the distribution and wishes to make sure that it is carried out properly to ensure the safety of the people it sends over. The Japanese government is being slightly reticent in certain areas and will not reveal if it has any concrete plans for distribution. The American scientists have worked out a simulation for the most efficient method of distributing a cure, but the plan needs accurate data on local conditions to make it effective."

Norio Kondo finished his coffee and pushed the cup away from him. "Have you been informed of this method? If we have an idea of its basic concept, it might help us provide more suitable information."

Bryant nodded. He had received a long briefing from Washington that morning. "Basically, the medication will be distributed from the outside in, as opposed to going directly to the center. This disease is population-dependent, which means that it needs people to pass it on. The idea is to identify the seriously affected areas and then create disease-free bands around them to prevent the disease from being passed outward.

The distribution will then work its way toward the center of these areas, continually increasing the width of the bands until it meets in the middle. This will be carried out with bands within bands to add to its effectiveness. For example, a massive band will be started around the Kanto region surrounding urban Tochigi, Ibaragi, Saitama, Gunma, Tokyo, and Kanagawa, and then smaller bands will be started in each heavily affected localized area within this larger band. The same thing will be happening simultaneously around the Kansai region and all other affected areas. The logistics of this are mind-boggling and the manpower required to implement it staggering, so the American government feels that Japan will be forced to accept its offer. It is therefore necessary for them to have precise details on the worst-hit areas and the areas where there are chances of distribution being delayed through blockages, hijacking, or other antisocial activities."

Toshio nodded his understanding.

"So," Norio Kondo said, "we need information on carriage rates and dangerous areas, right?"

"That is correct," Bryant replied. "But if possible, I'd also like news on road damage, blockages, anything like that. Huge quantities of the antidote will be delivered as close as possible to each area by sea and air, but after that we will be forced to rely on existing road and rail services. If the ground-transportation network is out, we will be back to square one."

Norio Kondo scribbled down a few notes and then looked up. "I understand. I will draft up an e-mail message outlining your requirements this afternoon and send it out to all members of the Tomonokai. That will amount to more than fifty people spread throughout the entire country. I will instruct them to post all of their observances at least once every day on the bulletin board, and you can write up your reports from the printouts of this. Is that okay?"

"That is absolutely wonderful, Kondo-san. You've no idea

how much I appreciate your help. Alone I would have been powerless. Thank you all."

"In addition to that," Kondo continued, "I think we should monitor the news on NHK." Ever since the start of the outbreak, NHK, Japan's premier broadcasting company, had been providing twenty-four-hour news coverage detailing updates on all aspects of the situation. "I'm sure we can work out a sort of shift system so that at least one of us is always watching. Anybody have any objections against that?"

All of those present shook their heads one by one.

"I am quite happy with that." Kazunori Matsuoka spoke for the first time. Bryant looked across at him in disbelief once more. His boss, for God's sake!

"However, I have one more suggestion, if you will allow me a few moments."

"Please go ahead, Totchan," Kondo said.

"I would like to ask you to recruit a new member for the Tomonokai. It is a friend of mine whom I have known since my junior high school days. He is a high-ranking executive who has Internet capabilities, but he is also an avid ham radio freak and has a network of contacts all over Japan. When I spoke to him of our predicament—in the strictest confidence, of course—he mentioned that he was in possession of equipment that would be able to intercept police and military radio traffic and offered his services. He would like to remain anonymous, however, so I cannot reveal his identity, I'm afraid. Not even to you, Gakusha-san. I realize that this goes against the rules, but given the situation, I thought you might consider it."

"But of course, Totchan," Kondo said expansively. "Such information would be invaluable! Let me know his handle and I will set up an account for him immediately."

"I will e-mail him later and ask his preference. I'll let you know when I receive his reply."

"Excellent. Now, does anybody else have any questions or something to say?"

Bryant raised his hand. "One more thing. I have been given some medication that may—or may not—help to protect us from infection. I'll translate the dosages into Japanese and let you all have them later on. I would be grateful if you all made sure that you follow the instructions to the letter."

"Fine. I'm sure you can rely on us there. Anything else?" Kondo looked around at everybody in turn to confirm that everything was clear. It was. "Then I understand Mr. Bryant—sorry, Peter-*san*—has a long list of questions to ask Totchan about this disease, so maybe we should leave them in peace."

Nobuyuki Akiyama crouched behind the counter and raised his eyes to heaven. He was not a practicing Christian, but he knew that this was the thing to do in such situations, and he was willing to try anything to help him out of his present predicament. In fact, had his knuckles not been turning white from the viselike grip he held on the large *hocho* knife that he used to clean fish, he almost certainly would have put his hands together in prayer. Another crash sounded on the door of the Koto Japanese restaurant, located just two minutes' walk from Leicester Square in London, quickly followed by the sound of splintering wood as the structure began to give way beneath the onslaught. Akiyama had no idea how many people were involved in the attack, but judging by the number of voices he heard raised in anger, there must be at least ten of them.

He wondered how long it would take for the police to arrive. If they ever did arrive, that is. He had heard from some of his customers that the police were not very sympathetic toward the victims of these hate crimes, and in certain cases they had even been known to turn a blind eye while Japanese stores had been looted and smashed beyond recognition. Was the same thing happening in all other countries of the world, or just in the United Kingdom? It certainly was not restricted only to London. The reports of Japanese companies being brought to their knees throughout the industrial north was the staple for the news programs recently, and the xenophobic "Buy British" campaigns were stirring up even more hatred of Japanese people. Didn't they realize that they were simply adding to their own unemployment figures? He had read in the newspapers of the picketing and victimization abroad, of course, but none seemed to be as bad as the situation in London. Although he was willing to admit that his proximity to the bullying rampant in the U.K. was probably giving him a biased view.

Another crash on the door had Akiyama scrabbling across the floor behind the counter toward his office. If he locked the office door and used his desk and filing cabinets as a barricade, he might be able to hold out until the police came. *If they came . . .*

Not for the first time, Akiyama thanked his lucky stars that he had had the good sense to board up all of the front windows and use bamboo halves for decorative purposes in order to give the restaurant an Oriental atmosphere. That, at least, gave him a few valuable minutes in which to establish some sort of line of defense. Had he left the glass in, as originally planned, the yobbos would have been on top of him minutes ago, and that certainly was not a thought to be relished.

Slamming the office door shut and placing the knife on his desk, Akiyama frantically began to put all of his weight behind a large wooden filing cabinet that stood to the left. It rejected his efforts at first, but slowly began to slide along the tiled floor until it was suitably placed to prevent the door from being opened, effectively providing a barrier against the yobbos should they get this far. Shaking both inwardly and outwardly, Akiyama sat down at his desk and stared at his makeshift barricade. If need be, he could reinforce it later with the desk and the chest of drawers that stood along the wall to his right. The office had no windows, so at least he didn't have to worry about his back. He was safe for the moment. He hoped that the gang would simply be content with smashing up the restaurant and then go on their way. He always left twenty pounds in five-pound notes in the register when the restaurant was closed in the hope that any would-be burglar would be satisfied with that and not bother to search for the safe in his office. But these were not normal burglars. They were a bunch of street yobbos whipped into a frenzy by the mass media, which made it sound as if punishing Japanese citizens for destroying the British economy and causing unemployment to skyrocket was the right thing to do. Hell, Akiyama had lived in London for fifteen years! He always paid his taxes on time, unlike some of these damn hooligans who wanted everything for nothing. Why couldn't the bloody government use some of his taxes to protect him? Surely he had a right to expect at least that.

Although it was only recently that he had noticed it, Akiyama was terrified of British youth. They were surly, bad-tempered, and seemed to have a mindless quality about them that induced them to destroy things for no purpose other than instantaneous gratification. He had seen them lop the heads off flowers in parks, throw stones at windows, and scratch knives and keys along the paintwork of strangers' cars for no practical reason whatsoever. The experts on television always explained away these malicious actions as being the result of the frustration that was building up over a lack of work, but from what Akiyama could understand, the last thing in the world that these kids wanted was work. With unemployment benefits and social security payments providing them with more cash than they could make from gainful employment, they all seemed quite happy to stay on the dole and destroy other people's property simply to satisfy their own warped sense of satisfaction. Akiyama had laughed the first time he had heard the Department of Health and Social Security referred to by its nickname, the Department of Stealth and Total Obscurity, but there was a hint of truth behind this sarcasm that sounded a chord of recognition deep within him. Not only did they hand out money in bucketfuls to every lazy bastard who refused to get off his arse and work, he had also heard stories of the DHSS dishing out money to the greedy and completely ignoring the needy. One of these stories involved the DHSS refusing to provide the sum required for an old lady to have her cataracts removed under private surgery, but paying for a family of six to have a two-week vacation at Butlins in Minehead while their house was being redecorated at taxpayers' expense. Why? Because the unemployed householder had complained that his daughter was being singled out at school for living in a tatty old house with the paper peeling off the walls. Now if that wasn't a candidate for totally obscure reasoning, what was? The whole damn country was crazy!

The sound of the gang of kids beating on the front entrance, muffled now that Akiyama was in his office, stopped suddenly, only to be replaced a moment later with the louder sound of the Koto Japanese restaurant being ransacked. Akiyama winced as he heard a crash that sounded mightily like one of his bar stools smashing into the mirror that lined the wall behind the counter. The kids shouted and screamed in glee as they willfully destroyed everything in sight, the foul language sounding almost medieval with a barbaric sort of take-no-prisoners quality that shook Akiyama to his core and had his teeth chattering in his head. If they managed to get through his barricade, he was a dead man, of that he was sure. Where the hell were the police?

Five minutes later, the attention of the youths turned to the office door. A few shouted commands to "Open up, you Jap bastard" preceded a hammering on the door, and Akiyama hastily pushed his desk over in front of the filing cabinet and pressed all of his weight up against it. He could hear the wood of the door splintering, but he didn't think they would manage to hack their way through the filing cabinet. It was made of sturdy wood and was at least two and a half feet thick. And even if they did managed to put a hole in the back, any hand reaching through would swiftly be introduced to the razor edge of Akiyama's *hocho* knife. He picked the knife up from the desk and held it at chest level.

The hammering continued for a further few minutes, and then, suddenly, silence reigned. Akiyama cautiously moved off the desk and around to the wall. He pressed his ear up against the side of the filing cabinet, but could hear nothing. Was it a trick, or had they really given up and gone home? He decided to wait for some time to make sure. He assumed that patience was not one of the scums' qualities and was confident he could easily outwait them.

But that was it! He'd had enough. It was time for him to return to Japan and wave good-bye to this godforsaken island. There was no way he was going to invest the money to have the restaurant done up, only to have the same thing happen a couple of nights after reopening. He had reached his limit.

The problem was, how would he get back to Japan? All flights in and out of the country had been halted, as had all shipping, and from what he had read in the newspapers, there appeared to be no direct route into the country. Akiyama sat down in his desk chair and lit a cigarette with shaking hands. He was stranded. Stranded in a country that neither liked him nor wanted him to be there. A prisoner in an enormous cell containing other prisoners who considered him to be fair game because of his nationality. The star player in the national game of pin-the-tail-on-the-Jap.

Akiyama sat at his desk for a full ninety minutes, contemplating his situation and tapping the knife on his knee between cigarettes. When finally he was convinced that the thugs had left his restaurant and he was totally alone, he dismantled his barricade and peeped cautiously around the side of the door. Nobody. He picked his way through the debris, his feet crunching and grinding the broken glass into the wooden floor, until he was out on the street, and then turned left to walk to the Leicester Square tube station, where he caught an underground train back to his flat in East Hampstead.

By the time the black-and-white panda car pulled up in front of the restaurant and disgorged the two uninterested policemen who were responding to the emergency call, Akiyama had been safe in his own living room for twenty minutes.

Peter Bryant submerged his head beneath the hot springwater and counted to twenty. The water was supposed to be especially beneficial for people who suffered from rheumatism and skin diseases, but Harumi Otsuka had also mentioned that the minerals contained in the water were reputed to add elasticity to the skin and prevent wrinkles from forming. Although still only twenty-nine years old and not yet concerned with skin elasticity and wrinkles, Bryant decided that he might as well hedge his bets and try to get the full benefit of his dip.

The bathroom in the *besso* was much larger than could normally be found in Japanese houses, but the presence of a constant and limitless supply of hot water pumped at no cost from the depths of the earth could usually be guaranteed to coerce owners into going to extravagant expense with improvements, the idea being that they would make the money back in the long run by saving on water rates and heating charges. Norio Kondo and Toshio Otsuka were no exception. The bathroom had been extended in size, and the actual bath, which was sunk three feet into the floor, made large enough for three people. Four, if they were on intimate terms. The floor of the bathroom and the bottom of the bath consisted of concrete, but the rim and back wall had been created out of rough-hewn rocks to give the impression of an indoor *rotenburo*.

A knock at the door startled Bryant. He grabbed the hand towel from the side of the bath and hastily plunged it underwater to cover his nakedness. "Yes?" he called.

The door opened and Kazunori Matsuoka entered, a wooden pine tray bearing a jug of warm sake and two *ochoko* cups balanced in one hand and a small yellow towel held modestly in front of him. Apart from the towel, Matsuoka was completely

241

naked, and Bryant was amused to notice his little potbelly protruding from beneath the tray. "May I join you? I have brought some refreshment."

Bryant relaxed and sat back in the bath with a grin of relief. The previous evening he had been caught unawares when Shigeko Kondo had entered without knocking to check if he had found the towels. "Please do. Refreshment of that kind is always welcome."

Matsuoka walked across to the bath, crouched down awkwardly in an attempt to retain his modesty, and floated the tray on the surface of the water. He then went over to the shower, turned his back on Bryant, and began to wash away the grime of his day.

"I shall never forget your face when I walked up the steps to the deck, Peter-san," Matsuoka shouted above the noise of the shower. "A perfect picture of conflicting emotions."

Bryant laughed, thinking back to his openmouthed surprise. "I wish you had told me earlier. I guess I'm not very good at hiding my feelings."

"I was tempted to let you know during our last telephone call, when you were considering sleeping on the park bench, but I was afraid that you would distrust me. It is not uncommon for young people to distrust their bosses. I couldn't take the chance."

Conversation dropped off as Matsuoka applied shampoo to his receding hair and scrubbed his scalp vigorously. Having rinsed the soap off his head and body, he replaced the yellow hand towel in front of him before walking across to the bath and stepping gingerly into the hot water. Bryant caught hold of the floating tray and poured a mouthful of sake into each of the two cups.

"Your good health."

"And yours, my friend." Matsuoka downed the drink in one go and poured two more. "It seems as if the Tomonokai will be very useful to your efforts, Peter-san. You will be able to get information from many different areas of the country."

"I just hope it is of some use. Things are getting worse, it seems."

Matsuoka settled his back against the wall opposite Bryant and took a small sip of sake, a look of pure contentment on his face. "Yes, but not for much longer. Goodness will soon rebound and things will get better."

"That's a very optimistic point of view. Do you really believe so?"

"Without a shadow of a doubt. At the moment evil is running rampant through every city, but goodness is waiting in the wings. For every criminal out there, there are ten thousand good people huddling in their homes, hoping they will go away. Soon, once they realize that they will not go away without encouragement, these people will band together and force them back into their holes. They will stop patronizing the black marketeers and form cooperatives to accumulate their own food. They will establish small barter systems where the owners of vegetables will deal fairly with the owners of meat. Civility will return, I assure you."

"I certainly hope you are right. Did you drive through Chigasaki and see the state of the area today? It's awful."

"Yes, Peter-*san*, it is awful. But soon the dregs will return to the bottom of the pot."

"Meaning?"

"Let us equate society with a huge cauldron of bouillabaisse. It looks tasty enough on the surface, but there are things lying at the bottom that are better not seen if you wish to retain your appetite. The meningococcemia disease has simply stirred up Japan's cauldron of bouillabaisse and sent those unsavory dregs to the top of the broth. Soon the goodness will return and the dregs will sink back to the bottom where they belong, hopefully never to be seen again."

"Mm, an encouraging thought. I certainly hope you are right."

"Oh, I am right, Peter-*san*. Have no fear. If evil were inherent to human nature, there wouldn't be a safe place on earth. You must have faith in the human race."

Matsuoka leaned forward and reached for the jug of sake.

"Kondo-*san* told me you were married. Where is your wife?" Bryant held out his cup and allowed it to be refilled.

"Safe in the family home in Kyushu, I hope. I will telephone later to make sure. I entrusted Joji Higashino with her safety. They left this morning by car."

"Oh, yes. I'd forgotten about Joji. How did you manage to convince him to contact me in the first place? When I spoke to him, he was adamant about not getting involved."

"His wife's mother is my wife's sister. It was I who acted as the go-between for their union. He couldn't refuse my request in case it got back to his wife and she made him see the error of his ways. Joji, I'm afraid, is not master in his own home, and he finds it hard to control the willful spirit of Kyushu women. I do believe she beats him, you know. Extraordinary!"

"Poor old Joji. When we first raised the subject, he gave us a ten-minute lecture on how society was blackmailing him into being loyal to the company. He seemed quite distraught."

Matsuoka laughed, a short, barking laugh that echoed around the bathroom. "He is mistaking society for his wife, although from his point of view, that is an understandable error. It is she who is blackmailing him into being loyal to the company."

"He said that he would not be able to pay for his house or send his children to school if he angered the company."

"Yes, that is his wife's logic, all right. I suppose we must sympathize with him. At this moment he is cornered in the same house with his wife, her two sisters, his mother-in-law, my wife, and her eighty-nine-year-old mother. Six Kyushu women and one Joji. I fear for his safety. He is probably washing dishes at this very moment." Matsuoka laughed again, enjoying the vision within his mind. "By the way," he continued after a moment, "did you send off your report?"

"Yes," Bryant replied. "Thank you very much for your help."

"I hope it proves helpful. I am not a technician, you understand, and simply told you what I have heard myself. Although I must admit to having studied the subject somewhat recently."

"There's one thing I don't understand about this disease."

"And that is?"

"The connection with the actual bacterium and this inflammatory cascade thing you mentioned."

"Ah, yes. The inflammatory cascade. Well, it is a runaway reaction by the body to something it doesn't like. It is not caused only by *Neisseria* meningococcus, but can be triggered by almost anything. You know when you catch a cold and your nose starts running, you get a headache, you start sneezing, your throat becomes dry, and you develop a fever?"

Bryant nodded.

"That is an inflammatory cascade. It is like a chain reaction where one thing leads to another. However, the severity of the cascade and the organs it affects are determined by the illness."

"How bad is it with this disease?"

"As bad as it gets."

The two men lapsed into silence as they contemplated this, the only sound coming from the spigot as it kept the bath topped up and overflowing with hot water.

"And what is it that finally kills the victim?" Bryant asked at length. "Organ failure?"

"Yes, that among other things. It really is a matter of what gains the upper hand first. Imagine being hung, shot, stabbed, garroted, strangled, poisoned, decapitated, and disemboweled—all at the same time. Which of these do you think would be the final act that ends your life? With this disease, you have as much chance of dying of pneumonia as you do of congestive heart failure. And even if you do survive, you will probably lose a few extremities to necrosis or gangrene, or you may go deaf, or you may develop arthritis or even grow abscesses in the brain. Who knows?"

"But that is incredible! How can they possibly find a cure for something like that?"

Matsuoka chuckled. "Oh, they can't, Peter-*san*, and they won't try. There is no such thing as a singular cure for the inflammatory cascade. Each ailment must be treated separately, and given the large number of different ailments that the victim will be inflicted with, that would be impossible. No, their target will be the bacterium itself, not the after-effects. The object of any vaccine or antidote they manage to develop will be to prevent the bacterium from penetrating the bloodstream and starting off the inflammatory cascade in the first place. That is the only way to control it."

"Do you think they will be successful?"

Matsuoka shrugged his shoulders and sipped his sake. "I was just about to ask you the same question."

The accumulated sum of the personal wealth belonging to the forty-three men who occupied the meeting room in Singapore's prestigious Goodwood Park Hotel exceeded $6.5 billion, but the amount they controlled with a flick of their fingers amounted to more than eighteen thousand times that much. All were chairmen, presidents, and CEOs of Asia's representative financial institutions, and all had been called to Singapore for a single purpose: to figure out a way of saving Asia's economy.

Mahathir Wong stood at the head of the elongated table and gently rapped his knuckles against the rosewood to call the meeting to order. "Gentlemen, good afternoon. I trust you all find your accommodation comfortable."

Everybody nodded in agreement. The Goodwood Park Hotel boasted 116 suites, and every person in the room had been assigned one of the more opulent two-bedroom suites.

"You all know the reason for our being here today, and I

would like to take a few moments of your time to explain the concept behind the plan that we have devised. I will shortly be asking all of you to pledge a certain sum of money on behalf of your banks and institutions that will be placed in a pool and used to try to stabilize Asia's failing economy. Every person in this room stands to benefit from this, so I am hoping you will all be as generous as rationality permits, as we require many billions, if not trillions, of dollars to ensure that our efforts are successful. Your pledges will be treated in the strictest confidence, with only myself and my closest aides being aware of how much each institution has contributed to the pool. Anything that is left in the pool at the end will be calculated into percentages and returned accordingly."

Wong cast his eyes around the table to ensure that he had everybody's attention. He had.

"Most of this money will be divided equally between us all. Then, when I issue the word, your institution will immediately begin to purchase the currency and stocks of all other member nations in bulk. There are forty-three of us here, representing eleven countries. That means that ten different locations of the world will suddenly begin to invest enormous sums of money in your country, hopefully stimulating other nations to begin bulk purchasing while the prices are still low. Considering the rates of our currencies at the moment, gentlemen, the risk is minimal and the potential returns great. Are we in agreement?"

A rumble of chatter broke out as everybody began to discuss the offer among themselves. Wong watched as each man in turn looked up at him and nodded.

"I must emphasize," Wong continued, "that timing is of the essence. Once the money has been distributed, my colleagues and I will work out daily schedules as to how the investments are to be made. These schedules will outline exactly how much money is to be invested in which stocks and which currencies and will be updated and sent to you before the opening of trading each morning. Every one of you will have different lists, and I ask you to make sure that the out-of-date schedules are destroyed the moment the new ones become available. The markets are fluctuating daily, and it is imperative that we place appropriate sums of this money where it will do the most good. When you receive your instructions to start buying, you must use the list that you received that day. Is that clear?"

It was. Wong noted with satisfaction the way in which the announcement was being received. Although small frowns could be seen on one or two faces, the majority were looking between each other to gauge reaction and then making small gestures of approval. Nobody took any notes.

"Excuse me, I have a question."

Wong looked across at the exquisitely dressed, middle-aged Indonesian banker. "Of course. Please go ahead."

The man pushed his chair back and stood up. "You mentioned that most of this money will be used as you describe. What of the remainder?"

Wong smiled and stretched out his hands expansively. "That," he said, "will be used to fight the cause of this recession at its roots. We will collect together the finest scientists and microbiologists the world has to offer and provide them with state-of-the-art facilities in which they will be required to come up with a cure for the meningococcemia disease. I am sure we will all agree that no matter how much money we pour into our own economies, there will be little effect unless we make a concerted effort to put Japan back on its feet. At the moment, a team of scientists at Western Washington University in America are working on this problem, but there is little doubt that the finest minds and a huge injection of cash will speed the process up remarkably. I have already contacted several of the world's leading scientists to offer them large sums of money for their participation, and all have accepted. We are currently involved in negotiations with the American government to allow us to finance this project with no strings attached, and there appear to be no problems. Together with our attempts to bolster our economies, one or two rumors will be released to indicate the fact that success is near to hand in discovering a cure for the disease, and this should provide the stimulation that the markets need."

The banker revealed a grudging smile and sat down.

"And now, gentlemen," Wong continued, "we come to the most important part of your trip to Singapore. All of you have been provided with a card with the name of your institution printed at the top and an envelope. I will now adjourn the meeting until five o'clock this afternoon. In the meantime, please return to your rooms and spend the next few hours deciding how much your institution can afford to pledge for this effort. I remind you that generosity is extremely important. I am sure you are all aware of the English saying about spoiling a ship for want of a ha'porth of tar. Secure lines have been established on all telephones if you need to discuss the plan with your head offices. I ask you to write down the sum that you decide on the card, seal it in the envelope, and return it to this box by four o'clock at the latest." Wong gently tapped with his knuckles on a square metal box secured with a sturdy padlock in front of him. "The total sum of all pledges will be announced at this evening's meeting. Gentlemen, I thank you."

Kazunori Matsuoka stared at the screen of the television, his eyes narrowing in hatred. "Bastard," he whispered.

Shigeko Kondo, whose turn it was to monitor the NHK news, looked at him out of the corner of her eye, but said nothing.

Matsuoka jumped to his feet and stormed from the room, closely followed by Gonta, whose mind was on the rice crackers that Matsuoka had fed him the previous evening. But Matsuoka did not turn into the kitchen. He walked to the stairs and ascended to the second floor, leaving Gonta staring up after him sadly. He turned right at the top of the stairs and knocked on the first door he came to.

"Come in." Peter Bryant's voice was muffled by the wooden door.

Matsuoka entered the room and sat down on the tatami next to Bryant, who was busy typing up his next report on the laptop computer. "Peter-*san*," Matsuoka said, "how would you like a trip into Tokyo tomorrow?"

"Tokyo?" Bryant looked at Matsuoka in surprise. It had been decided that none of the Tomonokai members would leave Izu Kogen unless essential. "Why Tokyo?"

"The demon is loose. Shigeru Hamada was released on bail this morning. He was just shown on television arriving back at his home, closely pursued by several reporters. He admitted that Hamada Seiyaku Pharmaceuticals had been closed down temporarily and that he himself was intending to leave Tokyo for safety before the end of the week. I wish to speak to him."

"But why? What good could speaking to him do?"

Matsuoka hesitated and fiddled with the satellite telephone, repeatedly extending and replacing the antenna. "I must know if he feels remorse. I have to look into his eyes, inspect his soul. I cannot rest until I know." Shifting his eyes from the telephone to Bryant's face, he continued, "Please, Peter-*san*. He is a violent man, and I might need help if he sees me as the enemy."

"Are you?"

"Am I what?"

"The enemy?"

Matsuoka lowered his eyes again. "Yes," he said softly.

"And, having looked into his soul, what if you see no remorse? What then?"

"I don't know, but I must look and see."

Bryant sighed, saved the file he was working on, and switched off the computer. Placing his hands behind him on the floor, he leaned his weight onto his arms and looked Matsuoka straight in the eye. "Yes, Matsuoka-*san*. I will accompany you. But it might be a good idea to take some form of weapon in case, as you say, Hamada recognizes you as the enemy."

"Thank you, Peter-*san*. I will visit the kitchen and see what I can find."

"All I ask is for your support," Shoji Kubota said dramatically, stretching his hands out to encompass the twelve cabinet ministers seated around the table. "I know that each and every one of you understands the implications of the chaos that Aizawa is inflicting upon the country, and it is our sworn duty to put a stop to it as soon as possible."

"Hear, hear," said Yoshio Saito, the chief cabinet secretary, clapping his hands rhythmically to add emphasis to his endorsement. "We have achieved absolutely nothing since being confined inside this damned building, and it is about time we reinstated a true government."

"The slight exaggeration overlooked, are you sure that a change in leaders wouldn't simply delay any good that Aizawa's policies have achieved so far?" Kayoko Inoue, the director general of the Science and Technology Agency, was still not convinced that a power struggle was beneficial at this point in time. She had always gotten on well with the prime minister in the past, and his recent determination to set the country back on the straight and narrow had impressed her. "You have to admit that certain areas are improving already. Now that the ground forces have been mobilized, at least we don't have to worry about breakdowns in utilities, communications, and transportation. We must give credit where credit is due."

Kubota smiled at her sympathetically. "Of course you are correct, Mrs. Inoue, but maybe it would interest you to know that it was I, in fact, who suggested this strategy to the prime minister."

Inoue raised her eyebrows in surprise. "Please excuse me, General Secretary. I had no idea."

"Unfortunately, few people have. Mobilization of military forces is the first and most logical step in handling a matter like this, and I must admit to having experienced a feeling of deep shock to discover that the thought had not occurred to Mr. Aizawa independently. Had I not spoken, we probably would be sitting here in the dark and relying on smoke signals for communications. I understand and respect your loyalty to the prime minister, Mrs. Inoue, but I'm afraid it is time to face the facts. He is incompetent and certainly not capable of the job that lies before him. We must assume power in his stead to assure that the country is saved from his administration."

A round of applause broke out around the table. Shotaro Maekawa, the minister of transport, rose to his feet in a standing ovation, swiftly joined by all other members of the meeting.

Kubota acknowledged their praise with a slight bow. Everything appeared to be going according to plan, and he truly expected them to be addressing him as "Prime Minister" within the week. "However," he continued, raising his right hand for silence, "we still have a few hurdles to overcome. The takeover will be much simpler if more join our ranks. It is for this reason, my friends, that I have summoned you here today. Please take your seats and hear me out."

The twelve ministers sat down and looked up at Kubota expectantly.

"None of us here are strangers to the art of lobbying. Correct?" He waited for the laughter to die down. "I now want to ask you to use your skills and talents by lobbying all of the remaining ministers, secretaries, advisers, and aides to bring them over to our point of view. I am sure there will be a few who will continue to side stubbornly with Aizawa, but these people will be replaced once we have power, and their jobs, as I'm sure you have already concluded, will be the bait with which we will lobby the others. Please feel free to use my name at will. Tell everybody you speak to that I have been keeping an eye on their work and am impressed with what I see. Tell them that I have the need of high-ranking officials to help put the country back on its feet. Tell them anything you wish, if you think it will help garner their support. We must have support. Can I rely on you?"

A chorused "Yes" echoed around the room, and Kubota smiled graciously upon his new followers. Of the eight remaining ministers, he expected that four would go against him, three with him, and the last one would be undecided unless promised something special. Something like the position of secretary general of the Liberal Democratic Party, for example. Yes, he would work on that minister himself. That would give him a total of sixteen followers and would be more than sufficient to initiate the takeover. Prime Minister Aizawa, he had already decided, would be confined to quarters until most of the problems afflicting the country had been solved, and then paraded before the nation as a scapegoat by being publicly tried on a charge of treason. That would teach him to get above himself and make an open enemy of Shoji Kubota. He would be made to pay for his insolence. Severely.

Chapter Eleven

Kazunori Matsuoka waited until Shigeru Hamada was almost level with the car before opening the door and stepping out into his path. Peter Bryant climbed out of the passenger side and stood watching the two men.

Hamada's eyes narrowed. "You . . ." he snarled, his lip curling in contempt.

"Yes, me. Are you surprised to see me?"

"No more surprised than I would be to see a cockroach in my path." He glared across at Bryant. "Two cockroaches," he amended. "I see you have teamed up with the *gaijin*, Matsuoka. I'm sure you are well suited: two cockroaches exuding false-placed loyalty and filth."

"Nice to see you too, Mr. Hamada," Bryant said.

"*Urusai!*" Hamada pointed a threatening finger at Bryant. "You are living on borrowed time, roach. Keep your mouth *shut!*"

Bryant shrugged and crossed his arms in an open act of de-

254

fiance. "Blow it out your ass, pal," he muttered in English, not knowing if Hamada would understand or not.

Hamada dismissed Bryant with a contemptuous wave of his hand and turned back to Matsuoka. "By deserting me, you realize that you have signed your own death warrant, don't you? You have seen my method of dealing with traitors, so you know what to expect. Maybe not today or the next day, but sometime soon. Very soon."

"If you have a chance to give the order, Hamada. You might be dead yourself before then."

Hamada threw back his head and laughed out loud. "What, you? Kill me? Ha, don't make me laugh. You are weak and timorous, Matsuoka. An aging businessman whose only enjoyment is golf and karaoke with young office girls who flatter you simply because you are old enough to be their grandfather. You are foolish and ridiculous. Take a look at yourself in the mirror and then tell me again that you are capable of murder."

Matsuoka pulled his arm from behind his back, revealing a long, sharp kitchen knife. "Maybe you would like to push me a little further, Hamada. Put me to the test, if you feel that confident."

"Armed, but not dangerous. If you wanted to kill me you would have done so already. Get out of my way, cockroach. I have business to attend to."

The steel flashed in the sunlight as Hamada pushed past Matsuoka. Hamada stopped with a gasp and looked down at the blood blossoming across his white shirtfront beneath his open suit jacket. He raised a finger to his chest, touched the shallow six-centimeter wound, and then moved the finger up to his mouth to taste the blood. "You will regret that," he said with menace. "As you observe, I am still alive. As I thought, you do not have the guts to finish the job. Now, if you'll excuse me."

The blade flashed again, this time drawing a line from Hamada's collarbone downward until it dissected the first wound. Hamada grunted with the stinging pain of the superficial injury.

"Get in the car!" Matsuoka barked the order, startling Bryant even more than when he had used the knife. He had forgotten that Matsuoka was capable of shouting orders. A vision of him as his boss floated into his mind. "Now!"

Hamada looked at him defiantly, rage boiling just beneath the surface. "How dare you speak to me like that!" he hissed. "If you want to kill me, do it now. I will not be taken elsewhere if my fate is already sealed."

"Ah, so you admit at last that I *am* capable of killing you. Well, if you must know, I have no intention of doing so. I refuse to bring myself down to your level, Hamada. I will kill you only if you try to escape. I simply want to take you for a drive. There is something I need to show you. Get in the car."

Hamada stared hard at Matsuoka, not knowing whether to believe him or not. Matsuoka opened the rear door of the black Cedric and gestured for him to get in. The knife glinted once again in the sunlight, and Hamada finally climbed into the backseat.

"Would you mind getting in the back with him, Peter-*san*? I need you to tie him up."

Nodding agreement, Bryant slid in beside Hamada and accepted the nylon cord that Matsuoka retrieved from the glove compartment and tossed over into the back. "Tie his hands and his feet to make sure he cannot move," Matsuoka said, watching Bryant fashion a slipknot and loop it over Hamada's hands. "That's it. Tighter."

"You will regret this, Matsuoka," Hamada growled through clenched teeth. "You would be advised to kill me now, if you know what is good for you. I will come for you. I will find you no matter where you hide."

Confirming that Hamada was incapable of movement, Matsuoka leaned over the seat and slapped him hard across the head with the palm of his hand, like a schoolteacher dealing with an errant student. Ignoring Hamada's screech of rage, he turned to Bryant and held out the bloodstained knife. "Here, Peter-*san*. You'd better take this. Keep an eye on his hands to make sure he is not trying to free himself. You have my permission to cut off one of his ears if he tries anything funny."

Chuckling at Hamada's oaths, Matsuoka sat back in the driver's seat and started the engine.

Fifteen minutes later, they were on the Wangan Expressway speeding toward Haneda airport, the Bayside Bridge and Yokohama beyond. Changing to the Yokohama-Yokosuka Highway at Hodogaya, they continued south until leaving the highway at the Hino interchange and driving through to Fujisawa and then down onto the Shonan coastal road. Hamada kept up a steady string of vows and expletives throughout the journey, but Matsuoka and Bryant remained silent. Bryant regularly inspected Hamada's hands to make sure he was not attempting to free himself, but apart from that, he sat contemplating the different side of Matsuoka that had been revealed to him. To say that he had been surprised at the ostensibly gentle Totchan's actually using the knife would be an understatement. His eyes had nearly popped out of his head when he saw the blood soaking through Hamada's shirt. That Matsuoka was sickened by the death and chaos caused by Hamada's actions, Bryant was in no doubt, but that his anger had reached such levels as to enable him to inflict physical injury on a human being he found totally out of character. It was not the Matsuoka that he had come to know and respect.

Matsuoka had also been deeply shocked by his own actions. Although he had taken the knife with the purpose of using it had the need arisen, he had not expected the action—or was it a reaction?—of slicing it through human flesh to come so easily. The knife had lashed out seemingly of its own accord, with little or no input from Matsuoka's own intentions. That had scared him. Was this the phenomenon that allowed normal men to become cruel and efficient killing machines in times of war? He imagined that it was, but the thought did little to console him. He had granted himself the right to become Hamada's judge and jury simply because he had convinced himself that the man was evil and deserved to be punished. Having come to this decision, his subconscious had taken over and entered seek-and-destroy mode, like a mindless, computer-controlled weapon designed for death and destruction. His body had revealed to him a part of himself that he would rather not have seen, and that was cause for concern. Deep concern.

The sunlight flashed through the trees lining the Chigasaki Beach annoyingly. The road was almost totally devoid of other cars, but burned-out wrecks dotted the roadside here and there. Matsuoka turned right to move away from the coast and penetrate the built-up area of the city of Chigasaki. Despite the scarcity of other moving vehicles, Matsuoka drove slowly, casting his eyes in all directions, as if wanting to absorb every detail of the catastrophe as it unfolded before them.

"Tell me, Hamada, what do you see?" he asked at length.

Hamada grunted, but did not reply.

"Look over to your right. Do you see those people hiding in that doorway?"

Still Hamada made no attempt to reply.

"Shall I tell you why they are hiding? They are hiding from us. They are afraid that we may be carriers of the disease. *Your* disease."

"You are crazy, Matsuoka," Hamada said, finally deigning to speak. "There are always sacrifices in the advancement of science. What is your point? Why did you bring me here?"

"You think creating a killer epidemic is an advancement of science?" Matsuoka shook his head wearily. "And you call me crazy? Do you not realize what you have done? Do you not realize how many people have been sacrificed for the advancement of your so-called science?"

"All right, you've made your point. Now let's get out of here."

Matsuoka turned left at a convenience store with no glass left in the windows. Something scuttled amid the shadows in the depths of the store before disappearing behind what was left of the counter. A little farther down the road he turned left and then pulled the car over to the curb next to a small pocket-handkerchief park, a one-block area surrounded by trees with a children's playground dominating the center. Several of the benches were occupied by mounds of tattered rags that fluttered in the wind blowing strongly off the sea. The mounds moved slightly as the car came to a halt, and eyes peered curiously from between strands of dirty fabric garnered from various sources in an attempt to keep the cold at bay. One or two failed to move at all, victims of either meningococcemia or hypothermia—it was impossible to tell.

Checking the rearview mirror, Matsuoka reached out a hand and released the lock on the trunk. He stepped out onto the sidewalk and walked around to the rear of the car. Grabbing a large black plastic bag from the trunk, he moved across to the entrance of the park and dropped it into the bushes to the right. The mounds of rags, overcoming their fear, began to edge toward him. Matsuoka then opened the rear door of the car and gestured for Hamada to get out.

Hamada looked up in fear. "What . . . what is going on?"

"Just get out of the car."

"No! I demand that you take me back to Tokyo. I am finished playing your games."

Matsuoka leaned closer and grabbed hold of the nylon cord tying Hamada's hands together. Nodding to Bryant, the two men pulled and pushed simultaneously until Hamada was standing on the sidewalk, hopping up and down on the spot to maintain his balance. Matsuoka slipped a hand into the inside pocket of Hamada's jacket and removed a mobile telephone, which he switched off and dropped into his own pocket. Then, placing a forceful hand between Hamada's shoulder blades, he pushed him across to the entrance of the park and returned to the car. The mounds of rags came closer.

"Wait! You can't leave me here. What do you want? Money? I'll give you anything you want! Just don't leave me here. Please . . . !"

Matsuoka turned around to face Hamada from a distance of three yards. "Hearing you grovel is all I want, Hamada. It is time for you to see the extent of the damage you have caused from close quarters. I think you'll find that most of your new-found friends"—he nodded in the direction of the rag-clad people gradually getting closer—"are in the early stages of the disease. I'm sure you'll have a pleasant time explaining away your involvement."

"Matsuoka, please! I implore you! Don't do this! I'll do anything you say. I give you my word! You cannot leave me here!"

"In case you are interested, that black bag contains as much food as we can spare and enough drugs for approximately one hundred people. Maybe you can convince them to let you have some, although I wouldn't raise your expectations too high. Once they see the letter that is also in there and discover who you are, they might not consider you worthy. I'll leave that decision up to them, however."

"Matsuoka, please. You are not thinking clearly. Leaving me here will solve nothing. Please take me away from here."

Ignoring Hamada's pleas, Matsuoka turned to Bryant. "Come, Peter-*san*. We should be getting back to Izu. It will soon be time for dinner."

The two men got into the car and drove off without a backward glance, leaving Hamada screaming in fear and rage as he tried fruitlessly to hop after them and away from the horrors that awaited him.

Professor Stanley Donnelly waved a hand at the driver of the truck and watched it drive toward the outer perimeter of the enclosure five hundred yards away, its tires kicking up billowing clouds of Maryland dust from the dirt road. He checked his clipboard to see how many other trucks could be expected that day before walking over to the small wooden hut near the construction site for a well-earned cup of coffee.

The window in front of his desk gave him a clear view through to the construction work. Not that a lot could be seen at the moment, of course. The prefabricated airtight compartments had already been delivered and set in place and most of the work was being carried out on the interior. The inspectors were due at three o'clock that afternoon by helicopter from Washington and Baltimore, but as the prefabricated structures were seamless and built to level four biosafety containment specifications before being delivered, he expected no problems there. The only inspection that was likely to take time was the negative air-pressure checks, given the fact that the entire complex consisted of nearly eighty compartmentalized sections. He hoped they would send a sufficient number of inspectors to get the job completed before the arrival of his guests the following day.

Donnelly was still having trouble believing that within twenty-four hours he would be leading a team of the world's foremost scientists in a project to identify a method of preventing the genetically engineered meningococcus bacterium from entering the bloodstream and triggering the inflammatory cascade. His own career, although not entirely spent in the shadow of obscurity, was nothing in comparison with those of the microbiologists and bacteriologists he was expecting from India, Portugal, the United Kingdom, Sweden, Germany, Israel, and Argentina. Every one of them, if not a household name, would be instantly recognized by anyone who had spent any time in the fields of microbiology, biology, and medicine. Between them they had probably published more books, papers, and essays than fifty other of their peers throughout the world, and Donnelly's own bookshelves contained nearly all of their works. If there were an Olympic event for microbiology, this would be known as the Dream Team.

And in addition to that, Donnelly himself was in line for receiving up to $2.5 million in bonuses. The project had been financed for a period of five months by an Asian consortium and authorized by Western Washington University via the White House, but the onus was being heavily placed on a swift solution. Donnelly would be paid a bonus of half a million dollars for every month before the end of the five-month deadline that a cure was found. In other words, he stood to pick up half a million if the cure was discovered in the fifth month, $1 million if discovered in the fourth month, and $1.5 million if discovered in the third month. If, as he was hoping, a miracle occurred and they made serious headway in the first month, his bonus would be a cool $2.5 million! The other doctors, he knew, were on a million-per-month bonus system. He had never heard of the consortium that was financing the whole affair, but they certainly were playing hardball. The cost of building and equipping the research and hospital facility with its razor-wire perimeter must be up near the billion mark, also. The state-of-the-art equipment being shipped in was the stuff dreams were made of, and sufficient to have any scientist in the whole world drooling in ecstasy.

The phone on Donnelly's desk rang. He passed his coffee cup to his left hand and picked up the receiver with his right. "Donnelly," he said. He listened for a few moments and checked his clipboard. "Okay, Joe, send them on through and tell them to take a right at the construction site and park in the grass field behind the bank of latrines."

Donnelly replaced the receiver in its cradle and finished his coffee before leaving the warmth of the office and heading toward the latrines. He could see the dust cloud generated by the convoy of eight luxury-accommodation trailers heading toward him and increased his pace so that he would be in position before they arrived. It was only a minor point, but he wanted to make sure that the trailers were parked with their cabs facing the south so that the interiors could take the best advantage of the daytime sunlight. A tiny detail, but, in Donnelly's opinion, nothing was too small a detail when it concerned the comfort of the Dream Team.

"More coffee?"

Peter Bryant looked up at Shigeko Kondo. "Yes. Thank you very much. Where is everybody?"

"Harumi is watching NHK in the kitchen, and my husband, Omotenashi, and Totchan are out foraging." Most of the houses in the area were weekend houses and consequently left vacant during the off-season. Many of them had stores of gasoline, kerosene, and other useful things in their garages, and Kondo regularly organized foraging expeditions to replenish their own supplies. Kondo kept a detailed list of everything removed from each house, with the intention of repaying the owners in full when they returned. "What are you doing?"

Bryant added sugar to his coffee. "Just finishing off a report to send to Washington. I'll be finished in about ten minutes if there's anything you want me to do."

"When did you last phone Michiyo-*san*?" Shigeko and Harumi were constantly nagging Bryant to telephone Michiyo at least once a day.

"A couple of days ago, but I'll get to that just as soon as I've sent this report." Bryant grinned. "You women do stick together, don't you?"

"Well, after you explained how upset she was about your being here, I can't help but sympathize with the poor girl."

"She's much better now, Shigeko-*san*. She just needed a little time to get used to the idea. I think she understands the reasons behind my motives a little better now."

"But she hasn't forgiven you entirely. . . ."

"No, not entirely," admitted Bryant.

Shigeko placed the coffee jug on the table and slipped into one of the chairs. "Would you like me to speak to her? I'm sure I could make her understand. Maybe she doesn't realize the importance of the job you are doing. Maybe a woman could explain it better."

"That's very nice of you, Shigeko-san, but I don't think it would do any good. The problem is not why I am providing America with information; it is why I am doing it from here instead of from Fukushima."

Shigeko nodded her understanding. She realized that she would probably feel the same under similar circumstances. "Then you must buy her a big, fat diamond ring when this is all over and tell her how much you love her."

"A big, fat one, huh?"

"Definitely. The bigger and fatter the better. One that fits on the fourth finger of the left hand."

Bryant looked at her in surprise. "An engagement ring? You crafty old schemer, you."

Shigeko smiled impishly. "Come, now, Peter-san. You are thirty years old and getting older by the minute. You need someone to look after you."

"I'm twenty-nine, if you don't mind."

"Almost an old man." Shigeko waved away his protests with a flick of her hand. "Marriage would be good for you, Peter-san. And that, if you want my opinion, is why Michiyo is upset with you now. It has nothing to do with your being here. She is waiting for you to pop the question."

Bryant grinned and released an exaggerated sigh. "I was right. You women *do* look after each other."

"Well, somebody has to look out for us. If we left everything up to you men, we would all end up neglected and miserable."

"Point taken. I'll phone her before dinner and buy her the biggest, fattest diamond ring I can get my hands on when all of this is over. Although I can't promise which finger it will fit at the moment. Fair enough?"

Shigeko closed her hand over Bryant's and looked deeply into his eyes, her mood suddenly mellow and serene. "Peter-san, I want to thank you."

Bryant raised his eyebrows at the sudden change in subject. "Thank me? Why?"

"For giving us the opportunity to help. Michiyo's loss is our gain. You have made us feel useful, needed, wanted even. Had it not been for you, we would have been stuck up here hiding under the tables and jumping at every small noise the wind makes as it rattles the trees." She paused and looked out of the window. Kondo's minivan was just turning into the driveway, and Gonta was dashing across the lawn as fast as his little legs would carry him, barking furiously at the joy of being reunited with his master after a prolonged separation that must have lasted all of three hours. Toshio Otsuka was the first to open the door and jump down onto the gravel, only to be almost knocked off his feet by the ecstatic corgi. Norio Kondo was next, closely followed by Kazunori Matsuoka. Each received the affections of Gonta in turn. "Look at that," Shigeko continued. "What do you see?"

"I see a successful expedition. They look like they've won the jumbo *Takarakuji*."

"What you are seeing, Peter-*san*, is contentment. Contentment at knowing that they are playing an active role in saving their country. Whether they achieve their goal does not matter. What matters is that they have tried. I have seen a dramatic change in my husband since we have been here. He is stronger, more focused. His mind's eye is fixed unwaveringly on a single target, and he is striding confidently toward it. He is enjoying the sensation of being alive and useful, as are we all. Thanks to you, Peter-*san*."

Bryant looked down at his computer keyboard in embarrassment. He wanted to tell Shigeko that he felt the same. That he, himself, felt alive and needed, and that in his mind, this was thanks to the Kondos, the Otsukas, and Matsuoka. It had nothing to do with him. He was simply a pawn who just happened to be in the right place at the right time. Instead he said nothing, knowing that Shigeko understood the sense of gratitude that he felt toward them.

After a moment's pause, Shigeko picked up the coffee jug and shook it. "Well, I've said my piece. I'd better go and refill this before the rest come in. And don't you forget to phone Michiyo, all right?"

"Yes, Shigeko-san. I understand. And thank you."

Left alone, Bryant added the final touches to his report, closed the file, and connected the satellite telephone to the back of the computer. He hit the send button and his file was "squirted" up into space and beamed instantly back to a different location in Washington D.C. A small beep informed Bryant that another file had simultaneously been downloaded into his computer. He opened the file and was scanning the contents as Kondo, Matsuoka, and Otsuka entered the room.

"Peter-san," enthused Otsuka, "we had an exceptional run today. Six extra cans of gasoline, two sacks of charcoal briquettes, soap powder, potatoes, carrots, rice, and even two pots of radish tsukemono pickling in miso."

"That's wonderful, Otsuka-san. The radishes should provide Kondo-san with plenty of ammunition for the tailwind gag. Maybe we should eat out on the lawn tonight."

"Ah, you can run, Peter-san, but you can't hide," Kondo said with a wink. "I shall simply save up my ammunition until we are inside again. How about your day? Any news?"

"Yes, as a matter of fact. I have just this minute received a message from Washington to say that work has begun in earnest on finding a cure for the meningococcemia disease. A special complex has been set up in Maryland manned by some of the world's leading scientists and microbiologists. The complex will also include hospital facilities where the victims of the disease in America can be cared for."

"There are victims in America also?" Everybody turned their attention to Shigeko Kondo, who had entered the living room bearing a tray of cups and the ever-present coffee jug.

"I'm afraid so, Shigeko-*san*. Most of the early cases have already died, but several new victims were discovered amongst the people who were evacuated from Japan. The scientists will use these people to discover if the antidote they develop works."

"But that's just awful!" Shigeko placed the tray on the table and rubbed her hands together in anguish. "I didn't realize that we were instrumental in killing Americans as well. How can they ever forgive us? Does that mean your country also has areas like our Chigasaki?"

"No, no, Shigeko-*san*. Most of the victims were discovered during a period of quarantine, and all sporadic outbreaks are being confined by swift action. Please don't worry. Everything is under control."

"Swift action," Matsuoka repeated wistfully. "What a wonderful phrase. Why is it that the Japanese government is incapable of swift action? It is heartbreaking sometimes to watch them play around with their committees and red tape while disaster looms. I have seen it so many times."

"You cannot blame the government totally, Totchan," said Kondo, pouring himself a cup of coffee and adding sugar and cream. "It is part of our cultural background. Our roots are in agriculture and commerce, and both of these require the consensus of the majority to succeed. In the olden days, a single farmer in a community could not change his crop from rice to wheat overnight, as the people around him relied on his rice crop. Without him they would have no rice. Besides, there was probably another farmer down the road who harvested wheat. He would be ruined. So the rice farmer would call a meeting in the village hall and air his ideas. The villagers would discuss it and maybe even discover that the farmer who raises wheat would rather raise rice. Problem solved by majority vote, the essence of Japanese culture. On the other hand, America's strength is its hunter background. Hunters must make decisions on the spot and follow them through. If the decision proves to be bad, they are willing to accept responsibility. We are just different people. We in Japan have a group mentality. Decisions are reached by consensus, not by individual initiative."

"America also has a history of agriculture, Kondo-*san*," said Bryant, enjoying the lecture. "Not *everyone* was a hunter."

"On a different scale, Peter-*san*. Your farms in America stretch as far as the eye can see. They are hundreds, even thousands of acres in size. A single farmer may have potatoes in one field, wheat in another, alfalfa in yet another. In Japan the average farm is no larger than one of your backyards in America. Twenty farms would make up a single small village that would fit into a baseball stadium with room to spare. The community was everything."

"That is very interesting indeed," said Bryant, watching Shigeko print something off the computer out the corner of his eye. "I have never thought of it in that way before. Yes, I believe it fits."

Shigeko walked across to her husband and handed him the printout. "This is where your theory falls to the ground, my husband. It seems as if the government is willing to take swift action after all."

Kondo examined the piece of paper, a look of concern spreading across his face. "Oh, dear," he said softly. "This is going to put the cat among the pigeons."

"What is it?" Matsuoka peered over his shoulder.

"It is a message from our friend Statesman." Statesman was the on-line handle selected by Matsuoka's ham radio friend. He had provided several interesting items of information since signing on with the Tokonokai and was proving invaluable.

"Well, what does it say?" persisted Matsuoka.

"It warns of an imminent power struggle within the government. It appears that Shoji Kubota, the general secretary of the Liberal Democratic Party, is poised to oust Kiyoshi Aizawa from power and assume the position of prime minister himself."

"When?"

"Early tomorrow morning, it seems."

Shoji Kubota sat behind his desk in the office of the speaker of the House of Representatives and waited for the next call. He had really wanted to claim the Emperor's Room, located at the top of the grand staircase leading up from the central hall, as his own, but explaining that away when the country returned to normal would not be an easy thing to do. No, it was better for him to appear humble in his new position and not create problems where none existed.

The telephone rang and he grabbed it from the cradle before the echo had died out. He listened in silence for a moment, a broad grin spreading across his features, and then hung up again. Everything was moving according to schedule. So far all of Aizawa's supporters located in the first and second members' office buildings had been confined to quarters, and his other staff in the Annex building were also under guard. That only left the third members' office building and the House of Representatives committee rooms. Aizawa would be the last to know of Kubota's rise to power, and Kubota had decided that he himself would be the bearer of this news. The anticipation created by the thought of how Aizawa would come to terms with this piece of information had Kubota mentally rubbing his hands together. He could hardly contain his impatience. He glanced up at the clock on the wall: four-twenty-two A.M. Twenty-two minutes since the bloodless coup had been launched. Twenty-two minutes for the pendulum of power to swing away from Aizawa and toward himself. Possibly the most important twenty-two minutes of his entire life.

The phone rang again, its guttural burbling seeming out of place in the early-morning silence.

"Yes?"

"All three office buildings secured, sir. No casualties to report."

Christopher Belton

Kubota replaced the receiver and steepled his hands together beneath his chin, only to hastily fold his arms across his chest as he realized that he had observed Aizawa assuming the same position on several occasions in the past. Four down, one to go. Two, counting Aizawa, but that was something to look forward to.

Rising to his feet, Kubota collected his jacket from the back of an armchair and brushed a piece of lint off the collar. He opened the door a fraction and addressed his personal secretary and the six military policemen who stood to attention without: "I shall be ready to leave in a few moments. Have you posted a guard outside of the state minister's room?"

"Yes, sir, Mr. Prime Minister," answered Susumu Ishibashi, his rimless spectacles glinting in the overhead lighting.

Kubota glowed with pride at hearing his new title for the first time, but held up a remonstrative finger. "Not quite, Ishibashi. But soon. Very soon."

Closing the door and returning to his desk, Kubota glared at the phone as if willing it to ring. What was taking them so long? As if in answer to his tacit question, the telephone gurgled.

"Yes?"

"The House of Representatives committee rooms are secure, sir. No injuries or casualties."

"Thank you, Sergeant. Remain in position until you receive further orders."

At last the moment had arrived. Kubota left his office and began to stride down the hall toward the west-central section of the Diet building, closely followed by his secretary, Susumu Ishibashi, and the six military policemen.

Pausing outside of the State Ministers' room, Kubota cleared his throat gently and forced himself to overcome the impulse to knock at the door. Mustering his most pleasant of smiles, he threw the door open and marched inside, leaving his entourage outside. The door swung closed behind him.

To his surprise, Aizawa was not asleep on the cot, but sat at his desk in front of a laptop computer, the only form of illumination being a desktop lamp.

"Ah, Kubota. What took you so long? I've been expecting you for thirty minutes."

Kubota's eyes narrowed, but he refused to take the bait. "I have some news for you, Aizawa, and I wanted to deliver it in person."

"Yes, I thought you might, somehow. Gloating would fit your character perfectly."

A hint of confusion began to diffuse Kubota's confidence. "You would be advised to select your words more carefully, Aizawa. Do you have any idea with whom you are speaking?"

Aizawa's shoulders shook as he chuckled. "You missed your vocation, Kubota. High drama has always been one of your fetishes, has it not, Mr. Prime Minister?"

"You know?"

"I guessed. You are not very subtle."

A storm of fury blew up within Kubota. He dismissed Aizawa's claim that he had guessed the situation out of hand, for if that was the case, how would he have known about the timing? Somebody privy to Kubota's plans must have been providing him with information. Despite the knowledge that he had a traitor in his camp, Kubota strained every fiber to suppress his anger. He was damned if he would give Aizawa the satisfaction of knowing that Kubota had been severely disappointed at being robbed of his chance to faze the ex–prime minister.

To provide himself with the time required to compose his features, Kubota walked across to the wall, picked up a chair, and placed it in front of Aizawa's desk. "You don't seem too bothered about the situation," he said once seated, calm again.

"Should I be? You have relieved me of a heavy burden. I am grateful."

Kubota, no longer able to contain his anger, banged his hand on the desk. "Don't play your games with me, Aizawa. You are in deep and very serious trouble. Pretending to be in total control of the situation is not only stupid, it is downright insulting. I would expect something like that from a kindergarten child, but not from a full-grown man. Admit it! You are shaking in your shoes. I know you are. You cannot fool me. Maybe knowing your fate once this is all over would wipe that smile off your face. Shall I tell you?"

"Save your breath, Kubota. Given the limitations of your imagination, I'm sure it would not be hard to work out for myself. Something like a charge of treason? Public humiliation? Paraded before the Diet in drab prison clothes, like the South Korean trials? Would that fit the bill?"

Kubota leaned forward, his face red and his voice wispy with anger and tension. "Do you want to know what I hate most about you, Aizawa?" Before Aizawa could reply, he continued, "You are supercilious. You carry with you a distasteful air of superiority that is unbecoming in a public servant. You exude slime that you confuse for confidence. You are *nothing!*"

"Well, it's nice of you to notice, Kubota. I appreciate it very much."

Kubota jumped to his feet, his patience suddenly depleted to dangerous levels. He pointed a finger at Aizawa, his arm shaking with fury. "You are confined to quarters until I can decide where else to keep you. Guards will be placed at the door and you will be allowed no visitors. Rot in your own slime, Aizawa. I have no further use for you."

Turning his back on Aizawa, Kubota stormed across the room and flung open the door, startling Ishibashi and the guards. "Organize a guard rotation. I want two people on this door at all times. Nobody goes in or out. Understood?"

"Yes, sir!"

"And you"—he pointed at Ishibashi—"follow me."

Back in his office, Kubota threw his jacket on the armchair and began pacing behind his desk. "Sit down!" he ordered.

"Yes, sir." Ishibashi sat in front of the desk and fearfully withdrew his notepad and pen. He had never seen the general secretary—no, the prime minister—in such a foul mood before.

"Inform everybody that there will be a cabinet meeting at nine o'clock. I want you to prepare an order for all military units to shoot looters, deserters, and sick survivors on sight in time for this meeting, where it will be reviewed. *And don't look at me like that!*" Kubota's anger was already near ignition point, and the last thing he wanted was for his decisions to be judged by a damned secretary.

Ishibashi lowered his eyes to his notepad and concealed his shock.

"I also want a facsimile giving details of the changeover in leaders drawn up, ready for dispatch to all governments of the world. Clear?"

"Yes, sir."

"Then get out!"

Chapter Twelve

The situations room in the underground complex of the White House was buzzing with activity when the president entered the area and took his seat at the head of the table. Aides rushed in and out, placing documents and folders in front of the people present and whispering conspiratorially into upturned ears. The technician seated at the console by the wall checked to confirm the arrival of a summarized document and clicked his mouse to display it on all of the monitors. Dale Lindley, the chairman of the Joint Chiefs of Staff, abandoned his discussion with CIA director Wayne Jeffers and took his place on the president's left-hand side. Secretary of State Patrick Watson clapped his hands once to indicate that the meeting was about to start. The aides hurried from the room and the door was closed behind them.

"Good evening, Mr. President. A summary of the report from Japan is available on your screen."

President Raymond DeBerry quickly scanned through the main points of Peter Bryant's report, displayed on the monitor in front of him. "Is it legal?" he asked at length, displaying no outward shock at the contents.

"The legality of the matter is difficult to ascertain with only this information, Mr. President," answered Watson, "but as this Shoji Kubota will be installed as the leader of the Liberal Democratic Party—the party currently in power—there is nothing that visibly goes against the constitution. The public votes in the party, not the leader, and I don't need to tell you how many times the prime minister of Japan has changed over the past fifteen years. It is one of their national pastimes, it seems. The leader of the party is elected by the other party members and becomes the prime minister by default."

"So there's nothing we can do?"

Watson shrugged. "Not as far as I can see."

"But this guy Bryant uses the phrase 'coup d'état.' Surely enforced takeovers are against the constitution."

"It could just be a turn of phrase for want of a better description. It's certainly not enough to run with."

The president nodded. "So tell me about this Kubota. What do we know about him?"

"You've met him yourself on three occasions at various events both here and in Japan, Mr. President. He is—or at least was—the general secretary of the Liberal Democratic Party and one of the so-called kingmakers. Very powerful. It is said that he orchestrated Kiyoshi Aizawa's rise to power himself."

"Is he stable?"

"Presumably, although he must be under a lot of stress and pressure to go as far as ousting the incumbent prime minister at a time like this."

"Psychological profile?"

"Maybe Wayne would answer that one. Wayne?"

Wayne Jeffers cleared his throat and sat forward in his seat. "Nothing that provides us with any deep insight, Mr. President. He is the leader of one of the largest factions. A die-hard politician who is probably intoxicated by power, but prefers to wield it from the background. That is what is so strange about this takeover. I can imagine him replacing the prime minister with another candidate of his choice, but seizing the reins of the premiership himself seems totally out of character. He is extraordinarily wealthy and has a reputation for collecting the largest amount of donations for the party coffers. There is a sort of competition that goes on within the parties in Japan to see who can collect the largest amount of donations, and Kubota has been ranked number one for seven of the past eight years. That requires a concerted effort and probably marks him as a man who hates to play second fiddle."

"Okay, so what do you suggest?" The president directed the question at Watson.

"I guess we have to work with him, Mr. President. The official notice of the takeover still hasn't arrived, but I doubt if it will give any indication that there will be changes in the ways things are to be run. As far as we're concerned, we just have a different guy to work with. Nothing much else has changed."

"Okay, that sounds fair enough. Write up the normal message about how we are looking forward to working with the new prime minister and send it off the moment the official notice arrives. Presuming, of course, that it is kosher. Now"—a broad grin was suddenly displayed on the president's face, his campaign trail expression—"tell me how the hell this guy Bryant is getting his information? What is he, some sort of superman?"

Jeffers laughed. "It's amazing, isn't it? Apparently he has established a nationwide network of contacts who are feeding him information on a daily basis. You wouldn't believe some of the intelligence he is coming up with. He is giving us precise information on the roads and railroads that are blocked, the areas that are badly infected, the regions that are crime-ridden, everything. It is like he has an overall view of the entire country. God knows how he managed to set it all up within such a short period of time. He's a damned genius!"

"How did you manage to get someone like that in place? I didn't think you had any covert operations in Japan." The question came from Jack Marchant, the secretary of defense.

"He is the friend of one of our embassy tykes in Tokyo, not one of our men. He is a translator specializing in U.S. patents, believe it or not. Just a regular Joe, really. He's young at twenty-nine, and speaks fluent Japanese. His mother, in fact, is a Japanese national. She lives in Los Angeles with her American husband. It was this guy—his name is Peter Bryant, by the way—who tipped us off to the outbreak in the first place. It was also he who established the link with the Japanese government *and* the one who passed us the information about how the bacterium was genetically engineered. God knows where he is getting all of this information, but man, he is solid gold."

"It looks to me like he is showing you how to do your job, Wayne," drawled Sterling Van Allen, the undersecretary for political affairs, a staunch proponent for reducing the CIA's budget. "There's the CIA with their satellites and multibillion-dollar gadgets, and this regular Joe, as you call him, is running rings around you. Makes you think, don't it?"

Jeffers refused to rise to the bait. He knew that the president had a short fuse when political squabbling broke out in his presence, so he simply shrugged his shoulders and made no comment.

"Did he mention where he got this information?" asked DeBerry, waving a hand at the computer screen. "How could he know of a takeover before it was made official? Has he got someone in the Diet building?"

"No, Mr. President," replied Jeffers, "he has somebody monitoring the radio waves. He has also provided us with a lot of excellent intelligence on military movements through the same source. As I say, the guy is solid gold."

"Incredible. Make sure you keep him safe, Wayne. I'd like

to meet this man when everything is under control and he's back in the States." He turned to the secretary of state. "Maybe we could work out some sort of award for him, Patrick. Maybe even a medal or something. What do you think?"

"Well, he certainly deserves it, Mr. President. I think that is an excellent idea."

"Right, get on it then. And keep me informed of any updates."

Rising to his feet, the president nodded politely to everyone and left the room. Three floors above, the official message from the Japanese government announcing the change in the leadership of the country was being received by the communications office.

By the time trading opened in the Singapore markets, the English-language *Business Times* newspaper had been on the streets for three hours. Despite a relatively small circulation of just under thirty thousand copies, the front-page announcement of a rumor that the team of leading scientists in America was close to finding a cure for the meningococcemia disease sent a surge through all Asian markets and had speculators scrabbling to fill their pockets with stocks and currencies at bargain-basement prices. At ten o'clock precisely, investors from eleven Asian countries began to purchase massive amounts of blue-chip issues and other Asian stocks as well as currency in huge volume, triggering an unprecedented session of panic buying that lasted through to the end of trading. Although suspecting this to be a coordinated ploy to stimulate buying, the European markets picked up where Asia left off and began to dump dollars, Euros, and other European currencies in massive sums in favor of Asian currencies while they were still comparatively cheap. With nowhere to go but up, investors could not *afford* to miss the opportunity that had been handed to them on a plate. Within twenty hours of the *Business Times* being issued, a noticeable blip of confidence had returned to the Asian markets and a lot of people had become very rich. On paper, at least.

Peter Bryant shuffled the computer printouts on the dining table and marveled at how accurate Kazunori Matsuoka's prediction of a return to civility was turning out to be. Of the forty-seven messages before him, twenty-eight described positive efforts by groups of civilians to put their lives back into some semblance of order. Groups of vigilantes were being formed to patrol and police localized areas, and offenders were being locked up and guarded. One of the biggest problems plaguing the urban areas had been the huge groups of *Bosozoku*—gangs of youths on motorcycles and souped-up automobiles that terrorized entire neighborhoods—but there was one message from a Tomonokai member in Kumagaya, Saitama prefecture, reporting that an organized group of civilians had raided a *Bosozoku* camp and punctured the tires and gas tanks of over a hundred machines. Bryant thought back to his conversation with Matsuoka in the bath and shook his head in wonder. It was uncanny. The man was a genius, Bryant decided, little knowing that this same epithet had been appended to his own name not a few hours before in the White House.

Unfortunately, not all of the messages had good news to report. The computer had beeped approximately thirty minutes previously and Bryant had watched in despair as a message from Statesman came in. The message had explained how Statesman had intercepted a radio transmission and discovered that all military units were being ordered to shoot deserters, looters, and sickened victims of the meningococcemia disease on sight. Apparently this had been the first official order that the new prime minister had issued, and it was to be put into effect immediately. Although Statesman had not deigned to include his own personal opinion of this action, his disgust had been apparent in the method and style of writing. Bryant himself knew very little of Shoji Kubota, but NHK had been airing past footage of the man since the official announcement of the takeover had been issued earlier that morning, and nothing he had seen had prepared him for the knowledge that the new prime minister was capable of ordering the indiscriminate death of countless people. NHK had depicted him as a tolerant, avuncular sort of figure who wielded tremendous power behind the scenes of Japan's house of representatives. He was the leader of one of the largest factions and had a vast number of loyal supporters. How could a man like that suddenly change into a cold-blooded murderer? He supposed there was a chance that Statesman was mistaken, but judging from the accuracy of every report he had sent through so far, Bryant doubted if that was a viable possibility.

Whatever the case, Bryant was obliged to send this information through to Washington as soon as he possibly could. Maybe the American government would be able to contact the new prime minister and dissuade him from this radical method of dealing with the situation. He hoped so.

He was halfway through typing the report when Kazunori Matsuoka and Norio Kondo returned from the garage, where they had been sorting out the supplies and stacking them in the appropriate order of consumption. Their daily foraging expeditions had yielded enough food and fuel to keep them alive for six months, and the previous evening Kondo had been ruing the amount of money he would need to fork out in payment for all of this once things got back to normal again. That had reminded Bryant of the money that Matsuoka had given him.

"Working at your computer again, Peter-*san*?" said Kondo as he walked through the living room and into the tatami room, jauntily followed by Matsuoka. "A man's work is never finished, right?"

Bryant laughed dutifully and turned back to the computer to finish off the report. Just as he hit the send button to transmit the file to Washington, he heard the loud ripping sound of a full-grown man breaking wind from the tatami room, and then Kondo's voice rose in a gleeful, "*Oikaze da!*" The man was incorrigible. Bryant shook his head and chuckled to himself.

Bryant carried the computer up to his room and collected the leather clutch bag of money that Matsuoka had given to him almost a lifetime ago. By the time he had returned to the tatami room, Matsuoka and Kondo had spread the day's messages from the Tomonokai members out on the low table and were reading through them and chatting quietly together.

"Ah, Peter-*san*," said Matsuoka, jubilantly waving a handful of the messages in the air, "the bouillabaisse begins to settle, I see. Did I not tell you so?"

"You certainly did, Matsuoka-*san*. I am impressed beyond words." Bryant settled himself down at the table. "But have you seen the message from Statesman?"

"No, not yet." Matsuoka hunted around amid the pile of papers until he found the message he was looking for. A frown etched deep lines into his forehead as he read through it. "This is serious," he said, passing the message across to Kondo. "Killing the victims of the disease is one way of preventing it from spreading, but hardly the most suitable. This could cause riots."

Kondo read through the message before throwing it onto the table in disgust. "Pah!" he exclaimed, "this is just typical of the Japanese government! Ignore it until it bites you, and then shoot it! Damn, but this is terrible! I have never trusted these people who wield power behind the scenes. They think of nothing but themselves, their own power bases, and their bank accounts. How could Aizawa allow this . . . this . . . this moron to take over?"

"I hardly think you can blame the former prime minister," said Matsuoka reproachfully. "Statesman called it a coup d'état, and NHK labeled it a forceful reshuffling of power and mentioned that Aizawa had been arrested and confined. I somehow get the feeling that Kubota didn't actually *ask* him if he could take over."

"*Kuso!* That's all we need, soldiers running about shooting everyone on sight. Do you think we are safe here?"

"Who knows?" replied Matsuoka tiredly. "Although I don't see any reason for the military to come to these parts. We have no reports of disease or crime this far up the mountain. We *should* be out of their sphere of interest and consequently safe. Who can tell?"

"I suppose this also corroborates Statesman's report of the other day stating that the Self-Defense Forces were being troubled by countless desertions," said Bryant, picking up the message and reading it again. "With a bit of luck, the whole damn lot will desert and nobody will be left to do the killing."

"Wishful thinking, Peter-*san*. The majority of these people are having a fine time with all this power they have been presented with. An order like this is a dream come true for them. Don't hold your breath."

"Have you sent your report on this to Washington yet, Peter-*san*?" asked Kondo.

"Yes, just a few minutes ago. I have suggested that the president contact Kubota to try to persuade him to rescind the order. External pressure might work better."

Matsuoka looked up at Bryant in wonder. "You are a very powerful man, Peter-*san*," he said. "Now it is my turn to be impressed. Let us hope that the president of the United States heeds your advice."

The three men lapsed into silence as they wrestled with their own thoughts and gently rifled through the stack of messages on the table, earnestly searching for any snippet of pleasant news that would dissipate the feeling of desolation that Statesman's message had generated. The dusk was falling rapidly behind the paper-screen windows, but nobody noticed the darkness until Toshio Otsuka returned from collecting wood and pulled the cord above the table to switch the light on.

"Why so glum?" he asked, seating himself on a *zabuton* cushion and surveying his colleagues.

Kondo passed him the message from Statesman and the four lamented once more over this turn of events, Otsuka's opinion matching everybody else's exactly.

"How did the stacking go?" Bryant asked once the subject had been exhausted and the room had lapsed again into silence. "Do we have enough supplies to last through the spring?"

"We have enough to last until Christmas, Peter-*san*," Kondo replied, "Although I estimate we will be down to rice and pickles by about the middle of the summer."

Bryant reached for the clutch bag that he had stashed beneath the table and brought it out into view. "I want you have this," he said, passing the bag across to Kondo. "It is to cover the cost of the food and fuel you've . . . um . . . borrowed. It contains both mine and Matsuoka-*san*'s share."

Kondo accepted the bag with a curious grin. "What is it? Money?"

Bryant nodded.

Kondo unzipped the bag and looked inside, whistling at the sight of the fat wad of banknotes. He looked up in confusion. "But this is far too much, Peter-*san*. In any case, I don't need any extra money. We have plenty."

"I insist."

Kondo looked across at Matsuoka. "And what is your connection here? How come Peter-*san* says it includes your share?"

Matsuoka shrugged. "That is between Peter and I, Gakusha. If you don't want it, give it back to him."

"How much is here?"

"Four million yen," replied Bryant.

Kondo looked thoughtful for a moment before finally saying, "I'll tell you what I'll do. I'll match this sum and place it in a pool. Whatever is left after all expenses are paid we split evenly between us. Fair?"

"Don't forget me." Everybody looked at Toshio Otsuka. "I'll

283

add my share, too. That gives us each a two-million-yen investment, right? I'm happy with that. If we're going to do it, let's do it together."

Kondo looked around at each person in turn. "That sounds fair. Everything that doesn't get spent gets returned. Is everybody agreed?"

"Agreed," said Bryant.

"Agreed," echoed Matsuoka.

"Definitely," said Otsuka.

Thirty minutes later, as Bryant was standing out in the garden watching the stars twinkling over Mount Omuro, Matsuoka came up behind him and placed a hand on his shoulder.

"Stargazing, I see," he said.

"Yes. It's a beautiful night."

"Even better since the factories have been closed down and the pollution has dissipated. I have never seen so many stars."

"Me neither. If it weren't so cold, I could stay out here all night."

Matsuoka looked down at his feet to see what was nudging against his legs. Gonta, the corgi, had followed him out to see if he was on his way to dig up a bone or a secret stash of food. "Was the full four million in that bag?" Matsuoka asked softly.

"Yes, it was."

"You spent not even one yen of it?"

"No. I was saving it for emergencies. I used my credit card for hotel bills and other things."

"And you regard Gakusha as an emergency?" Matsuoka laughed. "Yes, I see your point. If we are lucky, he might use some of it to plug that obnoxious *ketsu* of his and save us all from the indignity of further tailwinds."

Bryant laughed too. "No, no. Nothing like that. It just occurred to me that he was being put to enormous expense on my behalf and I thought the money would be better spent in his hands."

Matsuoka fell silent as he stared up into the dark, cloudless sky and watched the canopy of stars. "You are a good man, Peter Bryant," he said at length. "You have a noble heart, and I am a better man for having known you. When this is all over, I hope you will not forget us. I would like us to remain friends forever."

Bryant look at Matsuoka and grinned. "That, Matsuoka-*san*, I can promise you."

The knock at the door brought Kiyoshi Aizawa out of his dream world and back to reality. He had been sitting at his desk, pondering the future and seeing himself relaxing on the porch of the family home in Nagano, his two granddaughters laughing and squealing as they chased each other through the garden. He preferred this scenario to the one where he spent the rest of his days behind bars, and was beginning to dwell on it more and more frequently of late. He didn't bother answering the knock, as he knew the guard would enter anyway.

"Your dinner, sir," said his jailer, pushing a small trolley laden with a tray of food through the door. He positioned the trolley beside Aizawa's desk and left the room.

Aizawa reached across to swing the trolley behind his desk and moved the tray onto the top of his blotter. At least Kubota was not trying to further his humiliation by rationing his food intake. The layout was lavish and even included the small carafe of red wine that he had requested on a silver platter. Picking up the chopsticks and removing the lid from the soup bowl, Aizawa began to eat. The grilled yellowtail with its coating of teriyaki sauce was especially good, and he relished each mouthful. Alternating between the various dishes of fish, meat, pickled vegetables, and rice, Aizawa slowly but methodically finished off the food, pausing only once to pour himself a glass of wine, until all of the plates were empty. Replete, he sat back and reached a hand out for the carafe of wine. He raised it a few centimeters and removed the silver platter from beneath it. With searching fingers, he located a small clip on the edge and pressed it, allowing the platter to be split open like a circular book, held together only by a small and invisible hinge. A single sheet of paper fell out onto his lap. Closing the platter, he swiftly read through the note and clicked his tongue in exasperation. Taking a pen from his desk drawer, he turned the note over and wrote for several minutes on the back in distinctive but neat *kanji* before replacing it inside the platter and returning it to the tray.

Deciding that a drop more wine was in order, he refilled his glass and sat back while he waited for the tray and trolley to be removed. The boredom of confinement was beginning to fray his nerves, but there was no doubt that a good wine helped him relax and see things in a better perspective.

The telephone on the president's desk rang, and DeBerry picked it up immediately.

"Line test, sir. Would you mind saying something, please?"

"Mary had a little lamb; she tied it to a pylon. A thousand volts shot up its ass, and turned its wool to nylon."

"Thank you, sir. Now the interpreter. Would you say something, please?"

"Testing, one, two, three, four . . ."

"Thank you. Not very imaginative, but it serves the purpose. The call should be established within a few minutes. Please hang up and wait for the phone to ring again."

The line went dead and DeBerry replaced the receiver in its cradle. The line tests for secure overseas communications were causing him a lot of headaches, as he was nearing the end of his limerick repertoire. He made a point of using a different one for every test, and was recently finding himself spending more and more time on trying to recall a snappy one than he was on official government business. It was all crap anyway. Although the trace had to be run all the way through to Tokyo to make sure nobody was intercepting the call while he spoke with the prime minister, the fact that at least a dozen people would be listening in at both ends and that a further thirty or so would get to read the transcript afterward rather invalidated the concept of securing privacy and confidentiality. Still, it satisfied the consciences of his paranoid staff and allowed them to feel that the work they were involved in was more important that anybody else's, and that, in itself, was an important factor of life on the Hill.

The phone rang again, but this time DeBerry took his time answering it, needing to mentally prepare himself for the upcoming conversation. It was not common practice for the leader of one nation to offer open criticism to the leader of another nation on a man-to-man basis, and the president was not sure how Kubota would react to his probing. Such chores were usually the sole province of the diplomats and took months of careful planning, but in DeBerry's opinion, the time for diplomacy had passed.

He picked up the receiver and listened to the faint popping and crackling noises reverberating down the line.

"You're clear. Go ahead," said a voice.

"Good morning, Mr. Prime Minister. I trust I am not disturbing you." DeBerry could hear the interpreter at the other end of the connection translating his words into Japanese.

A moment later, a stream of Japanese filtered down the line from the other end, and the American interpreter immediately began a simultaneous translation.

"Of course you are not disturbing me, Mr. President. It is a pleasure to hear your voice. What can I do for you?"

"I wanted to welcome you to the premiership of Japan personally, Mr. Prime Minister. I am sure our two countries will continue to enjoy a long and lasting relationship under your guidance."

"That is most kind of you. I assure you that I think along the same lines."

"In which case, Mr. Prime Minister, you will not mind my mentioning that we are rather concerned about the order for military units to open fire on unarmed civilians."

A pause.

"I see," the interpreter said at length. "And may I ask how you came by this information? It has not been officially announced yet. Nobody outside of my cabinet knows of it."

"We have our methods, Mr. Prime Minister. I would just like to voice my protest of such actions and respectfully request that you reconsider. I realize that things are difficult over there, but murdering civilians will not solve the problem."

"Excuse me, Mr. President, but I resent the use of the word 'murder.' This is an internal affair and has nothing to do with the United States of America. I would be obliged if you would refrain from interfering in the affairs of a sovereign nation."

"I was hoping you wouldn't see it as interference. We are just concerned, Mr. Prime Minister. Deeply concerned."

"Then may I suggest that you direct your concerns back into your own country? Your crime figures are atrocious and the tales of judicial corruption shameful for an advanced country. I hardly think that you are in a position to explain the meaning of right and wrong to me."

DeBerry could feel the rage beginning to rise within him. He was making a concerted effort to be as polite as possible, but Kubota seemed intent on speaking his mind without preamble. "Mr. Prime Minister, you would be advised to reconsider this order. The United States is committed to doing everything within its power to help Japan overcome this problem, but it would be extremely difficult for us to overlook government-sanctioned genocide."

"Genocide? I must protest at your choice of words, Mr. President. The people who will be affected by this order are criminals. They are worthless creatures who are destroying our efforts to maintain civil order."

"I'm sorry, Mr. Prime Minister, but I cannot condone that. Neither looting nor deserting are crimes deserving of capital punishment. And what of the victims of the disease? How can you possibly label them criminals?"

Another pause. DeBerry presumed that Kubota was becoming more and more irate on the other end of the telephone, as he was himself. He had detected a slightly stronger inflection in the man's phrasing, despite the fact that the person delivering the message, the interpreter, was a female with a particularly emotionless voice that failed to carry the man's rage.

"I'm afraid, Mr. President," the interpreter continued a moment later, "that I must run this country as I see fit. Your suggestion has been noted and respectfully rejected, and I would be grateful if you did not try to interfere in the running of this country again. If you have anything constructive to offer in the future, then I will gladly accept your call. Otherwise, it might be better if you kept your advice to yourself."

"I'm sorry you feel that way, Mr. Prime Minister. I believe it is in the best interests—"

"I'm sorry, sir." The voice of an engineer came over the line, interrupting the president. "Japan has hung up, sir."

DeBerry stared at the receiver in open-eyed wonder. In three and a half years of his being the president of the United States, it was the first time that anybody had ever hung up on him, and he discovered that the new experience was not to his liking. "Bastard!" he muttered under his breath before slamming the receiver down in its cradle.

Shoji Kubota sat at his desk, clenching and unclenching his fists. The audacity of the president of the United States in presuming to tell him how to run Japan had astounded him, but not as much as had the news that he had a spy in his camp. That was the only explanation Kubota could think of for DeBerry's knowing the details of the execution order. Damn, he even knew that the disease carriers were to be targeted. He grabbed the phone and waited impatiently until it was answered by his secretary, Susumu Ishibashi.

"Yes, sir?"

"Check all communication data for the past three days," he shouted down the phone, his fury getting the better of him. "I want a list of every overseas call that left this building and the name of the person who made the call. Fast!" He slammed down the telephone.

If anybody was in contact with America from the Diet building, the list should be able to smoke him or her out. But what if it didn't? What would that mean? It could mean anything, from the United States government having the Diet building bugged, to an internal spy reporting to somebody who was in touch with the American authorities on the outside. However, no matter how it was being carried out, it would have to be stopped—and stopped quickly.

Kubota suddenly paused, the memory of something that might be important flashing into his mind: a report that he had seen the previous day and dismissed as not requiring any further attention. Could it be what he was looking for? He picked up the phone again and waited for his secretary to answer.

"Yes, sir?"

"Ishibashi, do you remember that report you gave me yesterday on unidentified satellite transmissions?"

"Yes, sir."

"Tell me about it."

"Two of our radars stationed in Odawara and Yamanashi have picked up unidentified satellite traffic on several occasions, Mr. Prime Minister. The transmission time was so short that it attracted the attention of one of the radar operators. Although satellite transmissions are not uncommon, the length would seem to suggest that certain compression techniques are being used, indicating a level of sophistication that is not normally found in the private sector."

"Military equipment, you mean?"

"A possibility, but not confirmed, sir."

"Can you isolate the satellite with which it is communicating? I mean, is it one of our satellites?"

"No, sir. It is a noncommercial satellite owned and operated by the United States government, sir."

"I see." A grin appeared on Kubota's face. "Tell me, Ishibashi: is it possible to pinpoint the location of these transmissions?"

"Yes, sir. We already know that it comes from somewhere inside the Izu peninsula, or possibly farther south toward Shizuoka, but we will require one more radar concentrated on the area to acquire an exact location."

"Listen carefully, Ishibashi. I want you to arrange for another radar to be set up immediately to pinpoint these transmissions. Once you have the location, I want the person or persons involved captured. Alive if possible, but if necessary they must be killed to prevent further transmissions. Have I made myself clear?"

"Yes, sir."

"Oh, and one other thing. I want you to keep this a secret from all of the cabinet members. Nobody, apart from you and me, is to know. Do you understand?"

"Understood, sir, but it will be necessary for me to explain the situation to the Self-Defense Forces."

"Of course it will, fool! What do you take me for? Just make sure that nobody inside this building gets to hear of it. All right?"

"Yes, sir. I'll get on it right away."

"You do that, Ishibashi. And let me know when the culprits have been captured."

Chapter Thirteen

Harumi Otsuka was the first to see the message from Statesman arriving on the bulletin board. She swiftly printed it out and took it through to the kitchen, where Peter Bryant and Kazunori Matsuoka were adding further details to the large map of Japan that was hanging on the wall. They had devised a color-coding system to indicate conditions within the country and provide visual information at a glance, and the entire map was littered with different-colored fluorescent ink. The areas shaded in fluorescent red represented heavily infected regions, the roads and railway lines shaded in fluorescent green were impassable, and the areas shaded in fluorescent yellow indicated high-crime or otherwise dangerous regions. Every morning Bryant and Matsuoka spent an hour or so updating the map from printouts of the messages that had come in from their contacts over the past twenty-four hours. Bryant would then compose his report based on the same messages and send it off to Washington.

"We've got trouble," said Harumi as she entered the kitchen.

Both men looked at her quizzically.

"Your satellite transmissions have been detected, Peter-*san*. Statesman says that we must never use this method of communication from here again."

"Damn, you're kidding! Let me see." Bryant took the message and read through it before looking up at Matsuoka helplessly, his shoulders sagging wearily. "They even know we are in Izu."

"But that is terrible! We cannot stay here. We shall have to get out as soon as we can."

"No, we are safe for the time being. Statesman says that they still don't know the exact area, but they are training the radars on this region and will easily be able to get a location if I transmit from the computer again. That means I can't contact Washington anymore."

"You have to send at least one more message, Peter-*san*. You have to let your people know the situation."

"But that's impossible. They'll get us for sure."

"They will if you don't."

"Excuse me?"

"What will the people who are expecting your messages do if you suddenly stop contacting them?"

"Of course! They'll phone me using the satellite connection. Damn!"

Matsuoka walked over to the refrigerator and examined the map of the Kanto region pinned to the door with two magnets. "We must go for a long drive and send the message from somewhere far away from here."

"Where do you suggest? It might not be safe to go too far. We might hit trouble if we run into one of those military units with orders to shoot on sight."

"Hakone," said Matsuoka, tracing his finger along the map. "We can use the Izu Skyline road. It runs straight through the mountains down to Lake Ashinoko and is well off the beaten path. Hakone should be far enough away."

"Okay, that sounds good. When shall we leave?"

"How about tomorrow morning? There is no point going until after you have prepared your report, and if we leave this afternoon we will have to drive back in the dark. I don't think that is a good idea, somehow."

"Yes, all right. They wouldn't contact me for a single missed report. Tomorrow will be plenty of time. I'll write out the report this afternoon."

"Just make sure it is a good one, Peter-*san*. It may be our last."

The first hint that success was in the offing arrived in Professor Stanley Donnelly's office in the form of a telephone call from Dr. Frederick Manswell of the Department of Biological Sciences at the University of Warwick in England, one of the leading members of the Dream Team.

"Professor Donnelly, I think you ought to come and see this."

"Certainly, Doctor. I'll be down in a moment. Is it anything interesting?"

"Very interesting indeed, Professor. I think we may have something."

"What?"

Donnelly slammed down the phone and hurried out of his office within the Maryland complex. The cream-colored walls of the corridor absorbed the sound of his footsteps, which clicked annoyingly on the carpetless floor made out of a bio-safe premolded-plastic compound. Arriving at Dr. Manswell's laboratory, he quickly entered the air shower and changed into the white protective clothing that resembled a baby's romper suit and covered him from head to toe. Finally, placing the special mask over his mouth and nose and slipping on the latex gloves, Donnelly entered the laboratory and walked across to where Dr. Manswell stood looking through a glass panel imbedded into the wall of the laboratory, dressed in an identical suit of protective clothing.

The Dream Team had been split up into three different groups to attack the problem of finding a cure for the *Neisseria* meningococcus bacterium from different angles simultaneously. Group A was working on a vaccine that would teach the body's natural killers to initiate a response to the bacterium, Group B was trying to discover a method of neutralizing the UL18 flag that tricked the body's NK cells into thinking the bacterium belonged in the body, and Group C was trying to come up with something that would destroy the bacterium while it was still in the victim's nasopharynx to prevent it from entering the bloodstream and releasing its endotoxins. Dr. Manswell was the leader of Group B.

"Ah, Professor Donnelly. Good of you to come." The doctor's British accent was soft and easy on the ear. He waved a hand at the glass panel fixed into the wall. "Take a look at that, Professor, and tell me what you see."

Donnelly peered through the glass into the miniature intensive-care ward containing four beds. On each of the beds sat a victim of the disease, although Donnelly had never seen the victims sitting up and acting this perky before. A nurse stood beside the bed of one patient taking a blood sample, her face concealed behind a plastic mask. Donnelly turned back to Manswell, a look of incredulity spreading across his features. "You've done it? You actually cracked it?"

The doctor smiled, hardly able to contain his own excitement. "Well, it is still too early to say with any certainty, but if you had seen the state of these people this morning, you could be forgiven for jumping to conclusions and saying that we finally have something with which to fight this monster."

"But how? How did you manage it?"

"It's a cocktail of several things, including first-line antibiotics and a bactericidal/permeability-increasing protein that helps the white blood cells neutralize the bacterial endotoxin."

"But we've already tried that. It didn't work."

"Ah, yes, but that was a result of the UL18 protein. Once that flag has been shut off, the other drugs assist the immune system in going to work on the disease."

"You managed to shut off the protein?"

Manswell nodded happily. "You could put it that way, although it is not entirely accurate."

Donnelly stared through the window in disbelief. One of the patients, a teenage girl, waved at him. He absentmindedly waggled his fingers and smiled in return. All of the seventy-three patients in the complex had signed releases to allow drugs untested in clinical trials to be used on them. An executive order signed by the president had also overridden FDA stipulations to allow the procedures of drug testing to be bypassed in this single, unique case. Time, it was decided, was of the essence, and there was a chance that this method, although not without its risks, could save the lives of countless people who would certainly be doomed if not treated expediently. "I can't believe this. It's incredible. How the hell did you neutralize the UL18 protein?"

"I didn't actually neutralize it, but I suppose the end result is the same. It was quite simple, actually. All I did was create a monoclonal antibody. Our original thought was to try to reverse-engineer the bacterium to remove it, but that was turning out to be both time-consuming and inconsequential, and the data we received from Japan was not helping any either. I then remembered that there is conclusive work being carried out on antibodies that 'sit' on proteins that are foreign to the host in order to trick the immune system into not recognizing that transplanted organs do not belong within the body, thus overriding the necessity of using anti-immune system drugs. Maybe you have heard of this work?"

"Yes, of course. It is used quite commonly in human organ transplants nowadays."

"Well, I then started experimenting with an idea in which

the antibodies do not block the immune system, but activate it instead. However, in order to do this, the antibody would have to be specifically designed for the protein against which it is to work. So I calculated the DNA code for the active sites of the UL18 antibodies, genetically engineered them into the E. coli bacterium, grew them in a one-liter fermentor, and then purified them out, if you see my point."

"I certainly do! It's so simple. And this is the result?" Donnelly waved his hand at the patients behind the glass panel.

"It most assuredly is, Professor," replied Manswell, his chest puffing out slightly. "The antibodies are basically designed to single out the UL18 protein and put a 'hat' on it in order to make it recognizable to the immune system. Once the system has been alerted to the danger, the natural killer cells will then go to work on the *Neisseria* meningococcus bacterium, aided by the antibiotics and bactericidal/permeability-increasing protein."

"Doctor, you are a genius!" Donnelly grabbed Manswell's hand and shook it vigorously. "I presume that it will be possible to mass-produce it?"

"Of course. If you use enough thousand-liter vessels, you'll be able to make it by the ton. Unfortunately, it is not a cure as such, and will not help anybody in the latter stages of the inflammatory cascade, but it will help the people in the early stages of the disease and stop the epidemic dead in its tracks."

"This is absolutely wonderful, Doctor! Is it conclusive yet? What I mean is, how long do you think it will take before I can announce this?"

"Almost immediately, really. Although I would like to monitor progress on the remainder of the complex's victims first of all. As you know, this killer hits so fast that any progress will be immediately noticeable. If you'll give the go-ahead for all of them to be treated with the antibody and other drugs, I'd like to keep an eye on them overnight and see what we have in the morning. If all goes well and these initial patients do not suffer any relapses, you should be able to contact your people before midday tomorrow."

Bryant was enjoying the trip across the mountains from Izu to Hakone. The weather was beautiful and the scenery breathtaking. Every now and then a tantalizing glimpse of the glittering ocean was revealed far below them, only to be snatched away again a moment later as the car entered another avenue of cedar trees or sped behind another outcrop of rock. The Izu Skyline was a toll road—although nobody had been collecting the tolls on this day—and consequently kept in perfect condition, and even with the regular bends and hairpins, Matsuoka's Cedric was able to maintain an average speed of nearly eighty kilometers per hour.

Two hours later Matsuoka left the toll road and followed the road signs down to the side of Lake Ashinoko. The car park was devoid of vehicles, and Matsuoka pulled up as close to a clump of trees as was possible. Bryant grabbed his computer from the backseat and the two men got out of the car.

"Hell, it's freezing!" said Bryant, hastily pulling the collar of his coat closer together under his chin.

"It's the altitude up here. The temperature is several degrees lower than at sea level. The wind whips over the lake, too, making it feel much colder than it is. The windchill factor."

They walked across to the edge of the lake and watched the swan-shaped pedal boats bobbing against each other in the stiff breeze beside a wooden pier, seeming strangely out of place without the hordes of tourists queuing up for an hour's rental. A large sightseeing boat decorated as a pirate ship was moored forlornly to the quayside several hundred meters to their right. Not a soul was in sight.

"Come on. Let's get it done and get out of here," said Matsuoka. "I feel somehow exposed."

Bryant sat down on a wooden bench and opened the computer on his lap. He reached into his pocket for the satellite telephone and connected it into the back of the computer. A few moments later the computer displayed the communications screen that he required. He highlighted the file that contained his final report and hit the send button. After the message had been sent, the machine beeped and a new file appeared in the directory.

"Ah, looks like we have a message from them, too." Bryant opened the file and scanned the contents, a look of incredulous excitement spreading across his face. "They've done it! Matsuoka-*san*, they've *done* it!"

"How pleasant for them. I hope they had a nice day for it."

"No, you don't understand. They have a cure! Everything's going to be all right!"

Matsuoka's mouth dropped open in shocked wonder. "But that is wonderful!" he exclaimed. "Are you sure?"

"Yes, yes, yes! It says so right here. Although they are not calling it a cure. They are calling it monoclonal antibody therapy. Apparently they have neutralized the component that tricks the body into accepting the disease so that it can be treated with conventional drugs. It won't help the people in the advanced stages of the disease, but it will prevent it from spreading further. Oh, my God, this is wonderful!"

"Now all we have to do is find a way of getting it here and distributing it. What I have seen of the new prime minister so far does little to instill me with confidence that he will go much out of his way to assist the American government. We might still have a fight on our hands, Peter-*san*. We must not let down our guard for a moment."

"Mr. Prime Minister? Ishibashi, sir. The radars have located a quick-burst satellite transmission from the banks of Lake Ashinoko."

Shoji Kubota gripped the side of his desk with his free hand. "When?"

"Just a few moments ago, sir. We have a two-vehicle ground

unit in the area, and they are currently speeding toward the location. I should have some news within a few minutes."

"Why Lake Ashinoko? I thought you said the transmissions were coming from the Izu peninsula. Lake Ashinoko is in Hakone."

"I have no idea, sir. Unless he was warned of the increased radar activity. Either that or he is mobile and not permanently situated in Izu."

"Damn! Oh, well. It can't be helped. Well done, Ishibashi. Let me know the moment the spy has been captured. Remember, I want him alive if possible. If we do have an informer here, I'm sure he would be more than pleased to tell us who it is with a little gentle persuasion."

Matsuoka was just driving out of the car park when two military vehicles came thundering down the hill leading to the lakeside right in front of them.

"Jesus!" exclaimed Bryant in panic. "Hit a left! Go left! Quick!"

Matsuoka heaved on the steering wheel and stomped on the accelerator when the car was halfway into the turn. The car responded instantly, and both men were thrown back against their seats as it roared forward like a racing horse given its rein. The sound of squealing tires was clearly audible as the two military vehicles careened around the corner in hot pursuit.

Bryant turned around in his seat and looked out the rear window. "A jeep and a truck," he said, watching the vehicles gain on them. "And they are really moving. Can't we go any faster?"

"Yes, but I'm no racing driver," replied Matsuoka, his voice loud with tension as he concentrated on driving. "I'm likely to kill us both if I go too fast. I'm not used to this, Peter-*san*. Damn, I should have asked you to drive."

"I would have refused. I don't have a license."

"That's ridiculous. Everybody has a license."

"Not me."

Matsuoka groaned and kept his eyes on the road, his knuckles pure white as he gripped the steering wheel. "Are they still there?" he asked, afraid to take his eyes off the road and check the rearview mirror even for a second.

"You bet they're still there. And gaining on us. Please, you have to go faster."

The road narrowed as it wended its way around the lake. To Matsuoka's eyes, the trees that lined the roadside were but a gray blur of nothingness. His field of vision took in nothing more than the black asphalt and the white lines running down the center of his own private hell. He gently aligned the car so that he was driving exactly in the center of the road, the white lines being voraciously gobbled up by the front of the speeding car. He then gradually began to increase the pressure on the accelerator and held his breath. He knew it was only a matter of time before he wrapped the car around something hard and immovable, killing them both instantly, and he dreaded the thought that around the next bend another car might be heading toward them. A bead of perspiration broke out on his forehead and ran down the side of his face.

Bryant noticed the increased speed and held on to the back of his seat more tightly. "Damn, they're still coming. How fast are we going?"

"I don't know," shouted Matsuoka. "I'm scared to look."

Bryant swiveled around in his seat and studied the speedometer. "Mercy! One hundred and forty per hour. Why aren't I praying?"

"Peter-*san*, this is not going to work. I'll never be able to outrun them. Can't you think of something else?"

"Start swerving, Matsuoka-*san*. Do it now!"

"What?"

"Start swerving. A soldier is leaning out of the window and pointing a handgun at our tires. Start swerving!"

Nearly weeping in fear, Matsuoka began to swing the steer-

301

ing wheel slightly to the left and right. The power steering kicked in immediately, and the Cedric's tires began to squeal in protest. "Peter-*san*, I'm going to crash. I can't *do* this!"

"Okay, okay," shouted Bryant, his mind racing to overcome his fear and concentrate on their predicament. "Listen, I think I've got an idea. Begin to slow down gradually. Not too slow. Try to keep the speed to about one hundred kilometers. I want them to think we are going to stop. Let them get as close to your tail as possible. Okay?"

"Okay, but they will only shoot us."

"Not if they think we are stopping."

Matsuoka did as he was bidden. He very slowly began to release the pressure on the accelerator and straightened the car once again in the middle of the road. True to expectations, the soldier in the vehicle behind pulled his arm back inside the car and sat looking grimly at them through the windscreen.

"Okay, now just before you get to the next bend, I want you to switch on your taillights and stomp on the accelerator at the same time. Got that?"

"Got it, but what good will that do?"

"When the lights go on, they'll think you've hit the brakes and the driver will respond automatically."

Matsuoka nodded eagerly. "Sounds a bit weak, but it's better than nothing. Okay, here we go. Hold tight."

The lake off to the left-hand side was suddenly obscured by another series of trees as they approached a bend that curved around to the right. The jeep was pacing the Cedric at a distance of only a few meters when Matsuoka switched on the taillights. Instinctively responding to the data his mind had been trained to accept, the driver of the jeep removed his foot from the accelerator and stomped quickly on the brake pedal as their quarry inexplicably increased speed and nearly stood on its side as it negotiated the curve. The driver of the small troop carrier behind was not as swift. By the time his foot hit the brake, the front of his truck was less than one meter from the rear of the jeep, and a moment later the quiet mountain air was rent with a deafening cacophony of noises as he tail-ended the jeep and sent it crashing into the trees at high speed. And still the truck's momentum carried it forward. The driver wrestled frantically with the large steering wheel, but the vehicle had entered a spin, and the laws of physics prevented the truck from making the curve. It slowly slewed around until it bounced over the edge of the road and broadsided a group of trees, where it finally came to a halt.

Shaking and dazed, the driver climbed over the passenger seat and jumped down onto the soft composite of the forest floor. He could hear the groans and cries of pain coming from the back of the canvass-topped truck, and walked around to the rear. Of the six soldiers who had been tossed around like Ping-Pong balls in a hurricane, only three were conscious, although all were groaning in agony over their broken limbs and multiple bruises. But at least they were alive. He looked over to the jeep thirty meters down the road and shook his head in despair. The vehicle had hit a single tree while traveling in excess of one hundred kilometers per hour, and from the driver's perspective, it appeared as if the tree were growing out through the center of the car. Nobody could possibly have survived that, so he didn't even bother checking for signs of life. What lay within the car was probably better not seen, anyway. Instead, he climbed back up into the cab of the truck and prayed the radio was still working.

"Well, are they still with us?" Matsuoka's voice was becoming reedy with the stress.

"I don't think so. I can't see them. Better keep up this speed for a bit longer, though. Is it possible to circle the lake and get back onto the Izu Skyline?"

"Yes, I believe it is. But we can't drive back in this car. They're sure to have radioed a description through."

"Damn, you're right. What shall we do?"

"Let's make sure we've shaken them off, and then we can

303

drive as far along the Izu Skyline as we dare. We should be able to avoid detection as long as we get rid of the car before we hit the main roads. We can find somewhere to hide it as we drive along. Phone Gakusha on my mobile unit and get him to come and meet us halfway in his car."

"Good idea." Bryant looked out of the rear window and scrutinized the road. "I think we've done it. I can't see them anywhere. Slow down a little and I'll keep my eyes out for them."

"Peter-*san*," said Matsuoka gratefully, "that is the best suggestion you've made all day."

Mahathir Wong watched the results of the day's trading scroll out on his computer monitor and breathed a deep sigh of relief. He could hear the noise of the champagne party through the walls of his office, and smiled gently at the voices raised in celebration. He would have to go out and join his staff in the revelry soon, but for the moment he just wanted to sit quietly and enjoy the satisfaction of a battle well fought, like a general intoxicated on victory.

The news of the cure for the meningococcemia disease had spread through the business world like wildfire and had had an instant and extremely gratifying effect on Asian stocks and currencies. In fact, the results were so good that Wong was expecting several countries to be in an even better situation financially than before the crash by the end of the week. Wong recalled a story he had once read. It was about a Polish farmer who visited his priest to say that he was at his wits' end and close to suicide. The farmer explained that he lived in a tiny one-room house, which he shared with his wife, four children, his children's wives and husbands, and their children. The constant noise and lack of privacy was torturous, and he asked the priest for advice. The priest suggested that he bring a goat into the house and come back and see him in a week. The following week, the farmer broke down before the priest and said he could go on no longer. The filth and smell of the goat added to the noise and crowded conditions of his house was just too much to bear. The priest told him to put the goat back outside again and return in one week. The next week the man returned in a much better frame of mind. Now that the goat was out in the yard, things were much easier in the house. It was crowded, admittedly, but that was bearable now that the smell of the goat had been removed. Although Japan was still in economic ruin and would require years to regain its preoutbreak level of economic stability and power, in finding a cure for meningococcemia, the scientists in America—financed by Wong's consortium—had succeeded in putting the goat back out in the yard.

Wong reached out a hand and switched off his computer. Trading in Asia had finished and the ball had been passed across to Europe, who would then pass it on to America later in the day. It was time for the rest of the world to fill their pockets with the Asian windfall.

Wong put on his jacket and went to join the party.

"Well?"

"I'm sorry, sir. We lost them." Ishibashi's voice was faint and he stared solemnly at the carpet one meter before him.

"Lost them? What do you mean, lost them?" Shoji Kubota's voice began to increase in power. "How could a trained military unit lose someone?"

"I'm afraid that is not clear, sir. We have two men dead and six injured, three seriously. The only coherent survivor is the driver of the troop carrier. According to his statement, the jeep in front suddenly slammed on the brakes, causing an accident."

"Damn, damn, damn!" Kubota slammed his fist onto the desk. "Why am I surrounded by incompetence? I will not stand for failure! Do you understand me, Ishibashi?"

"Yes, sir."

"You said 'them.' How many of these spies are there?"

"Two, sir. Probably both male. They were driving a Nissan

Cedric with a Shinagawa license plate. We traced the number and discovered that the car belongs to a Kazunori Matsuoka. He was one of the directors at Hamada Seiyaku Pharmaceuticals."

"Hamada Seiyaku? But that is . . ."

"Probably not a coincidence, sir. We are trying to check it out, but it might take time. Matsuoka's house is deserted."

Kubota nodded. "Yes, I'm sure it is. Find out if this Matsuoka owns any property in Izu, Shizuoka, or Hakone. Maybe we can track him to ground that way."

"Yes, sir. Right away, sir."

Kubota dismissed Ishibashi and prepared himself for his cabinet meeting. The escape of the spies was unfortunate and irritating, but it was not the end of the world by any means. Maybe they would be foolish enough to use the satellite to communicate again. They couldn't escape his clutches forever.

The twenty members of his cabinet were already seated in position when he arrived at the meeting room. Some looked tired, some looked defiant, and all looked wary. Kubota's style of administration based on fear and punishment had shocked each and every one of the cabinet ministers, and all—without exception—were regretting their decision to oust Aizawa in favor of the new prime minister.

Kubota took his place at the head of the table and shuffled his papers around until they were in a position that suited him. "Right," he began. "First of all I must inform you that we failed to catch the spies who have been informing the American government of our decisions and actions. We will get them in the end, however, so we can now pass on to the next item on the agenda."

Before Kubota could continue, an aide entered the room, bowed politely, and walked over to Naoki Hoshino, the director general of the Defense Agency. He whispered into his ear and passed him two sheets of paper before leaving the room

306

once again. Hoshino quickly scanned the sheets and rose to his feet.

"Mr. Prime Minister," he said, "I have just received news to say that a fleet of American navy ships led by the aircraft carrier USS *Kitty Hawk* and consisting of six vessels has taken up a position eighty kilometers off the coast of Niigata."

Kubota looked up in shock. "What? For what purpose?"

"Probably to effect a landing on the coast of Niigata to distribute the medicine for meningococcemia that they have developed. We received a message from the U.S. government forbidding us to take any preventive action."

"They what . . . ? How dare they!" Kubota jumped to his feet, his face purple with rage. "This time they have gone too far. I want that area fortified. Set up artillery installations along the coast of Niigata immediately, Hoshino. At the first sign of the Americans approaching, open fire. I will not be dictated to in this way!"

"But . . . but, Mr. Prime Minister," stuttered Hoshino, "I must protest. We cannot open fire on a friendly nation. You cannot do this. . . ."

Kubota's eyes narrowed and he stared fiercely at Hoshino. "You dare to tell me what I can do and what I cannot do?"

"Of course not, sir. But—"

"But nothing! I want heavy surface-to-surface and surface-to-air missiles installed on the coast of Niigata immediately! If America thinks we will sit back and make no effort to protect the country, they will soon discover that they have erred in judgment."

"But that will be construed as an act of war, sir. We cannot possibly go that far."

"Enough!" The shout reverberated around the room and had Hoshino and all of the other cabinet ministers quaking. "You will do as I say, Hoshino, or you will find yourself replaced by somebody who will. Maybe you would like to share a cell with Aizawa when this is all over. Do I make myself clear?"

Hoshino stared down at the papers on the table in front of him, struggling to find the courage to defy Kubota, but discovering—to his disgust—that his politician's sense of survival was winning the battle.

Before he could answer, however, Kayoko Inoue, the director general of the Science and Technology Agency, rose to her feet and stared at the prime minister with fire in her eyes. "You cannot do this," she hissed through clenched teeth, aware of the consequences of her rebellion but past caring. "If what my colleague here says is true, the American navy wants only to deliver the medicine. We must have that medication. You cannot continue to hinder every chance we have of putting the country back together again. I will not stand for it!"

"*You* will not stand for it? And who are you to tell me what you will stand for, might I ask? I do not wish to hear your childish outbursts, Mrs. Inoue. It might interest you to know that I consider the announcement that a cure has been discovered to be false. It is a strategy by the American authorities to fool the world and justify an attack on Japan. All it needs is for this cabinet to side with America and allow them to attack, and we will all find ourselves with American masters in the not-too-distant future."

"You are crazy, Kubota! You don't know what you are talking about. Power has gone to your head. You are not fit to run this country, and I want nothing more to do with you!"

As if a tap had been turned on, Kubota's blood pressure rose until his face was suffused with blood. "How dare you!" he screamed, crashing both fists down onto the table. "Your job is to protect this country, not play into the foreigners' hands! Get out of my sight! Now! Before I have you placed under arrest!"

Inoue began to pack up her papers and stuff them into a small attaché case. Ignoring Kubota, she stormed across the room to the door, stopping and turning around once her hand was on the handle. "You sicken me, Kubota," she spat, her voice tinged with contempt. "I voluntarily place myself under confinement. I can no longer be a part of this . . . this circus!"

She turned and left the room, slamming the door behind her.

Kubota sat at the head of the table, thoughtfully tapping a pen again his chin and allowing his anger to subside. "Anybody else?" he asked at length, the calmness of his voice belying the mask of fury that covered his face. "If you want to leave, now is your chance." He looked around the table at the remaining nineteen people in turn.

Wataru Okajima, the minister of construction, slowly rose to his feet, closely followed by Goro Fukui, the foreign minister. Avoiding eye contact with the prime minister, the two men walked across to the door, turned around to face the room, bowed deeply, and exited.

"Now," continued Kubota, "maybe we can get down to some work. Your very presence indicates that you have had a change of mind and will carry out my orders accordingly. Is that correct, Hoshino?"

The director general of the Defense Agency looked down at the table and nodded miserably.

"Fine. Then let us get back to work."

Chapter Fourteen

The antibody to prevent the meningococcal bacterium from releasing its deadly endotoxins into the bloodstream was being manufactured and added to the cocktail of existing drugs in laboratories spread throughout the world before being shipped across to the United States for final delivery. Military aircraft from allied countries plied the Atlantic and Pacific oceans with unprecedented regularity, and the overflow that could not be fitted onto these flights was loaded aboard commercial aircraft and delivered to the various airports around North America before being ferried into military installations by helicopters. Having reached American soil, the many thousands of tons of medication were then airlifted across the Pacific into the Yongsan Garrison of the 52nd Medical Battalion in South Korea, where they were stockpiled in huge hangars, awaiting delivery to the fleet of ships positioned in the Sea of Japan.

* * *

"How's this, then?" Norio Kondo held up a sheet of paper with large-font *kanji* characters written from top to bottom. "That should hit the mark. What do you think?"

The other members of the Tomonokai scrutinized the message that Kondo was holding up and nodded approvingly. It was Kazunori Matsuoka who had first pointed out that the Japanese government was not publicizing the availability of the new antibody for the disease. The fact that nothing was being shown on NHK regarding its existence had initially raised his doubts, and then they had been verified in a message from Statesman, who had also added that the new prime minister had cut off all lines of communication with America. No reason had been given for this inexplicable attitude, but each member of the Tomonokai realized how far-reaching the implications could be. Being out of contact with the American authorities themselves, they had decided to start their own nationwide campaign to advise the population of the antibody therapy's availability.

Norio Kondo had created a flyer that would be sent on-line to all members of the Tomonokai around the country, and these people would then print out thousands of copies for distribution around their localities. The flyer explained that a cure for the disease was now available and would be delivered to all military bases throughout Japan for use by military personnel only. Despite the fact that this was an out-and-out lie, all felt that it would be necessary to stress the point that the government had no intention of distributing it to the public in case people simply sat at home and waited for the authorities to get around to delivering it.

"I think it looks fine," said Harumi. "I especially like the piece about the government trying to pull the wool over everybody's eyes. If I received one of these, I'd be rioting outside of the Diet building before the day was out."

"I am hoping that it won't come to riots," said Kondo, placing the flyer in the center of the table where everybody had a clear view of it. "Riots could end in casualties and may inadvertently provide those armed fools with even more reason to shoot on sight. I have tried to design the wording to simply send a message to the government to remind them of their responsibilities and to provide the people with a little bit of hope. A touch of public opinion may force Kubota and his cronies to change their minds and allow distribution."

"I wouldn't bet on it." Matsuoka picked the flyer up and studied it. "It seems a little too heavily worded, in my opinion. We don't want to push them over the top and worsen the situation. What do you think, Peter-*san*?"

Bryant shrugged. "I really don't know. If, as you say, the government intends to keep quiet on the antibody, then maybe nothing we do will have any effect anyway. With or without this, NHK and all of the other broadcasting companies and media that are still operating are bound to hear about the cure sooner or later, and I'm sure the government has already taken that into consideration."

"They should have heard already. They certainly have the capabilities for monitoring overseas news. Maybe the government has forbidden the media to mention it." Toshio Otsuka's words silenced everybody around the table as they contemplated this. "After all, we are still technically under martial law, and the government has the power to censor public broadcasts if they so desire."

Matsuoka nodded. "That is a point I had not considered, I must admit," he said. "In which case, I suppose we have no choice other than to send this out and hope it has some beneficial effect."

"What about faxing a copy through to NHK and monitoring the news for a couple of hours?" suggested Bryant. "If it is ignored, we will know that the broadcasts are being edited."

"I don't think that will be necessary," said Kondo. "It won't change anything. If they run with the news they will simply be helping do our job for us, and if they don't broadcast it we will just have to do it ourselves anyway. It would only waste time."

"We could fax them a copy on the off chance that they might air it," said Matsuoka thoughtfully. "If they do use it, it will be good for our campaign, and if they don't, everything will still run according to plan. What is there to lose?"

"All right, that's good." Kondo stood up and walked across to the computer. He sat down at the keyboard and turned around to face everybody. "Are we all agreed?"

They all nodded and Kondo pulled up the mail screen to transmit the flyer and the instructions on its use to all other members of the Tomonokai.

Susumu Ishibashi cowered in his seat in front of Shoji Kubota's desk and waited for the prime minister's tantrum to burn itself out. He eyed the heavy glass paperweight situated on Kubota's left with trepidation. The prime minister had picked it up and slammed it down several times so far, and from where Ishibashi was sitting, it appeared to be only a matter of time before he flung it across the room in rage, and he wanted to make sure he was well out of the line of fire before this unsavory scenario unraveled.

"Do we know who is distributing this . . . this propaganda?" Kubota spat the last word out in contempt, as if he couldn't stand to leave the taste of it within his mouth. He waved the Tomonokai flyer in the air and then threw it back onto the desk with a flick of his wrist.

"No, sir. They have appeared in large quantities throughout the country, usually just placed on park benches and populated public areas for anybody to pick up. We have also discovered that they appear to be printed on different paper and in different typefaces, indicating that they were printed on different machinery in separate locations."

"Damn! Damn, damn, damn! I will not stand for this!" Kubota grabbed the paperweight and slammed it onto the desktop to add accent to each syllable. "And what of its effects? Are people believing these lies, Ishibashi?"

Ishibashi nodded and looked down at his notes. "I'm afraid so, sir. Thousands of people have begun to arrive at military installations all over the country demanding the cure. So far we have managed to avoid trouble, but there is a chance that riots could be sparked if we don't do something soon."

Kubota grabbed the flyer again and read through it. Screwing it up into a tight ball, he hurled it across the room as far as he could. "I think the Americans are behind this," he growled. "Have there been any more satellite transmissions from the spy?"

"No, sir."

"How are they managing to do this to me? Whichever way I turn, they are in my hair. I can't believe it!"

"There are also mumblings within this building, Mr. Prime Minister. The news of the propaganda has spread through the entire complex, and certain people believe that we are in possession of the cure but refuse to distribute it. Most of the people here have family on the outside, and fears are rising. I think we need to make a public announcement of some sort to allay these fears."

"A public announcement? What do you suggest?"

"NHK would be the obvious choice."

Kubota considered Ishibashi's suggestion. Maybe a public announcement would be a good idea. NHK had worked hard on painting a good picture of Kubota, and fifteen minutes before the cameras with gentle smiles and reassuring words might help calm both the public and the workers inside the Diet building.

"Okay, Ishibashi. Set it up for later today. Also, send me a speechwriter. I want to make it clear that the Americans are behind this and have planted spies in the country to spread these lies about a cure. I'll work with him on the script."

* * *

314

Peter Bryant looked up at the bird in the tree indignantly. Brown bulbuls were capable of a wide range of vocal utterances, from piercing shrieks to melodious singing, but ever since Bryant had stepped out into the garden to enjoy the early-spring sunshine, the bulbul sitting in the branch above his head had concentrated on a single word and was screeching it repeatedly from the treetops.

"Dweeb."

"Yeah, take a look at yourself, pal." Although it was crazy for him to be involved in an argument with a stupid bird, Bryant couldn't let the insult pass without comment. "How many points did you get on your SATs?"

"Dweeb."

"Jerk!"

"Dweeb."

"Pissant!"

"Dweeb."

"Scrote!" said Bryant, remembering a good one he had learned from Leonard Drake.

"Is everything all right?"

The voice, seemingly coming out of nowhere, startled Bryant. He spun around and saw Shigeko Kondo leaning out of the living room window, a look of worried concern on her face. He waved at her self-consciously, feeling his face turn red. "Everything's fine, Shigeko-*san*. Just talking to the animals. It's very relaxing. You should try it sometime."

Shigeko shrugged and disappeared from sight, obviously confused at this turn of events and wanting to seek council. He would have to be careful if he wanted to hang on to his reputation. He could imagine her hurrying into the tatami room and excitedly informing everybody that Peter-*san* had finally flipped his lid and was out in the garden swearing at the trees. Bryant chuckled to himself. Well, if she wanted craziness, she didn't have to look much farther than her own husband. At least Bryant didn't shout, *"Oikaze"* at the top of his voice every time he farted.

Bryant ignored the bulbul's continued insults and started on a slow stroll around the garden. The sunshine felt warm on his back, and the delicious fragrance of sun-baked earth put a jaunty skip in his step. Bryant was feeling pretty pleased with himself. He had given the American government Norio Kondo's e-mail address in the last message he had sent from Hakone, and that morning he had received mail from Mike Woodson. Although he hadn't realized it during the enforced silence, being out of contact with America had worried him deeply. The umbilical cord of shared communication had been thin and tenuous, but it had provided him with purpose, something to hold on to to prevent him from feeling helpless. Once the cord had been severed, he had been out in the world alone and had experienced a loss of motivation and self-esteem. It had made him realize that he was just one man among many millions who could do nothing more than simply *hope* that things would turn out for the best. What was the point of collecting information if there was nobody to pass it on to, nobody to verbally pat him on the head and remind him that he was a vital cog in an enormously important machine? When Woodson's e-mail had arrived, explaining that the antibody was being mass-produced and loaded onto a fleet of ships located off the coast of Japan, a jolt of happiness had coursed through Bryant and fired up his motivation once again. He was no longer alone. He was fighting for a common cause side by side with people who shared the same beliefs.

Reaching the barbecue area, he rested his backside against the bricks and looked up into the trees again. The bulbul's mate had appeared and the two were hopping around the branches contentedly, occasionally taking time out to remind Bryant that he was a dweeb. Seeing the two birds together made Bryant realize just how much he missed Michiyo. He had phoned her that morning to make sure she was all right, and her gentle voice drifting down the phone lines had inexplicably set his blood pumping—almost as if he were a teenager arranging his first date. He wanted to be with her. He wanted to lie beside her on a Sunday morning and chat about how they were going to spend the day. He wanted to follow her about the Ginza while she happily absorbed herself in shopping, dragging her protesting into coffee shops to ease the boredom that shopping for female attire instilled within him. He wanted to sit opposite her in the Hard Rock Café in the underground complex between the Landmark Tower and Queens Square and watch her eat giant hamburgers while ZZ Top slipped inside their sleeping bags. He wanted to drive her crazy by nibbling gently on her earlobe.

He thought back to the conversation he had had with Shigeko on the day they had watched Kondo and the others return from a foraging trip. *Then you must buy her a big, fat diamond ring. One that fits on the fourth finger of the left hand.* Was it time for him to think about marriage? Was he ready to commit himself to the confines of marital vows, as he had been promising himself ever since Michiyo had moved in with him? Maybe he was. The experiences he had acquired throughout the duration of the outbreak had matured him and made him realize that companionship and respect for other people were more important than anything else in the world. He certainly loved Michiyo. Of that he had absolutely no doubt whatsoever. Yes, maybe it would work. . . .

"Dweeb."

Bryant looked up into the trees and laughed. The damned avian was probably right. He was going off his chump.

The front door to the house opened and Kazunori Matsuoka appeared. He hurried down the steps and walked across to where Bryant stood leaning against the barbecue.

"Bad news, I'm afraid, Peter-*san*," he said the moment he was within earshot.

"What's happened?"

"A message from Statesman just came in. Shoji Kubota is planning to attack the American fleet."

"What! When?"

"They are setting up heavy artillery units in four locations along the coast of Niigata. The surface-to-surface missiles will be ready by tomorrow morning, and the surface-to-air missiles will be ready within forty-eight hours. They won't be able to get within a hundred kilometers of the coastline."

"Damn! But that will be like declaring war on the United States. What's the matter with the man?" Bryant pushed himself up into a standing position and began to pace in circles, his head bent in thought. "We'll have to warn them immediately. According to the message I got from Mike Woodson this morning, the fleet is holding position about eighty kilos off the coast."

"Statesman says they will attack only if the ships or aircraft try to approach any closer. He even suggested that the units be taken out before the surface-to-air missiles are functional. He has provided the coordinates for all four of the installations."

"Damn, I can't see America going that far. Japan is an ally, for God's sake. They wouldn't dare attack the military installations of an ally. But then again, how else can they get the antibody ashore?"

The two men fell into a frustrated silence. Everything had seemed to be going so well, and now they were as far away from controlling the epidemic as ever.

"Come, Peter-*san*. It is out of our hands. You could walk around in circles forever, but it won't help the situation. You must report on this immediately."

"You're right, of course. I'll do it now."

The two men hurried across the lawn to the house and disappeared inside, neither noticing that the brown bulbul had managed to get in the last word.

"Dweeb."

318

* * *

A large-screen television had been set up in one of the house of representatives' committee rooms, and ten minutes before the prime minister's speech was scheduled to commence, the room was filled with upward of a hundred people. Kayoko Inoue, the former director general of the Science and Technology Agency, stood at the back of the room next to Kyoko Mitsui, the minister of posts and telecommunications. Although she was under voluntary confinement, Inoue's movements were not being monitored, and she had slipped away from her room in the annex building without trouble.

"How are the plans going?" asked Inoue softly.

"As well as can be expected. Although many people are terrified of Kubota and refuse to go against him."

"I hope you haven't revealed anything. If this gets back to Kubota, we will all spend the rest of our lives behind bars."

Mitsui reached out a hand and gently squeezed Inoue's fingers. "Don't worry; we have just been testing the water. Nobody knows anything yet."

"That is good. How is the rest of the staff taking the news of this cure?"

"They are very angry. They believe the military has received shipments of the medication specifically for their own use. There have also been reports of civilians being shot while demanding the drug at the bases, and this is fueling their fear. Very few have confidence in Kubota anymore. It will be interesting to see how he handles this announcement." Mitsui nodded toward the television at the front of the room. The solemn NHK newscaster was sitting in front of the camera with a large photograph of Kubota displayed on a screen behind him, his voice muted by the sound of people conversing within the room. "I walked around the room a few moments ago," she continued, "and heard nothing positive about Kubota. Everybody seems to hate him with a passion. I would say the time is ripe."

Inoue noticed the labor minister standing by the open door and bowed. Teruo Nagata bowed back, nodded to the screen, and pulled his hand swiftly across his throat to indicate that he had little confidence in Kubota's ability to explain away events. Inoue smiled and turned back to Mitsui. "I have been in touch with Aizawa."

Mitsui turned to her in surprise. "The prime minister?"

"The *former* prime minister."

"Yes, yes. You know what I mean. How is he? Are they treating him well?"

"As far as I can gather. I didn't actually speak with him directly. Typically, he has befriended one of Kubota's aides, and the man delivers messages for him. His spirits appear high, but he is furious over the way Kubota is handling things." Inoue looked across at the television screen and noticed increased activity. "I think they are about to start. Shall we move nearer?"

The two women edged their way closer to the screen. A hushed silence fell over the room as Shoji Kubota was suddenly revealed on the screen, his hands clasped and resting on the desk before him. He had a gentle and seemingly sympathetic smile on his face. He kept the smile in place for a moment more before beginning his speech.

"It is with regret, my friends, that I sit before you today. It has recently been discovered that the United States of America has initiated a campaign of propaganda within Japan as a precursor to launching an attack against us. I realize that this will shock many of you, but I believe that part of my job is to keep you informed of events. A government that keeps secrets from the public does not deserve to be in power. It goes without saying that it is my fervent wish to solve this problem through diplomatic channels, but this, I regret to say, appears to be impossible. My staff and I have been in constant communication with the president of the United States for this sole purpose, but I am afraid that very little progress has been made.

As I speak now, a flotilla of six American warships is heading toward the coast of Niigata, where we understand they will try to effect a landing. However, I want to emphasize the fact that we are not yet in danger. Despite the negotiations having made little progress up until now, I can assure you that the government will continue to place its hopes in diplomacy and do everything within its power to prevent Japan from becoming just another American state." Kubota paused to allow the import of this item of information to sink in.

"He's good," whispered Inoue into Mitsui's ear. "A lot of people will believe this."

"The United States government," continued Kubota, "is also responsible for spreading the rumors about a cure for meningococcemia throughout the country. Let me assure you, my friends, that such medication exists only in the imagination of the instigators of this despicable propaganda. Our country is under siege, and we must fortify ourselves against misinformation. Many of you, I know, have been led to believe that our military is in possession of some wonder drug that will put an end to the epidemic, and as much as I would like to believe this myself, I regret to tell you that it is just not true. If you have been fooled by these lies and were intending to visit one of our military installations to receive your inoculation, then save yourselves a journey. A cure does not exist. If you have been fooled by these lies and are now outside one of our military installations, go home, I implore you. You are the victims of a vicious campaign that has been maliciously designed to add to your suffering." The camera zoomed out to show more of Kubota's office, its very neatness preconceived to have a calming and reassuring effect on the audience. Kubota wrung his hands before continuing, a sad look of despair on his face. "Our country is living through difficult times, and things are sure to get more difficult before they get better. But we, as Japanese nationals, have the right to decide our own future. We will beat this disease. That I promise you. We will over-

come our difficulties and return to our rich and comfortable
lifestyles. That I also promise you. But you must make a choice.
Will you believe that this government is striving under unprecedented conditions on your behalf to put the country back
on its feet, or will you believe the lies and terror tactics of
America? Remember, the government of Japan is on your side.
The government of the United States is not. Thank you."

The camera zoomed out further and then faded out, to be
replaced by the dour newscaster. The volume was turned down
and the room erupted into conversation. Kayoko Inoue swore
under her breath and began to push a path though the crowd
of people until she was standing beside the television. Mitsui
brought a hand up to her brow in anxiety. She had a nasty
feeling that Inoue was about to do something extremely foolish. She watched Inoue grab a chair, place it before the screen,
and climb up onto it.

"Attention, everybody," Inoue shouted loudly, passing her
eyes slowly over the many heads before her. The buzz of conversation gradually died down as everybody looked over toward
her in curiosity. "What you have just heard is a carefully designed but blatant package of lies."

The room erupted again as everybody tried to make their
opinions heard simultaneously. Kyoko Mitsui sighed in disbelief
and began to edge her way through the crowd. She had to get
Inoue off her podium before the guards heard the ruckus and
came to investigate. Kubota would not take kindly to being
called a liar in public, and Inoue was exposing herself to grave
danger. So much for her being worried about Mitsui's revealing
their plans to Kubota's followers.

"Will you please all listen?" Inoue's shrill voice carried, and
people began to turn their attention back to her. "This government is not in constant contact with America. He is lying!
Communications have been cut off by us. Kubota is having
people shot in cold blood. He is a murderer!"

Mitsui groaned anew and shook her head. She managed to

force a path through to the front of the crowd and was surprised to note that twenty or more men had formed a ring around her and were facing outward, as if protecting her. As she watched, more and more people began to break away from the main crowd and join the circle around Inoue's chair.

"It is my belief that a cure for this disease *does* exist," continued Inoue, her voice raised above the clamor. "I don't know if the military is in possession of it or not, but the reason for the U.S. presence off the coast of Niigata is to deliver the drug, not attack Japan."

A shout at the back of the room indicated that the guards had arrived. The pace with which people had been joining Inoue's circle suddenly picked up. They linked arms, and looks of solid determination appeared on their faces. Twenty people became forty people. Forty people became sixty people.

And still Kayoko Inoue's voice rang loudly through the room. "Do not be fooled by this pretender to the throne. Kiyoshi Aizawa is the elected leader of the party. He is the only man who can save Japan now. We cannot allow this madman Kubota to continue. We must bring him down and restore law and order."

Mitsui found herself a position at the front of the circle and turned around to face the guards who were struggling to force their way through the crowd. The back of the room was almost empty, but began filling up as more guards streamed into the room. Mitsui felt somebody link an arm through hers. She glanced sideways into the eyes of Teruo Nagata, the labor minister. He smiled reassuringly before turning his attention back to the guards.

"By supporting Kubota you are supporting mayhem and murder," shouted Inoue, profoundly moved by this show of support. "Who will support Aizawa?"

This final sentence was delivered as a scream and punctuated by Inoue's fist striking up into the air. The crowd immediately picked up the chant of "Aizawa, Aizawa" as the guards continued to force their way roughly through the crowd toward the instigator. Although the barrier was solid and determined, it was no match for the guards, who were not above using fists and batons to forge their way through.

The chant continued relentlessly as the guards finally beat a path through to Inoue and dragged her screaming and struggling off the chair while other guards linked arms and established a barrier through which she could be maneuvered. It took five of them to bodily carry her across the room and out the doors into the corridor, back into confinement—this time enforced.

And still the chant continued.

"*Aizawa, Aizawa, Aizawa, Aizawa.*"

Chapter Fifteen

The Kitty Hawk Battle Group, consisting of the USS *Kitty Hawk*, the USS *Chancellorsville*, the USS *Mobile Bay*, the USS *Vincennes*, the USS *Vandergrift*, and the USS *Curtis Wilbur*, all of the Seventh Fleet, was positioned a fraction under fifty miles west of the coast of Niigata in the Sea of Japan. Of the six vessels, the aircraft carrier USS *Kitty Hawk* was the most impressive. One thousand and sixty-five feet in length and with an average displacement of eighty-six thousand tons, it dwarfed the five other ships and resembled a mother duck navigating across a gigantic pond together with her clutch of ducklings.

Four F-14 Tomcats took off from the deck of the aircraft carrier and circled at four thousand feet while the four F/A-18E-model single-seater Hornets were connected up to the catapults on the 4.1-acre flight deck by the yellow-jerseyed air department personnel and launched into the sky one by one. Once all four Hornets were airborne, the eight aircraft turned east and headed toward the coast of Niigata, concealed from view by a shimmering haze. From the sky, the vast mass of the USS

Kitty Hawk was shrunken down to toy size until it was impossible to imagine that it was home to 5,500 members of the crew and air wing.

With their ability to track up to twenty-four targets simultaneously, each of the Tomcats was fitted with six Phoenix AIM-54A air-to-air missiles and a Vulcan MK61A1 20mm cannon to provide air support for the Hornets, whose job it was to drop their payload of AGM-8 HARM missiles onto the four radar and missile installations being set up along the coast of Japan.

At twenty miles from the coast, the aircraft split up into four groups of two and sped toward the individual coordinates provided by Peter Bryant and designated to each fighter in the attack plan. Just over two minutes later, the Hornets released their missiles simultaneously in a coordinated fire plan before banking around to the west and heading back to the *Kitty Hawk*, their mission accomplished. The Tomcats stayed in place for a few minutes longer, scanning the skies for enemy aircraft scrambled against the attack and waiting for the smoke to clear above the targets to acquire visual confirmation of a successful mission and obtain conclusive film for the postmission debriefing.

The four missile installations—one at Hayakawa, one at Muramatsu Hama, one at Yoneyama, and the last one at Tanihama—received direct hits by the HARM missiles and were, for all intents and purposes, obliterated from the map. Having confirmed that the installations no longer posed a threat to U.S. interests, the four Tomcats turned west and followed the Hornets back to the battle group.

The first fist-sized rock crashed through the window of the living room and flew over everybody's heads before smashing into the far wall and falling harmlessly to the floor. Before anyone had a chance to react, another rock, this time even larger, splintered the glass in all directions and landed with a thud in the center of the table. Gonta the corgi came rushing in from the kitchen, where he had been dozing, and stood just beyond the table, barking up at the window.

"Jesus Christ!" shouted Peter Bryant in English, leaping up from his seat and throwing himself in front of Harumi Otsuka to protect her. "Quick!" he continued in Japanese. "Move!" Grabbing Harumi by both of her arms, he dragged her to her feet and pushed her before him until they were concealed behind the jamb of the door between the living room and the tatami room.

The next rock flew soundlessly through the gap in the window made by the previous projectile and glanced off the back of Norio Kondo's head. Recovering quickly, Kondo grabbed hold of his wife's arm and pulled her across the floor to the tatami room, where Bryant, Matsuoka, and the two Otsukas were already taking refuge.

"What is happening?" cried Shigeko Kondo plaintively as she gently pressed a pocket handkerchief to the wound on the back of her husband's head. "Who is doing this?"

"I've no idea, Harumi-*san*, but whoever it is seems rather annoyed."

Another small rock crashed through the remaining glass panel and bounced off the table onto the floor. Gonta rushed at the rock and barked furiously.

"Gonta, get over here!" shouted Kondo, now holding the bloodstained handkerchief to his head himself. "Gonta! House! House, Gonta!" But Gonta refused to comply with the order to return to his mat in the kitchen and instead turned his attention back to the window.

Bryant peeked around the doorjamb and was the first to see the dark shadow outside lifting a thick stick above his head and bringing it down forcibly onto the shards of broken glass that protruded drunkenly from the frame. "Look out; he's coming in!" he shouted. "Is there anything we can use as a weapon?"

The shadow brought the stick down repeatedly on the window frame until every piece of glass had been smashed to smithereens and then lifted a leg across the sill.

Gonta rushed at the figure, his teeth bared and a guttural growl emanating from deep within his chest. The stick flashed once and the dog yelped and ran whimpering across to his owner with his ears laid flat back against his head. Norio Kondo knelt down to inspect the dog for injury and then stood up, satisfied. "He's not injured," he said in obvious relief. "Probably just bruised."

"Oh, my God!" exclaimed Matsuoka, staring at the apparition, who was now standing inside the living room, his shoulders heaving visibly as he frantically tried to force air into his lungs. "It's you! Hamada!"

"Yes, it's me," wheezed the president of Hamada Seiyaku Pharmaceuticals, hardly recognizable in tattered clothes and with purpuric lesions spreading over his face. He took a step forward, balancing himself precariously on the stick. "And now it's you, Matsuoka. I told you I would come, and, true to my word, I have."

"You're crazy!" Matsuoka spread his arms out to protect the people behind him, gathering them together into a small group and pushing them farther into the tatami room. "He's got the disease," he whispered over his shoulder. "Don't let him get near you."

Hamada took one more step forward and sneered at Matsuoka. "You thought you had killed me, didn't you? You should have finished me off with the knife when you had the chance. Now you will die, too. Slowly, as I am."

"Look Hamada, this is between you and me. Let's discuss it outside. It has nothing to do with these people."

Hamada threw his head back and laughed, the eerie sound echoing unpleasantly around the room. "No, Matsuoka. They will die, too, and all because of you. You will go to your own

328

deathbed knowing that you were responsible for the deaths of your friends."

Having made sure that the other members of the Tomonokai had retreated into the tatami room, Matsuoka left his position by the doorjamb and began to sidle into the living room in an attempt to lead Hamada away from them. Behind him, Norio Kondo handed Gonta's collar over to his wife and, silently gesturing for Peter Bryant's assistance, hefted the low table up onto its side and gently began to unscrew two of the legs with the use of one-yen coins pulled from his pocket. The corgi, now recovered from the slap on the butt, was straining at his collar and barking in uncontrollable rage.

"The disease must be affecting you more than you realize if you think you can kill six of us with a puny stick, Hamada," Matsuoka said, moving toward the rear of the room so he could put the sofa between himself and Hamada.

"My weapon is inside me, Matsuoka. My weapon is my breath." With that, Hamada opened his mouth and puffed air through his mouth into the surrounding air, his head swiveling around to cover all angles. "My weapon cannot be seen with the naked eye, Matsuoka, but it will kill you just the same." He blew more air out into the atmosphere before breaking down in a coughing fit that racked his body and caused tears to stream from his eyes.

Matsuoka brought a handkerchief from his pocket and placed it over his mouth and nose. He looked across to the tatami room and gestured for everybody to do the same. All followed his lead, except Shigeko, who had already used her handkerchief to blot up her husband's blood. Instead she pulled the collar of her sweater up until it covered the lower part of her face.

"How did you find us?" asked Matsuoka, turning back to Hamada.

Hamada eventually coughed up a large wad of phlegm and spat it over the table, where it splattered onto the screen of the laptop computer set up on the desk by the window. "You were too confident, Matsuoka," he said, his voice wheezing and cracking over his tortured vocal cords. "You said that you must get back to Izu for dinner, if you remember. How stupid! Once I got here I just asked around to see if anybody had seen a foreigner. Your own foolish mouth and the *keto* led me right to you."

"But how did you get away?"

"Money. You took my telephone, but you left me with enough money to buy my way to Izu. And now you will pay for your foolishness, cockroach."

Hamada took an unsteady step toward Hamada and blew air in his direction. Matsuoka continued backing up, but soon he would be at the wall and at the farthest point his retreat would be allowed to go without stepping out into the hall. The only option open to him was to slip through the door and collect a knife from the kitchen, but using a blade as a weapon would necessitate his getting close enough to Hamada to use it, and that would simply be suicidal. Matsuoka had no doubts that Hamada's breath was as deadly as he claimed. The trouble he was obviously having breathing was a perfect indicator of a respiratory disease, and the rash spread over his face and hands verified the diagnosis. No, Hamada was in the final stages of the disease and was as biologically deadly as any weapon ever devised for hand-to-hand combat. Getting close enough to disable the man with a knife would also sound Matsuoka's death knell.

Hamada took another step nearer and hawked up some of the liquid that was rattling in his lungs. Rolling the phlegm around his tongue, he suddenly puckered up and spat it as hard as he could in Matsuoka's direction. Matsuoka managed to dodge out of the way in time, and the bacteria-ridden phlegm hit the wall and slid silently downward as it obeyed the laws of gravity.

And still Hamada kept coming, a grin of pure evil evident

through the lesions that scored his face. Matsuoka shifted his eyes nervously from left to right in search of a weapon—any weapon—but nothing was available. Hamada had nearly reached the sofa when a brown-and-white ball of fur came rushing out of the tatami room and took a firm grip on the meaty part of his calf with small but very sharp teeth. Hamada screamed in pain and rage and tried to shake the dog off, but Gonta was in no mood for showing mercy. Gritting his teeth, Hamada moved his weight off of the stick and lifted it in the air above the corgi, but before he could bring it down, Peter Bryant had come charging out of the tatami room with a short but sturdy table leg raised above his head in a one-handed grip and swung it at full power into Hamada's forehead. The solid crack as the wood came into contact with Hamada's frontal bone rang satisfyingly around the room, and Hamada collapsed in a heap on the floor, for the moment decommissioned from his deadly agenda.

Before he had time to think about his actions, Matsuoka had rushed forward instinctively and upended the sofa so that it covered most of Hamada's torso and all of his head. He then jumped onto the top of it to make sure that the madman was pinned down and unable to move.

Not that it was necessary. Shigeru Hamada was unconscious and slowly drowning on the fluid that a severe case of pneumonia had built up in his lungs.

"Gonta!" Shigeko Kondo rushed into the room and grabbed hold of the corgi's collar, trying fruitlessly to separate him from Hamada's leg. Gonta kept up a continual growl in his chest, but passed inquiring eyes up to his mistress, as if surprised that she was willing to show the demon mercy. "Gonta, *hanase!*" she shouted, wagging a finger in front of the dog's face. "*Hanase*, Gonta! *Oriko, neh. Gohan tabe ni iko, neh, Gonta.*" Seduced by the promise of food, Gonta released his hold on Hamada's calf and stood panting up at Shigeko, his rear end swaying from side to side in delicious anticipation as he tried to wag his nonexistent tail. Shigeko grabbed him by the collar and took him out to the kitchen, where she connected his leash and tied him up to the door handle.

Peter Bryant stared at the table leg in his hand as if seeing it for the first time. He looked up at Matsuoka and raised his eyebrows. "I guess I hit him," he said in surprise.

"You certainly did, Peter-*san*. And rather well too, if I may say so. Our only problem now is what to do with him."

Norio Kondo knelt on the floor and peered beneath the sofa. "He looks out cold. I don't think he is going anywhere for the time being. Just as long as nobody suggests mouth-to-mouth resuscitation, I am quite happy to leave him here until he rots."

"You shouldn't get too close to him," said Shigeko, arriving back from the kitchen. "You don't want to catch the disease."

Kondo moved away from the sofa and surveyed the room in despair. "Well, he's trashed the room. We couldn't possibly use it anymore. What shall we do?"

Matsuoka sighed and climbed down from his position on top of the sofa. "We'll have to board the place up and move out. The whole place could be contaminated. Nobody take their handkerchiefs away from their mouths. We'll have to leave a large sign on the front door to prevent anybody from coming in while we're away."

"Where will we go?" Toshio Otsuka stood forlornly beside the door to the tatami room, his voice muffled by the dark blue handkerchief pressed tightly in front of his mouth and nose.

Matsuoka looked across at him. "Any one of these empty houses around here. This place will have to be professionally decontaminated before you can ever use it again."

Otsuka nodded but said nothing.

"And what happens when he wakes up?" Harumi Otsuka pointed to the sofa in disgust, as if the object that lay beneath it were a particularly loathsome insect. "I somehow doubt that he will allow us the time to board up the house and move out leisurely. Maybe we should call the authorities and have them come and take him away."

"I think you'll find, Harumi-*san*," said Matsuoka, "that the only authority we need is an undertaker. The wheezing stopped a few moments after I pushed the sofa on top of him."

"I killed him?" Peter Bryant's eyes opened wide in terror. He looked back down at the table leg still in his hand.

"I doubt it, Peter-*san*. The disease killed him. He was dead before he entered the room. Don't let it worry you."

"Well, we can worry about all of that later," interrupted Norio Kondo, gingerly touching the cut on the back of his head. "In the meantime, we should get out of here as quickly as we can. If Harumi and Shigeko would start packing what we need, the rest of us will start boarding the place up and loading up the van."

Susumu Ishibashi stared at the facsimile as it streamed out of the fax machine, and scratched his head despondently. Kubota was definitely not going to like this. Ishibashi just hoped that he would not expend his wrath on the messenger, as was becoming the norm over the past few days. The seal of the president of the United States was placed at the top of the message, and the president's signature became visible as the paper scrolled out of the machine with a faint whirring sound. It was addressed personally to the prime minister, and the contents were short and to the point. America would be delivering the antibody and other drugs for the meningococcus disease to Niigata by sea and air within twenty-four hours, and any attempt to launch an attack against American property would be construed as an act of war and dealt with severely. The prime minister was warned to keep all military aircraft on the ground or risk the consequences.

Ishibashi removed his rimless glasses and polished them absentmindedly with the end of his necktie. Was there any way he could get this message to Kubota without actually having to pass it across himself? He could get one of the other aides to deliver it, but that was not fair to whomever he chose. Kubota's paranoia had hit new heights since the near-riot the night of his televised public announcement, and it was becoming more and more difficult to inform him of bad news without his blowing a fuse and lashing out at the person nearest at hand. He had also become aware of rumors regarding a plan to overthrow him, and he no longer trusted anyone. He eyed everybody furtively and refused to even use his consultants. Every word that left his mouth was a command, spat through lips contorted by the constant fear of being ousted and forced to take responsibility for his actions.

No, there was no way Ishibashi could subject some poor, unsuspecting aide to that fate. He would just have to grit his teeth and deliver the message himself.

Replacing the spectacles on his nose and straightening his jacket, he placed the message in a red leather folder and walked out of his office and down the corridor to the speaker of the house of representatives' room, where Shoji Kubota was busy tallying up the number of supporters who remained staunchly behind him.

On the fingers of one hand.

Bryant was carrying his rucksack and computer down the stairs to the front door when the satellite phone began to ring. Startled, he looked down at Matsuoka, who was pinning a message to the boards that were nailed across the door frame to the living room. The message had the two *kanji* characters for danger written in large letters at the top and an explanation that the room contained a biohazard in smaller characters below. It even had a hand-drawn illustration of the international symbol for radioactivity on it. Matsuoka returned Bryant's look and shrugged his shoulders.

At the bottom of the stairs, Bryant hunkered down and removed the telephone from a pocket in the side of the rucksack.

Extending the aerial, he pressed the button to connect the call and held the unit to his ear.

"Bright light rubies," said a voice that Bryant recognized instantly.

"Mike! What are you doing calling me on this line? I told you they had radars trained on the area."

"I had no choice, Peter. You weren't answering my e-mail," said Mike Woodson.

"I'm afraid we lost the computer. It is in a room contaminated with the bacterium. We couldn't risk using it, and I was afraid to use the laptop because of the satellite linkup being monitored."

"Well, I guess that explains it. But I had to tell you to get your ass out of there and move up to Niigata as fast as you can. The antibody will be delivered ashore within the next few hours."

"That's great news, Mike! Hold on." Bryant cupped his hand over the mouthpiece of the telephone and excitedly passed the news onto Matsuoka, who smiled in relief and hurried out of the front door to tell the others. "Mike?"

"Yeah?"

"That is wonderful news, man! What part of Niigata?"

"About fifty kilometers north of Niigata city, just south of Murakami. We are going to set up a massive field hospital right there on the coast. If you can use your contacts to pass the word around, we have enough for everybody. The more the merrier."

"Jesus, Mike, that's great! What about the Self-Defense Forces? Aren't they going to be a little pissed about that?" Bryant heard the clatter of feet and looked behind him as the other five members of the Tomonokai entered the front door with big grins spread across their faces. He smiled in return and gave them the thumbs-up sign.

"We've warned the government that they will be blown away if they try to interfere. Any military aircraft that gets off the ground is toast. How long will it take you to get out of there?"

"We are ready to leave almost immediately, although we weren't originally planning on moving so far. It'll probably take us about an hour to load the cars up with supplies and gasoline to get us to Niigata, but it might be a good idea if we evacuated for an hour or two to make sure the satellite communications have not been monitored. We nearly got caught the last time I sent you a message."

"Okay, do that. Just remember that those beers are still waiting on the bar, and they're getting flatter by the minute."

Bryant groaned in fake ecstasy. "Don't mention beer, Mike, please. You're torturing me. See you in D.C., man. I'm looking forward to it."

"You'll see me before that. I'm on board the *Kitty Hawk*. I'll be in Niigata before you, although we might have to wait until we get back to Washington for those beers. I don't think they can spare the manpower for setting up the bars yet."

"So I'll see you tonight?"

"Yup."

"That's great, Mike. I can't wait. If you can't get the beers, make sure the coffee's brewing. We ran out a couple of days ago and I've been living on green tea ever since."

Woodson laughed. "You're on. Coffee it is. Take care, Peter. I'm looking forward to seeing you."

"Me too, Mike. See you."

Bryant disconnected the phone and rose to his feet.

"Well, what else did he say?" Matsuoka asked, leading the others along the hall and clustering around Bryant.

"A large field hospital will be set up just south of Murakami in Niigata prefecture and the antibody distributed to everyone who can get there."

"Oh, Peter-*san*. That's wonderful!" Harumi Otsuka pushed her way through to Bryant and grabbed hold of his arm excitedly. "When do we leave?"

"Soon, but first we have a couple of things to do. One is to send a message to all Tomonokai members telling them where the hospital is so they can pass the information around. The second is to load up the cars for the journey."

"Right, let's start straightaway."

"Wait!" Peter held up a hand. "We have to assume that more military vehicles are heading toward us at this very minute. If they managed to get a location when we transmitted from Hakone, they are sure to have gotten one this time too. We have to move away from here for a couple of hours to make sure we are safe."

"I agree," said Norio Kondo. "Let's take the van for a drive down toward the tip of the peninsula. I will create an e-mail message for all Tomonokai members on Peter-*san*'s computer as we drive. We can send the message when we hit the end of land, and then drive back."

Everybody agreed. Locking the front door behind them, they quickly boarded Kondo's van, and, having checked that there was sufficient gasoline in the tank, they put Izu Kogen behind them and headed south.

Norio Kondo sat in the seat directly behind Matsuoka, who was driving, and next to Bryant. He opened the laptop computer on his knees and began to compose a message that he would send throughout the country. He read it aloud and made a few suggested amendments before saving the file and opening a new message screen.

"Just one more message to write," he said, studiously ignoring Bryant. He read the message out loud as he typed it. " 'Dear Kyuryo-Dorobo. I wonder if you would be so kind as to do me a favor,' " he read. " 'On your way from Sendai, would you please pick up a passenger and deliver her to Niigata? Her name is Michiyo Kato and she is staying in Aizu Wakamatsu.' " He broke off and turned his head to Bryant, who was having trouble concealing his excitement. "What is Michiyo's address again?"

*   *   *

"Would you please present the prime minister with my compliments and inform him that we have intercepted a satellite transmission from Izu Kogen and are now mobilizing a unit to enter the area? We should have the miscreants captured within thirty to forty minutes."

Susumu Ishibashi looked up at Kyoko Mitsui and raised a hand to indicate that he would be only a minute or two. "I'm terribly sorry, General. There must be some mistake," he said into the receiver. "The order to track the satellite transmissions was rescinded several days ago. I'm sure you must have received it?"

The line went silent as this piece of news was digested. "By whom?" the voice asked at length.

"The prime minister himself, General."

"I see."

"Please accept my humblest apologies, General. I am afraid that we have been experiencing several breakdowns in communications over the past few weeks, but I can assure you that we are striving to ensure they don't happen again."

"So what am I to do?"

"Nothing at all, General. It has been confirmed that the people transmitting the satellite messages are not a threat to state security. Please demobilize the unit and ignore all other transmissions. I will have the prime minister contact you personally later today to confirm this, if you think it necessary."

"No, that won't be necessary. Although I would appreciate it if you would fax me a copy of the order for my files."

"Of course, General. It might take a few hours, though. As I say, we are experiencing a few communication problems here."

Ishibashi hung up the connection and turned to Mitsui. "Sorry to have kept you waiting, Minister."

"What was all that about?"

"Oh, nothing at all. Just a little misunderstanding that had to be cleared up."

"Do you have the keys?"

Ishibashi reached into his pocket and lifted a bunch of keys into the air.

"Good. Then let's go."

Kyoko Mitsui walked out into the corridor and waited for Ishibashi to join her. They walked in silence until they reached the west-central section of the Diet building, and then turned along the hall until they reached the State Ministers' Room. The two guards saluted and stood at attention.

"At ease," said Ishibashi, slotting a key into the door and turning it. "Remain at the door until somebody comes to relieve you."

Ishibashi looked along both lengths of the corridor before pushing open the door and disappearing inside with Kyoko Mitsui.

"It is time, Mr. Prime Minister," said Mitsui.

Kiyoshi Aizawa rose from behind his desk, nodded, and smiled. The guard's uniform fit him perfectly, and he cut a striking figure. Placing his hat on his head and pulling it down slightly over his eyes, he made a mock salute, winked, and followed them out the door.

Returning the salutes of the two guards, Kiyoshi Aizawa followed Ishibashi and Mitsui through the halls of the diet at a distance of two paces, as was fitting for a military officer in the presence of a cabinet minister. As they arrived at the committee room, three other people walked toward them from the opposite direction. With the silver wig and camel overcoat, Kayoko Inoue was almost unrecognizable. She bowed in the direction of the prime minister and they all entered the room. The people already present rose to their feet as one and bowed deeply. Katsumi Higuchi, the education minister, started a round of applause, but Aizawa hushed him with a finger to his lips.

Inoue was the last of the twenty cabinet ministers to arrive. She removed her disguise and took her place with the other nineteen people seated around the large table. Ishibashi helped Aizawa change out of the guard's uniform and into a blue serge suit. He watched the prime minister take his seat at the head of the table and then waited by the door while six guards quickly filed into the room and took up positions along the wall to his right. At Aizawa's nod, he left the room and went to collect Shoji Kubota.

Eight minutes later, Kubota stormed into the room ahead of Ishibashi and walked toward his seat at the head of the table, a frown of concentration on his face. The American attack on the missile installations on the coast of Niigata had enraged him, and he had called the cabinet meeting to formulate plans for retaliation. He was only three meters from the head of the table when he noticed that somebody was sitting in his place, and halted his progress. Not yet understanding the situation, he looked around at the people sitting at the table in confusion, until his glance fell on Kayoko Inoue.

"You," he hissed, his eyes narrowing in puzzlement.

Passing over Inoue, he looked back to the head of the table and took an involuntary step backward as he noticed who was in his chair.

"I'm terribly sorry, Kubota," said Aizawa pleasantly, "but this cabinet is taken. You'll have to go and find one of your own."

"What is the meaning of this?" Kubota's voice boomed around the room. "What are you doing here? I'll have you flung into a prison cell for this, Aizawa."

"I'd like to see you try. You see, I have been reinstated back into my old position. You, it appears, have been fired."

A look of fear flashed across Kubota's features, and a touch of hysteria entered his voice. "You can't do this to me. Guards, arrest that man!"

Nobody moved. Kubota spun around to face the six guards

who stood against the wall, his face contorted in fury. "Did you not hear me?" he screamed. "Arrest that man!"

"Tut, tut, Kubota. I can see your blood pressure rising from here. Why not just accept the fact that you have lost and I have won?"

Kubota turned back to Aizawa, his eyes flashing with impotent rage. "You cannot do this! I forbid it!"

"I'm afraid it is already done, Kubota. That is the beauty of democracy. A leader who is not capable of handling the job will not last long. All members of the cabinet took a vote, and it was decided unanimously that I should be elected back into power. I am the current prime minister of Japan; you are the *former* prime minister of Japan. Now, if you'll excuse us, we have a lot of things to cover before we can start undoing your wrongs."

Kubota stood clenching and unclenching his fists. Susumu Ishibashi crept up behind him and stood close by, but out of Kubota's line of sight. True to Ishibashi's expectations, Kubota suddenly leaped at Aizawa with a roar of rage.

But Ishibashi was quicker. He swiftly lashed out a foot that caught the side of Kubota's right shoe, causing him to trip over his own feet. Kubota went sprawling forward on his hands and knees, and before he could regain his composure, three of the guards detached themselves from their positions by the wall and hauled him to his feet.

"Arrest that man, please," said Aizawa, his eyebrows raised sardonically at the comedy of Kubota's fall. "He has no right to be in this room."

"Wait!" Kubota shouted, his eyes darting between Aizawa, Ishibashi, and the guards. "We can work this out. You need me, Aizawa. We must work together. You cannot disgrace me after everything I've worked for. I can be of use."

Aizawa looked wearily around his cabinet and sighed. "All right, let me show you the power of democracy. All those in favor of accepting Kubota as a respected member of this government, raise your right hands."

Everybody sat defiantly looking at Kubota. Nobody moved to raise their hands.

"Democracy has spoken. Get him out of here!"

"Wait! Please see reason, Aizawa. You can't do this to me!"

But the guards were already doing it. A pair of handcuffs were snapped sharply onto Kubota's wrists, and he was led struggling from the room, spitting expletives and vowing revenge.

Chapter Sixteen

It was nearly dark when the van containing six members of the Tomonokai and one corgi pulled into the driveway of the house in Izu Kogen. The trip to and from the tip of the peninsula had taken nearly three hours, but they had sent the messages successfully without running into any trouble. Then, having returned to Izu, they had parked one hundred meters up the road from the house in darkness for an additional ninety minutes while they monitored the area for any signs of military personnel or vehicles. Satisfied that they were safe, Kazunori Matsuoka drove up the driveway and parked just in front of the garage.

Having alighted from the van, Bryant, Matsuoka, and Otsuka busied themselves with sorting out and loading supplies from the garage into the van while Norio Kondo topped up the gas tank with gasoline from a red plastic container. Shigeko and Harumi took a walk around the garden to stretch their legs, stiff from so many hours cramped up in the van, accompanied by an enthusiastic Gonta.

"We'll soon be off. Isn't it exciting?" said Harumi Otsuka, pulling gently on Shigeko Kondo's sleeve. "If it weren't for the Americans, who knows what might have become of Japan?"

"We're not there yet, Harumi," replied Shigeko, more in tune with reality than the optimistic Harumi. "Remember that the Self-Defense Forces still have orders to shoot on sight, and we have a long journey before we get to Niigata."

"Oh, don't be so morbid. If the American forces have landed, everything is sure to be fine. We'll be all right. You'll see."

The two women wandered around the side of the house and traced a path along the edge of the small copse of trees that marked the boundary of the property at the back. Gonta disappeared into the woods in quest of anything that might be even vaguely edible. The warm spring sunshine of the day had heated up the ground, and the fragrance of the mountain rejoicing in the birth of new life wafted up around them, despite the chill of the evening breeze.

"I love this time of the year," said Shigeko, wistfully dragging her feet through the scattering of leaves that remained unswept from the previous fall. "It is almost as if God had looked down upon us and deemed us worthy of one more cycle of seasons. As a child, I used to worry that the spring would never come again. That God would decide that we did not deserve the reward of fresh verdure and new life. That we would have to suffer through a millennium of winter until we had re-earned the right to enjoy the warm sunlight once again."

Harumi smiled in the darkness, her mind extending a telescope back into the past through which she was able to peer myopically at her own childhood fantasies and anxieties. "I remember loving the winter up until the New Year, and then hating it until spring. There was something refreshing about the first half, but gloomy about the second half. But even now, the sounds and smells stay with me, even more so than the sounds and smells of any other season. Do you remember waking up on dark, frosty mornings and hearing your mother chopping vegetables in the kitchen for breakfast? The sound of the knife as it crunched through the radish and then made a noise like a woodpecker as it hit the wooden chopping board? The smell of the warm rice and miso soup?"

"Ah, yes, I do. And the one hundred and eight bells from the local shrine ringing in the New Year. The sharp fragrance of the tangerines placed in a wooden bowl in the center of the table. The sound of the pinewood spitting and crackling in the stove. The smell of sake on my father's breath."

The two friends lapsed into silence as they fondly remembered their pasts. Gonta reappeared from the woods, his foraging having produced no results, and capered ahead of them as they rounded the front of the house until they were once more in view of the men loading the van. Peter Bryant looked across at them and waved cheerily, the knowledge that he would soon be reunited with Michiyo adding purpose to his actions. Harumi and Shigeko waved back.

"I suppose we will always remember this winter," said Harumi softly. "Some awful memories, but also some pleasant ones. Peter-*san* is such a nice man. I hope we never lose touch with him."

"Yes, you are right. For some reason, he brings out the mother in me. I do hope he has chosen well in Michiyo-*san*. It would be terrible if she were one of these modern women who think only of themselves and forget that marriage is a partnership of mutual respect that must be worked at if it is to succeed. I would hate to think of him as unhappy."

"I think we can trust Peter-*san* there. If she is the woman he has chosen, you can guarantee that she is as perfect as perfect can be. He is a very shrewd man."

"He is also very naive and has a tendency to see good in everybody he meets. I hope you are right, but I think it is our duty to take this Michiyo aside and make sure she is suitable."

"Shigeko-*san*!" exclaimed Harumi in feigned shock. "You

345

sound like an old woman. That is the responsibility of his mother, not us. And besides, he is nearly thirty years old. He may not take kindly to us interfering in his love life."

Shigeko laughed. "I *am* an old woman, Harumi-*san*. And so are you. As long as he is in Japan, we are his mothers and we must look after him. After everything he has done for us, we cannot let him become involved with an unsuitable woman and ruin his future. It is our obligation."

"You are right, of course. He is under our wing, and there he will stay." Harumi linked arms with Shigeko, and the two increased their pace until they had joined the men.

"How much longer before we are ready?" asked Shigeko as she drew near.

Norio Kondo stopped what he was doing and looked up fondly at his wife. "Five minutes ago, if we'd been offered some help."

"Ignore him, Shigeko-*san*," said Peter Bryant, bringing out the last of the suitcases from inside the front door. "We'll be ready any minute and will be able to—"

Bryant broke off midsentence, dropped the suitcase, and rushed to Shigeko's side, anxiety clearly defined on his face. "Shigeko-*san*? What is it? What's the matter?" he shouted in alarm.

Shigeko raised a hand to her forehead and stumbled back two paces, her eyes rolling in confusion. "I . . . I don't know. I suddenly feel faint."

Norio Kondo leaped to his feet and put his arm around his wife's shoulders to support her. "Shigeko! Are you all right? Quick, help me get her into the van."

With Bryant's help, the two men assisted Shigeko up into the van and sat her down on one of the seats, her arms flopping limply onto her lap. "I'm sorry," she said, her voice reedy and shaky. "It must be the excitement. I'll be fine in a moment, really."

Matsuoka and Otsuka came out of the garage and walked

over to the van. "Problem?" asked Matsuoka as he saw them fussing around Shigeko.

"I don't know," replied Kondo worriedly. "It's my wife. She just had a dizzy spell."

"Let me see."

Matsuoka climbed up onto the first step into the van and looked deeply into Shigeko's eyes. "Her irises are down to pin-points," he said, reaching out a hand and placing the palm on her forehead. "Damn, she's burning up! Quick! Get me something to cover her with."

Bryant, Kondo, and Otsuka immediately took off their coats and passed them to Matsuoka, who supported Shigeko's back as she lay down on the double seat and then covered her up.

"What do you think it is?" asked Norio Kondo, his eyes wide with anxiety. "Could it be something she ate?"

Matsuoka turned around until he was looking directly into Kondo's eyes. He said nothing, but the look of helpless sympathy on his face told the whole story.

"Oh, no!" mumbled Kondo, averting his eyes from his wife's supine form. "She hasn't . . . ?"

Matsuoka laid a hand gently on his friend's shoulder. "I can't be sure, but I'm afraid that's the way it looks, Norio-*san*. We have to get her to the doctors in Niigata as soon as possible. It seems that Hamada's weapon has claimed its first victim."

The sand on the beach was whipped into a blinding storm of frenzied particles by the hovering helicopters as they released their cargo of marines and then skimmed back across the waves to the USS *Kitty Hawk*, situated two miles out to sea. Together with the landing craft that delivered both men and equipment, the helicopters managed to put eight hundred soldiers onto the coast of Japan within a period of forty minutes. One hour and twenty minutes after the first man had stepped ashore, fourteen acres of grassland had been secured and a human perimeter established.

F/A-18 Hornets flown by Carrier Air Wing Five's VFA-27 Squadron and F-14 Tomcats flown by the VF-154 Squadron crisscrossed the skies above, their radars searching for any aircraft stupid enough to be fixed on a heading that intercepted the area. The pilots and radar-intercept officers were experienced, and none allowed his attention to waver for even a moment.

Once a defensible razor-wire fence had been erected along the entire perimeter, work began on assembling the tents and prefabricated huts that would make up the giant field hospital. The marines and engineers worked hard and fast. For many of them it was their first time to set foot on Japanese soil, but they worked as well as—if not better than—during their training sessions in the United States. All had a job to do, and everyone knew how to do it. Huge banks of portable latrines and shower cabins were set up close to the beach, and a gigantic tent that seemed to stretch as far as the eye could see was erected parallel to the ocean to serve as the kitchens that would be required to produce tons of hot food and drink on demand twenty-fours of every day. The hospital tents were set up in three distinct clusters, each separated from the others by at least one hundred yards of open land that was sporadically punctuated with more portable latrines, showers, and huts in which the medical supplies were to be stored.

And then came the equipment, ferried in aboard countless landing craft and helicopters that shuttled back and forth between the battle group and the beach: thousands upon thousands of collapsible cots, sheets, blankets, pillows, chairs, tables, desks, lightbulbs, stretchers, and bedpans. And still it arrived in an endless stream: delicate life-support systems, monitoring equipment, X-ray machines, operating tables, lighting rigs, surgical instruments, syringes, hypodermics, bandages, cotton swabs, and dozens of miles of suture.

And then came the antibody for the meningococcus disease, together with thousands of large boxes containing antibiotics and other medication. Massive stocks were delivered to each of the three hospital tent clusters, where they were ticked off on lists and then distributed to predetermined areas spread throughout each enclave. Each tent had sufficient medication to treat eight thousand patients, but far greater stocks were stored on the battle group two miles out to sea, from which they would be ferried in when necessary.

And last but not least came the doctors, nurses, orderlies, and administrative staff required to provide the treatment so desperately needed by an entire population. Many were military personnel, but a large number of civilian volunteers were also among their ranks. They arrived in droves and were immediately transported to their places of work, where they spent the remaining time familiarizing themselves with the layout of the equipment and supplies and organizing environments in which they could work most efficiently in anticipation of the influx of patients.

The largest field hospital in the history of man was two hours away from the commencement of operations.

"You have to put it on, Norio-*san*. Please."

Norio Kondo looked at the proffered hand-fashioned mask and shook his head sadly before turning back to his wife and squeezing her hand encouragingly. Peter Bryant clicked his tongue in exasperation and placed a hand on Kondo's shoulder. "Please, Norio-*san*. If you don't wear a mask, you'll catch the disease."

"I don't care. If Shigeko dies, I have nothing to live for anyway. I understand and appreciate your concern, Peter-*san*, but this is the way I want it."

Bryant lowered his head in resignation, his shoulders slumping in pity and frustration. Realizing that no amount of pressure would coerce Kondo into accepting the mask, he stepped down from the van and walked across to Matsuoka and the two Otsukas, who were standing by the steps leading up to the deck.

They looked at him expectantly, but he shook his head and wearily pulled his own mask down off his face so that it hung just beneath his chin.

Matsuoka was shivering uncontrollably, his face deathly pale in the glow provided by the porch light. "This is all my fault. I have killed them," he stammered through chattering teeth. "If I had not gone after Hamada, this would never have happened. Oh, what have I done? How could I have been so stupid?" He covered his face with his hands and pulled downward, stretching the skin under his eyes as if trying to rub away the misery that had penetrated the depths of his being.

Harumi Otsuka stretched out a hand and placed it gently on his chest. "It's not your fault," she said, her voice soft and compassionate. "You must not torture yourself like this. She is one victim among hundreds of thousands. We don't even know for sure that she caught it from Hamada. She probably would have caught it anyway."

"No, you're wrong. She caught it from Hamada, and it was I who led him here."

"Then you must include me in the blame."

Matsuoka looked up at Bryant in confusion. "You? Why?"

"Because I had the chance to stop you and didn't. If you insist on blaming yourself for this, then remember that I was with you and played a role in leading him here."

"Oh, Peter-*san*, Peter-*san*. You are a good man, but totally transparent. I appreciate your attempt at trying to ease my feelings, but you are completely blameless. Remember, it is I who have been involved in this terrible tragedy since the beginning. It is I who was employed by the company that caused it in the first place. It is I who was part of a team to cover up the grisly details, thus allowing the disease to spread and kill countless people. It is I who tried to rectify my own mistakes by appointing myself the judge and jury for Hamada. It is I who have ended up being instrumental in killing my own friends. This blame will not be shared. It belongs to me."

Bryant nodded and looked down at his feet. He kicked languidly at the grass, his right foot drawing a small spiral on the lawn. "So we are looking for things to blame you for, are we?" he said at length. "How about blaming you for saving my life? Or what about blaming you for providing me with the information that alerted the rest of the world to the disease? And we could blame you for telling me how the bacterium had been genetically engineered to speed up the process of manufacturing a cure. Oh, yes, and we mustn't forget to blame you for inviting me into the Tomonokai and providing a means for America to have a clear idea of conditions within Japan so that the cure can be distributed as quickly as possible."

"You are wrong, Peter-*san*—"

"Oh, and then there is Statesman," Bryant interrupted. "We mustn't forget him, now, must we? If you hadn't introduced him to the Tomonokai, we all would be dead anyway, killed by a military unit tracing our satellite transmissions. And then there are the artillery installations along the coast of Niigata that would have blasted the American navy to hell and back if your friend hadn't tipped us off."

"Peter-*san*, please listen. That was my duty as a human being. This is different."

"Different, my foot!" Bryant spat, tiring of Matsuoka's indulgence in self-pity. "Single-handedly, you are responsible for saving the lives of millions of people, Matsuoka-*san*. Do you hear what I'm saying? You are a *hero*, damn it!"

Matsuoka stood dumbstruck, awed by Bryant's raised voice and flashing eyes, like a rabbit mesmerized by the headlights of an oncoming car.

"Were it not for you, there would be no antibody therapy available. Were it not for you, the people of Japan would not know that an antibody is now available. Were it not for you, Harumi-*san* and Kondo-*san* would already be dead! Now, you can either spend the rest of the night here wallowing in self-pity, or you can get in that van and drive us all to Niigata, where we have a chance of saving their lives. What's it to be, Matsuoka-*san*? Think on your feet!"

Before Matsuoka could answer, Norio Kondo put his head out of the van door and shouted across to Bryant, "Peter-*san*. Your telephone is ringing."

With a final glance at Matsuoka, Bryant broke away and trotted the few steps across to the van. Kondo handed out his rucksack, and Bryant swiftly unbuckled the side pocket and pulled out the satellite telephone.

"Hello?" he said.

"Peter, it's Mike. Listen, the hospital is almost up and running. How far away are you?" Woodson's voice was raised in an effort to make himself heard above a loud *whup-whup-whupping* that indicated powerful machinery operating in the background.

"Still in Izu, Mike. We have a problem. One of us has contracted the damned disease."

"Oh, God, no! Then I suggest you get here as soon as possible. Why are you hanging about?"

"We'll be leaving in a few minutes. If everything goes smoothly, we should be there by daybreak."

"How bad is the victim? Will he last that long?"

"It's a she, actually. And I don't really know. At the moment she has a fever and a sore throat. I don't know enough about the disease to say how bad that is."

"Well, get out of there as soon as you can."

"Gotcha, Mike. Where are you?"

"I'm in the air at the moment. I'm in a chopper being transferred from the battle fleet to the field hospital. I'll be waiting for you at the main gate and rush you though."

"Great, Mike. Is that the reason you phoned?"

"Yes and no. I also wanted to let you know that Kiyoshi Aizawa has resumed power of the government and promised to assist in distributing the antibody. The entire ground Self-Defense Forces have been placed at our disposal, so you don't have to worry about avoiding military units on your way through to Niigata."

"That's great news, Mike!" exclaimed Bryant, involuntarily raising his voice in response to the clatter of the helicopter rotors leaking through the telephone connection. "I must admit that running into patrols was worrying me. We might be able to get there quicker under those circumstances."

"The quicker the better, Peter. I'll have a doctor on standby."

Something clicked in Bryant's mind. The word *doctor* combined with the sound of the helicopter triggered an idea that seemed worth following through.

"Mike," he said, "how much authority do you have?"

"How much what? What do you mean?"

"I mean, do you have sufficient authority to commandeer a chopper and bring a doctor on down here to pick us up? You could get here in less than an hour, and it might save my friend's life."

A silence met this request. Bryant could imagine the gears of Woodson's mind turning as he examined the suggestion. "Gee, Peter, I don't know. I could give it a try. Hold the line for a second and I'll see if I can get an authorization."

"Tell whomever needs to know that the victim is one of the group who has been working for the U.S. government with me."

"Roger. Hold on."

Bryant covered the receiver with the palm of his hand and explained what he had heard about the Japanese government to the eager ears around him. Matsuoka and the Otsukas had moved across to the van to see whom Bryant was speaking with, and they stood in a small group just beside the van's open door. Matsuoka seemed to have recovered from his previous mood, and color was returning to his face, although he stood there with his lips pursed and a decidedly sheepish look on his face. Bryant didn't mention his idea of the helicopter

353

in case it was refused. He didn't want to build up their expectations unnecessarily. He could hear Woodson's muffled voice down the line and crossed his fingers while he waited. If they could get a doctor to examine Shigeko within the hour, it would increase her chances of survival a thousandfold. From what he had heard of the disease, he knew that speed was imperative if Shigeko was to conquer this infection. There was not a moment to lose, as there was no telling what condition she would be in after an eight-hour drive to Niigata. Shigeko's own survival notwithstanding, Bryant was also aware that the other members of the Tomonokai would be placing themselves in grave and mortal danger by sharing a confined space with her on the trip. Masks or no masks, the chances of several or all of them contracting the disease during the journey were high. He tapped his fingers rhythmically on his knee as he waited impatiently for Woodson's voice to flow down the line.

"Peter?"

"Here, Mike."

"Okay, it's all authorized. The pilot says he has enough fuel on board for the round trip, so we'll just stop briefly at the field hospital to pick up a doctor. We'll be with you in less than an hour."

Bryant heaved a huge sigh of relief. "Thanks, Mike. You've no idea how good it is to hear that."

"You'll need to tell us exactly where you are and find an open space where we can land the chopper. I have a map on my lap here. Tell me where to look."

Bryant frowned. He could direct the chopper to Izu Kogen without problem, but all he had seen of the area so far had been trees, trees, and more trees. "Find the Izu peninsula first. It's the larger of the two peninsulas just southwest of Tokyo and Yokohama. The farthest one. Got that?"

"Okay, got it!"

"Now trace a line along the eastern coast about halfway. Look for the city of Ito."

"Ito, Ito, Ito. Right, I've found it."

"Then go a little more south around the bulbous bit and then inland for a few kilometers. Izu Kogen should be around there somewhere. That's where we are."

Only the sound of the helicopter was audible down the line for a moment or two. Then Woodson's voice reappeared. "All right. I've got you located. Where shall we pick you up?"

Bryant hesitated as he tried to envision a mental picture of the locality. He tried to remember a park or even a children's playground large enough for a helicopter to land, but drew a complete blank. Asking Woodson to hold the line, he pulled his mask up over his mouth and nose and climbed into the back of the van. Once seated, he leaned over and tapped Norio Kondo on the shoulder. "Norio-*san*, I've arranged for a helicopter to come and pick us up. They will bring a doctor to give the cure to Shigeko-*san*. She is going to be all right."

Kondo swung around in his seat and stared into Bryant's eyes. "How long before they get here?" he asked, his hopes visibly inflating and lighting up his features.

"About an hour, but they don't know where to land. Are there any open spaces around here?"

Kondo paused and looked out the window, as if expecting the trees to suddenly wither and provide a landing strip. He thought for a moment and then smacked his hands against the back of the driver's seat. "The mountain," he said simply, turning back to Bryant. "The mountain has a crater at the top. It has no trees, just grass and bushes. It's perfect."

Peter smiled his thanks and spoke into the telephone. "Mike, look for Mount Omuro; it's just beside our location."

"Mount Omuro? Okay, got it."

"We'll be inside the crater at the peak. Apparently there are no trees to hinder your descent. We'll take some heavy-duty flashlights with us and will be there before you."

"Okay, Peter. I'm with you. We're just coming in to land, here. The doctor should be here any minute. We'll take off the moment he gets here and be with you within the hour."

"Cheers, Mike. I appreciate this."

"My pleasure."

The line went dead and Bryant turned to Kondo, who was leaning across his wife whispering encouragement into her ear.

"She'll be fine, Norio-*san*. I promise."

Kondo turned around to face Bryant, the tears of emotion spilling freely from his eyes. "Thank you, Peter-*san*. Thank you."

Bryant looked away self-consciously, surprised to discover that the look of pure gratitude on Kondo's face was tickling his own emotional reserves. A hand came up from the below the seat and covered Bryant's. He looked over into Shigeko's eyes and saw the gratitude there too. He smiled encouragingly before climbing out of the van to replace the telephone in his rucksack.

"Peter-*san*?"

"Yes?" Bryant climbed out of the van and faced Matsuoka.

"Once again you have taught me a lesson. I apologize for my selfish outbreak. You are right. We must look forward, not backward."

Bryant smiled and hefted his rucksack back into the van. "Your apology is accepted, Matsuoka-*san*. Now, maybe we should find us some flashlights and get up that mountain. Otherwise the chopper will be there before us."

By nine o'clock at night, a small portion of the gigantic hospital nearest the main gates was up and running. A vast reception tent had been set up and was manned by Japanese speakers who interviewed the first of the victims in their native tongue to avoid unnecessary delays that would be unavoidable if everybody were interviewed in the English language. An ever-lengthening queue was forming outside the complex as word of the cure spread rapidly through the locality. Once the victims were allowed through into the first tent, their name, sex, age, and address were written on the top of a small slip of paper, and then they were asked for their symptoms. The people who had simply arrived to receive the medication as a preventive measure were given the top copy of the slip and told to report to the eastern enclave, where an army of doctors greeted them and gave them the required shot and medication before shooing them out of the rear of the facility and back into society. The people who were showing flulike symptoms with fever, dizziness, and coughs were given the slips and directed through to the central enclave, where they were treated and placed in cots for overnight observation. And the people who were obviously displaying symptoms of the inflammatory cascade were placed in the custody of orderlies, laid out on stretchers, and wheeled through to the western enclave, where they were linked up to life-support equipment and received intensive care. Some would survive; many would not.

Shortly after the hospital began operations, a squadron of Japan's ground Self-Defense Forces arrived and was immediately assigned to constructing and manning the furnaces that would be used to cremate the unlucky victims of the inflammatory cascade. The personnel not required for this task were provided with vehicles fitted with loudspeakers and ordered to patrol all built-up areas to make sure that everybody in the vicinity was aware of the availability of the cure. This swelled the number of people milling about outside the facility, but as the rest of the hospital came on-line and began to help with the workload, the speed with which the queue was swallowed up by the main gates increased and nobody was forced to wait in line for more than thirty minutes.

Japan was on the road to recovery.

"I think I can hear it," exclaimed Harumi Otsuka, huddling inside her coat against the stiff breeze with a hand placed behind her ear. "Quick, switch on the flashlights."

Bryant, Matsuoka, and Toshio Otsuka switched on their

flashlights and began waving them in the air. At 581 meters above sea level, Mount Omuro was not a huge mountain, and the peak was easily accessible, but a cold wind blowing in from the north made it seem as if the group waiting for the helicopter were camped out on the upper reaches of the Himalayas. The sweat drying on their bodies from the hand-over-hand climb up the mountain with the use of a rope strung below the cables of the chairlift didn't help any, either.

The buzz of the helicopter came closer, although it was impossible to tell from which direction it was approaching. The group stood back-to-back in the center of the wide crater—Shigeko supported by her husband—and kept their eyes on the rim, which was faintly visible against the backdrop of the dark, star-sprinkled sky.

"Here it comes," shouted Toshio Otsuka as the beam of a powerful searchlight became visible from the northern side of the crater. A moment later a heavy, cumbersome-looking aircraft swept over the peak of the mountain and came to a halt, hovering approximately one hundred meters above their heads.

"Down here!" shouted Harumi, jumping up and down and waving her arms. "We're here!"

"They can't hear you, Harumi," said her husband. "They've seen our lights, anyway."

The helicopter began to fall gently out of the sky toward them. Bryant and Kondo both extended their arms around Shigeko to protect her from the wind and dust being kicked up, dervishlike, by the rotors, and Toshio and Harumi huddled close to Matsuoka in a separate group. All squinted their eyes and tucked their chins into their collars as minitornadoes blew up all around them. Gonta crouched on the ground with his back legs laid out flat behind him, whining in abject terror. It was his first-ever meeting with a helicopter, and the experience was proving a little too rich for him. The noise of the rotors became louder and louder, until the helicopter finally touched down on the grass twenty meters away from them, scattering the archery targets set up at the bottom of the slope leading up the side of the crater wall. The door slid open, and Mike Woodson, a huge smile spread across his face, waved them across.

The inside of the helicopter was large, with six seats lined up on either side of the fuselage. A navy medical officer was sitting on one of the seats beside a stretcher gurney collapsed down to floor level. He nodded a greeting to each in turn and then helped to get Shigeko up into the body of the helicopter and strapped onto the gurney.

Bryant watched as each member of the Tomonokai was pulled up into the aircraft, and then passed Gonta up into Woodson's waiting arms. The dog was not convinced that climbing inside the machine was in his best interests, and wiggled like a bagful of eels. Once the struggling corgi was securely restrained on Toshio Otsuka's lap, Woodson returned to the door and held out a hand to Bryant, who shook it heartily before allowing himself to be heaved up inside the aircraft.

With the door closed, it was possible to hear conversation if shouted close to the ear.

"Peter," yelled Woodson into Bryant's ear. "It's good to see you, man! You look great!"

"You too, Mike. Thanks for coming. What's the delay?" asked Bryant, noticing that the helicopter was still sitting on the ground.

"The doctor asked the pilot to wait until you've all had your shots before taking off. In addition to the antibody, he has some sort of serum that has to go straight into the bloodstream to help the white blood cells kick ass, and he doesn't want to jab around and give you all multiple puncture wounds during a bumpy flight."

Bryant looked across at the doctor and gave him a thumbs-up sign. The doctor grinned back and continued his examination of Shigeko. Norio Kondo sat beside them, holding Shigeko's hand and looking worriedly into the doctor's face. The doctor busied himself with a nasal spray, then three white tablets, which Shigeko chugged down with mineral water from a small bottle, and then swabbed her forearm for the jab. Wiping the entry point with a cotton swab, he leaned across to Kondo and said something into his ear. Kondo's face lit up and he grabbed hold of the doctor's right hand with both of his own and pumped it furiously up and down. Although Bryant couldn't hear what they were saying, he presumed it was good news, as Norio seemed on the verge of covering the doctor's face with passionate kisses.

One by one, the doctor administered the drugs to Kondo, Otsuka and his wife, and Matsuoka, and then beckoned to Bryant. Grimacing at the thought of the shot, Bryant moved across to the seat beside him and allowed himself to be treated.

"Thanks, Doc," shouted Bryant once the procedure had been completed and the doctor had closed his bag of instruments. "I really appreciate your coming to get us. I'm sorry to have taken you away from the action in Niigata."

"My pleasure, son," replied the doctor, leaning toward Bryant so he could be heard. "Mike here has told me one or two things about you on the way down, and I am mighty glad to make your acquaintance." He held out his hand, and Bryant shook it. "When we get back to the States and your face is spread all over *Time* and *Newsweek*, I'll be able to tell my kids that I was given the honor of watching you squirm on the end of a needle."

Bryant laughed and leaned close to the doctor's ear. "I have a favor to ask, if you don't mind."

"Sure, anything you want."

"I think our dog might need treatment. He came pretty close to a victim in the final stages of the disease, and I want to make sure he's okay."

"How close?"

"As close as it gets. Right down to the bone, in fact."

The doctor grinned his understanding. "I can't do anything

here, but wait until we get back to the hospital. We have a vet there for the rescue dogs. I'm sure he'll be able to do something."

"Great, Doc. I appreciate it."

Bryant moved back over to Mike Woodson and strapped himself into his seat. Woodson checked that everybody was securely belted in before going forward to give the pilot the okay for takeoff.

Three minutes later the helicopter rose from its position on top of Mount Omuro and turned north in a wide banking movement that had everybody holding their breath in exhilaration. The trip to the field hospital lasted fifty-two minutes and took the helicopter over Kanagawa, Tokyo, Saitama, and Tochigi before entering the airspace over Niigata prefecture, where it proceeded northeast to the field hospital.

From the air it was possible to appreciate the size of the hospital. Powerful halogen lamps lit up the entire area like a Christmas tree, and helicopters were constantly landing and taking off from a large fluorescent orange ground pad laid out several hundred yards south of the nearest hospital tent. They remained hovering in position for a few minutes, awaiting permission to land, and then swooped in toward the orange pad. The moment they were on the ground, a white field ambulance with a large red cross painted on either side and two jeeps broke away from the vehicles parked alongside the landing position and sped toward the helicopter. Shigeko was taken off the chopper on the gurney and loaded into the back of the ambulance together with Norio Kondo and the doctor, and the others jumped into the back of the jeeps and were whisked through the rapidly forming streets to a series of administration huts constructed to the south of the kitchen tent.

"It's a bit spare in here, but the heat should be operating," explained Woodson, ushering Bryant, Matsuoka, and the two Otsukas inside the wooden structure. "It will eventually be fitted out with desks and turned into an office, but in the meantime, please feel free to use it. I'll have some cots and partitions brought in later."

"It's great, Mike. Thanks very much. Can we go and visit Shigeko?"

"It's probably best to wait until she has been examined. I'll get somebody to let us know her condition the moment we have news. And don't worry. She is in fine hands. She'll be okay."

Bryant translated this information into Japanese for Matsuoka and the others while Woodson collected some of the collapsible chairs that were leaning against the far wall and set them up around one of the tables. Then, using the internal telephone that was hanging from the wall, he ordered some hot coffee and sandwiches to be brought in.

"So where do we go from here?" asked Bryant when they were all seated around the table and he had gratefully drunk his first cup of coffee in several days. Gonta, typically, found a spot under Toshio Otsuka's chair and promptly went to sleep, the excitement of the evening obviously having no lasting effect on his ability to nap whenever the chance presented itself.

"That's up to you, Peter. You can return to the States whenever you wish, or you can stay on here for a bit longer. Although I might add that the president of the United States has expressed a specific wish to be introduced to you, and it might not be a good idea to keep him waiting."

"Me? What do you mean?"

"You are being hailed as a hero. The newspapers are full of you. The president wants to be seen shaking hands with you in the Rose Garden. It'll be good for his image."

"Get out of town," said Bryant incredulously.

"It's true, Peter, I assure you. There's not a man, woman, or child in the entire country who doesn't know your name."

Woodson smiled at the look of shock on his friend's face. "Your fifteen minutes of fame has not only been assured, it has been extended a millionfold. Even your parents have been interviewed by the networks. You're hot stuff."

"But why?"

"Are you kidding me? You brought this entire catastrophe to a happy ending. You're a hero, man!"

Bryant shook his head and turned to the Otsukas to translate the news of his instant rise to stardom. Before he had completed the first sentence, however, he was interrupted by a knock on the door. Woodson went to answer it.

"I understand you have a dog that needs attention, sir," said a young marine, saluting smartly. He held up a dog leash for all to see. "If you could lead me to him."

Bryant hauled Gonta out from his position beneath the chair and led him across to the door. "Thanks very much. I don't know if he has caught anything or not, but he could certainly do with a checkup."

"Yes, sir. The vet will see him straightaway. I'll report back as soon as I can."

Giving Gonta a final pat, Bryant watched the marine attach the leash to his collar and lead him off. Seeing the corgi obediently trotting beside him caused a wave of tiredness to wash over Bryant, threatening to knock him over onto his ass. Over the course of the past few months he had lost his job, been forced to leave his home, been beaten up, shot at, been the target of a bomb attack, been separated from his girl, and been attacked by a lunatic with lethal breath. The excitement and responsibility of coping with these situations had provided him with the zest to continue on a day-to-day basis, but now that his subconscious was aware that he and his friends were safe and that even the dog was in good hands, a deep sense of relief and weariness swept through him, seeming to have an adverse effect on his balance. He closed his eyes until the feeling had passed and then raised his eyes up to heaven as he counted his blessings.

All he needed now was to set eyes on Michiyo and his life would be complete.

Of course, Michiyo!

"Mike," he said suddenly, breaking out of his reverie and turning back into the room. "Can you find out if there is any word from Michiyo yet?"

Woodson nodded and walked across to the telephone. Four minutes and three calls later, he returned to his seat. "She hasn't checked in for treatment, but that doesn't mean she isn't here. People are allowed through the gates at will, but it's only when they seek treatment that they're required to provide their names and other details. What time are you expecting her?"

Bryant turned to Kazunori Matsuoka and asked the same question in Japanese.

"Kyuryo-Dorobo will pick her up on his way down from Sendai, but I have no idea when he was planning to leave. If he left immediately after Kondo-*san* sent the message, they could be here anytime. On the other hand, he might not leave for a couple of days."

Bryant relayed the answer to Woodson and then considered the situation. They were expecting a lot of Tomonokai members to arrive at the camp, but nobody knew what they looked like or even what their real names were. Given the size of the entire complex, they could be here for days and nobody would ever know.

"Listen, Mike. Would it be possible for us to stick up a notice board at the front entrance directing the members of the Tomonokai here?"

"The what-o-kai?"

"The Tomonokai. I told you in one of my e-mails. The nerds' association. Remember? These are the guys who provided us with information from around the country. We told them all to get here, but without some sort of notice board requesting them to contact us, we won't know them from Adam."

"Ah, yes, the nerds' club. No problem. Tell me what you

want to write on it, and I'll get the carpenters to put one up right away."

Bryant spoke to Matsuoka for a moment and then turned back to Woodson. "It'll have to be in Japanese. We don't know how many of them speak English. If you could let us have a board and some paint, Mr. Otsuka here will do the honors."

Thirty minutes later, Toshio Otsuka stepped back from his handiwork and surveyed the results. Smiling in smug satisfaction, he passed the brush to a uniformed carpenter, who painted in a rough map directing visitors from the main gate to the administration hut. The board was four feet wide by three feet tall and would be placed at the main entrance, where nobody could miss it. It simply asked all members of the Zen Nippon Otaku Tomonokai to report directly to Gakusha in the hut indicated below.

The board was carried out for positioning, and the five once again sat down at the table.

Matsuoka poured himself some more coffee. "You know, it will be nice to meet up with the other members of the Tomonokai. I have been conversing with them on-line for several months now, but I don't have a clue what any of them look like. Present company excepted, of course." He waved an apologetic hand at Otsuka.

"Me, too," agreed Otsuka, pushing his cup forward to accept the coffee being offered by Matsuoka. "I'm especially looking forward to meeting your friend Statesman. He has done so much to help us that he feels like an old friend."

"I'm afraid you probably won't get the chance, Norio-*san*," said Matsuoka. "I very much doubt if he will come to Niigata. He is an extremely private man."

Bryant looked up in disappointment. "Oh, no! Can't you persuade him to come, Matsuoka-*san*? We owe him so much. Not least of all our lives."

"I'm afraid not, Peter-*san*. Hopefully he will prove me wrong and knock on the door sometime soon, but I really can't see it. If you knew him you would understand."

"Understand what?"

"Understand why it would be difficult for him to leave Tokyo."

"What do you mean? He sounds intriguing. Who is he?"

Matsuoka chuckled and shook his head. "I'm afraid I can't tell you that, Peter-*san*. Suffice it to say that he is not totally out of the public eye and his connections with the Tomonokai are better left concealed."

"Now I *am* intrigued. Can't you give us a hint?"

"I'm afraid not, Peter-*san*. Maybe you will understand sometime in the future, but for the moment, please don't ask me to betray Statesman's anonymity. That his identity would remain confidential was one of the conditions when he agreed to help us in the first place. Please understand my position."

Bryant nodded reluctantly and turned to Woodson to translate the gist of the conversation. It seemed strange that somebody so involved in getting the antibody onto Japanese soil would be so reticent at being hailed for his contribution, but if that was the way he wanted it, Bryant had no right to force the situation. Hopefully, as Matsuoka had suggested, he would learn of his true identity sometime in the future.

The hours passed slowly, but for Bryant and the other members of the Tomonokai, that was not a bad thing. The exhaustion generated by fearing for their lives for so long was their paramount feeling, but it was not an unpleasant sensation, and all reveled in a sense of freedom. Woodson ordered more coffee, and they were all thinking that they couldn't possibly imbibe yet another cup when the phone rang. Woodson answered it and stood listening for a few moments. Hanging up the phone, he walked back to the table. "Good news," he said. "The dog's fine. Not a trace of the bacterium anywhere, although the vet will keep him overnight to make sure."

Bryant heaved a sigh of relief. "At least that's one thing that poor old Norio-*san* won't have to worry about. Let's hope the same is true for Shigeko-*san*. How long will it be before we know how she is?"

"Probably by the morning. The only way to tell if the disease is spreading is by monitoring the patient for a certain period of hours. If no new symptoms crop up, then they are probably in the clear."

"By the morning, you say?"

"Yes."

"It already is morning." They all turned their eyes to the windows and saw the gray light of dawn illuminating the previously invisible roofs of the huts and tents surrounding their own hut. Bryant checked his watch. "It's five-forty-five. We've been up all night. No wonder I'm so darned tired."

"You want to stack a few?" Woodson waved a hand at the partitioned-off sleeping cubicles that had been set up at the back of the room during the night. "I'll wake you if I get any news."

The idea of a few hours' sleep was tempting, but Bryant was eager to hear of Shigeko's condition. He asked the others, but apart from Harumi, they decided that they would stay up a little longer. Woodson showed Harumi to her cot behind one of the partitions, and five minutes later the steady rhythm of her breathing could be heard throughout the hut.

The following few hours were once again taken up with desultory conversation. Bryant filled Woodson in on everything he could remember ever since they had parted by the side of the Tama River, and Woodson gave them all an outline—translated by Bryant—of the actions initiated by the United States and other countries of the world to not only fight the disease, but also to rescue the currencies of Asia. By nine-thirty they were all talked out. Toshio Otsuka had laid his head on his arms and was snoring gently, and Matsuoka, despite his body's screams for mercy, was drinking coffee by the gallon and regularly pacing up and down to shake off his sleepiness.

The door being flung open to reveal a gleeful but obviously exhausted Norio Kondo took them all by surprise. The noise of the door hitting the wall of the hut brought Otsuka out of dreamland with a start, and he sat there with surprise written all over his face.

"Norio-*san*!" exclaimed Bryant, rushing forward and clasping the man into a hug. "I'm so glad! When will she be released?"

"You know?" Kondo seemed disappointed.

"It's your face, Norio-*san*. It tells the whole story. When will she be released?"

"They want to keep her for another day or two. She has a slight chest infection, but the doctors say that will clear up with antibiotics in due course."

Matsuoka and Otsuka hurried over to give their congratulations. Bryant turned to Woodson to explain, but before he could open his mouth, Woodson said, "You don't have to tell me, Peter. At least, I'm hoping you wouldn't all be that happy if she'd croaked. She's all right, right?"

"Right."

"Tell him how pleased I am for him."

Bryant relayed the message, and Kondo walked forward to shake Woodson's hand. Turning to Bryant, he said, "Please express my deepest gratitude for everything Mr. Woodson has done. The doctors told me that Shigeko would not have made it if we had been a couple of hours later. It was Mr. Woodson's helicopter that saved her life, and I am forever in his debt."

Bryant passed on the message, his eyes clouding over with moisture in his happiness for both Norio and Shigeko. When he had finished, Kondo turned to him.

"And you too, Peter-*san*. It was your idea that brought the helicopter. How can I ever thank you?"

"The knowledge that Shigeko-*san* is safe is more than enough for me, Norio-*san*. Although I think Mike here would be most interested to hear the *oikaze* gag, if you could manage it."

Kondo narrowed his eyes and scrutinized Bryant's face to determine if he was joking or not. Shrugging his shoulders and turning on a mischievous grin, he said, "Well, if you think that Mr. Woodson would be *that* interested, then how can I refuse? But you'll have to give me a few moments to prepare myself."

"Take as much time as you need, Norio-*san*. Have some coffee, if you think it will help."

They all sat back down at the table and Kondo allowed Bryant to fill a cup with coffee for him. He asked after Gonta and was assured of his safety. Ten minutes passed before the next interruption, this time a knock at the door.

Bryant waved Woodson back into his seat and stood up to answer it. As he pulled open the door, his jaw dropped several notches as he took in the golden apparition that stood without. Michiyo Kato grinned at him, placed her hands on her hips, and gave her butt a sassy wiggle. "Hello, sailor. Remember me?" she asked cheekily.

Choking down his emotions, Bryant extended both arms to her as if in a dream.

Behind him, a loud noise split the air and Norio Kondo's voice echoed after it: "*Oikaze da!*"

Prime Minister Kiyoshi Aizawa rubbed his knuckles into his eyes and then stretched his tired frame until several joints popped in protest. He had done enough for the day and was looking forward to the arrival of the whisky he had ordered. It would still take a long time for Japan to get back on its feet and regain the confidence of the world, but at least a systematic start had been made, and there was no doubt that the country was heading in the right direction. Now that the monoclonal antibody therapy was being distributed on schedule throughout the country and the spread of the epidemic had been halted, he was hoping to put an end to the state of emergency within the next two weeks. Not that that would be any consolation to the eight and a half million victims of the disease—6.5

percent of the entire population! That was a figure that Aizawa was destined to take with him to the grave, indelibly branded on his mind in uppercase characters.

"Enter," he called in reply to the knock at the door. He had already turned down the lights of the State Ministers' room, and the only illumination left was provided by a lampstand on his desk and the glow from his laptop computer.

The door opened and a young man in rimless spectacles entered, a bottle of Jameson Irish whiskey, a crystal glass, a small bucket of ice, and two bottles of Suntory mineral water balanced on a silver tray and held reverently before him.

"Ah, Ishibashi. Thank you very much. Maybe you'd care to join me?"

"Thank you, no, sir. I still have some duties to attend to, if you don't mind."

"As you wish."

Aizawa watched as Susumu Ishibashi poured out two fingers of whiskey into the glass and then added the ice and water. "I am feeling Irish this evening, Ishibashi. I need something bright and cheerful to help me get through this difficult period. Tomorrow I must meet with the South Koreans to persuade them to reopen their embassy in Tokyo. Scotch whisky will not work tonight."

"I understand, sir."

"Ah, do you, now? Are you sure? Would you like me to tell you why Scotch whisky will not work tonight, Ishibashi?"

"Yes, sir. I would be most interested."

Aizawa reached out for the glass and took a sip. He rolled the liquid around his mouth luxuriously before continuing. "Scotch whisky is a religion, Ishibashi. It is made by solemn men who worship their creation. It is dour and staid, and revels in its own perfection. It is an icon, there to savor and cherish, not to cheer. It provides solace for the soul and refuses to be taken lightly. Irish whiskey, on the other hand, is full of cheer and instills life in the inanimate. It generates images of young girls skipping joyfully to jigs played by old men in whiskers. It frees the soul and allows it to wander barefoot through fields of heather. It stimulates desire and holds the promise of better things to come."

"I understand, sir."

"I wonder if you do, Ishibashi. I wonder if you do. Tell me, how long has it been since you rescued me from that dreadful meeting with a blank piece of paper?"

"Close on three months, sir."

"Do you remember my words at that time?"

"Yes, sir. You said that I would go far."

"And so you shall, Ishibashi, so you shall. Under the right direction you could be one of the future prime ministers of Japan."

"Thank you, sir. I am honored that you think so."

"Oh, I think so, all right. But before we elect you, let me ask you a question. If you were the prime minister of Japan and had to be equated with a particular brand of whisky, what would you prefer to be? Scotch whisky or Irish whiskey?"

Ishibashi raised his eyes to the ceiling in thought. "Given your explanation, sir, I would say Irish whiskey."

"And *that*, Ishibashi, is my point exactly. This government has had enough Scotch whisky. It is time for us to dance to the jigs of public opinion and not simply create more icons to be worshiped. Thank you, Ishibashi. I won't be needing you any further tonight."

Left alone, Aizawa cradled the glass across his chest and inspected the contents. He still felt the occasional twinge of guilt at adding ice and water to pure perfection, but that was the way he liked it. He would not be bound by tradition. If he decided that the beverage was improved by simple additives, then that was the way he would drink it. And that, he decided, was the way in which he would run Japan, neither bowing to tradition nor kowtowing to staid beliefs. He took another sip and exhaled in satisfaction. He had one more job to finish before he could turn in, and now he was in the correct frame of mind for it. It only required sending a thank-you note to some acquaintances, but a relaxed mind would help him find the correct words to express his gratitude.

Placing the crystal glass on his desk, he turned to his computer and logged on to the Internet. Once the connection was established, he pulled down the menu of bookmarks and selected one. He waited until the screen was displayed, and then moved the cursor to the log-in field. He began to punch out his handle, mouthing the letters out loud as he typed each key.

"S-T-A-T-E-S-M-A-N."

EAST
OF THE
ARCH

ROBERT J. RANDISI

Joe Keough's new job as "Top Cop" for the mayor of St. Louis has him involved in more political functions than investigations. But all that changes when the bodies of pregnant women are discovered on the Illinois side of the Mississippi. Suddenly Keough finds himself on the trail of a serial killer more grotesque than anything he's seen before.

When the offer to join a special statewide serial killer squad comes his way, Keough has to make a decision that could change his personal and professional life forever. But through it all he continues to work frantically, battling the clock to find the perpetrator of these crimes before another young woman and her unborn baby are killed.

ANDREW HARPER
RED ANGEL

The Darden State Hospital for the Criminally Insane holds hundreds of dangerous criminals. Trey Campbell works in the psych wing of Ward D, home to the most violent murderers, where he finds a young man who is in communication with a serial killer who has just begun terrorizing Southern California—a killer known only as the Red Angel.

Campbell has 24 hours to find the Red Angel and face the terror at the heart of a human monster. To do so, he must trust the only one who can provide information—Michael Scoleri, a psychotic murderer himself, who may be the only link to the elusive and cunning Red Angel. Will it take a killer to catch a killer?

Dorchester Publishing Co., Inc.
P.O. Box 6640
Wayne, PA 19087-8640

_5275-X
$6.99 US/$8.99 CAN

Name: _____

Address: _____

City: _____ State: _____ Zip: _____

E-mail: _____

I have enclosed $_____ in payment for the checked book(s).

For more information on these books, check out our website at www.dorchesterpub.com.
____ _Please send me a free catalog._

TARGET
ACQUIRED

JOEL NARLOCK

It's the perfect weapon. It's small, with a wingspan of less than two feet and weighing less than two pounds. It can go anywhere, flying silently past all defenses. It's controlled remotely, so no pilot is endangered in even the most hazardous mission. It has incredible accuracy, able to effectively strike any target at great distances. It's a UAV, or Unmanned Aerial Vehicle, sometimes called a drone. The U.S. government has been perfecting it as the latest tool of war. But now a prototype has fallen into the wrong hands . . . and it's aimed at Washington. The government and the military are racing to stop the threat, but are they already too late?
